As she replaced the receiver, the double-wide, etched glass-and-oak door opened with a squeak. Natalie jumped. She gathered her composure and donned her best hospitality smile.

The doorway filled with a set of wide shoulders covered in plaid flannel and long legs encased in worn blue jeans atop scuffed hiking boots.

"Nat?"

She squinted, wondering who belonged to the disembodied voice of the tall man stepping from the porch's shadows into the lobby.

"Nat," he repeated. "Sorry I'm late."

His voice was guttural and familiar. Her heart plummeted to the pit of her stomach, like a thundering rockslide. Only one person called her Nat. That same person spewed constant apologies for being late. She locked her gaze on the recognizable aqua eyes. "Brad?"

Sixteen years.

He'd gone from a slender, clean-cut captain of the football team to a buff guy sporting a days' scruff of chestnut-brown beard.

In a flash, her thoughts transported to the senior girls' jealousy stemming from the *big man on campus* asking the *big-city, new girl* to the prom. Her reflection reverted to summers growing up in Vermont, and the instant bond she developed with her aunt. Earlier to a time when climbing trees was cool, boys and girls could be best friends, and true friendship went unimpeded by those things the genders let get in the way. And before she decided to remain in Mistletoe Falls her senior year, when her heart filled with love, and *long* before her heart smashed to smithereens.

Praise for Delsora Lowe

"In THE INN ON GOOSENECK LANE, author Delsora Lowe proves you can come home again—and find that one true love lost to you. A winner all around."

~Kat Henry Doran, Wild Women Authors

~*~

"Set in Vermont, this story is about a sweet second chance at finding love and everything they've been missing…"

~dianamcc, Romance Junkies

~*~

"A heartwarming sweet romance with the magical feel of winter in Vermont. … Can they find their own second chance at happiness by opening up the past that will reveal the secrets hidden…?"

~Vera, reader

~*~

"Delsora Lowe has given us a new verb for our romance vocabulary "snickerdoodling. …and descriptions of scones, fudge, and hot chocolate that make your mouth water… Absolutely blissful reading!"

~Cathy, reader

~*~

"Enemies to lovers romance… a satisfying read"

~5 Stars, Zara West Romance,
My Favorite Romances for 2020

~*~

"…short, enjoyable read about second chance love."

~4 Stars, Judy Kentrus,
author of BLUEBERRY TWIST

The Inn on Gooseneck Lane

by

Delsora Lowe

This is a work of fiction. Names, characters, places, and incidents are either the product of the author's imagination or are used fictitiously, and any resemblance to actual persons living or dead, business establishments, events, or locales, is entirely coincidental.

The Inn on Gooseneck Lane

Contact Information: info@thewildrosepress.com

Cover Art by *Diana Carlile*

The Wild Rose Press, Inc.
PO Box 708
Adams Basin, NY 14410-0708
Visit us at www.thewildrosepress.com

Publishing History
First Edition, 2022
Trade Paperback ISBN 978-1-5092-4418-8
Digital ISBN 978-1-5092-4419-5

Published in the United States of America

Dedication

Special thanks to my best high school friend, Leslie, whose life-long friendship and law office work stories were inspiration for the heroine in this story. And to the Unity College students who worked for me in the admissions office and whose stories of their adventures in their majors of Adventure-Based Environmental Education and Adventure Therapy were inspiration for the hero. To my Maine Romance Writers chapter, whose members have helped me every step of the way. And lastly, to the sweet town of Brandon, Vermont, the setting which was used as inspiration for this story.

Chapter One

"You what, Aunt Mary?" Like her days of playing high school softball, Natalie Thomas suffered the slam of Mary's announcement like a misfired throw in the center of her chest.

Her aunt fluttered like a wounded butterfly before she placed a hand on Natalie's cheek. "Everything will be fine. You'll see."

Despite her aunt's comforting and warm gesture, Natalie's gut churned. She suppressed a groan and tempered the tight press of her lips into a smile.

She'd arrived late yesterday afternoon at the Inn on Gooseneck Lane, the place she called home, for a much-needed rest. After an exhausting day, she crashed under the warm quilt. She woke when the thin sliver of sun slipped through the window to caress her face. Pushing from the soft pile of pillows, she peered outside. The view of forest behind her bedroom, winged thoughts to childhood. She'd felt so grown-up with her own room, next to her aunt and uncle's in the renovated carriage house.

At the tiny sink, Nat splashed cold water on her face and donned flannel-lined blue jeans and a sweatshirt. The hug of the worn clothing confirmed she was truly home. Bracing Vermont air, breathed deep during her short walk from her childhood room to the inn, eased her heart of the stress she'd left behind in

Washington, D.C.

This morning at breakfast, she lowered her shoulders and edged her breathing to a steady, comfortable pace. Until this moment. Her aunt's announcement trapped breath in her lungs. Her heart pounded in time with the thump-thump-thump of the industrial mixer beating bread dough in the nearby kitchen.

Natalie sucked in cleansing, yoga breaths. "Aunt Mary, I'm sorry. I'm tired from my trip. Let's sit." She snagged a chair at the table in the inn's guest dining room, where she'd been gulping coffee and typing law exam study notes.

Mary refilled Natalie's mug, then set the pot on the warmer, before smoothing her skirt.

She endured her aunt's habitual hovering until Mary perched. "So, this plan of yours?" Sporting her signature peering-over-her-glasses expression, Mary's pointed look sparked shivers along Natalie's spine, a remembrance of her own childish practice of constantly speaking out of turn. Not that her question was impudent. But tempering her tone would lead to more productive talk. "Tell me your plan."

"Honey, planning the program won't be hard."

Natalie glugged a fortifying gulp. She placed her half-empty mug on the table and waited until her aunt continued. She didn't. Instead, Mary extended her sweet, but disarming, smile, which usually worked toward defusing her childish outbursts. Not this time. "Won't be hard?" Blood pounded through her veins. A heated path blazed across her cheeks. Again, she sucked deep, cleansing breaths. "Less than eight weeks remain until Christmas. What were you thinking?" She prayed she conveyed cool, calm, and collected.

"Oh, darling. No fretting." Mary leaned her elbows against the table and flashed a smile. "You're a worrier. Walter Ketcham assured me the Mistletoe Falls Senior College is rounding up participants for our senior ski week. They're handling the registration. He'll clarify details when he comes later this week."

Natalie opened her mouth.

"Walter, he's the director of the program at the Community College."

A tinge of pink bloomed on Mary's cheeks. Did her dear aunt have a bit of a crush on this Walter guy?

Mary brushed her hand through her short, gray cut. "Walter called Green Mountain Sports looking for a leader for the cross-country ski lessons and trips." She hauled in a deep breath after her monologue.

"Eight weeks to plan an event that normally takes a year."

"So you said, dear. We've had a planning meeting. Concentrate on the positive."

Natalie jumped from her seat and paced around the spacious dining room. Thank goodness the room was empty. "Why didn't you tell me about the event earlier?"

Before I took a paid sabbatical which includes me working.

She needed every minute of the two months to finish the online prep course for the January certified paralegal exam. Never mind time to breathe in country air and help restore enthusiasm and energy for her job.

Mary stood and skirted the table. She wound her arms round Natalie.

Her aunt's tight hug infused warmth like a well-wrapped, knit shawl. Her breath soothed into an easy rhythm. She relaxed. This woman acted more a mother than her own. Mary welcomed her every summer and the year Natalie fell in love with Brad, begging to spend twelfth grade in Mistletoe Falls. The decision was the best solution for her own sanity and dearly cost her. Her parents abhorred her independence, and in the end, made her pay.

"You're in laid-back, Vermont, not Washington. And…" Mary rubbed a hand along Natalie's spine.

Her aunt kissed her cheek, conjuring memories of comfort offered for scraped knees and hurt feelings.

"We help each other. None of that city competition. This week of activities will work. You'll see." Mary retreated.

But her lilac scent swirled over Natalie, easing her worry a tad. Even with her plate full, she couldn't dismiss this harebrained idea. "What's the reason for taking on a large event last minute?"

"Honey, I didn't want to tell you—"

"What?" Regretting her gruff demand, she steepled her fingers and breathed through her nose, then out through her mouth, before she cradled her aunt's hands. "Tell me what's wrong."

Mary dropped her gaze toward her low, black pumps. "We don't have many customers. We need the business."

For a split second, Natalie inhaled, her breath catching in a paralyzing grip. "I-I didn't know. Is the inn in trouble?" She circled her aunt's waist in a hug. They both could use the comfort of an embrace. This beautiful inn was her aunt's home.

"The inn might close."

Natalie pulled away.

"Don't you worry." Mary patted her cheek. "We have the perfect solution for a full house at Christmas. Hosting groups will become part of the inn's new offerings."

"So, this ski-week is make-or-break, Aunt Mary?"

Her aunt rolled her eyes. "Oh, for goodness sakes. Call me Mary. Tacking on *aunt* makes me sound old. We're partners."

Aunt Mary ignored the make-or-break comment. She forced a sigh down. *Partners? What have I signed up for?* She slumped against the chair, before she straightened, ready to stay positive and focus on the challenge. "You're right. We'll make this event happen." She didn't work for a hotshot law firm in Washington for nothing. Although working on financials and property acquisitions for the elite seemed easy compared to Mary's mad scheme.

"What's wrong, honey?"

Mary's fingers circled her wrist, imparting her love, just as she had done throughout her childhood. "Sorting things. You know how I work—in my head." No way would she divulge her own workload.

"No one ever understood where you were coming from until you sorted through the puzzle, then let us in on the secret."

"I'm not—" She swatted the air with the back of her hand.

"You are, honey. You keep everything deep inside. And then you complain your friends give you a hard time."

"Or give up on me…" The memories of senior year when the local kids resented the *uppity* newcomer slipped through her in a chilled trail of best-forgotten recollections.

"You're speaking of high school. Oh, honey."

Mary's voice lowered to her soothing maternal tone. Her aunt's veiled reference concerned the break-up with Brad. The worst day of her life. The day she should have been flying high—graduation and the standing ovation following her valedictory speech. The first visit from her parents since she rebelled and stayed in Vermont.

Then they ruined the joy by orchestrating her present—her flight to Europe the next day. They added punch to the gift by disabling her phone, claiming they would make communication accommodations in Europe. She never believed their story. Her parents were experts at plotting manipulation, demanding her cooperation, and in the end blackmailing her with the threat of refusing to fund college.

After what Brad did, she'd come to a point where she didn't much care. Her disappointment was wiped away by the years. Or so she thought until the twinge of memories squeezed her heart. No way would she ask after Brad.

Her aunt's sympathetic gaze homed in. Her usual optimistic smile was gone. Just because the pain from sixteen years ago still leached from her every pore when memories resurfaced, Natalie refused to cause her aunt distress. "I'm fine." She squared her shoulders. "Just give me time to jot notes. When will Walter meet with us?"

"Day after tomorrow. He'll have registration forms and outline his role and ours."

The last remnants of her frustration bubbled in a

sigh.

"You'll do fine. Organization is your expertise. You'll fit together the pieces." Mary sat and shuffled her stack of papers. "Honey, your trip is fortuitous."

"Of course. I'm yours." How could she tell Mary she needed rest, a break from routine, and time and energy devoted to her own law work? Natalie stood and paced, hoping the movement would allow her to focus. "Okay, let's start with big pieces. Walter sent a notice in the Senior College newsletter, right?"

"A third announcement will be distributed in the Senior Colleges of New England Association's next newsletter. We've received more calls expressing interest from our advertisement."

"Good." She tugged her sweater, sat, and logged into a popular Internet-based spreadsheet. "We need tabs for promo, reservations, meal planning, event programming, vendors—"

"Vendors?" Mary pressed the tips of her fingers against her lips.

"People to lead activities, provide meals—" With the scent of their chef's fresh baked bread wafting through the dining room, Natalie hugged her stomach to suppress the growl. She took a sip of lukewarm coffee, hoping to tamp hunger pangs.

"We'll cook right here, of course."

"Can Chef Heidi handle off-site location catering while cooking three meals a day for guests? We could be at capacity with this extra group."

Mary leaned on her elbows. "We *will* be filled."

"Heidi needs more wait staff and another cook." Oh, brother, how will they pay salaries?

"Oh, I didn't think… We have Jeremy, her sous

chef." She fluttered her fingertips to land against her mouth.

Natalie bit her bottom lip, to restrain negative responses. No wonder the inn was in trouble. Her aunt wasn't a businesswoman. Ever since her uncle passed and the inn's manager took another job, things slipped downhill fast.

Sitting in the cozy dining room by Mistletoe Creek, the sun warmed her. Instead, she *should* be in her room with an open computer and head down, immersed in sucking up knowledge and ensuring she nailed her exam and won the promotion. For eleven long years, she'd worked hard toward obtaining executive assistant to the founding law partner.

Why had she opted to work in the sunny dining room? A roil of anxiety sparked every nerve. She plastered on a smile and pressed a hand against her mid-section. The pressure of resurrecting this business outweighed the day job stress. She understood the routine, laws, and procedures. International million-dollar, corporate monetary exchanges for high-powered clients were a piece of cake compared to running an inn.

Home less than twenty-four hours and already a bombshell derailed her plans. She pondered organizing an already publicized event with no tangible strategy. Her hands trembled. A rush of dizziness encompassed her, as if she tumbled in a barrel, bumping over creek rocks, headed straight for the waterfall at the end of town.

Like water over the falls, the plan was in motion. Expiring on the spot wouldn't help. To decelerate her racing heart, she reverted to the slow intake and exhale of her yoga breathing. She handled this sort of event on a regular basis, although the usual prep time was more than two months. She centered her spinning mind. If she were sitting in the boardroom, she'd tell the partners no task was too daunting. Big events were her thing.

Imagining the corporate Christmas party for high-powered clients would make this task easier. Granted, the planning took a year to execute and followed fifteen years' worth of notes.

She *could* plan the event. She could *plan* the event. She could plan *the event*. *The Little Engine That Could.*

Natalie flopped against the chair. With her head resting against the top rung, she closed her eyes. Remembering childhood summers at the inn added to the *I can do this* mantra silently circling through her mind.

Aunt Mary read the story so many times Natalie memorized the book. The two snuggled under the fluffy, goose-down comforter in her aunt's big bed. Mary's rhythmic voice and words of wisdom schooling her in the power of optimism now gave her comfort.

Anxiety from the taunting little voice repeating *planning an event is too much to handle* leaked away, drip by drip. Then why did the dread continue to shoot through her like an electric bolt, frying every brain cell?

Concentrate.

Heartburn bubbled and burned. Pressing a palm against her sternum, she visualized cat stretches and downward-facing dog positions and drew in deep breaths to dispel the pain. Relaxed, she flexed her fingers. *I can make this work.* "You're right, Mary. We *can* create a successful week." She rattled off tasks and timelines, keeping pace taking notes.

Mary jotted her own comments in longhand.

She nailed the highlights of their discussion into the spreadsheet. Her fingers flew across the keyboard, toggling between spreadsheet pages, thanks to building dictation speed while recording every nuance of corporate meetings.

I think I can. I think I can. I know I can.

After a half hour of discussion, incessant typing, and another coffee refill, Natalie glanced at the time. She drew a deep breath and expelled to the slow and steady beat of ten.

Mary tossed her pen and covered her powdered cheeks. "Oh my, I never imagined events had so many moving parts."

She forced the corners of her mouth to lift. "We *can* do the event." Rather than focus on the big picture, which without mistake caused Mary stress, she zeroed in on one important item. "Okay, who did you speak with at Green Mountain Sports?"

"Walter called. His name is here…" Mary fumbled through her papers. "Brett or Brian or Bill."

"Leave your notes with me. I'll get them organized, and you and I will meet this afternoon."

"Here's my notation. Oops, I only wrote *B*. He's the new owner." She tapped her notes. "He's coming today at two." Mary's head bobbed between her document and Natalie. She dropped her pen to the table and squeezed her hands. "Heavens, I forgot my hair appointment. But you can handle the meeting."

"What am I supposed to handle?" Her voice pitched an octave higher than normal. A brief moment of stomach-churning panic replaced the benefits of her controlled breathing. She straightened, pressed against the slatted chair, and mumbled her mantra. *I. Can. Do. This.*

"The notes are right here— what Walter and I talked about." Mary shoved her untidy stack across the table.

She glanced at a half page of her aunt's less-than-flawless penmanship. Weren't ladies of her generation supposed to write perfect cursive? Natalie checked the time on her cellphone. Half past eleven. Two-and-a-half hours to get her ideas organized before the new owner, whoever the heck he was, arrived. She hoped this guy produced stellar solutions to Mary's harebrained scheme.

Yup. Make-or-break. No worries.

****

Brad Matthews shoved shut the cash register drawer and heaved a sigh to rival Old Man Winter breathing down his neck. He studied the well-stocked store. Too well-stocked, which meant insufficient customers of late. Three weeks until Thanksgiving, and the woman exiting Green Mountain Sports was his first customer today.

He strode across the floor to tidy the one shelf of men's shirts his last customer rifled. Every other display sat pristine, as the perfect piles hadn't been touched this week. Brad prayed business would pick up with pre-Christmas shopping.

Business had slowed to the agonizing crawl of a water-deprived, desert nomad. Sales were steady September through mid-October from leaf peepers crowding into town to view the spectacular display of leaves changing to their autumn reds, yellows, oranges, and purples. A few eager beavers booked ski rentals and cross-country ski lessons for the coming winter.

Bring on the snow.

Over the years, his little town grew into a hub for four-season outdoor activity. The cash registers rang summer into fall with bikers, canoers, and mountain climbers who made southern Vermont a destination, including a few, late season hangers-on, such as the kayaking daredevils who braved the icy creeks in late fall.

Brad glanced at the ceiling and counted tiles, breathing in deep to stem the anxiety crawling through him which tended to compress his chest at unpredictable times. He sucked in a gigantic breath and held the inhalation close before expelling the air in a whoosh. He had nothing to worry about. Every business had their slow seasons.

Yup, keep telling yourself, buddy.

Dealing with business concerns was the time he most missed his dad, his consummate cheerleader and advisor. He'd run his own garage and accomplished more than breaking even. The town valued his business acumen. He served on the town council and as president of the chamber. He'd opened his heart and mind for everyone's benefit.

Brad rubbed a hole in his sternum to relieve the pressure. He had huge shoes to fill and a reputation to recover. He imagined his father would have been pleased. One thing Brad prided himself on was not second-guessing his decision to return to Mistletoe Falls or buy Green Mountain Sports.

Not much.

Maybe between two and three a.m., when he

catapulted into high-alert mode and his troubles scrambled through his mind. Coming home was his dream and his one chance to show everyone he was successful. Because everyone in town knew he'd disappointed his dad.

Switching gears, he strode past the racks of apple-red, lime-green, and lemon-yellow kayaks. "Hey, Will."

His assistant poked his head from amidst a rack of personal flotation devices, in the same array of bright colors as the kayaks. "What's up, Boss."

Brad cringed at the moniker. "Snag the price-gun and lower the price on these. A shipment of newer styles arrives after the holidays. Maybe folks will buy PFDs for presents." Anything to get the business through the season.

This little scheme of Mary's could be the solution. Advertising GMS taking lead on the inn's ski trips could inspire area athletes to find their store. The solution—get off his hiney and do the work to ensure their program happened, prove he could be a team player, and if nothing else, a hero to Mary…and his mom.

Brad marched into his small office and paced. His attempt to dispel the constant internal nag reminded him of his past failures. His father never forgave him for heading west instead of college. He hadn't forgiven himself for neglecting to return home to make amends. Not seeing his father before he passed sent Brad to his knees.

For years, he bemoaned his failed ability to make peace with his internal battle and reach out. His plan was to grow roots in his hometown and help his mom while she regained her health and strength.

He scanned the sales floor from his office. "Will, take over. I've a meeting across town in twenty."

"Sure, Boss."

Brad tossed a half-serious glare at the cocky kid who'd rather be climbing the cliff edge of Hazelton's Peak than dealing with retail. Will needed the money, and Brad needed his expertise in rock climbing, kayaking, and wilderness first aid. The boss comments reminded him of the immense challenge and weighty responsibility of taking over a business which ebbed and flowed with the seasons. Talk about rock climbing without a safety harness.

Today's meeting was designed to pad the coffers for those days between fall and winter sports. The extra income provided a cushion for the upcoming, slow late-spring season, when the ground became a mud bath from melting snow, the trees were barren, and the sun weak.

He prayed Mary Packard got her act together. Even though he loved her like an aunt, at times, she tended toward spacey. With a little over seven weeks until the event, he hoped Mary's idea jelled.

Striding through his office, he slammed past the rear door. His mind churned with random event ideas which might have a chance of succeeding. After strapping on his helmet and shrugging into his leather jacket this balmy first week in November, he mounted his bike, turned the key, and pressed the pedal. In seconds, the engine revved. The initial growl, followed by the incessant purr as he roared through the streets, soothed his soul.

The short trip toward the outskirts of town, along Mistletoe Creek to The Inn on Gooseneck Lane, would settle his worries. Heck, maybe the planned Outdoor Adventure Con for the over fifty-five crowd would be a huge success.

Because the alternative didn't bear thinking about.

Chapter Two

Mary fluffed her hair. A last-minute cancellation at the hairdresser cemented her little white lie. Not so small. Luckily, she scribbled *B* instead of *Brad* in her notes. She prayed Natalie was distracted enough not to search the Internet for GMS owner's name.

She understood her niece. She'd carried the hurt for sixteen years. Brad, too, according to his mom, Sylvie. But enough was enough. Soon, Natalie and Brad would meet for the first time since high school graduation. She prayed neither would run once they discovered she set them up.

Crossing Main Street, she meandered up Townsend, to pause in front of her friend's house. Worry knotted her stomach. She squared her shoulders, strode up the sidewalk, rapped on the door, and entered. "Sylvie?"

"In here."

Mary followed the voice and scents of vanilla, pumpkin, and chocolate toward the kitchen. "What in the world are you doing?" She shucked her coat on a kitchen chair and rushed toward the stove. "Let me." She seized a set of hot mitts.

Raising a gloved hand, Sylvie bent by the oven. "I'm able to make cookies on my own."

"I know, but—" Mary leaned toward Sylvie. Whether her friend needed assistance or not, she intended to help.

"No buts. The doc said go ahead and resume normal activity, within reason."

Mary straightened. "*Within reason* being the operative words."

Sylvie slid the hot baking sheet on the butcher block. "See?"

Her proud expression spoke of strength and determination.

"I promise I'm pacing myself. I made and chilled the dough last night. Pumpkin chocolate chip are Bradley's favorites."

"Speaking of Brad…the kids should be meeting."

"I hope sparks fly. And not in a negative way. They belong together."

"Time will tell. At least our scheme got them over the first hurdle—in the same room."

They each removed their oven mitts and rubbed their hands in perfect timing, like matched cartoon villains. All through school, as fast friends since the cradle, kids teased them as the Bobbsey twins because of their brown-eyed, brown-haired coloring and identical height.

"However, I think we'll have to nudge, discretely of course, to ensure they give this thing a chance."

Mary's laugh echoed in the small, tidy, kitchen. "They don't yet know this thing *is a thing*."

"Soon enough, they'll figure they still love each other. They're destined. Come, let's make a pot of tea and share the cookies I decorated earlier."

"Pacing yourself?" Mary raised a brow.

"Morning. Afternoon." Sylvie flipped her wrists. "I told you, I'm icing the cookies in shifts. Besides,

Bradley loves the orange-iced pumpkin shapes. So, I *have* to decorate them."

"You realize he's thirty-four?"

"He'll always be my baby." Sylvie laughed.

Mary bit into a pumpkin-spice-infused cookie and moaned. "Your baby might be grown, but he does deserve these cookies—he deserves a second chance with Natalie."

"We're nudging them. I pray our good-natured meddling works."

A flutter of worry pulsed inside Mary's chest. "Our little scheme *will* work. I don't want you fretting. Tell the truth—are you doing okay? I can't help my concern."

"My six-month mammogram was fine. I'm still low energy, but I've beat cancer. Plus, I've *decided* my evil disease will *never* return."

Mary's laugh bubbled to wrestle with cookie scents. She enveloped her best friend in a sisterly hug. "You've decided? When you make up your mind, Sylvie Matthews, nothing can beat your resolve." She searched the cupboard next to the stove. "What kind of tea did you have in mind?"

"Today is a bergamot tea kind of day." Sylvie plated more cookies, then transferred the whistling tea kettle from the stovetop to a trivet. "You pour the tea." She pointed to the delicate white teapot and matching cups covered in tiny pink roses. "I'll take these into the sitting room and stir the fire. Grab the milk and honey, will you?"

"Right behind you." Mary put two teabags in the teapot and poured the hot water. She placed Sylvie's grandmother's pot on the tray with the milk pitcher and honey pot. She loved the quaint ritual of tea with her dearest friend. "We'll plot next steps in getting these two kids to face their inevitable future. The timing couldn't be more perfect. I didn't fathom Natalie intended to come to Vermont for two months."

As Sylvie left the kitchen, she tossed a glance over her shoulder. "You know if they ever find out, we're dead, right?"

"So, we make sure they never find out." Mary winked. Inside, her gut churned.

****

Natalie stood behind the high-backed registration desk which served the same purpose since the 1890s when her great-grandparents opened the inn. She was amazed her aunt could see over the relic.

Fiddling with the fringe on her silk scarf, she waited for two guests expected soon. Worry gnawed a hole in her stomach. The Inn had full-paid staff scheduled, to say nothing of a stocked kitchen to serve a handful for dinner. They should be close to full every night. She jotted a reminder. *Lure locals to dine.*

Once this planning meeting ended, she would suggest to Mary alternative, front-of-the-house staffing. The kitchen, already understaffed, had no extra help, nor budgeted money, to cover days off. Cross-training employees seemed probable to cut overhead and ensure vacation and unplanned coverage.

The pressure intensified to guarantee the senior college event would fill the inn for ten days at Christmas and safeguard their future. The weight of her new responsibilities sparked her nerves.

If their event worked, Mary could plan others. Baby-boomer weekends for spring and summer. Family vacation specials. Events associated with the town's biking and kayaking seasons, as well as supporting the town's artist community. Those markets should be crucial pieces to the inn's promotion agenda and bring extra income to pay experts to implement new activities.

Worries worked tentacles through her stomach, causing her lunch not to sit well. No amount of yoga breathing helped. Mary and Natalie's inheritance must survive.

First agenda item, bust her gut to work with the new guy and craft a sure-fire Christmas week success. After spending the last few hours reviewing her aunt's scrawled meeting records and putting them in a semblance of order, she hoped the illusive *B*, owner of GMS, would fill in the blanks.

The rotary-style phone clanged. The unfamiliar sound caused her to jump. Decorative and adding historic ambiance to the top of the desk, the outdated phone was more of a hindrance in a modern-day inn. She scrawled the new registration information in the large, musty, and time-worn, leather-bound ledger, making sure her writing was legible. How much would a computer system cost to help the inn run efficiently?

At least, they'd filled another guest room. As she replaced the receiver, the double-wide, etched glass-and-oak door opened with a squeak. Natalie jumped. She gathered her composure and donned her best hospitality smile.

The doorway filled with a set of wide shoulders covered in plaid flannel and long legs encased in worn blue jeans atop scuffed hiking boots.

"Nat?"

She squinted, wondering who belonged to the disembodied voice of the tall man stepping from the porch's shadows into the lobby.

"Nat," he repeated. "Sorry I'm late."

His voice was guttural and familiar. Her heart plummeted to the pit of her stomach, like a thundering rockslide. Only one person called her Nat. That same person spewed constant apologies for being late. She locked her gaze on the recognizable aqua eyes. "Brad?"

Sixteen years.

He'd gone from a slender, clean-cut captain of the football team to a buff guy sporting a days' scruff of chestnut-brown beard.

In a flash, her thoughts transported to the senior girls' jealousy stemming from the *big man on campus* asking the *big-city, new girl* to the prom. Her reflection reverted to summers growing up in Vermont, and the instant bond she developed with her aunt. Earlier to a time when climbing trees was cool, boys and girls could be best friends, and true friendship went unimpeded by those things the genders let get in the way. And before she decided to remain in Mistletoe Falls her senior year, when her heart filled with love, and *long* before her heart smashed to smithereens.

The memories swirled through her—some good, some bad. She sucked in another deep breath, pushing her fingertips against her abdomen to quell the bubbling panic at setting eyes on Brad for the first time since… "I thought you lived in Colorado."

"Not anymore."

Stepping beyond the desk, she stared. "I see the prodigal prom king returns home." His smirk morphed into his signature arrogant grin.

"Prodigal prom king?" He strode toward her and crowded into her personal space. "You *know* I was more to you."

She tamped the sudden urge to fidget with her scarf…or run. His gaze scanned her, from her brown kitten heels to linger at the bottom of her knee-length, matching skirt, before a slow perusal of her pumpkin-colored sweater. She'd put together the casual outfit in fall colors, with hopes of showing the new sporting store owner she meant business. She'd forgone her usual crisp, city business attire so she wouldn't appear intimidating in this small, laid-back town.

"I see nothing's changed since you were a hormone-riddled teen."

Smiling, he lifted his smug gaze to settle on her face. "*I see* you're dressed for a Vermont winter."

She retreated a step and crossed her arms. "If you must know, I'm dressed for a meeting with the new owner of Green Mountain Sports."

Moving closer, he fingered the tip of her angled-cut bob.

His warm hand grazed her neck below her left ear. A spark of shiver slipped along her spine. His scent, so familiar, dispersed the tingle through every nerve in her body.

Brad leaned against the desk. "What you see is…well, you know the saying…what you get."

"What?" She shook her head to dislodge the spiral of dread, replacing the sensuous shiver of moments earlier.

"The new owner."

The timbre of his deep voice tunneled through her. She glanced up. He'd gained a few inches and bulk on his school-age, six-foot frame. "You? But Mary said B—" *Start using your brain, Natalie… "Your* name starts with B."

"You remember."

His deep drawl shouted sarcasm. He narrowed his eyes, drilling holes through the stiff and stoic persona she'd constructed with care. The dissolution of their high school love had ended on a low note to beat all. In caps and gowns, lined up, holding hands, they marched into the school's gym. On their special day, the added staging decorated with their class year banner and flowered shrubs snatched her breath. Their future soared ahead of them, like a hot-air balloon filled with possibilities.

After the ceremony, he curled his fingers against her palm before the warmth of his grasp disappeared and left her cold. Left her alone, she discovered, when without ceremony, he dropped his news flash—bombshell a more appropriate description. He wouldn't attend her graduation party. His other plans hadn't included her, either.

With Brad standing in front of her, years later, grown and more handsome in a scruffy, woodsy way, she transported to the past. Her heartache welled inside. Since his betrayal, she'd stuffed the overwhelming sorrow to the deepest recesses of her heart. Today, the hurt teemed to squeeze her chest.

"Remember? Hardly." Her dread at the moment of recognition switched to reality. Brad was the man she must work with to make their December program a success. The guy who would help save the inn, and stood in front of her, cocky and yummy and showing no remorse, was once the boy who destroyed her.

After the ceremony was the moment she died inside. Her parents whisked her off, then handed her tickets to Europe—her graduation present. Later, her father divulged Brad moved to Colorado. Mary said he'd taken the year before college to lead rafting trips and teach ski school. Sylvie indicated he wanted to find himself.

As a couple together with a future, the two planned to attend Northeastern. He never did show at college—even a year later, despite his promise to his mom. In fact, he never contacted her. At this point, too much time passed to ask why.

She straightened. She refused to let Brad see the effect of his betrayal.

She'd put her best foot forward rather than risk her aunt losing the inn.

Make-or-Break. Do whatever you have to, Natalie.

More than once, she pretended to like law clients. Plastering on her best fake smile, she pretended to play nice.

****

Challenging Nat on whether she remembered him was the last thing Brad should have done. He sounded arrogant. But Natalie Thomas had to be the last person he expected to run into. Man, she stunned him, even dressed in her designer outfit, disguised to look business casual. A fancy-schmancy haircut replaced her beautiful, long, black hair, but she had the same slim figure. He couldn't put a finger on what else was different. Maturity? How had she become more beautiful since high school? Before she broke his heart.

Stepping from the circle of her heat and enticing mint-laced, vanilla scent, different from high school, he replayed his mission. Bottom line, he was here to work with her to keep his business in the black. That meant placing the past in the rearview mirror. “We have catching up to do.” Meaning to disarm her, he flashed his best customer-service grin.

She glared.

He stepped aside.

“We’re here for one reason—to do business.”

She was a high-powered executive assistant in a big law firm in the nation’s capital. Why the heck was she here? Charming her wouldn’t work. He glanced at his phone and flashed the time. “Then let’s start. I’m due at the store by three-fifteen.” Two could play this game.

Collecting her laptop and file folder off the counter, she strode across the Oriental carpet.

The rug, faded in places, didn’t quite cover the scuff marks on the wide-planked wooden floors. The old inn, usually polished, drifted toward decay. *Sad.* He shook his head and followed Nat through the wide casing.

She stopped at the first round table, shoved aside the place settings, positioned her computer, and gestured toward another chair.

Neither sat. They each played the power advantage. “Sit. I’m being a gentleman.” *As stubborn as ever.*

“I don’t need chivalrous gestures.”

She squinted, her lips drawn in a pursed smile, before she yanked her chair, ending the stand-off.

Nat opened the folder to study her papers. Or avoid his scrutiny. He’d bet on the second option.

“To recap, according to Mary, you two have agreed to this half-baked idea. We’ve no time for organized publicity. No other solid plans are in place. The way I see—"

"You weren't in previous meetings."

"I have Mary's notes with Walter—"

"I, on the other hand, attended the meetings *with* Walter. I have my own records." He opened his three-ring binder and flipped to the middle tab. "I'll tell you how the planning went down. Then you can critique."

Her mouth opened.

He held up a hand, then gestured toward her laptop. "Take minutes, so you can't argue later." He sounded steamed because he was. After these past years, and what Nat and her father stole on graduation day, he owed her nothing. She betrayed him and tossed aside every plan. He did, however, owe his mom and her aunt. "Ready?"

"Fine. I've started a spreadsheet for the areas we need to address."

Her smile was phony, unlike the one she'd used to greet the unknown owner of GMS. "*Fine.*" He couldn't restrain the mimic or sarcasm. Obstinacy seemed to be a habit he'd developed in the last ten minutes. "After I reel off what we've done and you've entered notes in the spreadsheet, you can send me the doc. Then we'll be on the same page."

A flash lit her eyes. He didn't wait for her retort. He read her the plan, item by item, without giving her one second to interject.

If the rapid click of keys was indication, she kept pace. Each time he glanced, the top of her head bobbed above her computer. He stopped reading. Within seconds, she met his gaze.

Her mouth clamped in a signal nothing had

changed since he last saw her. She continued to hold everything tight, process things first, assess, and then spew her opinions. He chafed at her initial animosity and meeting takeover. But then, her fancy law firm job must have taught her the art of dealing with presumptuous clients.

"To recap." Mimicking her again, he regressed to a pesky twelve-year-old. *Sheesh, grow up, man.* "We've ID'd various partners, outlined a work schedule, started a publicity blitz—"

"Without nailing a final okay from the partners or solidifying an activity schedule. Never mind taking into consideration the strain on resources of *said* partners—both financial and human." Without looking at her laptop, she tapped a few keys.

His own hunt-and-peck method resulted in misspelled and missed words, even when he stared at his computer.

"Your email address?"

He stuffed his anger and reeled off his email.

She finished recording as he stopped talking. Man, she was fast. "Done. I've sent an invitation so you can view the document. We have a ton to nail down. A timeline to put together so we can ensure the pieces get done on schedule. And—"

"I leave in ten minutes." *View the doc?* No way would he ask. Will would know.

"What?"

"I'm running a store, and my employee's shift ends in one hour." He'd taken all he could of her attitude.

"You only have one—"

Now she acted like a freakin' snob. Were one-man operations below her notice? He'd show her who could be the bigger person. “I can return after I close—six-thirty.”

She glanced behind her.

Did she look for a realistic excuse or plan on bolting through the kitchen door?

She shoved the chair, stood, and plunked her hands on her hips. “We’ll be in the middle of dinner service.”

Her tone carried a tinge of superiority. He cocked a brow. *Okay, enough of being nice.* “You’re a server, too, on top of registration desk duties? You’re the *one* employee?”

Oh, how the mighty have fallen.

Chapter Three

The meeting did not end well. Brad owed Nat an apology, but he couldn't wrap his tongue 'round the words. Instead, he seized the event binder and marched from the inn.

At GMS, he slammed the binder on top of the growing pile on his desk, then scrubbed a hand across his chin stubble. Exhaustion screamed through his shoulders and across his neck. Between the two-day camping-trip he'd led earlier in the week, and running the store, his energy level hit rock-bottom.

Tonight, he'd deal with being thrust into planning a half-baked, screwball, ten-day-long mess of an event. And…grapple with the shock of seeing Nat after so many years.

Crawling into a cave and hibernating for a few months was his best bet. Nevertheless, life moved forward and sleeping away his days would do no one any good.

Brad sucked in a deep growl. He'd cash out, run home to clean up, buy a bottle of wine, and return to resume their meeting. With the few hours of space, maybe both he and Nat would cool off.

Each had been caught off guard. He could be civil. He hoped Nat agreed. Despite being roped into working on the event together, the two shared a common goal.

Sharp pain gripped his heart. He scrubbed his hand

across his chest to ease the hurt resurrected from the past. Maybe hiding in a cave was okay for the next two months.

In an attempt toward optimistic thoughts to reverse a fiasco in the making, he imagined a positive outcome. This joint project was his opportunity to reconnect with Nat and discover why she abandoned long-ago summer plans. She blamed him for running off to Colorado when she was the one to change course.

Had she expected him to sit in Mistletoe Falls throughout the summer knowing she'd never return? He loved her. Maybe the sole extent of their experience was a first-bloom kind of love. Yet, the memory and eventual hurt stuck with him for years. His entire life was planned and spread in front of him for the taking. She left without a word. His heart turned to granite and hadn't softened since.

He'd been such an innocent.

Now he knew better.

All his hopes and dreams crashed to the ground, left him as helpless as the pilot of a leaking helium balloon veering into a mountainside. Lesson learned. Since, he'd never committed to a relationship.

Brad shook off the grief and anger, which at times coursed and tumbled through him like the snow-melt filled rushing Mistletoe Creek. Water over the dam. Time to move beyond his past. His reason for coming home was to set free his ghosts and take care of his mom during her cancer battle. His first step, if he wanted to reclaim the good graces of his family and friends, was to make amends with the *girl* he once loved.

Leaning over, he planted his palms against his

knees, then sucked in and held a huge breath. He stood, air blasting from his lungs. He would work beside Nat and wrangle from her what the hell happened sixteen years ago. She owed him.

At eight, he hoofed up the wide granite steps to the porch surrounding three sides of the stately inn. A bottle of Vermont-made wine, his peace offering, was tucked under his arm. He and Nat could manage to work together to resurrect two businesses. Right? The two were adults. Time to step to the plate and make amends. First on the agenda—set aside his hurt and bottled anger and offer to do anything to make this event successful.

Brad strode across the porch and reached for the doorknob.

Mary swung wide the front door.

She was sweet and generous and, yeah, a bit scattered, like a butterfly afraid to alight in one place for long. But she'd do anything to assist the people of Mistletoe Falls. In return, he planned to help her restore the good reputation of the inn.

"I hear things didn't go well." Despite the smidgeon of scold in her words, Mary smiled.

"Nat told you?"

"And I spoke to your mom. I know both sides. You two kids have a lot of time, and hurt, to make up for."

Kids. They were thirty-four-year-old adults.

"Go make yourself comfortable." She gestured toward the parlor. "I'll call Natalie and get you kids a pot of coffee."

He hoisted the wine bottle, ignoring another reference to *kids*.

"Wine glasses." Mary grinned. Minutes later, she

returned carrying an old wooden tray.

Brad stood. "Let me. What in the world—?"

"Natalie skipped dinner. I bet you did, too."

He held the tray while she set place mats on the round dining table in the turret alcove. The scent of garlic and brown butter wafted as Mary lifted two steaming plates—covered with medium-rare slices of roast beef, green beans almondine, and mashed potatoes topped with a pool of melted butter—and set them on the cozy table. His mouth watered, and a distinct rumble moved through his belly.

Nat picked the very moment to stride from the lobby.

Her mouth opened, wide as nearby Butler's Cave.

She reached over her aunt's shoulder to move aside the Tiffany lamp. "What in the world, Aunt Mary? We—I don't need dinner."

"Of course you do, dear. Brad's a growing boy, and you both expend lots of energy. Sit." Mary situated a glass pitcher of au jus. She added two wine glasses, salt and pepper shakers, and silverware rolled in cloth napkins. "You kids eat first, then work."

Brad stared at Mary. *What was she up to?*

"A pleasant meal between old friends does wonders to bridge a divide. Eat."

Now she read minds? Mary glided from the room like she floated on angel wings.

Before she closed the pocket doors, sealing them in the comfy room with a roaring fire, she winked.

Brad took Mary's order to heart.

Nat snorted a huff.

"Sit." He pulled her chair and motioned.

She pressed her lips into a rigid line, before she

laid a hand against her stomach. "I'm not sure I'm hungry."

Brad ignored the faint rumble. Was her claim of no appetite from nerves, or because she couldn't face Vermont-size portions? In high school, she'd been on the slender side, but today she was skinny. "Seems you have no choice. I guarantee your appetite will kick in. Everything smells great."

Nat's glance slid toward the closed doors before she sat and flipped her napkin across her lap. Eyes focused on her plate, she picked up her fork, speared a single green bean, and slipped the bite into her mouth.

A perfect mouth, in his opinion. Brad ignored the tug on his heart. Instead, he poured each a half glass of wine, then forked a chunk of meat, chewed, and waited for her to take another bite. She peered up, her silly longer length of hair falling over one eye.

"What?"

He refused to call her on her dainty eating. Noticing would stir smoldering embers into a new flame. "I owe you an apology."

"Why?"

"Today, I goaded you. Not okay."

"You have the bad habit of having to apologize."

What did she mean? Pulling a reaction from her—positive or negative—was a constant effort. "Apologize?" His gruff voice was sure to set her on edge. "When?"

"When you were sorry for being late."

"Right." He forked another bite.

She bit her lip, then she set her fork on the edge of the plate. "I might have done the same."

"Apologize?"

"Goad you."

His grin widened. Her admission seemed a lame attempt at *maybe* apologizing, but hey. "Call a truce?"

She nodded. Her hands dropped toward her lap, and she locked her gaze with his.

He swept the edge of his napkin across his mouth.

Still, she stared.

"What? Gravy on my face?" He swiped the entire cloth across his stubble.

"You're different."

"Different?"

"You were continually confident and cocky in high school. You earned the right. Nowadays …"

He *was* different. Life threw him a few curveballs since they'd been friends…and more. Leaning against the chair, he held his breath before expelling on a slow roll.

She displayed a tiny furrow between her brows when she thought hard. The crease deepened. His overwhelming desire was to run his finger down the indent and ask what precipitated her thoughts.

He swore he saw wheels spinning through her mind as she worked to form the right words. *Nothing's changed.* Still contemplative, although skinnier and edgier and distant. She'd forever been quiet and introspective, but she also exhibited a liveliness, attracting him from the earliest days.

Tonight, her scrutiny was different, as if she judged him versus second guessing his thoughts. Once upon a time she never censored her words. Currently, the circles dipping to her cheeks and the tiny lines edging the corners of her mouth and eyes spoke reams on what she left unsaid—stress and something else.

Another puzzle to piece together—later. Tonight, he planned to encourage a cordial working relationship. He dragged another chunk of meat through the pool of au jus and tower of potatoes, and popped the piece in his mouth. For a moment, he found himself lost in the bold, grassy flavor of the roasted meat mixed with the buttery bite of potato. He must compliment the chef. He grinned. Heidi would probably faint. They'd spent a lifetime, as best friends, sparring.

Nat speared another bean.

They ate in silence, as one minute stretched into five.

Her head bent, she forked one morsel at a time. A myriad of emotions shifted like shadows playing across her face. She shook her head, and her short haircut didn't move except that weird point. He recognized her expression from their youth, when ideas swirled while solutions circled through her mind.

For an instant, the problems of today disappeared. In their place, the rush of thoughts regarding commencement invaded the peace of the intimate dinner. She'd worn her hair long with wavy curls, the sides pinned up under her cap and cascading behind her. Throughout the ceremony, he ached to run his fingers through her hair and kiss her. Back then, he spent hours kissing her, as his lips angled and met hers over the gearshift of the car his dad refurbished for his sixteenth birthday. Remembering vividly other kisses under the stars in the swing on the inn's front porch, during hikes up to Butler's Cave and along Mistletoe Creek, and under the gym bleachers during dances, made him wish he could go back in time.

He recalled every sweet, innocent kiss and

cherished the scent and taste of her, spicy, earthy cinnamon and cloves. Did she still taste like gingerbread cookies?

Shaking off remnants of teenage ardor now roaring to life, he wanted nothing more than to lean across the table and touch his lips to hers—test his premise regarding a new scent and taste. Instead, he sucked deep his regrets from long ago and polished off the remains of his dinner before setting aside his fork.

She'd made a microscopic dent, the only empty spot on her plate where the beans once laid. Still, she picked, taking a small bite of beef or dragging her fork through the potatoes until a thin layer stuck to the tines.

Her head rose. "You're finished?" She set aside her fork.

"We're not starting our meeting until *you* finish." He gestured toward her two-thirds full plate. He lifted the bottle of wine and replaced with a splash the two sips she'd taken. He refilled his own—liquid courage to combat the daggers she threw his way. He smiled, settled, and sipped. "You said I've changed. How?"

Shaking her head, she lifted her fork, her concentration on her plate. Her utensil slid through the tower of potato, leaving a tiny dent in the mound. "I'm not sure. Still confident, but…sad?"

Her voice lowered to three decibels below quiet on the last note.

He shoveled in a mouthful to avoid asking why she used the word sad.

She scooped another molecule of potato, sucking the fork clean.

Before more memories of kissing her resurfaced, he counted backwards from ten.

"Defeated."

He lifted his head and glowered. *Defeated?*

"Your mom? You're worried, I'm sure. But Mary says she's in good spirits and doing well with her treatments."

Defeated. He had to deflect her scrutiny, because, as usual, she nailed her observation. He plastered on a grin. "Mom's a trouper. Still, hard not to worry. After Dad died, she struggled. She's bouncing back, and her energy amazes me." He wouldn't mention the guilt he carried with him for never having spoken to his father before he died.

"Your mom's amazing."

She flashed the smile he remembered from years ago when they spoke with ease.

"With everything she's done for Mistletoe Falls, everyone supports her with huge numbers of prayers, taxiing, and healthy casseroles…"

Her glance appeared from under long lashes, before she raised her head.

"According to Mary…" She paused.

A grin lifted the corner of her mouth. Her eyes lit like crackling sparklers on New Year's Eve.

"Sylvie is a strong woman. She'll beat this cancer. Right?"

Afraid if he spoke his voice might wobble, he nodded. He'd missed watching Nat's eyes spark when she spoke with passion. And that optimism came from her affection for his mom. As a kid, Nat spent a lot of time with Sylvie. She acted as much an aunt to Nat as Mary played the role for him. His heart had been so closed off to love for years. But listening to Nat and watching the affection cross her face took the once filled-in chasm and opened the fissure a bit wider to let in the light.

He shuddered. Nat cast a spell over him…once more…but soon she'd leave to go home. The world she'd built without him.

She forked a few bites, then shoved aside the plate.

"You should eat more." The second he spoke, her head lifted in a sharp jerk. He'd overstepped. "I didn't mean to sound bossy. I'm worried. You're skin and—uh, small."

"And too tired to eat." She shoved her chair and stood. "I'm ready to drop where I stand."

"Mary's working you hard."

She shook her head. "The last few months at the firm have been rough."

Standing, he moved the plates to the serving tray.

She gathered silverware and glasses.

"Go. Grab shuteye. I'll clear. I know where to find the kitchen." In one fist, she clutched the handful of utensils, and in her other hand, she gripped two glasses. She stared. *Earth to Nat.* "Do you have time in the morning? We'll discuss details."

A mask of forced nonchalance descended over her features. The prospect of facing him in the morning seemed no better than dealing with him today.

She stepped toward the tray, deposited cutlery and glasses, and nodded. "By nine or ten, breakfast ends and most guests are checked out."

"Good. I'll stop by after I open the store." Knowing he epitomized a thorn she wanted to yank, he handed off the wine. "For a nightcap."

The forced proximity in the overheated parlor resolved nothing, despite Mary's attempt to give them a romantic dinner. His biggest wish was to get to know Nat and discover what happened to yank them apart. They had to work together over the next weeks on a harebrained idea with a ton of moving parts and no cohesive plan. She didn't trust him. He didn't trust her. Time to set aside the past and put his best foot forward to show her what he was made of.

I'll see you tomorrow." Without glancing behind, he shouldered the tray like a pro wait staff and headed to the kitchen.

Tonight, he'd formulate a plan to ensure success for the project and their partnership. Somehow, he had to earn her trust. And…find a reason to trust Nat.

Chapter Four

Going from sound asleep to wide awake in seconds, Natalie lifted her head in a jerk to scan the room. The half-moon shone a bright path through her sheer curtains to cross her pillow, like a laser beam sent to wake her. She glanced at the red numbers on the digital clock beaconing two a.m.

Fluffing her pillow, she shut her eyes and willed sleep to come. Instead, dinner with Brad invaded her thoughts.

First thing, she'd read Mary the riot act for the matchmaking stunt.

Second on her agenda, reconcile awakened stirrings for the one guy she'd ever loved. Her mission—quash any interest.

Despite their tense meeting, she couldn't quell the spin of emotions. Both had changed. Both traversed different paths. Both displayed traces of anger.

Her lids drooped. She drew in a deep breath and, with a slow, methodical sigh, prayed sleep to overtake her. Instead, the tiny changes in Brad's features loomed large behind her lids. His chestnut hair was longer than he'd worn as a star athlete. Throughout dinner, the scrub of darker whiskers gracing his face tempted her to skim her fingers along his jawline. His vivid aqua gaze followed her every time she spoke, and now, in her imagination.

Trying to dispel his image, she squeezed her eyes tight. A poem rambled through her mind, the lines skittering as she was thrust into Frost's "The Road Not Taken."

One distinct factor—she and Brad chose different paths. Did they choose, or did circumstances guide them separate ways? They'd have to discuss how they each arrived at this point. The reason they'd separated stood as the single most important obstacle in allowing her to move forward.

For sixteen years, she remained stagnant and stymied in the love department. Not moving forward was her own fault. She took the easy way out, by ramming every memory deep and closing off her heart.

Her mind spun with images of how she continued to live her life. Point of interest—Wes. They'd dated for two years, until this break. Wes was one more man she chose who couldn't commit. Except…neither could she. What did a fear of commitment and a string of surface-only get-togethers say? Did she sabotage her own relationships?

Now wide awake, Natalie shoved aside the bunched pillow to lean against the headboard and ponder her evening. Self-reflection winged throughout the room. Had she also sabotaged meaningful conversation with Brad once he apologized? No. The weariness drove her upstairs before their second meeting ever started.

She fell against the pillows. A good night's sleep was crucial. Tomorrow, clear-headed, she'd work on her relationship issues. She shoved Wes and Brad from her mind. Her lids obliterated the swirling moonlit reflections. To sooth herself, she counted pinecones, like the ones she and Heidi collected hours earlier to fill baskets by the fireplaces.

The rockin' buzz of her alarm shook her from another dream starring Brad. Several moments passed before the get-out-of-bed signal penetrated the fog. One more minute, then she'd tackle another long day.

Half hour later, she walked the long way to the inn, allowing the crisp air to clear her head. Stopping by the front steps, she lifted her face to meet the sun's warmth and breathed deep the citrusy scent of evergreens until she relaxed. With forced vigor and a scrap of confidence, she sprinted the steps.

Bless Heidi. Insulated carafes of regular coffee, decaf, and hot water stood at attention in the dining room, awaiting weary soldiers to attack the pumps. A Continental breakfast was disbursed with a bell next to a calligraphy note alerting guests to ring for a full breakfast.

With coffee circling the rim, and in imminent danger of spilling, Natalie sipped the scalding brew before wandering into Heidi's sanctuary. Mouth-watering aromas of bacon and baked goods wafted. Natalie's stomach grumbled.

"Mornin', sunshine."

Heidi's cheerful voice grated like fingernails on a chalkboard. "You're way too upbeat for my taste." She tried to brush aside the cobwebs wrapping any semblance of clear thinking.

"Too much wine and fun last night?"

The chef, a former classmate of her and Brad's, raised a sculpted brow. Truth remained she'd taken two or three sips of wine. "How did you—never mind. Mary, right?" Her friend's hazel eyes sparked with humor, tossed with a bit of meddling.

"Dish. I want to hear the scoop before we're interrupted."

Her temples throbbed with tension. "Nothing to tell." She set her coffee on the counter.

"Come on."

Heidi's fists rested on her tiny waist, as her extra four-inch height hovered over Natalie.

"Since when don't you tell me everything?"

"When there's nothing to tell." Natalie waved a hand before her best friend argued. "Zip. *Nada*. *Fini*s. If anything is worth telling, you'll be the first to know. You dish. What's Mary up to?"

"I have no clue what you're talking—"

"Mary's scheme to throw me and Brad together—twice." Natalie stepped into Heidi's personal space, and plastered her fisted hands to her side, mimicking her friend. Heidi rolled her eyes like she'd done as a kid every time she lied.

"Scheme?"

"Don't tell me you're involved. Thrusting me into spearheading an insane event. An event, I might add, which we should have planned a year ago. Knowing this cozy little arrangement would keep me and Brad glued to each other until New Year's Eve."

"Wow." Heidi scowled. "You think I'm in cahoots with Mary?"

"I don't think. I know. I *believed* you were my bestie." She thumped her chest with a fist. "I. Am. Wounded."

Laughing, Heidi turned to pull the last pan of scones from the oven and almost dropped them.

"And a tad bit dramatic."

Heidi's belly laugh added salt to the realization she remained complicit in Mary's scheme. And she'd bet Sylvie represented another partner in the plot, as one did nothing without the other.

"Drama—not your usual style." Heidi handed her tongs. "Help me get these pastries plated before folks appear for breakfast."

"Diversion," Natalie muttered.

"I heard you. Get to work."

"Only if I can nab one of these." Before Heidi could respond, she swiped a cheddar-bacon scone off the sheet pan cooling on the counter. "My all-time fav."

Heidi waved the tongs toward another baking sheet. "Cranberry-vanilla bean used to be your favorite."

"They are to die for. Save me one for my afternoon sweets fix. Give me cheese and bacon any morning and I'm a happy innkeeper."

She and Heidi organized sweet treats and savory offerings. Ten minutes later, she refilled her coffee and snatched two more scones. "I'll be in the office if you need help." Bookkeeping and early check-outs awaited her before Brad arrived for their postponed meeting.

"You're working too hard. We got along fine without you."

"Thanks a lot. You're telling me what I've done isn't lightening Mary's work?"

Heidi held up her palms. "You know what I mean." She seized a brush from the sudsy water bucket. With a swoosh across the stainless steel, she scrubbed in ever-widening circles. "You're supposed to take a break after almost eleven years working non-stop." She tossed the brush in the bucket, wiped the stainless dry, and placed the cutting board on the counter. Then she clutched a wide-edged culinary knife and attacked a pile of carrots.

"You think I can lounge while Mary needs help? Problem is, I missed clues the inn ran on limited staff. I should have visited regularly." Natalie rested her hip along the doorjamb, her hands full. "The inn is Mary's life. And yours too. You know I can't sit and observe."

"Promise me you'll take time for yourself. You're tired already."

Natalie saluted with her refilled coffee cup, sloshing enough to dribble the length of the cup and drip onto her blouse. She drew in a breath. "Truth is I arrived tired."

Minutes later, after dabbing her blouse with a damp cloth to battle the stain, she dove into work. She spent the early morning running between office, front desk, and kitchen. Soon, a group of locals crowded into the lobby, looking for the dining room. Good for business. Bad with the inn short-staffed. They ordered breakfast off the limited, hot dish menu rather than indulge in the Continental buffet, which meant waitress duty.

If she dragged her feet several days in, the next two months would prove long. No way could she tell Mary her own work was due. Her aunt's tendency toward fretting and hovering, in the guise of helping, only added to Natalie's pile of stress. The resulting vicious circle did no one any good.

By ten-thirty, with twelve plus hours still to work, she wanted to crawl into bed. She must have run throughout the inn at least a gazillion times. Her morning step count alone had to compare to a week at the law office. She stretched her toes, but her shoes constricted the movement. She kicked her wedged heels to land in different directions under her desk, plucked the napkin from the third scone—okay, so they were minis where three equaled one—and clamped the tasty morsel between her teeth. If she persisted in this bad habit, her hips would grow by inches before she returned home.

She shook her head and vowed to concentrate on work. A brilliant idea percolated. With speed and determination, she typed a quick overview before the thought disappeared.

The front door slammed, as a frigid breeze spiraled. She groaned and toed on a shoe.

A large set of shoulders in her doorway obliterated the hallway light, before her foot made contact with the second shoe. If she could determine how to hide the coffee stain and pretend her feet were dressed, she might look as though she had her act together.

She swallowed. The scone, perched between her lips, triggered a coughing fit.

"Rough morning?"

Brad's bass reverberated through her. Her heart performed a hop, skip, and jump.

Rough morning and rough week. As if time stood still, she wanted nothing more than to seek solace from the man who'd been her best friend and love of her life, before all hell broke loose. His lopsided, teasing grin catapulted contradictory, acrobatic emotions through her belly. Nothing new. Brad honed the art of twisting a knife and grinning simultaneously. Even through the most dramatic senior year moments when she wanted to bury her head and pretend everything was fine, he'd dragged forth a laugh. She despised the unwanted emotion skittering through her belly.

She swallowed a sip of tepid coffee to wash down the last of the scone. “Don’t stare. I know I’m a mess.”

“I’ve a cure.”

“For what? Me? Or the mess I’m in?”

“Both. Come on.”

“I’m busy.”

He strode the three steps across the office and offered a hand.

Before she could decide how to respond, he clasped her hand and tugged her from the chair. She teetered on one shoe, then fell smack into his solid chest covered in soft, comforting flannel, and scented with wood-fire smoke and pine. With her free palm wedged between them, she straightened. His warm palm anchored her shoulder. He dropped her hand and lifted her chin with his finger.

“You okay?”

“Tired. Stressed. Half dressed.”

“You look fully dressed to me. Unless…” His gaze moved over her.

“Ha, ha, Matthews.” She glanced toward her one shoeless foot. Setting her stockinged foot on the floor and thrown off balance again, she clutched his arm. He cupped her elbow. As soon as she was steady, he released his hold, leaving her chilled.

“Go. Change into warm clothes.”

Too shocked by the order to argue, she stared.

“Field trip. And before you debate, our outing relates to the event.”

“But—” His warm fingers pressed her lips, an effective way of shutting her down. The gesture shot a tingle of heat straight through her middle.

"I checked. Mary and Heidi will stand guard."

Molten anger burned through her muscles to tighten her stance. She gripped his fingers to dislodge his attempt to sway her into going. "You checked with Mary and Heidi? Before asking me?"

His other hand crossed her mouth.

"Calm down. This expedition is replacing our meeting you agreed to last night."

She had no choice. Planning every detail of the ski weekend would ensure success and save the inn, even if the mission meant spending time in cramped quarters with the guy who'd stomped on her heart years ago.

"Fine."

Swatting his hand, she marched past him and exited the confining space filled with Brad's smoky, pine scent. No way she'd admit she blanked the meeting or that being alone with him elicited raw emotions.

Keep your mind on the mission. The Inn needs saving.

****

Brad paced across the lobby. His patience slipping, he flipped his wrist to note the time, then accelerated his steps. *Why do women and quick changes not mix*? Ten minutes was plenty of time to jump into a pair of jeans and throw on walking shoes. Did she plan on returning?

Getting Nat alone might give them time for genuine catching up, minus the well-meaning manipulation of relatives. They had tons to discuss. Explaining the mystery of where their lives had taken each between past and present would be a start to the conversation. Learning what she'd done the last sixteen years would go a long way to filling the deep hole gutting him each time they met.

He'd lived with the rockslide of emotions for so many years, no one had been able to excavate his over-filled crevice—until now. Seeing her opened a gap in the fortress barricading his heart.

The day he expected to meet Mary, he'd been unprepared for the pain slamming him head-on when he confronted his past. Today, seeing her sad expression, brimming with fatigue, he wanted nothing more than to attach her to his guide rope and help her climb toward the sunshine. Instead, he gave her space. If she thought he rushed to rescue, she'd revolt.

They were a pair. If he took on her problems, he'd have to share his own. Not a good idea. The ol' trust issue reared its ugly head.

Nat banged through the kitchen door and screeched to a halt, inches from his tapping boot toe.

He breathed in relief.

"Sorry."

His eyes narrowed. "For what?"

"Taking so long." She nibbled a nail. "Heidi had a dinner question."

"I thought you'd run off." He grinned, hoping to temper both his mood and hers. He tugged on her hand to save the poor nail nub.

Her shoulders dropped. "Where are we going?"

"Going?"

"Your thoughts on another planet?"

"Huh?" He refused to dwell on emotional wounds. Today was for new beginnings. "Calculating how to ascend from a crevice."

She shifted from one foot to the other and met his

gaze. “One of your guide trips?”

“Yeah. You ready?”

“Let me fetch my bag—”

“Also, your event planner.”

She palmed her cell and waved the thing in the air. “All right here.”

“We won’t have reception where we’re going.”

Her raven eyebrows arched toward the ceiling. “I can still take notes, and the tablet is in my bag.”

He shrugged. Yup, two different worlds. Hers, corporate, connected, high heeled, and high tech. His, independent, unconnected, booted, and low tech. He’d been boots on the ground for so long, scrabbling over rocks, avoiding deep crevices, and navigating rapids. Although, he imagined they both had scrabbling, avoiding, and navigating in common. Likely she *scrabbled* plenty in her D.C. office.

Nat climbed into the truck, buckled, and turned to stare. “So?”

As he shoved the key into the ignition, and the truck roared to life, he glanced toward the passenger seat. “What?”

“You never answered. Where are we going?”

“You’ll see.” He patted his notebook wedged between the seats. “It’s right here.”

She reached for his three-ring binder.

He wrapped his palm over her soft, warm hand. “Typical.” He ignored her long-winded sigh as he guided the truck onto the two-lane road. The quiet in the cab settled like a comfortable, well-worn sweater across his shoulders. Like the good ol’ days. They didn’t have to fill the space stretching between them with chatter to still the silence. Twenty-minutes later, he parked and rounded the truck, intent on opening Nat's door.

She jumped from her high seat.

The top of her head grazed his chest as she landed on solid ground. He palmed her shoulder to steady her. The brief touch scalded him. He withdrew his hand.

What am I thinking?

He wasn't. He stepped from her scent, a soft mixture of vanilla and mint, so different from high school. Then, her hair perfumed by a cinnamon and sugar-scented shampoo matched her taste when he kissed her.

"Wow. They repurposed the old train station."

Brad returned his concentration to the present. "Mistletoe Falls' business community spruced up the area and refurbished the old train cars."

She stood with one hand cradled along her mid-section and gestured with the other. "They did a beautiful job with the storefronts."

"For local crafters."

"A funky, full-time flea market. Brilliant."

Her description made him grin, settling his nerves. "Come on." Despite trying to maintain distance, he clutched her hand, warm from the truck's heat. Surprised and pleased when she didn't yank her hand from his, he climbed the steps to the station's sprawling front porch. Wooden rocking chairs, pots of chrysanthemums, and pumpkins in every size and hue lined the length of the deck. The sun warmed his shoulders. The musty and earthy scents of late fall wafted on the light breeze.

Once inside, hand-in-hand, Brad guided her toward the train schedule display lining one wall. "They run every day in the summer into fall leaf-peeping season. Then other runs for special occasions, like the Easter Bunny Express and the Thanksgiving through New Year's holiday celebration tour. Santa's involved."

She faced him. "Santa?"

Her eyes brightened, before her mouth quirked into a frown. He'd wager a million bucks she regretted the playful expression escaping unhindered. He bet she didn't want to be dragged under the spell of the coming holidays. Or maybe she was reluctant to display emotion in front of him.

"Where does the train go?" She turned to gesture toward the map.

Back to business. "Circles around the base of Hazelton's Peak and winds along Mistletoe Creek to Chelsey. See." He pointed over her shoulder, past the ticket counter and wall filled with a collage of Christmas photos from the two towns.

She marched to the map and ran a finger along the train's journey.

Years back, she used to trail her finger along his cheekbone to his jaw when she wanted his attention. A shiver slipped through him.

"Wasn't this railway line the old route to Burlington?"

"You, ah…" The catch in his throat thwarted words. As memories swirled of their youth spent together, he sucked in a calming breath. "You remember. American Train Corp travel gained more popularity, increasing their routes north. Freight trains did the same. See this? They upgraded the main tracks and abandoned the little ones throughout the state."

"This track only runs between two towns?"

Vanilla and mint swirled. He ached to hold her close. Pulling in a breath, he modulated his response. "Yup."

Her brow quirked.

"Gives visitors a travel adventure while benefiting both towns. During climbing and ski seasons, the train stops at the base of Hazelton Peak. What do you think?" Nat's puzzled expression made him itch to touch her warm skin and run his finger down her nose, to soothe the lower lip caught between her teeth.

"As one of the week's activities for our event?"

"Yeah, for our OAC.

"OAC?"

"Outdoor Adventure Con."

"We're naming this-this…?" She waved a hand through the air.

Fiasco? He wanted to finish her sentence, until his epiphany. Together, they could ensure a successful event. "You have a better idea?"

She shrugged. "OAC it is."

For a second her smile widened, and he swore he heard her teenage voice say "what'ev'a" in her youthful Boston accent. Today, her vernacular connection to Boston was faint at best.

"So, the activity?"

"The group boards the train for an afternoon of lunch and shopping in Chelsey."

"But the cross-country ski theme of the week… Mary said—"

"Look, Nat, they can't ski all day, every day." He anchored his palms against his hips. Would she let him do his job—figuring the best way to lead trips and plot itineraries? "I spoke to the conductor. After breakfast, we'll board our group for the nine a.m. run. They'll stop midway at Hazelton Peak. We'll lead a ski excursion along the base of the mountain. The group will reboard the train on the second trip to Chelsey at noon, then they'll lunch and explore town. Return trip is four-thirty."

"I-ah…" She lifted her chin. "I love your idea!"

The light caught the sparkle in her eyes. Her smile lit the old flame deep in his belly. "Let's go." Before he stroked her cheek, he stepped to the porch and trotted the stairs to the parking lot. He turned as she followed. "At Hazelton Peak, we'll supply thermoses of hot chocolate in the warming station by the tracks. The train has a locked storage compartment to store skis until they return to Mistletoe Falls."

"You've considered everything."

Her smile reached her eyes, and Brad was a goner. Plans jelled and the two were in sync.

"Should we make reservations at one restaurant or let each choose? Chelsey must have three or four options." She raised a palm above her shoulder to slap a high-five.

He grasped her palm in his fist. "Good, right? We make a great team." Relaxed, his fingers curled into hers and locked.

"Yeah. So far." She tugged her hand.

The momentary scorch of heat disappeared, leaving him cold, despite the sun beating his shoulders. "Right. Let's head to the base of Hazelton Peak. Then we'll hit Chelsey."

"I-ah, I can't." She stepped from reach. "Too much to do at the inn."

"Which ran itself without your help."

She pressed her lips tight. "You've been talking to Heidi?"

He shook his head. What was she getting at?

"Mary worries me. I didn't realize how hard she works."

He narrowed his gaze as he ducked to look into her eyes. "Aren't you here to take a break from work?"

"I am, but—"

Brad plastered a finger on her full lips, still warm from the building's heat. "Mary and Heidi told me they've got the inn under control. You're supposed to be on sabbatical."

"The very definition means I have work to do…for the firm."

He raised a brow, instead deciding to stay on point with their mission. "If we don't continue, we'll need to conduct event research another day. Time runs short…and we're halfway to Chelsey."

"Fine." She heaved a sigh. "I'll rearrange my to-do list."

Yes. Score one for team Brad. Appealing to her need for organization and time-management won the argument. "We'll lunch in Chelsey to study options and return by two at the latest."

She bit her lip and glanced at the brochure map she'd grabbed inside.

Her hesitation signaled her usual MO—her need to escape more time together. After whisking her from the inn, he wasn't yet willing to let her go. "We're over halfway. We'll plan itineraries after we explore town."

"You're right. Do *not* let my agreement go to your head." She snapped photos of the station and train cars. "Promo. We'll build excitement on social media and blast out photos."

She spouted off social media names—stuff he knew little about. He looked skyward. "Yeah, right. Okay." He'd been in the western wilderness too long with little Internet connection and no need to promote his trips. The outfits he worked for took care of the administration end. At GMS, he left promotion to Will. He couldn't even remember what media sites she'd rattled off—pins and insta-something.

He'd ask Will for a down-and-dirty lesson on stuff Nat mentioned. Before he made her mad, he had to reactivate the few social media pages he had, if he remembered how.

"You don't want to do promo? Brad, we have to."

"I didn't disagree."

"You certainly haven't added to the conversation." She raised her chin.

"Nat, I—"

"No, Brad, we have to be on the same page."

He shook his head. "Nat—" His belly churned like white water on a grade five kayak adventure.

She turned on her heel and marched off.

His shoulders tightened. The base of his neck curled into a tight knot. He didn't have time to learn the aforementioned *stuff* he had little use for, and he sure as hell didn't intend to tell her how little he understood.

Chapter Five

The old phone jangled. Mary reached for the receiver. "The Inn on Gooseneck Lane. How may I help you?"

"Spill. What happened last night?"

She tugged the phone to desk level and leaned into the comfort of her father's wooden and leather swivel chair. "You couldn't wait to hear, could you? Brad arrived with wine."

"Do tell."

Sylvie sounded breathless on the other end. "Are you okay?"

"Fine. Never mind me. What happened last night?"

"I left dinner and a roaring fire. Brad brought wine. I closed the parlor doors—you know, for privacy"

"And?"

"I'd planned to replace the top panels with glass."

Sylvie sighed. "We'll never know what happened. How long did they stay?"

"Heidi said an hour."

"Not much time to eat, discuss the event, and…"

"And what?" Mary huffed. What was Sylvie getting at?

Her friend giggled. "Sharing kisses."

"*La, la, la, la, la,*" Mary sang into the receiver and held one hand over her ear.

"Oh, come on. A few kisses start them on the path

to rekindling the fire once burning."

Mary stared at the ceiling and shook her head. "Dramatic, but you're right. Those kids are grown up. I don't want details."

"I know. The point—they're different. They need to get reacquainted," Sylvie said. "What's our next plan?"

"In process. Brad arrived and asked me to staff the front desk. He took Natalie to lunch…in Chelsey."

"Wonderful. In the car, alone, then Chelsey eating at a romantic restaurant."

"Where Brad told me they would finish last night's meeting."

"Still—"

"You're right. We couldn't have made better plans." Mary laughed.

"What's next?"

"We meet tomorrow. They'll be thrown together. I'll clue in Walter on the escape plan, so we leave the kids alone."

"Escape with Walter? Sounds like fun."

Mary straightened. "Don't you go reading anything."

"Why not? Walter's sweet and intelligent, plus, tall and handsome, with a full head of silver hair. Oh, my, his eyes—sparkling sky blue. What could be the harm? Harry passed five years ago. And Walter's Angie, six."

"Oh no." Mary swiped the air with her hand. "I'm not ready to think relationship. Harry and I spent a good life together."

"Of course, you did. Do you think your Harry would want you alone? He'd want you happy."

The door swept open. "Guests arriving. Bye."

"Fine, Mary. We are *not* finished."

Sylvie never let subjects drop. Mary wasn't certain how she viewed the whole idea of regarding Walter as more than a friend.

Mary pasted on a smile for her guests, as she ignored her friend's *threat*.

****

Agony was being crammed in the pickup cab with Brad. His scent of pine and campfire smoke and something distinct to Brad swirled, catapulting Natalie to blissful days of stolen kisses, furtive glances, handholding, and innocent, young love. Between memories of days prior to the emotional bomb explosion, and every future dream she and Brad planned, her belly twisted with tangled nerves.

On edge, she refused to blurt, Why? What happened? and wait for Brad to fill in the blanks. Not a good time to confront the past, stuffed in a small, intimate space with the man who'd been her future. Fleeing was impossible.

She vowed to survive these next weeks without rousing drama. Then she could orchestrate her escape to D.C. and a job filling every waking hour and often disturbing sleep. A position that afforded little time to obsess on her personal life, much less attempt to enjoy one.

The Vermont trip was meant for much-needed space and figuring out her relationship. She worked well with Wes and liked him but never sat on pins and needles until their next date. Neither did he—the reason for their break from each other. Had time arrived to cut the personal connection cord and stick to a strict, work-only association?

Glancing at Brad, only a console between them, she longed to stroke his arm or circle her fingers around his strong wrist. Any touch to feel his warmth. Daydreaming over what they had was a mistake. Looking forward to her return to D.C. proved preferable to focusing on the grip of yearning-for-the-past.

Leaning her shoulder into the seat, she watched the scenery whiz past. Vowing to bury desire coursing through every vein, she resolved to shove her longing into the deep well of memories.

Wes and she had a mutual vision, including shared values, goals, and life expectations. He was the type of man she needed, even if the two separated. A man who understood the stress of a harried work life and appreciated her need for space to accomplish her own professional goals. For the last few years, Wes stood by her side while she planned and executed every step to attain her dream promotion. His doggedness drove her to achieve her goals.

Maybe she did belong with Wes. Not in a soul-draining love match that could burn itself out, but a relationship of mutual respect and common goals. Love came in many different forms. The two had built a foundation. Maybe their love could grow.

"Hey."

Brad's rumble crashed through her *illogical* deliberations. Reality roared to the forefront. Her strained relationship with Wes worked only in her head and while they were separated by five hundred, culturally different miles.

"Penny for your thoughts?" Brad waved a gold-foil covered, chocolate coin.

Pulled from pondering her D.C. relationship, she

turned. "Where did you get chocolate?"

"The train station knit shop."

She stretched until her forefinger and thumb grazed the slippery foil. Brad yanked the coin from reach. His warm chuckle moved through her, reminding her of his incessant teasing in high school. He knew her weakness for chocolate. She curled her fingers, like a toddler's wave. "Gimme."

"No sweets until you confess your thoughts."

"Mary and the inn." She didn't blink at the fib. She wasn't ready to discuss her pseudo-relationship with Wes or face what happened years ago.

"It's good you're home. Mary worries about holding on."

She swore her heart skipped a beat. Finances must be worse than she thought. "She told you?"

"Mom squealed."

"The inn is Mary's inheritance. My legacy. I must find solutions, and fast." Like being slammed with a rockslide, her belly convulsed. She cradled her middle. After her father turned against his Vermont upbringing, she was the one family member responsible for helping Mary.

How would she assist and still maintain her studies? Attaining the promotion was the one reason she headed to Vermont, believing the inn a safe-haven where she could one-hundred-percent concentrate on reaching her dream promotion. Not only a logical step in her career-path, but the boost in pay ensured she could finance repairs on a general manager's salary.

"Our region is hopping with winter outdoor activities."

Brad's comment cut into her musings. "What?"

"Where'd you go?"

His grin telegraphed he caught her pondering. "Thinking."

"Our event will capitalize on this area's seasonal outdoor activities. Our efforts should enhance the inn's reputation as *the* place to stay for city folks escaping to the country. We have to ace this event to help both our businesses."

As various promo angles for reeling in out-of-state customers spun through her mind, Natalie bobbed her head. "The key—convince clientele to embrace Vermont winters by showing the inn as a comfortable, homey place to rest your head and enjoy the area's outdoor offerings. That's where GMS is key—corralling town businesses to work together promoting the concept on our social media. Win-win."

"You've covered publicity, right?" His fingers drummed the steering wheel.

"I'll design, but GMS must take the lead on dissemination." The look of terror he tossed her way confirmed her suspicion he didn't *do* social media—a subject to explore another day. "GMS promotion catches the attention of outdoor adventure-seeking visitors. On the promo…at lunch, we'll wrangle our to-do list into an action plan." She glanced at Brad to gauge his reaction, but he stared straight ahead. "By the time January hits, I'll have exciting photos to share for advertising future events."

Brad rolled his truck to a stop in front of a low-slung structure at Hazelton's Peak.

"Wow." She leaned forward. "Picturesque. You mentioned a warming shelter, but I envisioned the same old falling-down, three-sided, wooden relic. Remember our hikes?"

He nodded.

Why did she mention the past? Before he could spout memories to make her sad, she gestured toward the stone structure, wide open in front. "Tell me about— Oh." She opened the door, jumped, and strode toward the new building. Brad's door slammed. In a few steps, he reached her elbow. "Look…a fireplace in the back." She pointed. "I love the rough, hewn-wood benches."

"Another improvement. Our Mistletoe Falls and the Chelsey outdoor-adventure clubs spent years fundraising…together." His shoulder bumped hers. His breath feathered her neck.

"The planners solicited building-material donations and volunteers to lay stone and landscape."

"Wow. Wasn't Chelsey our big rival in ice hockey and football?"

"Still are, big time. Makes sense the chambers of commerce and downtown business groups cooperate. Both towns are off the beaten path. Outdoor sports enthusiasts routinely bypass us for the national forest or northern lakes and mountains. Attracting the tourists to southern Vermont is a must."

His signature grin set off butterflies.

"It's beautiful. My parents never understood the appeal. Dad discounted his upbringing, even though Mistletoe Falls provided a convenient dumping ground for me every summer."

"Dumping ground?" His brows knit.

Her chest tightened like a fist to her sternum. *My big mouth.* "Work and social life were priority. The live-in nanny cared for me during the school year. Mary was the summer *hired help.*"

"You know, she cherishes you like she would her own child."

"Of course. And I love her for caring. She's more a mother than—" Waving a hand, she swatted the illusory fly of childhood loneliness that continued to buzz her head.

Brad's arm weighted her shoulder.

"Why have kids?"

The question emerged as a mutter under his breath. She didn't have an answer. "Let's get lunch." Blinking tears smarting behind her lids, she forced a smile.

When Brad tugged her to his side, she sank into the comfort of his familiar touch. They hiked to the parking lot. For those fleeting moments, Natalie felt as though she'd never left. He'd been her lifeline since childhood.

He opened the passenger door and offered his palm to steady her as she climbed into the cab. She sucked in a calming breath and focused on the now, not the past.

Once Brad was seated and he buckled his seat belt, he glanced over. "Ready? I'm starved." Fifteen minutes later, a large, green-and-gold-embossed *Welcome to Chesley* wooden sign heralded a greeting. Brad veered into a parking spot along the main drag.

He yanked open her door before she could unbuckle. The cold air raised goose bumps to dance over her arms. Gripping her hand in his warm one, he helped her from the high cab, then fob-locked the truck. "Which way?"

"More to see toward town hall." She pointed left and towed him along the sidewalk. The two stopped in front of a wooden-framed shop with a glass-recessed door. Both Chelsey and Mistletoe Falls' downtowns had a quaint vibe. She wiggled her hand from his grip and shivered, not realizing until then his hand warmed her entire body.

Natalie fished for her phone. In front of one, bow-shaped window, she snapped a photo of bright-colored, fur-trimmed parkas, then moved to the next, for close-ups of patterned scarves and striped mittens in the same bright colors. The outdoor wear appeared perfect for strolling through the winding park paths by the river. She stepped to the edge of the curb, leaning solid against Brad's pickup door, to take more photos, then keyed descriptive words into her phone. "Let's go inside."

His eyes widened. "Here?"

"Look at you." She laughed. "You'd think I just demanded you eat a full plate of Brussels sprouts."

"I'd rather eat Brussels sprouts—"

"Than scope women's fancy clothing?"

"It's not—"

Laughing as she thrust a thumb toward the display, she stepped closer. She wagged a finger. "Fear? You're scared, Matthews."

"I'm not a shopper."

"Yet you own a sporting goods store." She nudged an elbow into his ribs.

He held up a palm and stepped from range. "Coming into GMS is *not* shopping—it's an adventure."

"Keep telling yourself. Great tag line though."

He cocked his head. "Tag line?"

"You know...promotion." She signed quotation marks. "Green Mountain Sports...An Adventure."

Scratching his chin, he studied the store sign above

him. “I like the way you think. I should put your tag line on my website. You know, right at the top.”

“What do you have now?”

“Our name, I guess. I let the kid take care of promo.”

“Kid?”

“Will. My employee.”

“How old is he?”

“Twenty?”

She couldn’t believe he didn’t have a handle on his own promotion. “And you let him have his way with your website without checking?”

Brad stopped in his tracks and glared.

Maybe she’d overstepped, but his marketing problem sounded as though he needed more help than a twenty-year old, unsupervised *kid.*

“I check the site every Sunday, once Will works his magic.”

“Not close enough.” With her hands perched on her hips, she stepped into his space. “Think, Brad. If you scan without noticing much, what do you think your customers do?”

“You can’t glam up a sporting-goods store.” He opened the door and stood aside.

“You can *glam* up anything.” She breezed by him and turned. “Our mission, besides configuring the event agenda, is to notice marketing. And learn.” She locked her gaze with his. “For both of us. I’ll take notes.”

He tossed a sideways glance.

“Come on. We’ll get ideas. Once we have specifics on town offerings, we advertise the train trip as one of the highlights.”

“It’s a cross-country ski week. Why will they want

to do anything else?"

"One-track mind with a one-track outdoor agenda does not an adventure make. An hour ago, who suggested we add variety? Isn't this why we came to Chesley? Huh?" She nudged him again. "We can use this promo year-round."

As his chin dipped, he raised a brow. "You're planning on being here next year?"

She detected a hint of cynicism and shrugged. "The beauty of the Internet. Promo can be done from anywhere." She towed him into the store, past the casual clothes, into the depths of lingerie and formal clothing, to the racks of outdoor wear. "See," she whispered. "This shop could be considered part of your competition."

He smoothed a hand over a parka sleeve, then sauntered to the next rack. Unzipping another, he looked at labels, fingered the lining, and studied prices. "We need to get going, or I won't get you home by check-in time."

On the sidewalk, she extracted her phone and accessed the notes page. "Well? Your opinion of the outdoor clothing?"

"Good quality." He drew on his gloves and faced her. "Overpriced. More for strolling Main Street than skiing an open, windy field."

"Why?"

"Why? The temp rating for one. Outdoor sports clothing needs ratings appropriate for climate and activity. These products are more a fashion statement used for running from the house to the car and shopping. Not for prolonged outdoor exposure and exertion where you build up a sweat."

"Sweat?" Goose bumps skittered over her arms.

"Certain materials absorb moisture. If not, you freeze to death."

"An extreme prediction."

"Not if you get lost in the wilderness."

"Point taken." She grasped next to nothing associated with outdoor trekking. She sucked her lip between her teeth. When she looked up, Brad stared at her mouth. A shiver slipped down her spine. "Let's go. Things to see."

They stepped into several stores. One sold tasteful, touristy, Vermont handcrafted products—moose-themed mugs, alpaca hats and scarves, maple sugar candy, and natural mint scented hand cream. Natalie jotted notes and snapped photos. Another store featured local art and pottery. In a deli case by the register, she noted Vermont cheeses, butter, local yogurt, and goat's milk.

"A strange combination of products." Brad held open the door. He waited until she stepped to the sidewalk, then followed.

She shrugged. "I imagine, since most of the pottery is geared toward household and kitchen use, selling comparable, local food products explains the oddity."

"Point taken. I'm not versed in pottery and the use of—"

"You eat, don't you?" She elbowed him, like they used to do as kids. "Or do you only concentrate on the outdoors and tin plates?"

"You making fun of me?" He returned the nudge.

She skipped sideways in time to escape the noogie on her head. She should have expected his reaction. Even as teens, when she teased, he flung his arm around her neck and inflicted the childhood punishment. Beyond arm's reach, she changed the subject. "Chelsey's downtown is pretty. A big change."

"Yup. Mistletoe Falls and Chelsey made concerted efforts to entice visitors year-round. We're close enough to Boston and on the route to the Adirondacks. Makes sense to take advantage of the tourist influx year-round and help the local artisans."

"How do you know so much concerning the area?" With the sweep of her hand, she showcased the panorama of storefronts. "You lived in the west all along, right?"

"The nature of the work is seasonal. I nabbed positions wherever I found work. After Dad died, I made an effort to land jobs in the New England area."

She gripped his forearm. "I never told you how sorry I was to hear of your dad's accident."

He shrugged off her hand and glanced over her shoulder. "I'm hungry as a black bear. Let's eat."

She got the hint, big time, and repeated her mantra. *No talk of families. No getting close.* She had an end date. Problem was, today she caught a glimpse of the Brad she fell in love with.

To outrun her thoughts and forgotten dreams, she turned and marched toward the nearest restaurant.

Chapter Six

Brad stared, his heart pounding at the notion of once again sitting opposite Nat. He never took her to fancy restaurants, except dinner before prom. Instead, the two hung at the Shake Shop. If he'd grown up with Nat's family money, he could've treated her to the finer things. And…they might have ended up together. He shook his head.

"What? Nothing you like?"

He caught her gaze. *Oh, I see plenty I like.* "Still deciding. You?"

Her finger skimmed the list of menu items and stopped. "I'm splurging on mushroom-shrimp risotto. Dinner happens after the dining room closes. Usually, I'm too tired to eat. Risotto should hold me."

"No wonder." He scanned what wasn't hidden by the table. "You're skin and bones. Find time to eat."

"How?"

She snapped a glare like a red flag stopping a race—don't order me around. Then her gaze locked on her lap, her face softening.

"I've decreased employee hours until the holidays."

"Things bad?"

"I didn't realize until I arrived. Mary needs help."

Her whisper cut deep. "Will staff return as needed?"

"I made sure they found temp work, so, yeah. If we can co-sponsor outdoor tour groups for the rest of the winter and spring, we might keep business steady until summer. Not big like this event. Maybe winter skiing weekend trips or spring canoeing or bike riding, partnering with adventure tour guides. They—as in you—plan the trips. We provide the beds, breakfast, and dinner."

Brad fisted, then stretched, his hand over and over to dispel the stress. Growing up, he considered the inn his second home. He must help Mary…and Nat. Her idea…good for both businesses, but at best, a long shot. The plan also meant adding staff to manage trips.

For a second time, his stomach growled. He signaled the wait staff, and they each placed orders.

Their server presented fresh-baked rolls with a ceramic pot of farm-churned, local butter.

Once she buttered her own, Nat bit into hers and issued a low moan.

The sound hit Brad like an arrow straight to his heart. He rubbed his chest to dispel the pain of longing.

Nat bent over her tablet, tapping the keys to awaken the ever-present spreadsheet.

She was oblivious to his discomfort—a good thing. He placed his file folder, front and center. He listened to her chatter as she tapped notes, while he scratched reminders along the meeting minutes' margins. At this rate he'd need more space than the margins provided. He pulled a yellow pad from his folder.

They were from two different planets. Brad shook off thoughts of the intimate lunch being about the two…together…as a couple—a date. He willed his attention back to the ballgame. This project seemed like playing for the World Series. The ultimate goal to ensure both businesses winners would provide solvency.

"So, arrival on December twenty-third, cocktail mixer, and a buffet." Without looking from her tablet, Nat talked and typed. "Good?"

"Yup."

"We should feature local, New England fare. Several guests mentioned they can't arrive until the twenty-fourth."

Nat looked over his shoulder, her gaze far off in the world of planning and organizing. He recognized her contemplative, thinking through each step to the rightful conclusion expression. As a go-for-the-gold type of kid without a plan, her pondering drove him crazy. Today, he appreciated the value.

"Heidi has great recipes for wassail, hot spiced wine, and eggnog, plus we'll offer non-alcoholic. Maybe dark hot chocolate with nutmeg and cinnamon and mulled cider. Not an open bar, but festive. What do you think?"

"Truth? I'd go for beer." He tapped the local liquor menu.

She bobbed her head. "Good idea."

Without looking up to confirm he meant local, she continued typing.

"Vermont-brewed beers and holiday spiced ales. December twenty-fourth—a big, Vermont-style brunch. Introduction to the week, fit everyone for skis, and a ski lesson."

"Last-minute Christmas shopping?"

She raised her head and snagged her bottom lip between her teeth, before she threw a sideways glance.

"You're such a man. They'll have finished shopping."

"Maybe not. I'm entertained by last-minute shopping. A challenge—like a sporting event."

"I repeat, such a man. Fine." She kept typing. "Van into town for the afternoon?"

He scratched a few notes on his yellow pad.

Her decisiveness alerted him to her big-city work style. For a split second, he vowed to release this foolish notion of the two of them—a couple, with similar interests and skills. In Vermont. Together.

"Takes the pressure off staff."

He lifted his head. "What?"

"Taking guests to town gives staff time to ready the Christmas Eve dinner. For those who want to relax at the inn, we'll open the library slash game room."

"Or skiing and snowshoeing."

"Your proposed outdoor schedule means you or one of your staff should be available."

He nodded and scratched another note. "Once we finalize our schedule, I'll staff up."

She bit her lip. "How?"

"I have a list of summer and holiday student helpers."

Nodding, she poised her fingers above the keypad. "Okay, Christmas Eve, cocktail hour and heavy hors d'oeuvre buffet." She typed faster than her spoken words. "Acoustical guitar or something in the library after dinner. Early to bed. Unless—folks attend evening services."

"We'll need on-call vans. Music suggestions?"

She shrugged. "I don't know the area."

"Will might know." Brad jotted more notes.

“We need sedate.” She bent her head over her tablet. “And not too young.”

He crossed his forearms to lean against the tabletop. “You’re kidding, right?” He shook his head. “Just because they’re a fifty-five plus crowd doesn’t mean they only listen to their kind of music.”

“Not what I meant.”

“Then we ask Mary and Sylvie for their suggestions.”

“Of course.”

She pursed her lips in the put-out way he knew too well. She wanted to argue he was wrong. He waited for her to instruct him on what to ask the ladies. She didn’t. “I’ll call Ralph’s Tavern about local musicians.”

The meal arrived.

She closed her tablet.

The server presented Nat with a heaping bowl of risotto. In front of Brad, he placed a large plate covered with marinated skirt steak, a mound of mashed potatoes, and a medley of fall vegetables.

“I won’t need dinner.”

After each commented in sync, Nat laughed. Once she finished a few bites, she moved her meal to the left and opened her tablet. “We have the two days before Christmas planned.”

Could she get through one meal before shoving aside her food after two bites? “Eat. Work can wait.”

“Can’t. Time’s running out. Christmas—unhurried morning brunch.” She typed then forked in another bite.

He watched her beautiful mouth, then shook his head. He wasn’t here to rekindle what the two left behind.

“Stocking exchange?”

Pulled from his thoughts, he lifted his head.

"Or a gift bag under the tree for each guest? Or both?"

"Overkill."

"Maybe you're right." She took another bite. "This risotto is heavenly. Creamy and cheesy and filled with shrimp, with just the right touch of garlic."

At least she ate. He waved his fork. "On second thought, you can never have too many presents."

"After we collect merchant donations, we'll decide." She tapped the tablet to life. "Breakfast followed by cross-country skiing. Early evening, the big dinner."

"Whoa." Eating while working was a recipe for a stomachache. "Don't overwhelm the guests. The name of the game—relaxation."

"They paid for a cross-country ski week. I assume our guests are active. Anyone can opt out. We'll have quiet options."

"No wonder you're stressed. Tons on your plate. My end is easier."

"Not what I want to hear."

"Mine is cut and dried. You're juggling a ton."

"I have help at the inn."

"Why don't we eat first? Then work?"

She shoved aside her tablet, inhaled a deep breath, and straightened. "Brad, we have seven days to plan."

"After you eat." He spent the next half hour regaling her with his western adventures. As usual, she picked at her food.

Halfway through her risotto, Nat pushed her bowl to one side…again.

"I'll need a to-go container."

"What happened to storing your food intake to get you through dinner rush?"

She laid a palm against her stomach. "You make me sound like a squirrel with my jaws filled with acorns. If I finish the huge serving, I'll have to go into hibernation on the parlor couch." She opened the tablet. "We need goodies for the guests."

Refraining from eye rolling, he leaned his forearms against the table edge. "At least finish the seafood."

She stabbed a shrimp and brandished her fork. "Want one?"

He gestured to his nearly empty plate. "I'm stuffed. Take more bites. Then we'll work."

Looking down her nose, she dropped the shrimp back in her bowl.

He leaned back in his chair. "I vote for small vendor gifts and coupons in the stockings. No gift totes. Both is overkill."

Anchoring her palms against the table, she straightened. "I spent money already ordering totes with the inn's logo. We'll give them later in the week. My bet—we'll have enough giveaways to fill both. Now…to source stockings."

"Mom and Mary make hundreds of felt stockings for the toy drive. They might make extra."

"Perfect." Clapping her hands together, she grinned. "I spaced on Mary working evenings decorating them."

"See. Two great minds." He snapped his fingers. "The renovated church slash community center hosts a concert Christmas afternoon—bell ringers from one church, a choir from another, the local teen chorus. The entire town attends."

Her eyes widened. “Fun. Scratch Christmas skiing. Instead, a late brunch, so people can go to church early. A traditional Christmas Day dinner after the concert. Skiing on the twenty-sixth.”

“One day at Hazelton Peak, then lunch and shopping in Chelsey.”

“I think we need a mellow day using the inn trails the day after Christmas, then Hazelton on the twenty-seventh.” Nat tilted her head.

He nodded. Even though he wasn’t used to mellow on his trip excursions, the organization of this event seemed intense. “I bow to your expertise.”

“Okay then…” She reached for her bowl in the middle of the table and spooned more risotto.

To refrain from highlighting the obvious, he pressed his lips tight. She needed to continue eating to keep her strength. Some tiny voice in her head, and not a full stomach, told her to stop eating. He wished for the old Nat—the one who ate with gusto and enjoyed every bite.

She scooped in another morsel and moaned.

The unrestrained sound caused his heart to constrict. Brad clung to every ounce of strength to refrain from leaning over the table to touch his fingertips to her lips.

She dropped the spoon in her bowl and jumped into typing. “We should build in quiet days with activities. And alternatives for bad weather.”

“Agreed. Mom might have ideas. My steak is stellar. Want a bite?” Brad offered a forkful.

She hesitated, then leaned and closed her lips over the fork, chewed, and sighed.

He angled toward the center of the table, before

jerking back. Had she noticed? What was he thinking? He almost kissed her. *No*. He had to stop fantasizing and stick to business.

She settled in her seat.

Judging by her closed lids and the barest of a smile tipping the corners of her mouth, she savored the steak.

She opened her eyes, and her gaze homed in.

He diverted his stare to the breadbasket.

"What?" She pressed her forearms against the tabletop.

"Lost in thought."

"Ideas for bad weather activities?"

"No. Maybe. I'll talk to Mom." No way could he reveal watching her mouth sidetracked him.

Her gaze swept over him.

A shiver slipped along his spine. Once upon a time, she had him pegged. They had no secrets. Their friendship was solid, and their love grew in maturity. Then the perfect relationship tumbled to the gutter.

"I took notes on other ideas." Her voice drifted.

Yeah, she had pegged him dreaming of *them* instead of business.

She pulled her bowl, front and center, ducked her head to stare at her meal, then dipped her spoon into the creamy concoction of rice and cheese.

He swallowed his smile. When she wasn't conscious of what she did, she ate with abandon.

"I'll check the spreadsheet and fill in ideas for the last few days. Okay?" She glanced at him, narrowing her gaze.

Could she still read his mind?

"Let's concentrate on New Year's Eve—the big day. Maybe a morning off with a combined continental breakfast-lunch, so guests can eat whenever they want. They can sleep longer for a late night." She waved her spoon.

The spoon she'd seconds earlier removed from her mouth in slow motion. He fixed his gaze on her lips…once more. He couldn't help himself. With a mental slap at his rioting desire, he forced his focus on project preparation before his imagination was eaten by more kissing fantasies. Praying thoughts of snow and ice would keep him on track, he concentrated on a list of winter sports. "We could mix up the program with snowshoeing."

"Might be a fun change of pace and new experience. Some can still ski. They'll know the inn's trails by then. Right?"

"Yup."

Head down, she jotted more notes.

"We need a bonfire and a late lunch outdoors, if weather is decent?"

"The bonfire is already planned for evening, Brad. I say simple, help-yourself fare inside throughout the day, like soups, salads, and sandwich makings. Outdoor activities and quieter indoor options." She flipped her wrist.

He grinned at her use of the same gesture with which she might swat a pesky mosquito.

"Easier on staff if folks make their own schedule—downtown Mistletoe Falls, read by the fireplace, or nap. We'll set up puzzles and games in the parlor with crock pots of hot cider and chocolate in the dining room. They'll be outdoors that evening."

"Easier on staff?"

"We each have limited employees." She waved a

hand between Brad and herself. "We need pause days between skiing. Otherwise, we burn out."

Brad's head spun with details. This entire affair was akin to orchestrating a three-ring circus—more like juggling seven rings. His job sounded simple in comparison—one trek, one destination, one menu before heading home. Then start over on the next trip. He stalled for a second, trying like heck to remember what they were discussing. Ah, hot chocolate, reminding him… "Remember Heidi's mom's famous peppermint pie?"

"Oooh." The tip of her tongue grazed her upper lip.

He lost his concentration. "What?"

"The one with a chocolate crust and drizzles of fudge sauce. Fabulous idea. Mini tarts and pies for nibbling."

As if a typing marathon depended on her winning, Nat raced fingers over the keyboard. "How can you type so fast on those little keys?"

"Practice." She raised an eyebrow.

Realizing his question bordered on inane, he spread his broad fingers and glanced at her slender ones tapping the letter icons. Maybe not so absurd a question.

She glanced at her phone.

She made him dizzy switching between gadgets.

"Sending Heidi a text for her ideas."

He leaned on his elbows. "So, midnight? What leads up to the main event?"

"A sleigh ride?" She swiped the face of her cell, then flashed the screen. "Look. Perfect. The weather app says full moon on New Year's Eve. Pray for a clear night."

"I'm praying for a week of clear days and nights." He swore a curtain descended over her bright eyes, making them dull and…swimming with worry. "No prob. Skiing in a little light snow on the inn trails will be fun. We have standby plans…remember? You—we've—got this." He slid his hand across the glossy wooden table and ran a finger over hers hovering over the keypad.

"Ah, r-right. Reminder t-to self—add to agenda for next meeting."

He tried his almighty not to grin. If he wasn't as affected from touching her, he'd have barked a laugh. Sliding his hand from the table, he sucked in a steadying breath. "Here's an idea. Using the ice arena for a bad weather day."

A picture scrolled through his imagination of skating with Nat on family skate Sundays. Her cheeks were pink with excitement and the invigorating cold air. His arm slipped around her shoulders. Her cinnamon-sugar scent accosting him. His other arm crossed in front to lace together their gloved fingers to achieve the wonderful sensation of gliding arm in arm, hip to hip in total sync, skating as one. *Those were the days.*

"Aren't they booked with ice hockey tournaments and family skate hours during vacation week? Remember high school…"

He shook off his reflections.

Deep in thought, she scrutinized a far-off corner of the dining room. Nat wiggled her fingers over her tablet.

He reached to still hers, by wrapping his fingers round her wrist. The warmth seeped into him. "We couldn't—" With a cough, he cleared his throat of emotions from long-ago memories. "—get enough of skating, clinging to each other in public."

Color tinted her cheeks.

"Every Sunday— Ah, w-we do need to concentrate on…." She tugged from his grip.

He missed her warmth.

"Not relive moments long forgotten."

Did she try to erase their past? "Are they, Nat? Forgotten? I remember with vivid—"

"The arena and our guests—" She tucked her hands under cover of the table. "Could we book hockey tickets one night?"

With the rebuff, he shoved aside fantasies of long-lost love. "I'll check the dates for the playoff tournament. Give our guests a sense of small-town life and team spirit."

"*Love* the idea." Her voice rose on a high note. "The event room overlooking the arena? We could…"

Nat's gaze rose to catch him staring. Her eyes lowered as she stretched her fingers, then resumed typing. He couldn't help grinning. He loved getting a rise from her, whether a blush or stutter or averted eyes.

She paused. "You don't like the event room? Come on. Makes perfect sense."

With a beguiling wave and her fluttering painted nails approaching his face, he let his mind roam one hundred percent in a different direction—to high school. She painted her nails to match her outfit or season. Today, they were light orange, with a pumpkin on each thumbnail. Once, he peered into her bedroom. Nail polish in every color of the rainbow lined her bureau. They held hands, and he ran his thumb over the smooth surface of her nails. He yearned to touch her hand, but she'd made clear that shouldn't happen.

"The room is heated. Plus, we can set up food."

"What? Um, sure. Fine." He scratched another note, because sure as shootin' he would forget every idea and command she spouted. His entire inventory of brain power centered on pinkened cheeks and polished fingernails. Straightening his spine to stare at the ceiling, he distanced himself from memories and focused on exploring the use of the arena. "Agreed. Food. Great idea. An old-fashioned, New England baked bean pot and hot dogs—right?"

"Susie's Diner can cater." Flattening her palm against her heart, she leaned. "Her maple syrup baked beans are to die for. Plus, venison chili and, oh, her local bratwurst and sauerkraut. A hearty, down-home, game-day, Vermont buffet. What do you think?" She straightened.

Then she flashed that sweet smile he could never resist. Brad grinned. Nat, the city girl, fitting into small town life. "You've done your homework."

"Aunt Mary likes her once-a-week outings to Susie's."

"You don't have enough food at the inn?"

"Great food. However, we need a break every little while. Heidi's cuisine is different."

With his hands crossed over his stomach, he reclined. "If I weren't full, I'd hit Susie's on the way through town."

Her eyes sparkled and she sat forward. "We'll tell Mary our idea. Tomorrow, we can stop before the lunch crowd."

He loved the way she lit when she was excited. "And eat?"

"And eat, *if* we have time."

"You're a task-master, Ms. Thomas."

"What's the time? We have to go." She shoved her chair.

He signaled their server.

"We have more planning to do, including adding a daily dose of skiing." She gathered her belongings.

"Will and I can generate a location list."

"If I have downtime tonight, I'll organize today's notes. Are you on the spreadsheet doc yet?"

He glanced at the brick wall and sank his teeth into his lower lip before he swung his gaze to meet hers. "About the spreadsheet. I have no clue…"

"I sent the link. Can't Will help?"

"Can't you just *print* the spreadsheet?" The second he spewed the testy comment, he owned his ignorance. He flashed one hand. "I—"

"Won't work." She planted both palms on the table and stood. "These documents are fluid. We continue to add new ideas. You need to check them daily. And add your own ideas, update me on your assignments—like the arena situation."

With an apology sitting on the tip of his tongue, he changed his mind. "I'll call you."

"Not the point. We're both too busy to waste time discussing every detail—the reason why everything is on a document we each can access." Nat turned and strode toward the door.

He snatched the receipt tray from the server and scribbled a tip and signature. He stalked after her. "What's your beef about, Nat?"

"You. I need *you* to get with the picture on technology. I can't handle the entire event myself."

"An excuse." He clenched his jaw to the point where he feared a chipped tooth. "I'm owning my end. You and I both know our disagreement isn't over spreadsheets. You're running scared of what we—You're avoiding me. I thought we'd progressed."

"Progressed?" She straightened and faced him. "With the event, yes. You and me…we'll never advance past the graduation episode. You *hurt* me."

And you hurt me. "Right."

Not having a clue how his not knowing how to work with a floating and ever-changing spreadsheet suddenly became a blame game, he ducked past her and headed toward the door.

Boots and heels. How would they ever meet in the middle?

Chapter Seven

The ride to Mistletoe Falls was chilly—and not the cab temp. Brad's good-bye bordered on frigid. No hopping from the truck to do his usual being-a-gentleman thing. Just a nod and a curt "later," before he roared along the wide circular drive, past winter's remnants of summer's lush gardens.

She swore a black bear sat on her chest. The region of her heart throbbed. Why had she started a fight over their past?

Because she was tired.

And frustrated.

And still hurt.

Natalie stared after him, until the truck moved from sight, leaving only glimpses of snow-covered fields and the meandering Mistletoe Creek. Soon, the racing water would ice over…like her heart.

The heart that finally showed signs of thawing. Until she blew the evening's camaraderie.

What ate at him?

More like what troubled her? He was right. She ran scared.

The past reared, slipping trickles of chills along her spine. The same ice immobilized her on graduation day. He couldn't run fast enough, and he never answered her multiple emails and calls.

This time, a marginal disagreement had him

running, stemming from the stress of working together. Was tonight's behavior any different from sixteen years ago? They each ran—and still ran.

Her rib cage constricted. Nothing had changed in the intervening time. Natalie pressed a hand against her chest to stay the incessant, rapid beat.

Returning to Vermont was a mistake. Letting her aunt rope her into taking lead on the event was a bigger blunder. If she had confessed to her aunt the truth on why she was home… Instead, she was stuck with Brad. She glanced the length of the driveway—not even a distant engine rumble.

Once more, the graduation scene rushed forward. His announcement and disappearance, followed by her rushed trip.

The European tour was anything but a celebration. The romance of Paris, the historical beauty of Rome, the ghostly sadness of Pompeii, the passion of Spain, and their trek through the Portuguese vineyards and wine caves were lost on her. The whole summer left her heart a shattered spider web of tiny cracks—breaking up with the guy she loved with her entire heart. She still ached. Brad saved her years ago. And then, together as friendship wove into young love, the two made plans for the future.

Misery mounted with endless, boring days. The throbbing heartache and isolation of being unable to contact Brad still haunted her. She never discovered why he ran.

Problem was, despite differences as the two worked together, Brad saved her again. She shook off memories, and today's problems dragging her low, and climbed the wide steps to the inn. Wooden chairs and a porch swing graced the long veranda, bringing forth so many memories, leading straight to Brad.

Not going down this road.

Focusing on the present, she homed in on a portico needing paint. *Note to self—touch up front of inn before weather turns cold.* She eyed the swing, devoid of bright summer cushions and laughter from long childhood days spent giggling with Brad over lemonade and cookies. And later…

Don't go there. Walking memory lane of warm nights snuggling with Brad would do her no good. No reminiscing stolen embraces, his arm looped over her shoulders, snuggling her to his warm side, and kisses in the moonlight. And none of hot afternoons, their toes dangling in the cold mountain waters flowing along Mistletoe Creek, and later swinging on *their* glider on the long, wide porch, making plans for their future—together—college in the big city and Boston and dreams of what would follow graduation.

She opened the door, sucked in a bracing breath, and willed her mind to settle. Bottom line, she had a job to do—save the inn and refuse to allow thoughts of Brad to interfere.

Ready for battle, she straightened, thrust high her chin, and entered the lobby. The area appeared deserted, until her petite aunt's head bobbed behind the bountiful, autumn spray of flowers set on the large front desk. The nicks and scars from the past decades of use were evident beneath the gleaming finish. The old focal point of the lobby was a vestige of their heritage. Both a reminder and warning she must streamline the inn workings.

"There you are." With a massive grin, Mary shifted

her gaze to the left, then skirted the desk. "Did you two have a good day? How was lunch?"

"We worked. The outing wasn't a date."

Mary's expression shuttered.

Natalie forced a smile. Before Mary answered her tart comment, she continued. "We have tons of ideas. Tonight, I'll print the details for you. Plus..." She had to smooth over her reaction to Mary battering her with questions. "We need input from you and Sylvie."

"Oh, good."

Mary's smile returned to light her face.

"I can't wait to see your plans. In the meantime, two more reservations for tonight. Your outreach with discounts to families visiting area schools is paying off."

"Great!" Her shoulders dropped a tad. Connecting with the community was imperative. "This coming year we'll beef up our promo and research untapped sources."

Mary's smile slipped. "You won't be here."

"I can work from a distance. Computers. Internet. Remember? And I'll visit."

Mary cupped her jaw, then patted her cheek. "I treasure your visits, you know. If you ever tire of the city, I'll welcome you."

"I, ah..." Her throat tightened. "I'd love to come home. Maybe—"

Heidi strode into the lobby. "You're here. We've a ton of reservations, and I need a substitute sous chef."

"A ton?"

"Eleven. Thirty-two people total. We haven't been that busy since summer."

"Ooo-kaaay?" She wasn't exactly sous chef

material. Natalie rubbed her hands together. “Let’s get started.”

“Routine stuff you can handle. Jeremy’s baby is sick.”

“Oh, no. Is she okay?”

“Sniffles and a slight fever. His wife is stuck at the hospital with an emergency. She must see the case through, until the next shift is up and running.” Heidi sucked in a deep breath and glared toward the ceiling. “Jeremy hopes to get here sooner than later.”

Natalie glanced at Mary. “You okay to staff the desk?”

“I’ve been doing the job for years. Run along.”

After she changed into old clothes and sensible shoes for kitchen work, Natalie strapped on an apron and rewashed her hands. “Ready for orders.” Heidi’s intake of breath was a sure sign she was stressed.

“Carrots peeled and grated on the big-holed disk. Then celery chopped—quarter-inch or so.”

She grinned. “You’re making Waldorf salad?”

“My version.”

“My fav. I haven’t indulged in years. You don’t often see Waldorf on menus anymore.”

“Stick with me, kid. Plus, we’re in Vermont. Apples are a staple.” Heidi opened the oven door and stirred a huge casserole.

The hearty aroma of roasting meat mixed with subtle scents of lemon and rosemary wafted, reminding her of her aunt’s traditional Easter dinner. “Lamb stew?”

“Good nose. Tonight’s special.”

“I wish I’d refrained from eating a huge lunch. Had I known…”

Heidi closed the oven door, placed the big spoon on the holder, and removed her mitts. "I'll save leftovers for tomorrow's lunch. Speaking of—how was the date with Brad?"

Natalie lifted her chin. "Not. A. Date."

"Seemed like a date. He begged us to cover, so he could whisk you off…" Heidi shot her a wink.

The mischievous expression meant give me the goods or trouble will be a-brewing. If she didn't spill, Heidi would hound her. "Business. We hashed out program components for December. Didn't you get my text?"

"I did." Heidi closed the oven door.

"Then you know we worked."

"So, no fun at all? Even a smidge of nostalgia over old times?"

She shrugged. "Okay. A bit, and not in a good way."

Heidi leaned a hip alongside the counter. "Look, I love you both. I also know you're both miserable."

"We are—*I* am *not* miserable." The chef sent her the glare of an old friend who could read between the lines.

"Yeah, you are, deep down. Until you two discuss the past, neither will have good relationships."

Long ago, she thought Brad was her future. Now, she kept the notion buried. She tossed the half-scraped carrot on top of the cutting board. "We're not reuniting, believe me."

"Would be nice. However, I meant finding your own with others. Neither of you can get beyond the hurt to trust or let a new person into your life."

"Not so." She blew a wayward lock of hair from

her eyes, and she crossed her arms. "I've had plenty of—"

"What happened to each?"

"We've gone down this road. I know your opinion. Button your lips." She opened the walk-in and disappeared. She refused to admit she'd never fallen in love. Or that any man she'd had semi-serious relationships with bordered on platonic, including her two-year stint with Wes.

She never allowed herself to get close to falling in love. The longest was with Wes. Despite working well as a couple, their relationship was not one of deep passion. A peck on the cheek, a pat on the hand, a kiss after romantic dinners or special occasions, but no sparks erupted. They were perfect for each other in every other way. She assumed the comfortable connection would one day transform into a safe love.

Comfortable? Most of the time. Safe? Yes. Equal partners on the team? No. One more reason to stay clear of one-on-one moments with Brad. She couldn't guarantee keeping her heart safe. Comfortable and safe with Wes worked for her.

She emerged from the fridge.

Heidi pounced. "What were you thinking?"

"Nothing."

"Uh-huh." She grinned. "I rest my case."

She lifted her palms to shoulder height and huffed. "How in the world do you continually know what I'm thinking?"

Heidi dumped the risen dough on the bread board and kneaded.

Natalie shook her head. She never could pull one over on her bestie. Now, she'd have to put up with her interference, along with matchmaking efforts from Mary and Sylvie. She didn't even want to contemplate their machinations to ensure she and Brad were continually thrown together.

****

After an hour, Natalie left the inn behind as sous-chef Jeremy circled the kitchen, his apron strings flapping. Seeing the bustle soothed her, as Heidi and Jeremy performed the dance of chefs behind the prep table. Everything was under control, and the inn continued to make money.

She slumped with her spine pressed against the bedroom door. Her breath expelled in a slow hum. Between Heidi's relentless grilling and the building tension between her and Brad, the day was endless. She glanced at her clock radio—only seven. Fatigue gripped her—the usual state these days. With fingertips, she massaged her forehead, hoping to dispel a Canadian-sized headache.

Cracking the window, she plunked into the comfy recliner, closed her eyes, and cocooned her head against the chair. She pulled deep into her lungs invigorating air and willed her mind to declutter and settle.

After a half hour power nap, she changed and settled in the office to await arriving guests. She compiled the lunch meeting notes, saved the summary, and minimized the doc in case she had additional inspiration.

Perusing the budget, she found additional revenue to put aside for security cameras and an alarm system. She raised her hands in jubilant celebration. To surprise Mary, she planned to supplement the inn's extra income with her monthly savings account contribution.

Once she checked off her list, the weight of today's activities and those of last week lifted. She stood to stretch. With energy renewed, she reopened today's meeting notes and scanned them one last time before she sent them to Mary. Her aunt hadn't yet embraced technology beyond email and a bit of online shopping. Hopefully, she could give Mary a lesson. Pointing out gently the necessity of learning the latest technology, she could ease her aunt into the right decade, before she returned to D.C.

Natalie laid cool fingers against her temples to work a gentle massage near her hairline. Despite the vanishing headache, stress pressed her shoulders. Here at the inn, so much more was at stake, and no one else could help carry the burden. One of the perks of working with five hundred others was the shared distribution of pressure and workload.

Earlier she'd been harsh with Brad, challenging his tech ability. She had no right to judge. He spent sixteen years trekking the wilderness and now running a store. So, why had she been so stubborn and defensive? And why had she given her aunt a pass, and not Brad? No wonder he'd meted the silent treatment. Obsessing about their little tiff wouldn't help.

She glanced at her summary notes and pasted each into the relevant tab on the spreadsheet, adding the additional ideas that popped into her head as she'd mindlessly grated carrots for Heidi. With a flourish, she finished with a hard-plunked period. She addressed an email to Mary and Walter and attached the shared Internet link to their event folder. *Done.* Guilt spiraled through her heart and squeezed as she poised her finger above the Send key. She added Brad's name.

Next, she printed the notes to slip in the office binder. The extra steps seemed overkill. Still, she'd vowed to be sympathetic to other's skill sets, hadn't she? Plus, once she returned to D.C., Mary and Brad would have a record to be duplicated for future events.

She glanced at the time and peeked through the slot in the wall. She couldn't lock up until diners departed and overnight guests arrived, so she downloaded the road-trip photos. Tomorrow, she'd craft a public relations message and send emails to Chelsey store and restaurant managers, explaining the Outdoor Adventure Con and seeking photo-use permission.

Standing, she stretched before she popped into the kitchen for a cup of chamomile tea. Her cell vibrated in her pocket. She wasn't ready for any more questions from her assistant. "Hello." Sounding testy, she tempered her voice to sweet. "Natalie speaking."

"I'm sorry."

"Brad?" He usually called the inn phone.

"I shouldn't have blamed you for my ignorance and ineptitude of everything tech."

He read her email. She mopped her free hand across her forehead. "I-I'm the one to apologize. I was tired and short-tempered. We each have strengths. I can't claim knowledge about leading outdoor activities and group events."

"I'll learn tech. Finding time is the problem. Nowadays, I'm juggling an event while building my business and ensuring I'm open next year."

"Is your store in trouble?" She set her cup on the desk and settled against the chair.

"Not yet."

His sigh did not project optimism.

"The previous owners had a good following. If I don't stay on top of every opportunity to lure engaged customers, I might go the way of most new business owners."

"And old business owners." Her musing emerged in a mutter—thoughts she'd meant to keep close to her heart.

"I'm sure you'll resolve the inn's issues. Everything, including business, is cyclical"

"How?" The ramifications of failing to stop the inn's financial downturn whirled through her mind. "In two months? I have to return to my job." *If I have one.* She prayed she found time tonight for class work. Maybe after the last guest arrived, she could ask the server to keep an eye on the front desk and call Nat, if needed. Time to practice resourcefulness with staffing options.

"We're partners."

Brad's words yanked her to the conversation.

"Working together, we'll attract customers to both businesses. Guaranteed."

"Guaranteed, huh? Strong language, buster."

"Christmas season. Of course, more business is guaranteed."

His laugh moved through her like her favorite holiday music—cheery, optimistic, and familiar. "Oh-kay."

"Miracles happen, Nat. Together, we'll build our profiles."

"Fingers crossed. A ton rides on this event."

"Have you considered hiring a manager, so the work doesn't fall on Mary's shoulders?"

Like wishing for a fairy godmother with a magic

wand? "We have no extra for an executive position."

"You might find money if you tie future employment to meeting external goals. The manager doesn't produce, then no job come spring. The person produces, the profit helps pay the salary. Add a raise incentive if profit increases over the break-even mark."

She leaned against the desk. "T-the idea could work. How did you get so smart running businesses?" Brad's self-deprecating laugh caused her to straighten. They each understood little concerning the other. At one time the two had been tighter. They knew every intimate detail of the other's life. Nowadays…well, she knew next to nothing regarding Brad.

"We'll discuss over dinner."

"I-ah, we'll see." She hadn't pressed him on anything personal. The simple reason, she didn't care to spew details of her life since high school. Baby steps. Inevitably, the two would learn more over the next seven weeks. Then, time to head to D.C. and leave behind the past.

"Trial and a lot of error."

"What?" She shook off memories to concentrate.

"Learning the business."

"Sounds like my future. Trial and a lot of error." Brad's graveled laugh sparked a need to catch up with the past.

"Plus, mentors who took time to handhold a novice. Owning a business is different. I'm responsible entirely for this shindig. Time to search for the new and innovative, which means learning technology."

"I'll help. And maybe…" She hated to ask for help. Still, collaborating made sense. "Can you continue with business advice?" His pause sounded like a drumbeat pounding out, can I trust, should I get involved, and will I absorb everything I need to know? Or, more likely he didn't want to take time to school a novice in business. "Anyway…thanks for your advice." She fisted the phone…and held her breath.

"Deal."

After several beats of silence, she questioned whether he'd hung up.

"Nat, I'll share what I know." Another beat, with an inhale of breath echoing over the line. "I'm no mentor, but I'll help. Ask questions. Lots of them. I, ah, appreciate your tech tutorial offer."

Relief expelled as a whoosh from deep in her chest. "Great. Deal. I'll walk you through the spreadsheet and other new social media tools." She allowed the silence to linger.

"Yeah, thanks. Listen, have to run. Tomorrow after the inn's dinner hour? Can we compare notes?"

"Sure."

"Gregory's Bistro? Seven?"

Her heart raced. Many more hours would be spent up close and personal with Brad. What had she gotten herself into?

Chapter Eight

The next afternoon, a continuous flow of customers flooded the store.

Brad scrubbed a hand through his hair. He wasn't complaining. Extra foot traffic was a major bonus, except for failing to schedule reinforcement staff. Who knew?

His line stood five deep. As the next person stepped to the register, he glanced at Will hoping for assistance. With one customer inspecting climbing gear, while two others waited for Will's expert service, Brad marshaled his energy to tackle the deluge.

After the tense night with Nat, the sudden surge of business sapped his waning energy. Crawling into a hollowed-out tree stump and hibernating for a few months suited him. That wouldn't happen until after tonight's *date* with Nat. He plastered on his smile to focus on his customer. "Did you find everything?"

"More than I needed."

The gentleman, he guessed in his early fifties, unloaded the pile from his cart. "What brings you to Mistletoe Falls?"

"They bused us from a conference at the Mount Gilman Hotel." The customer waved his hand toward the crowded store.

With renewed energy, he straightened. His tension and exhaustion disappeared. A busload of conference goers—a new market—sent his imagination into high gear. He couldn't wait to tell Nat. She'd spew off promotional ideas, as she typed madly into whatever electronic gadget she brought.

"Interesting. What type of conference?"

"New England high school phys ed teachers. The focus is individual outdoor sports for school-sanctioned outing clubs and basics for year-round outdoor activities. Trip planning, that sort of thing."

"Wow. Wish I'd known. I could have presented options on wilderness experience training and demonstrated equipment."

"I'll mention the idea to the conference coordinators for future workshops." The man gestured toward the store's interior. "You offer great products. You sell online?"

"We're designing a system but haven't established formal online presence." He bluffed his response. A new website task for Will. He drew a business card from under the desk. "Call if you have questions or need products shipped."

"Great." The customer scanned the card. "I'll let others know."

"Or questions on outdoor adventures. For years, I led all-season trips in the West and New England."

"You ever lead small group seminars?"

"I've trained trip leaders and facilitated seminars." He handed the man extra cards and a stack of brochures. "Please distribute these trip listings in case anyone needs hands-on experience before they counsel teens. I can conduct on-site or online, in-depth workshops for any trip, or guide a leader's overnight experience."

"I'll be in touch." He tucked the brochures and cards in one full-to-the-brim bag, handed Brad his card, and clutched his haul in both fists. "My district couldn't get the funding for other teachers. I can round up a group. We're in New Hampshire, two hours east."

Brad nodded. "Not a problem."

"I'll put together a district proposal to contract you for next spring's teacher-education day."

In a miraculous shift, Brad's mood lightened. "Happy to meet any group needs. Send me an overview on your programs, and I'll put together workshop blurbs for your proposal."

"Excellent. I'll touch base over the holidays. Email is on my card. Give me a nudge if I don't connect before January." The guy shrugged. "Too many balls in the air."

"I hear ya."

The end of the line advanced fast. Within the hour, customers departed like a hoard of locust headed for greener foliage.

Jazzed, sore feet and overtaxed mind a thing of the past, he leaned on the counter and jotted seminar notes on a paper bag and speculated organizing local community college adult ed programs.

"Wow, Boss, what a rush."

"Unexpected." Despite his use of *boss*, Brad flashed Will a grin. "Let's restock." While the two lugged merchandise from the storage room, Brad broached his ideas. "Any way you can come up with a list of classes for adult ed? Or presenting programs on outdoor adventure in schools?"

"Solid. I can scrounge my trip shoots and work up a digital presentation, no prob."

"A what?"

"Boss."

Will's tone signaled people of Brad's advanced age were far gone.

"On the computer. You know—slides with photos and topic notes."

"Oh yeah. Great idea" Another thing to ask Nat about. "Let's get the plan in place before holiday traffic ramps into high gear. Show me what you've got." If Will came through, he could ditch bothering Nat. The less time looking foolish in front of her, the better. "Time to fill these shelves."

With his final restock load, Brad descended the stepstool. He placed the merchandise on the growing pile in his pull-cart.

"Boss. Visitor," Will called from the doorway.

The second he sauntered into the showroom expecting to see Nat, he detected the cloying scent of gardenias. His stomach roiled. The only person who never understood the concept of moderation, and gassed him every time she drew near, stood front and center and hard to miss decked in the latest fashions running antithesis to rural Vermont culture.

Celia.

What the hell? How had she tracked him to Vermont?

Her ring-covered hand clutched his forearm. One ring sporting a pointed jewel twisted and dug through his sleeve. The bangles halfway up her wrist clanked. He didn't have the option of barreling through the rear door to the alley. He yanked his arm from her grasp.

"Brad-ley."

She purred his name. He'd once found her breathy

voice alluring.

"Long time."

Not long enough.

The tone rasped a path along his spine—a warning like the sandpaper lick of a dangerous, big cat. "What do you want, Celia?"

"Can't an *old…friend…*stop by to say hello?"

Again, she stepped close. "Friends, yes. You, no."

Behind the register, Will's eyes widened like a full moon on a dark night.

Celia's hand tightened on his wrist like a python ready to squeeze out his life. No, wait—she'd crushed him years ago. He twisted from her grasp.

"You wound me, Brad-ley. Time to let bygones be bygones."

"State your business. I've got a store to manage." She scanned the sales floor with her cold, icy-blue eyes. At one time, those exotic eyes entranced him.

"Your customer service lacks. No wonder this place is empty."

He didn't give her the satisfaction of answering. If she believed for one minute, he had a successful business, she'd dig those talons and fangs deeper and never leave. "Down the street are stores suitable to your tastes. I've got work." He turned on his heel, caught Will's open-mouthed gasp, jogged to the storage room, and kicked the door shut.

Chicken? Yup!

The fox attacked the hen house. Any sane chicken would retreat. Whatever Celia's scheme, he refused to provide opportunity to set in motion her warped plan. He sucked in a lungful, then doubled over to expel the breath tightening his chest. Celia's habit of sticking close until her mission became clear and she reached her goal caused a bolt of worry to rocket through him.

His door eased open. Will peered in. "She's gone, Boss."

"Thanks. Next time, I'm not here. Understand?"

Will saluted.

Celia's hasty exit gave Brad time to research and plan his strategy. Whatever enticed her to town must be splashed over social media. If he still lived in Colorado, he'd have reinforcements. Although, his trekking buddy, Jeff, might give him clues to Celia's plans.

Time to call his old friend.

****

Several hours later, Brad emerged from the double-wide shower stall with triple heads—his favorite part of the apartment. Standing under the hot, pelting spray normally refreshed him. Tonight, Celia's appearance plummeted him into the past. Her three-year-old betrayal and hurt roared forth to form a cloud over the rest of the day, made worse following Nat's betrayal.

He called Will to open the store in the morning, so he could take a short hike. Outdoor activity was the tonic to thinking through his troubles. Tonight, he'd suss out Celia's motive with Jeff. Tomorrow, with a clear head, he'd face his other demons and confront Nat.

With concrete plans, Brad's stomach settled. Wearing a towel tied at his waist, he detoured to the kitchen to crack open his favorite local winter ale. The first lingering taste of malty sweetness and warmth slid down his throat in welcome relief. Beer in hand, he strode to his bedroom. Swigging more beer settled his nerves. He donned the heavy comfort of his well-worn sweats, confident his plans would work. Seizing his cell off the charger, he padded barefoot to the living room, intent on ordering pizza and watching part of the ball game before calling his pal.

Brad scrolled through his contacts for Tessa's Pizza. His Bruce Springsteen "Born to Run" ring tone jolted him from relaxation mode. "Hel-lo."

"Weren't we meeting at Gregory's at seven?"

Shoot. Nat sounded angry. "We are." Brad glanced at his watch. Seven-fifteen. "I am… Lost track of time. I'll be there in ten." He swiped off his cell and groaned. How did he get so side-tracked he forgot the date he obsessed over before the rush hit his store mid-afternoon?

One, he was exhausted.

Two, he dealt with Celia.

He looked at the ale with longing, downed a few swallows, strode to the kitchen sink, and poured the remainder in the drain. After donning jeans, a heavy cabled sweater, and his broken-in, Wyoming-made, cowboy boots, he jogged the stairs to his truck. Ten minutes to the second, or close enough, he marched into Gregory's. "Sorry."

Nat tilted her head.

He couldn't tell if she was angry or accepting his third apology in recent days. Being on the defensive was *not* a good habit. Although, if he were honest in his assessment, he'd been perpetually late and saying he was sorry since they were kids. He grinned to lighten the mood, until he registered her expression. She looked beaten down. "Rough day?"

"I'm not hungry for a big meal."

She glanced at him, deep circles rimming her

bottom lids.

"Can we order a few tapas and call this a night?"

"Sounds good. I could use a beer. Want anything?"

She shook her head, before giving a short nod. "Maybe a beer will help dislodge this headache."

He leaned in and grasped her hand, ice cold to the touch. "You, too?"

Nat sighed.

Laying his other hand atop hers, he rubbed warmth into the tips of her fingers and over her palms. The motion calmed him, as well. After today's craziness, he needed the connection. When she didn't pull from reach, surprise shot through him like the first blast of fireworks spray on New Year's Eve.

Silence floated—not uncomfortable, but the opposite. Like the years separating the two never happened, he reverted to the days when neither saw the point of filling every moment with chatter or activity. They were a team against the world, in a time when each trusted the other with their deepest secrets and their hearts and accepted silence.

He released her hand to lean on his elbows and rest his chin atop his fists. "How 'bout we stash the day's trials and enjoy ourselves? Kick these headaches to the side of the road." The slight tip of a smile graced rosy lips he'd lived to taste senior year—lips that still haunted him with questions of *what if*. Brad shook his head to dislodge memories turned to cobwebs clouding his brain and threatening to weave around the present to encase his heart.

Focus on dinner.

The two decided which four small plates to share.

He swigged the first few sips of icy beer, warming

as the hearty liquid slid past his throat. He slathered dense, chewy peasant bread with the house pâté manufactured at a nearby farm, then handed her the slice. He prepped his own, before slouching against the soft, brass-colored leather of the booth.

Nat bit into the thick slice of bread.

Her sweet little sigh wedged deep in his heart. He'd bet his inventory she'd eaten little today. "Feeling better?" He raised his mug to tap hers.

She gave a slight nod.

The gesture indicated she hadn't yet released her stress. Some things never changed. Nat was wound so tight, encouraging her to relax was an ongoing challenge. His gaze locked with hers. "What's up?"

"Nothing. Everything."

"Spill." He slathered another piece and offered the slice to Nat.

She shook her head.

With no time for lunch, he wolfed the bread. "You used to tell me everything. I'm still a good listener." Her worry sketched tiny lines between her brows.

"More stress than I envisioned."

"What kind?"

Her brows rose toward her hairline as she glanced at him. "My D.C. job is tough. I do know what to do in every instance. Still, client demands are often wacky, but not much surprises me anymore."

"But?"

Her arms circled wide. "Huge learning curve. Being an innkeeper is like juggling a hundred balls bouncing in opposite directions. Mary isn't much help."

"Your aunt and uncle ran the place…forever. She grew up at the inn."

"She's great with the customers and works hard. Mary understands all aspects of registration and check-in. Problem is, she doesn't have the head for business needed to take the inn to the next level."

"Then why are you taking on the work? Delegate. Make a schedule and place her in jobs utilizing her skills—the customer-service end."

She glanced at the ceiling, then frowned. "What happens after I leave?"

"You're streamlining. Each week show her something new. Keep a notebook she can consult—"

The server arrived with the first two small plates, placing them in the middle of the table.

After dreaming about pizza this afternoon, Brad wasn't convinced tapas would be enough. He asked for a refill on bread.

Nat raised her fork and polished the handle with her fingertips.

Up and down. Back and forth. Brad imagined wheels spinning through her mind.

"She worries me. She's still energetic, except her mind wanders the longer the day lasts. Not sure if her energy is waning or she's tired of the day-to-day grind. This inn has been her whole life. Maybe she needs a break."

"Have you broached the topic of selling so she can retire?"

Nat's shoulders lowered as she slumped against the chair. "I can't imagine Aunt Mary getting rid of her homestead. And…without the inn's income, she can't afford to keep her legacy."

Brad gestured toward the plates. "Eat." He forked a chunk of grilled ahi tuna off one plate and set the fish on his own. The aroma of a Mediterranean spice mix wafted. "I'm hungrier than I thought."

Nat helped herself. "Smells wonderful."

"The tuna is excellent. Here's a thought—maybe hire one of the high school kids to staff the front desk afternoons? Give Mary a break from worries."

"Or…" Nat set aside her fork and steepled her fingers under her chin.

The pose made him yearn to cup her chin in his palm and press a comforting kiss on her lips. She squinted, and he wondered if she read his mind.

She sat with her fingers clasped and resting against the table. "I've cut staff hours and picked up the slack. Maybe I can work the numbers to keep one server between lunch and dinner. Adding a new employee would cost more."

"Great idea."

She glanced at the ceiling, then straightened. Her gaze locked with his. "I know, minimal, yet every penny saved… Truth? This wasn't what I signed up for. I had no clue the inn was in trouble. Or any idea Mary planned a big event."

He narrowed his eyes. "Didn't Mary ask you to come home?"

Nat's gaze slipped to her lap. "No." She bit her lip.

The gesture sent Brad's heart racing.

"I was desperate for a break after eleven years." She glanced at him before her gaze drifted behind him.

He waited.

"I'm home for another reason."

Like the thin wisps of smoke from the candles, the silence circled them.

"I'm up for a huge promotion. Still, I have a lot to

learn." She looked him in the eye.

Silent seconds passed. He pressed his lips tight to hold his sympathy and to give her time to assess first before solving things on her own.

"My boss awarded my sabbatical to study for the certified paralegal exam. I need to edge past others applying for promotion. I thought Vermont would be a quiet retreat."

"But you've had no time for your course." His wasn't a question. The dark circles under her eyes induced him to slide the next plate closer. He wouldn't *order* her to eat. He learned his lesson such techniques didn't equate to a show of caring—just the opposite.

She glanced at the citrus-basted scallops sprinkled with cilantro.

He hoped the colorful presentation enticed. Forking one scallop, he planted the tasty bite on his plate. "Your idea is good, Nat. Utilizing current staff gives you a break and affords time to study." He cut the fragrant scallop in half, popped the bite in his mouth, and relished the combination of salty, spicy, and tangy flavors. "Man, this is tasty."

"I must catch up on the inn's paperwork and expand our social-media presence."

She ignored his hint to dive into dinner. "Not everything should be piled on you. Can Mary do simple back-end work while she waits for check-ins? And the afternoon wait staff—can they tackle social media! Kids are whizzes."

"What made you so smart? I hadn't considered…"

The corners of her mouth tipped skyward, as the grin won out. "I've always been smart." He didn't bother to temper the flirt in his voice. He added a wink to throw her off balance and nix the work topic.

Her wide-eyed, contained expression caught him off-guard. She looked as innocent tonight as she had the moment he met her. At age seven, she showed excitement at being in Vermont, running through the inn property, climbing trees, and catching frogs in the creek. They had so much history. They were best friends, long before they loved each other. "You appear— I don't know. Angelic?" He grinned, hoping to diffuse her reaction to his description.

She placed her fork on the plate edge, gripped the edge of the table, and laughed.

The unfiltered, genuine laugh he'd loved long ago was unexpected.

"Angelic. I don't think so."

Catching her fingertip between his thumb and forefinger, he gave a playful tug, before he caressed her finger, then enveloped her hand once more. Her shiver slipped sparks up his arm to tag his heart. "I call the scene like I see the picture—the candlelight sparkling in your eyes, the soft lights haloing your hair. An air of wonderment envelopes your face while you puzzle a problem. I saw an angel. Corny, I know. Except…"

She slid a glance toward his palm covering her hand.

Had he gone too far? His observation bordered on the schmaltzy side. However, he managed to pull forth a wide-open grin from Nat. He removed his hand, regretting the moment he lost contact. "All I meant is you used to gaze off into nowhere each time you mulled an angle."

"Mary says I think everything through. My contemplative nature used to drive you nuts."

He nodded. Yeah, her never-ending, deliberation-fest on each little subject had driven him over the top. "I'll admit, I wondered what you were thinking. You tend to be close-mouthed."

She glanced at her lap before pinning her gaze to meet his. "Did my behavior drive a wedge?"

"Never. You had stuff going on with your dad. And you confided a lot, *after* you pondered solutions. Still, I could have helped if you hadn't kept everything close to your heart." *Like today.*

She said nothing.

He knew better than to press her further. He dove into the woven straw basket between them, snatching up warm bread, content to fill his belly. The quiet enveloped them. At least he told himself silence was the answer. As they each chowed on bread and picked at the delicacies on the small plates, the silence loomed.

After a few bites, Nat settled her tablet on the table. "Tomorrow we have our next meeting with Walter. Let's discuss logistics besides registration updates and tasks Walter and Mary can take off our plate."

"Thought we wrapped things last week." Thank the stars on a clear night she changed the topic to neutral, despite having declared they should enjoy a night off from work.

"Not quite. Lots to do. Finalize the activity schedule, set up the van schedule, and—" Her hand fluttered toward the mountains, the inn, then toward Chelsey. "We need to plan next steps on promo. Tons of details."

Brad groaned.

"What?"

"Nothing. Tired. We agreed to put work to one side

for tonight." Although, they did have to ensure a stellar event. Bonus—planning equaled time spent with Nat and discovering who she'd become. Darn, he shouldn't think about Nat in any way other than a work partner, not after— "You must be chomping at the bit to get home to D.C. You got a guy waiting?"

Where did the question come from?

The dark point of hair caressed her chin as her head lifted and her glare pierced him with a direct hit. Like maybe her personal life was none of his business. "Making conversation is all. Sore point? The real reason you're here in Mistletoe Falls?" He arched his brows in a warped attempt to tease. "To escape both?"

Her gaze bolted to her lap.

"Look, Nat. I—" His silent apology hovered between them.

After a moment, she lifted her head to meet his gaze. "No. You?"

He curbed a laugh. The expression on her face was typical, have-to-think-about-my-response-so-I'll-divert-conversation MO by boomeranging his question. She wouldn't appreciate his warped humor. Not after the frosty glare. "An ex. Not a wife. A girlfriend. Old, *old* news." *Until today.* He prayed Celia would leave town without causing trouble. "So, Walter… What else do we need for the upcoming meeting? What's the date?"

She widened her eyes. "Are you kidding me? Did you not read my memo? Monday at eight a.m."

He couldn't hold his grin. At least he railroaded her off personal topics. A conversation he foolishly started.

"What's so funny?"

"You."

"Me? You're the one who can't—"

He leaned over the table and pressed two fingers across her lips. "Hold your rant, before you get us both in trouble. Yes, I read your notes. Pushing buttons works every time. You never could take a joke."

"Well, the *joke* wasn't funny."

A grin slipped to part her luscious lips. Seeing her beautiful smile was reward enough.

"Okay, I guess your comment was funny. You have a warped sense of play. Your attention-getting side."

He leaned in his chair. "Attention getting?" He winked. "Certain things never change." To diffuse the tension, he angled to get in her space, leaning his elbows on the tabletop. "We did have fun. We could continue to have fun if you'd retreat from your always-have-to-be-in-control mode."

She bared her teeth.

Pressing his luck, he laughed. "Yup. Things never change. You think you can settle in and enjoy the evening?"

Before she could emit a retort, the server placed the second two of their entrée plates between them.

The server glanced between them. "Another beer?"

He could use a dozen. Instead, he shook his head. "Nat? Another?"

The next hour eased by in benign conversation as they sampled the grilled asparagus wrapped in prosciutto and butternut squash ravioli in brown butter sauce. Despite his earlier need for a cheese-laden pizza, he found these dishes satisfying and oddly filling. Maybe the unique combinations of choices sustained him, but he'd bet the company nourished him more.

The food must have aided Nat, as she became more

talkative. Every once in a while, Nat let slip her job details.

“So, why’d you decide to be a paralegal?”

“I’m stuffed.” Her palm rested just below her ribs.

“D.C? Paralegal? Why?” He hoped his question didn’t intrude on the ease of the evening. They’d circled their past lives. He wanted more. He didn’t want to waste one opportunity to get to know the *today* Nat and resolve past issues. Would seven weeks be enough?

Her fingers slipped over her spoon, polishing like she’d done with the fork. She stared at the utensil.

“During my trip to Europe, I observed so much poverty off the beaten path.” She heaved a sigh.

He braced for what he’d learn regarding the ill-fated waste of a summer—the summer she left him bereft.

“Limousines that fit ten chauffeured us between appointments, where Father negotiated mergers to make more money than he needed. The sadness of what I saw broke my heart—the haves and have-nots.” She replaced the spoon on the table and took up the edge of her napkin. “I’ve been groomed to follow my father’s footsteps into law my entire life, despite my rebellion when I applied to art schools.” Her chest rose, before she exhaled, long and slow.

Brad didn’t utter a word, waiting to hear the story he’d been desperate for the last sixteen years.

“I couldn’t abide the notion of law school and corporate law. I wanted to help people.” She dropped her shoulders. “In the end, I had no choice.”

He flexed his hands under the table. He longed to touch her, soothe her, and dispel her pain. Her father was a controlling piece of work. Until now, he never understood the extent of the guy's overreach. "And yet, here you are working for a law firm specializing in corporate and business law." His statement was meant to elicit a reaction.

Her lids shuttered as she nodded.

Schooling his features, he kept his mouth shut, hoping she'd open.

"I studied art. Obtaining my paralegal certificate was my concession. Much to my parents' horror, I worked with a neighborhood nonprofit helping people improve their circumstances."

"Like?"

"Outrageous rent hikes, tenant-slum lord disputes, and a variety of domestic and employment issues." Nat glanced at her plate. "Our meal was delicious. Just enough." She folded the napkin to a pristine imitation of the original fold, before she scanned the room. "It's clearing. We should go."

He met her gaze. "And?"

"What?"

"We'll go"—he signaled for the check—"once you finish your story."

"I'm finished."

"You work for Klein, Abbot, Murphy, and Thompson. Seems like we're in the middle of your story. Can't leave until I pay."

"We're splitting the bill."

"I invited you. I'm paying. No more stalling."

"Fine. A funding freeze, budget cuts, and my job was eliminated. I volunteered until I depleted savings. Now…Klein, Abbot, Murphy, and Thompson."

"Why them?" The slow blink of her eyes followed by her steady gaze pierced him.

"The only firm to hire me. Seems I'd been blackballed across the city."

"Your father?" He refused to censure the disdain lacing his voice.

"I suspect."

He squeezed her chilled hand to stop her fidgeting with the napkin corner. He swallowed the nasty words concerning a father who undermined his daughter. Nat didn't need to open old wounds. She'd dealt with the specter of her father her entire life. "I'm sorry."

The server swept in to leave the bill.

Brad checked figures and deposited his credit card on the tray. "So, Europe, your graduation trip, steered your life in a new direction?"

Her face paled in the muted candlelight.

He wanted to snatch back the question. His need to know what happened trumped the discomfort stringing between the two. The question remained, how could he encourage a truthful response?

Chapter Nine

Natalie battled a headache. The pain slammed the base of her neck, tightened her shoulders, and spread like a wind-fueled wildfire up her face to lodge in her temples. Fatigue leached through her muscles and settled in her bones. She summoned energy to massage the tension-induced knot with arms heavier than a wildland firefighter's hose. She should have ended the evening long before Brad's questions.

Brad lowered his hand to the center of the table, palm turned up. He lowered his eyelids to half-mast.

He must have experienced the same long-ago pain. Still, she wasn't ready to meet him halfway. The urge to escape the blaze of pain licking her face and singeing her deliberations intensified.

"I understand why you went with your parents. You had no choice." He glanced toward his lap. "Why didn't you contact me?"

"Why didn't *you* contact *me*?" She spat venomous words, her protection from the conversation she dreaded since she first recognized the infamous *Mr. B* sauntering through the inn's front door. She didn't mention the disconnected cellphone. Now she realized he'd never tried. "I have to go." She shoved her chair from the table.

He was on his feet in a flash.

The touch of his hand scorched her wrist. She

shook off his hold and stood.

"I refuse to apologize for circumstances not my doing. Your father—"

She cradled her neck, willing off the tension slamming her forehead and spiraling through her shoulders.

"Don't let your father get between us. Not this time, Nat."

"What does my father have to do with—?" She waved her free hand, missing striking Brad's chest by inches.

He circled behind her.

His warm hand and strong fingers supplanted hers and massaged deep.

"There's the nasty knot."

She yearned to lean into his touch and let him take care of her, but trust, eroded long ago, was hard to find. With regret, she acknowledged he was right. If they didn't talk… "What did my father say?" He stepped from range, leaving her neck chilled, as he faced her.

"We'll talk. First, let's get you outside in the cold."

She never stopped loving his protective side. He was the one who rushed to the rescue of the underdog—the one who saved her in high school. No longer was she a victim. She turned to tell Brad she could take care of herself, and others, and had been doing so for years. He sidetracked her by plucking her coat from the chair. The soft and soothing merino wool blanketed her shoulders. The lapels tightened by his grip infused her with heat emanating off his chest. His arms looped her in a protective hug. For a split-second, she was desperate to accept his comfort. Common sense prevailed. She retreated from the snug circle of his arms.

He stepped beside her and tugged on her hand.

Having someone care for her was a nice change. Her parents rarely helped, unless nurturing was the required route to a purpose. The only person who cared continuously for her was Mary, until Natalie met Brad. Even as a kid, he was kind and protective.

Wes—not so much. She was the one tasked with tending to his needs.

By instinct she leaned into Brad, not because she had to and not because he asked, but because, for a change, relying on a once-trusted friend outweighed the constant need to prove her strength and independence. Plus, she had to gain the trust of that same friend. The idea frightened her. Despite her alarm involving dependence, and her wounded heart from their past, confidence slipped from beneath her defenses.

The restaurant's front door swung inward as a couple entered.

Chilled air caught her breath, while the cold caressed her aching temples like a welcome ice pack.

Brad stepped in front of her. "Shove your arms into your sleeves." He tugged closed the collar of her jacket. With his forefinger, he lifted her chin. "You okay?"

"Better. Fresh air helps." A shiver assailed her.

With a tug, he drew her zipper to her chin, then cupped her cheek.

His palm was warm and soothing.

"Come on. Want hot chocolate? The warmth and caffeine will relax you."

She wanted to argue. The last thing she needed, as tired and overwhelmed as she felt, was more time spent with Brad.

He grasped her hand.

And she could not say no.

A block from Gregory's, he opened the ice cream parlor door.

In a flash, Natalie stepped backward in time. Throughout their senior year, she and Brad frequented this place. The display case was precisely as she recalled—a kaleidoscope of colorful tubs filled with most every flavor imaginable. Her gaze locked on the bright pink tub. She could almost taste the sweet, cool flavor of mint.

"Peppermint candy?"

Brad's breath tickled her neck. She turned to face him. "You remembered."

"Who could forget the embarrassment of ordering hot pink ice cream?"

"You never said…" His warm fingers pressed on her lips.

"Teasing." He spun her.

Both palms curved over her shoulders. His breath feathered her ear, and his heady scent enveloped her like the familiar comfort of a favorite wool cape.

"I would have done anything for you. I love—loved you. I was proud to have cash in my pocket to buy your favorite ice cream every week."

A bubble lodged in her chest. She stuffed a swallow. His words evoked their differences—his dad a small-town mechanic, hers a big-city corporate attorney. Still, she loved him with all her heart. Until his graduation day declaration ripped a wide hole in her core—a crater which took eons to heal. The edges of scar tissue still pinched in pain.

Each time she breathed in his smoky, pine scent, or

heard his husky voice behind her, she hurt. Every time she was close enough to absorb his heat, her heart constricted in a deep throb. When he touched her with a brush of his shoulder, the caress of his finger on her cheek, or the warmth of his hand enveloping hers, she ached. Every tiny touch reminded her of the pain she suffered at his defection. She retreated. How could she believe he'd loved her once?

"Peppermint hot chocolate? Not pink. I promise." He grinned.

To avoid getting sucked in by the tiny dimple adorning one corner of his mouth, she nodded. *Too late.* His grin slipped through her, warming her and sending sparks where sparks shouldn't go. She forced a smile, while sheltering her heart. "Agreed. Too cold for ice cream. Hot chocolate works."

Brad placed the order and returned to stand by the wide windows.

"The lights are beautiful. I haven't been downtown this week."

He pointed to the nearby lamppost sporting a jaunty wreath. "These days, the maintenance crew and firefighters get an early jump."

"Decorations never used to be displayed until Thanksgiving weekend. Kind of sad. You know—the breaking of tradition." The sting from this minor change scurried through her. Holiday traditions were never a big part of her childhood, except her senior year. Why did she now mourn what she wasn't conscious of missing?

Most Christmases her family flew to tropical destinations. Lights twinkled from palm trees. Jolly Santas in red board shorts with white fur cuffs at their knees were everywhere. Senior year her parents flew to Switzerland for an international corporate meeting and spent the holidays skiing the Alps. She was ecstatic to spend a real small-town Christmas with Aunt Mary.

"Remember—"

The server hollered thirty-seven.

Saved by the bell.

A minute later Brad returned, his palms encircling the festive paper cups decorated with peppermint sticks.

She studied his long-limbed gait.

"I withdraw my promise. We have pink."

"Funny, because I was never a pink kind of person."

"No, you weren't. Red, blue, and bright green."

He remembered. The weight pressed against her chest eased.

"This should help."

"What?"

"To warm you."

He switched into protective mode. "Yes." She sipped the scalding liquid. "And to help the headache."

"Want to take a short stroll toward the town square to see the lights?"

"For a few minutes." She hesitated. "I should head home. I have work."

"Inn's *that* busy?"

"My D.C. work. I'm behind."

"No wonder you're exhausted and have a massive headache. Why didn't you tell me? I could have delivered food."

She snorted. A dribble of hot chocolate slipped off her chin.

Brad chuckled, as he dabbed the spill with his

napkin.

His scent overpowered the sweet aroma of her drink.

"I guess you have plenty of food at the inn."

She giggled like a teenager. "You might say that."

"You making fun of me?"

Laughing eased the tension, as did the caffeine and cold and company. "It's nice to get out."

As he pointed at window displays, Brad linked their arms.

Even in the bitter cold, his heat radiated through her. "T-this town does rally for the holidays. Our guests will enjoy Christmas in town."

"Remember…?" He raised a brow.

He mimicked her own words which had minutes earlier blocked desperate memories best left unsaid.

Walking memory lane with Brad—a terrible idea.

A blast of icy wind hit the two head on.

He drew her close. His gaze settled on her face.

In a split second, the weight of his palm on her back warmed her, and she leaned into him.

"You said earlier—remember?"

"Nothing."

"Come on, Nat" He nudged a hip against hers. "Tell me."

"The tree in the town square—"

"The tree lighting?"

His whisper, warm and sensuous despite the innocuous words, grazed her neck. Goose bumps slid over her arms…and not from the arctic blast. "I remember the tree lighting…and the caroling."

"Oh yeah."

His words, a murmur of long-forgotten memories,

tickled her cheek and sent a shiver straight to her toes.

"The countdown to zero, and the tree lit up to spotlight us kissing behind the gazebo. Principal Murray made quick work rounding the crowd."

She laughed, the cold air catching on the way to her lungs. "His face was ablaze like the star atop the tree." He pressed an arm over her shoulders, drawing her so close the two merged almost as one.

"We can laugh tonight, but I took weeks of ribbing from the guys."

Natalie never revealed the grief she experienced from girls' jealousy over their relationship. The new girl in town stole the big man on campus. Her sidestep added a few inches between them. Still, his arm remained slung over her shoulder. What if they had followed through on their plans? Where would the two be today? With each other? Most likely, each off in different directions, their love burned out, hating the other.

He ran a finger the length of her nose. "Those were the good days, before…"

She couldn't reminisce—not about the *good* days or the aftermath. She stepped from his scorching touch and the scent settling over her. "I need to go home."

Reaching, his hand grazed hers.

She turned, methodical in maintaining three feet of space, and strode to Gregory's and her car. No way would pondering the past do either any good. Best she kept her distance from Brad—both physical and emotional.

****

Brad shoved the grocery cart to a stop next to his truck and opened the door. A chilly breeze ruffled his hair, tickling his neck. He scrubbed his hand through the mop covering his head. Between running the store, helping Nat finalize event details, and seeing to his mom's needs he was worn straight through to his achy bones—no time for haircuts.

His mom grew stronger. Still, he worried. Adding to his full plate the anxiety over achieving strong year-end sales, plus organizing ski-trip details for event week, and his exhaustion drifted deep into brain-ache zone.

The impasse with Nat added another layer of concern. They'd not spoken in two days. He yearned to clear the air, but timing was wrong with her burning both ends of the candle. He rubbed his sternum, willing his stress to evaporate.

A day of tromping the woods—alone—would boost stamina and clear his brain. Despite his vow to escape, carving time from his schedule proved fruitless. Instead, he stuffed another grocery bag into his pick-up's filled-to-the-brim rear seat. Next, he hefted the twenty-four pack of toilet paper, the eight pack of tissues, and the mammoth jug of laundry detergent and plopped them in front. Keeping his mom's pantry stocked was his way to keep her safe during wintry weather.

Brad leaned against the truck's open door, the heat from the early winter sun cloaking him in comfort. For a few moments, he stared downhill toward Mistletoe Creek snaking through downtown. Shards of ice glued together the brown and flattened remnants of low growth along the stream. Seemed like yesterday, the green and gold grasses waved in the scented summer breezes, and birds chirped a harmonious chorus. He loved the cyclical Vermont seasons, despite missing the variations in the western mountains and the ebb and flow of his former life—every day a new adventure, meeting new clients, teaching and guiding, and being one with nature.

A twinge tugged his heart. He scanned the snow-topped mountains bordering the town's eastern boundary. For a split second, he fantasized dropping his to-do list responsibilities, strapping on a pair of snowshoes and his backpack, and roaming the peaks until the sun dipped toward the horizon.

Shaking off the tickle of despondency weighting his limbs, Brad raised his face to the sun. The heat warmed his spirit, draining off each burden. He valued his business and didn't begrudge taking care of his mom. He loved her and his life in Mistletoe Falls.

But resentment occasionally crept in when his numerous problems converged. Then, life anchored him to the base of the mountain he longed to climb and stand atop to scan the view. As the days had been when he almost lost his mom, the pain from those wearisome months still settled like a deep throb in his hands, the way stress always did. The same tight-fisted aches as they waited for the prognosis, then the outcome after surgery, coursed through him today.

Despite the melancholy momentarily slithering through, he straightened. He spread his hands in front of him, stretching his fingers to work free the kinks. Breathing in the fresh Vermont air, he set his mind on his list. Determined to stuff his worries, he shoved the grocery cart into the carriage port, slammed the truck's rear gate, and gunned out of the parking lot.

Minutes later, his cell bleated "Born to Run."

Glancing at the wireless connection perched on his dashboard, he directed the phone to answer. After dinner with Nat on Friday night, he'd put in a call to his buddy. "Jeff, what've you got?"

"You were right. She's up to no good."

"Lay the bad on me." Today couldn't get worse. The black mood had sucked him under since dinner with Nat and dragged his attitude to the depths.

"From my sources, Celia's money and luck are depleted. The big guy kicked her out."

Brad's gut somersaulted. "I swore they were a match made in heaven."

"Nope. She used him for his money."

"No brainer. Been there." Brad tapped a rhythmic drumbeat against the steering wheel. His stomach churned. He almost felt sorry for the guy. Except for the fact the fallout meant Celia once more homed in on Brad. "Time to get tough."

"Doing what?"

"No clue, except a one-way ticket from town." He growled.

"You tried once."

Jeff's voice echoed from the cellphone with the same defeated tone as Brad's. This whole episode smelled. Time to get rid of Celia…again. "In Colorado. Not in Vermont." Dead tired, not in the best sorts, he must rally to dish out retribution, before she did the same. He reminded himself Celia deserved anything he threw at her.

"Will anything stop her?"

"Once she's done damage she'll split."

Jeff's cleared throat punctuated the silence.

The sound reverberated through the interior of the

vehicle. "What're you thinking?"

"My buddy needs help. My next job starts mid-January. You up for company?"

"You serious?" He pumped his fist. "You up for a part-time holiday gig?"

"Bingo. That's the right combination. Can you put me up?"

He sucked in a deep breath. The dark mood lifted so fast he'd be dizzy had he stood upright. "You bet. Small apartment. You mind the pull-out couch?"

"Works for me. More comfortable than hard ground."

"Thanks, man. You're saving me in more ways than one." After stowing groceries at his mom's and then at home, he headed to work. Two more weeks of slow-season Sunday hours, then he'd brace for the Thanksgiving weekend onslaught. Jeff's presence was a welcome addition to his staff and his wellbeing.

Plus, hatching a plan with his buddy to get Celia to leave was top on his personal health and safety list.

Chapter Ten

Monday morning, Walter arrived on the dot of eight.

Aunt Mary stood front and center to greet him. She looked like she'd been getting ready for hours. Natalie grinned, waving hello from the dining room. The two stood yards apart, wearing goofy smiles.

Hmmm.

Walter ambled a few steps closer. "Mary." He breathed her name. "A fine-looking color on you."

A rosy blush covered Mary's cheeks, matching the color of her angora dress.

Brad breezed through the door.

Mary put her arm through Walter's and guided him toward the parlor and blazing fire.

Cocking a brow, Brad tipped his head toward the couple.

Natalie shrugged.

"We'll get the coffee." Brad strode by the parlor. He turned to Natalie and winked, before he drew her close to link their arms.

"Aren't you taking this—you know—*matchmaking* too far?" She wasn't in the mood to joke.

"I might learn a thing or three from ol' Walt." He grinned.

"Meaning?" She ignored the tiny flutter elicited by his smile.

"How to treat a lady the way she deserves."

A rockslide hit her stomach. "Like you did sixteen years ago."

"Nat. Don't." He shuttered his eyes. His joking grin of moments ago took a downturn into scowl territory.

"We need to talk. First, let's get through this meeting." As if he slipped on a porcelain mask, the cool tone of his whisper matched his veiled features. She should apologize. But she couldn't make herself utter *I'm sorry*. Not after the hurt from earlier years. Last night she relinquished her guard. Today, she'd shield her heart.

She tugged free her arm from the crook of his elbow and marched past the few guests lingering over breakfast. For a moment, she was captivated by Brad's playful charm. She never could resist him. This morning, she refused to get drawn in. Not until they cleared the air about her father. She was afraid clarity and forgiveness came much too late.

The kitchen door swung wide as Heidi backed through, her arms loaded with breakfast goodies. She placed platters of cheddar-bacon scones and fruit on the buffet table.

Reaching over Heidi, Natalie tried to snatch a scone.

Heidi swatted her arm. "Stay away from the merchandise." She flashed her best-friend, teasing smile. "I have a tray ready in the kitchen."

Natalie followed her to the cheery kitchen, intent on helping Heidi and escaping Brad. Instead, he dogged her steps. She glanced toward the ceiling, as if a Zen-like calm would magically sprinkle upon her. Even

Heidi's butter yellow kitchen didn't present the usual joy and sense of peace and safety.

"Here." Heidi thrust a tray into Brad's arms, holding four mugs, sugar packets, a pitcher of milk, plus tea and coffee carafes. "Take those." She pointed. Natalie looked toward a basket filled with a variety of scones and another with a pot each of butter and jam.

"Now go and—"

Heidi shooed them. Her expression beamed mischievous merriment.

"Keep an eye on the lovebirds."

"You knew?" Despite her full hands, Natalie nudged her friend with an elbow.

"Ever since the two concocted the harebrained idea a few months ago to collaborate between the inn and the senior college, the attraction has built. I think she's succumbing to Walter's charms. Cute, right?"

Natalie refused to roll her eyes. Just because she no longer trusted love, after years of widowhood Mary deserved to find a sweetheart. Why not? Walter was a great guy. She hauled the two baskets through the lobby.

Brad, his tray balanced on the counter, stood by the registration desk. "You think maybe this thing between the two is why Mary seems worn down?" Although he pursed his lips, his eyebrows lifted.

Not in the mood to joke about her aunt's burgeoning relationship, Natalie glared. Then she floated into the parlor where the group settled close to the fire. "I come bearing breakfast."

Walter's eyes lit. "Love Heidi's scones. Why do you think I vote for meetings here?" His gaze shifted to Mary. "Although nothing beats Mary's apple strudel."

Like a blushing teenager, the color rose on Mary's cheeks.

Watching Walter and Mary, she stopped taking notes. "Sorry, Walter. What did you say?"

"Seventeen registrations. Five couples. Seven singles."

"We might be at capacity with four single rooms." Natalie ran to the lobby. She returned with the registration book.

Brad leaned over Walter's shoulder. He pointed. "Two women from the same town registered on the same day. Did they mention sharing a room?"

"I-I'm not sure we gave an option." Walter shook his head. "We did give them a choice of single or the pricier double rooms, with the caveat rooms were first come, first served."

"Here's what we have." She laid open the registration book to December twenty-third. "With the usual clientele registrations, and putting three singles in double rooms, we'll be at capacity." She sank into the chair cushion, worry racing through her mind. "We hoped for twenty to make the event profitable."

Brad skimmed a finger over Walter's list. "Four men and three women singles. If we call the two women from the same town and the men and let them know they'd save money if they opted for a roommate, several might decide why not."

She nodded. "Even with four singles doubling, we open rooms. Walter, can we add the roommate option to the online registration form and start a waiting list?"

Walter flashed the high sign.

"I'll make calls to singles. However, no pressure exerted." Even with seventeen, the inn would have a good start on planning the spring season. Natalie glanced at Mary. “We have extra rooms in the carriage house.”

Mary’s eyes widened. “They’re not ready for occupation. The rooms need work to make them livable. They’re filled with linens, furniture, rugs, and supplies.”

Natalie shrugged. “We’ll move things.”

“Natalie, honey, putting guests with the help wouldn’t be fair. Even if we charged less.” Mary pressed her palms against her cheeks. “They’ll want to be together. Plus, they’d share your bathroom.”

A reduced fee beat no fee. “I suppose you’re right.”

“Reminds me.” Brad glanced between Mary and Natalie. “I have a buddy arriving from Colorado to work the Christmas season. Jeff’s an expert outdoor trip leader and can help with the event.”

“Great. You’ll have time to devote to the store.” Which meant less time spent with Brad. She swallowed the urge to expel another hefty breath of relief.

“The thing is…I just have a pullout sofa. Any chance if I help clear the carriage house rooms, he can rent for the next six weeks?”

She straightened. Having Brad’s friend living close meant possibilities of running into Brad. “I’m not sure—”

“Why, Brad darling, what a wonderful idea. How nice to have a man helping again.” Mary grinned, turning to pat Natalie on the hand. “He can help with heavy lifting.”

“I’m not sure, Mary. The rooms are filled with old furniture.” She had to redirect the conversation.

“Pish.” Mary waved a hand, grinning at Brad. “We

can reorganize. If your friend helps at the inn, we'll comp his room."

"Ah, Mary..." She wanted to mention their staff had no time to rearrange the carriage house, and the inn couldn't afford donating free rooms. Although, unpaid help might be worth having a stranger bunking nearby. Besides, once Mary latched on to an idea, the battle was lost. "Great. Settled. Other loose ends?"

"Yeah," Brad said. "Brainstorming alternate activities in case of inclement weather."

Mary raised a hand. "The remodeled church has a combination flea market and craft fair during the holidays and is perfect for Christmas Eve shopping."

She noticed the uplift at the corner of Brad's mouth as their gazes connected. She pictured an annoying bubble over his head with the word *ha*.

Brad flashed a wink. "Great idea."

Natalie quelled the somersault in her belly and concentrated on the cinnamon-sugar scent wafting from the kitchen. Snickerdoodles? Or was it the new candles Mary ordered to spruce up the lobby?

"Many shop owners set up tables."

She snapped back her concentration to Brad's comments.

"We'll ask merchants to offer a ten-percent-off coupon with each purchase. Does the old church sponsor other activities?"

"Quite a few artisans rent tables every weekend, year-round," Walter said. "Mary?"

Natalie noticed the flash of adoration crossing Mary's features.

"The local writing group sells books. Many crafters stay through next week to capture post-holiday shopping."

"Brad, you up for contacting vendors?" Walter snatched another scone.

"On it. Recap—the twenty-fourth, a shopping trip to the community center."

Natalie keyed in ideas. "Brad to contact downtown merchants."

Brad scratched a note on his yellow pad.

Walter glanced at Brad. "Can we use Ben Johnson's hay wagon and horse team for the New Year's Eve sleigh ride?"

"All in," Brad said. "Ben's neighbor, Martha, donated use of her old sleigh. Ben's horses can haul both."

"Her sleigh only seats…" Mary flashed two fingers.

Walter steepled his hands under his chin. "Still, the sleigh adds ambiance. Someone from the inn should lead the way."

After she typed in the last note, Natalie paused. "Walter, you and Mary should take the lead."

"Oh, sweetie. I'm too old for sleigh rides. We'll help Heidi set up. Ben's son, Ethan, will have the bonfire blazing by the time you return. You two take the lead. Martha's old sleigh will add magic."

"You two?" Natalie turned her attention to Mary.

"Yes, dear."

Mary looked over her glasses.

"You. And Brad."

Natalie swore Mary grew reindeer antlers with each attempt at meddling. "We'll make assignments later. Moving on." Natalie glanced at Brad. "Is Truman's set for the firework display?"

"Yup. I've rented benches to surround the bonfire. Heidi will provide hot chocolate, champagne, and assorted sweets at midnight."

"We have plenty of old blankets to keep everyone warm," Mary said.

"Our event sounds complicated with people doing different things." Walter tapped his notebook. "We need a chart to outline responsibilities."

"Done." Natalie hit the key as a punctuation mark. "I've added new ideas to a chart at every meeting. When I email everyone, I'll attach the link."

Brad faced Walter. "Let's powwow transportation needs. GMC has a van."

Walter flashed a thumbs-up. "The college has two that won't be in use over the holidays."

"We need flexibility on van availability, depending on weather."

"Noted." Walter straightened. "I've contacted the school district transportation director. Their three drivers are flexible and willing to transport."

"Wonderful." Mary laid a hand on Walter's arm. "It's a good thing you have connections."

Once more Mary's cheeks turned rosy. From the hint of color on Walter's face, Natalie bet he noticed.

"Looks like we have everything under control. Walter will update the website with waiting list information. I'll call the singles. Everyone think of alternate activities for bad weather days." Natalie swiped off her tablet.

If the stars were aligned, she could avoid alone time with Brad and shoo him to work, before he revisited their unfinished Friday-night conversation. Even though she owed him an apology for this morning's behavior, she wasn't entirely over her disappointment or her mad.

****

Brad left the wake of a swinging kitchen door. "Let me clear the trays."

"Clean-up is under control." Nat gestured toward the dirty dishes. "You have a store to open." She turned to clear trays and pop dishes into the industrial dishwasher.

What could he do to defuse her anger?

"Here." Heidi put the leftover scones in a plastic bag and strode across the kitchen. "Share with your crew."

"Yeah?" Brad grasped the bag.

"I can't re-serve them. You'll save them from being dumped."

"The crew will bless you. Anything else?"

Heidi surveyed the kitchen. "I, ah—"

"We're set," Nat called from the dishwasher.

"I guess everything's under control." Heidi shrugged.

Despite Nat's attempt to prod him into leaving, he refused until they talked. *Alone.*

Nat shoved another tray into the industrial dishwasher. "What else?"

Heidi glanced up from pot stirring. "Nothing."

Nat wiped her hands on a towel. "I'm heading to work."

"I assumed you'd been working." Heidi set aside her spoon.

Heidi squinted her eyes in that motherly, you're-in-trouble, look. An expression Brad knew well—a veiled attempt to shoo Nat, so he could have her to himself.

"She never stops." Brad forced a laugh.

Nat spun. "You're still here?"

"Not leaving until we talk." Heidi shot Nat what looked like the *whuh-woh* face. A look she bestowed on Nat and Brad since their childhood summers. The trio got into constant trouble. In fact, causing mischief together cemented his and Nat's relationship on a whole different level. Later, when Heidi started dating Evan, he and Nat admitted they liked, then loved each other.

Nat flicked her hand. "Nothing to talk about. We covered everything during the meeting." She edged along the far wall and shoved open the double doors.

He swooped into the dining room and caught her hand. "A private place?"

She tugged.

He held her hand in a tight yet gentle grip.

"I don't have time."

"Too bad. Your office?"

She turned. "No. Mary's working the front desk."

"Where then?" He pinned his gaze on the straight line of her mouth.

"Don't you have a store to open in fifteen minutes?"

"Will is opening. Where?" He couldn't contain the gruff-and-losing-patience edge. His molars ground together, until he set his jaw.

Nat strode toward the lobby.

Brad dogged her steps.

"Mary, can I have the key for room seventeen so Brad can see the layout?"

"A single? You'll want to show him a double, too."

"Why not." Nat marched up the stairs, clutching the keys in a tight fist.

Despite her ire and his annoyance, he couldn't help admire the gentle sway of her hips.

She opened room seventeen and entered, before she revolved to face him. "What is so important the conversation can't wait? I'm busy."

He set his palms on the curve of her shoulders and stroked to catch her elbows. "You. Us."

Like a spear, her glare pierced his armor.

He dropped his hands.

She stepped back until her thighs hit the edge of the sleigh bed.

He followed her step by step.

"No *us*." Nat worked on her own teeth-grinding action.

Not to be deterred, he invaded her personal space, which she hated. He didn't intend to intimidate her, but he had a mission. He refused to allow her to avoid the discussion they never finished. "Yes *us*, whether or not you wish to acknowledge the vibe stringing between us since that first event meeting."

"Your imagination." She poked his chest.

Hard.

"I'm not moving until you answer my question." She poised her finger once more, hovering opposite his chest.

He tugged the tip, his grip tightening. Her finger might be slim and delicate, but with the long, hot-pink, polished nail, damage was done. No way would he allow another strike. He folded his palm over her fingers to keep her captive. "Why did you break up and then disappear to Europe without an explanation?"

"Me break *up* with *you*?"

Nat's voice rose to a piercing exclamation. Why

did she insist on pretense—rewriting their history? "Answer the question. A simple one. Why?"

"You escaped to Colorado to find your inner mountain-man."

"How did you conjure up such a myth? You wanted to break up, so I fabricated the story."

Her eyes widened. "But…you went to Colorado."

"I did." He nodded. "Later. I couldn't stay in Mistletoe Falls. Not after I heard you abandoned our summer plans, and you didn't plan to return. I had to save face."

She retreated, plopping to the bed. Tears swam in her lower lids.

His resolve to badger the truth from her slipped. He sat and bumped his shoulder against hers. "Nat. I'm, ah, sorry." Man, he hated dealing with crying women. Nat continued to put up a solid front, until she folded in front of him. The Nat he remembered was *not* a crier. Maybe over the last few weeks he'd put a few cracks in her wall of resistance.

"Dad told me what you were too chicken to tell me yourself." A fist pounded her thigh. "Then he handed me my graduation present—plane tickets to Europe—and we left immediately."

"Too chicken to tell you what?"

"About Colorado."

"You're blaming me?" His breath clogged his throat. "You didn't think to ask me? I told you—I invented the story after you dumped me with no explanation."

"Dumped you?" She faced him. "I-I loved you. I didn't break up with you. You changed *your* mind."

"You could have called."

"Why?" She stood and paced the small space and stopped by the window. "Clearly you didn't want to talk. Why else would you tell my dad you were leaving town, instead of speaking to me?"

"I-I never told him I would leave. I was too stunned to speak. I told you I didn't plan to leave for Colorado until after your father confronted me." His fingers scraped his chin scruff. "He must have overheard and changed the story so he wasn't caught being the bad guy. I left for Colorado in August, after Mary told me you weren't returning. I lost my school deposit that I couldn't afford to blow." Brad stood and stalked toward the old, varnished oak door to gain distance. He planted a palm against the cool surface. The solid door stood in polar opposition to his brain turned to mush and a body on the verge of collapse. He dropped his hand and stretched wide his fingers to relieve the throb of nerves. Her father lied to them both. The last thing he should do is blame Nat for his disgust over what her father did.

He ached to slouch against the solid door for support and forget the past hurts he'd suffered. Nat suffered, too. He stepped toward her, stopping short of the window with a view of the creek, and sucked in a huge breath of calm. "I never told your dad anything. Your dad marched up to me after the ceremony and told me you needed your space. Said he planned to take you to Europe for the summer. I asked—"

His voice hitched, as if he were still in high school. Straightening, he drew on his resolve. Sixteen years. He shouldn't be struck mute. "I-I asked to speak to you. Your father told me you didn't want to see me…ever."

Nat gasped a sob, then her arms wrapped her waist.

She straightened and squared her shoulders. "H-he told you I-I didn't want to see you? No. I-I don't believe—" She slumped into the wingback chair by the window. Brad swore the chair hugged her tight, folding her into its comfort.

She leaned forward, her elbows planted on her knees and her face buried in her hands.

Pacing the length of the room, to give her breathing space, he sank to the edge of the bed. What happened to them years ago finally made sense. Her father set up both. Each wasted years being hurt, hating the other, and, according to Heidi, running from relationship to relationship. How did each fix this years-old dispute and learn to trust?

He stood and advanced toward the chair to squat in front of her. He tugged her hands to look into her eyes. "Can we agree, no more sniping at each other? I want us to start fresh and build a friendship." Who did he kid? He was already half in love with her…again.

They each needed time to digest the whole situation. The *situation* had ruled the direction of his life these last years. He imagined the past had done the same for Nat. Not wanting to let go, he enveloped both her hands with one palm. His finger caught the tear trickling down her cheek. "Nat?"

She nodded.

The depth of sadness shimmered in her beautiful eyes, and a blink told him the moment realization slammed into her. She lifted her head, her eyes wide and blank, like an accident victim who wasn't sure where she was or what had happened. He'd seen this shock reaction a *million* times in his trek leader and wilderness responder work.

She knew. She believed that years ago her father lied. He'd manipulated her and, in doing so, changed the direction of her life…and his. He squeezed her hands in a gentle gesture of comfort. The reassurance he aimed to give her was also meant to assure himself life would move forward in a positive way.

He, too, had been betrayed.

He, too, needed comfort.

He was desperate to enfold Nat in his arms, absorb her warmth, breathe in her scent, and swipe the damp lock of sable hair off her cheek. Pretending the last sixteen years never happened could allow each to return to the way life was before her father's betrayal—innocent and in love with their entire lives ahead of them—together.

Withdrawing her hands from under his, she reached to curve her palm against his cheek.

"Nat?"

"We could each use a fresh start. Today, I need to be alone. Okay?"

"Right. We have a ton to mull over." He swiped one more tear and stood. "Call when you're ready." He strode to the door, fighting his need to turn and hold her in his arms.

Instead, he yanked on the doorknob, and, without pulling closed the door, he beelined from the inn. His gut churned. He had his work cut out for him.

Chapter Eleven

The next morning, Natalie swiped a hand across her eyes. Tilting her head, she studied her reflection in her grandmother's antique mirror and glued on a smile, vowing to keep the perky expression in place no matter what.

Six weeks left to pretend everything was fine.

After jogging the carriage house steps, she circled the inn to prolong facing the inevitable. Turning, she gazed past the fields and breathed the bracing mountain air. Here she had a sense of peace that never happened in D.C.

She shook off thoughts of change, strode through the door, and hustled to grab coffee. Her hope was to avoid Heidi, who was nothing if not tenacious in dragging forth Natalie's every thought. She loved her friend, but no way did she wish to rehash the last few days.

Avoidance did nothing to stem the swirl of anger and regrets. Confronting her father was the only way to reconcile the past. The showdown would happen. *Someday.*

Much needed to be considered before a face-off. She could lose her prestigious career in D.C. Then again, she accepted sacrifice might be worth the pain to regain her dignity and live the life she dreamed about. Still, the thought of moving to a different phase scared the stuffing from her. In equal measure, the fantasy of living her dream buoyed her heart.

Seated on the old wooden chair that rocked and creaked each time she leaned, Natalie rolled the chair flush with the desk. She swigged a bracing gulp of coffee, the smoky, nutty roast burning a path to her stomach. She plunked the mug filled with lifesaving elixir on the desk. Remembering to breathe, she opened her laptop.

First, make a to-do list.

—Apologize to Brad

—Formulate groveling plan. He'd been a victim too

—Immerse her head in the game. She owed Mary and the inn her ceaseless concentration.

—Explore life options.

She minimized her list and worked on new, event-related tasks. With notepad in hand, she ducked behind the registration desk and perused the book. In several days, the inn would near capacity for Thanksgiving weekend.

Strolling to the parlor, she circled the room. Logs were set in the fireplace and ashes removed. She swept a finger across the side table and the lamp shade. Not a speck. She jotted reminders to thank the cleaning crew and distribute holiday bonuses.

Shoving aside the longing to crawl into bed and hibernate, she strode toward the dining room to grab more coffee. A quick glance showed disarray left from last night's dining service. She straightened chairs and added meal breakdown instructions to the list.

Ideas percolated for enticing overnight guests from afar and encouraging locals to dine. Setting goals to market winter and summer getaway options and extend the promotion range past Boston to New York City, Philly, D.C., and Montreal was a priority. By keeping the occupancy rates high year-round, they could restore the inn to the glory-days.

Not enough hours existed to implement her idea. If she left a plan for Mary, ticking off tasks one-by-one over the next year or two was plausible. Key to success was positive thinking. She lifted her head, straightened, and smiled. With new ideas and plans on the list, she set aside her worries and concentrated on the day-to-day with a renewed confidence.

Once she powered through Thanksgiving weekend, moving to the top of her list was catch-up on neglected studies. Her plan sounded easy, until she stopped in the middle of the lobby. The responsibilities swirling through her mind crushed her chest as if buried by an avalanche.

For a flash, she wished Brad's firm, warm palm eased her muscles and his voice calmed her terror. She turned her concentration from wanting Brad close to lists—only six short weeks to remedy problems.

Organizing was her forte. She donned her little-engine-that-could hat, stood tall, and breathed in the clean, crisp Vermont air.

She. Could. Do. This.

The key— categorize notes in a binder so Mary had step-by-step plans. The process—one pot of coffee and a few uninterrupted hours.

She concentrated on staying positive. Instead, a giant, icy, snowball of worry barreled down the mountain to lodge in the pit of her stomach. Aunt Mary couldn't run the inn alone. A niggle of a thought emerged over wasting years of hard work at Klein, Abbot, Murphy, and Thompson and starting over to take on the family inn. Living in Vermont might afford her time to dabble in art, her primary love. This wasn't the first time she daydreamed an alternate universe.

Glancing around, she marveled at the old, polished-to-a-gleam, carved, oak staircase, the beautiful, rough-cut, river-stone fireplace surrounds, the etched glass doors leading to the dining room, and the pocket doors closing off the parlor to make a cozy, private space. Beautiful, but everything needed refurbishing. The creak of the floor above, as guests moved about, pulled her from long-forgotten fantasies of taking chances on outgrown, ludicrous dreams.

She'd been happy with her D.C. life, until she stepped through the front door of the inn and found herself thrust into her aunt's plan to save the old place.

Enough wool-gathering, as her uncle used to say when she daydreamed. *Focus on the present.*

Natalie cleared the cobwebs of nostalgia clouding her perspective. With straightened shoulders, she opted to look forward—a big Thanksgiving weekend filled with holiday scents of pine and turkey, and a full house, requiring over the next few days her apt attention.

Moments later, she scripted cleaning notes and the announcement for the Tuesday staff meeting, and placed both on the clipboard hanging off the office door.

A chill overtook her. She yanked her sweater sleeves to cover her hands. So focused on work, she'd forgotten breakfast. Striding through the inn, she shoved open the kitchen swinging door.

Heidi spun. "Amazing what the cat dragged in,

sneaking through the front."

"I didn't sneak. I had work."

"Without coffee?" Heidi swiped her hands on her apron, leaving a trail of flour.

"I had coffee." She wouldn't mention the lukewarm, half-drained third cup sitting on the edge of the office desk she'd sneaked from the dining room. Or that not consuming food gnawed a hole in her belly.

"You look like you need intravenous." Heidi filled a mug and handed the steaming cup to Natalie. "Here you go."

Heidi's fake falsetto caused Natalie to shake her head. The thought of more coffee agitated her empty stomach. Instead, she would take a tiny sip and deflect Heidi's mothering. "You're too cheerful."

"What's not to smile about? Thanksgiving prep is on schedule. The inn will be filled. And…I have a date tonight."

"Spill. Who?" She ignored her growling stomach. "When, what, where, how, why?"

"The new ski instructor. Last night. Human. At Ricky's Tavern. We struck up a conversation and… Why? Because he asked me to dinner tonight."

"Wait. Human?"

"You asked what? How else would I answer? Leprechaun? Super hero? Mountain lion?"

"*Wha*t questions you having a date."

Heidi smirked. "I already told you I have a date. No need for a what."

She rolled her head to work the kinks free. Her friend made her crazy. They'd played word games since childhood. Heidi was the wild child. Natalie was cool, calm, contained, and never defied dictate.

Why did she never challenge law and order? Now was not the time to wander the path of reflections involving her parents. Not today and not here in the kitchen where Heidi would note her mood.

She flashed her best friend a grin. “All right, crazy girl, you win. So, does this guy have a name?”

Heidi shook her head.

She sucked in a huge breath and held the air until the pressure in her lungs burned to burst free. “You don’t *know* his name or not telling?”

“You ask too many questions.”

“So, you’re not telling me.” Natalie slugged down coffee.

Heidi winked. “Racer.”

She choked. “He…races?”

“Racer’s his name.”

The teakettle shrilled, adding to her irritation. “First or last.”

Heidi shrugged. “He introduced himself as Racer. I didn’t ask for clarification.”

“Whoa. You’re going with a guy named Racer, no last name, new in town. I hope you’re meeting him in a public place, because you should not be getting in his car until you learn more, including his real name.” She paused for breath.

“Come on, Natalie. If Stan Mills hired him for Hazelton Peak Resort, you bet he vetted both the man’s work and personal credentials.”

“You’re right. Stan is nothing if not diligent. Still—”

“Relax, *Mom*. I’m meeting him at Ricky’s, then we’ll stroll through town, where I might add, I know everyone. We’ll scope options and decide where to eat.

Speaking of—you need a night out. Since you're worried for my safety, call Brad. You two can meet me—My *wingman* and bodyguard—the three musketeers."

"No can do." Natalie swiped two scones, inhaling the tangy scent, and set them on a plate. "New flavor?"

"Blue cheese, rosemary, and pecan. Tell me what you think? Experimenting. Did you try the cranberry-jalapeno-ginger scone?"

"Sounds great. I'll grab one in the dining room. Bacon?" She raised a brow.

"Gone. Why not come with me tonight?" Heidi lowered her chin and flashed the schoolmarm look. "You don't have anything going on."

"Lay off. I am not asking Brad on a date."

Heidi wiped her hands on her apron. "A get-together, not a date. A friend thing. You two probably have important items on your to-do list needing discussion."

Natalie swallowed a groan. Her friend was dogged. "I am not looking for excuses to see Brad. I don't need complications. I'm leaving soon. Wes and I are still *a thing*." Or so she'd told herself, until Brad's big revelation.

"Have you heard from him?"

"Of course."

Heidi removed a baking sheet from the stainless-steel rack. Over the surface, she sprayed olive oil then sprinkled cornmeal. She arranged three shaped loaves of French bread. "When—the last time?"

"He texted. He's working a case."

Heidi walked to the sink to rinse her hands, before she snatched a clean dishtowel. "When?"

"Last week."

"Last time you spoke?"

Natalie gripped the edge of the counter to quell the urge to wipe away Heidi's cocky grin. "You sound like a broken record. When? When? When? What difference does our conversation timeline make? We keep in touch."

"*When*?"

As Heidi took up her warrior stance, legs spread wide, hands planted on her hips, and lips pressed tight, she swallowed a laugh. "Must you beat a subject into the ground?"

Heidi placed the baking sheet in the oven, then leaned against the counter. "Sounds to me like hanging on to a long-distance relationship with a person who doesn't have time to stay in contact isn't worth sacrificing the chance to see where this thing goes with Brad."

"I told you—no *thing*. Besides, why would I explore a relationship destined to become long distance? I am *not* sticking. I have a career, a life, in Washington." Although, not fifteen minutes earlier she'd contemplated reevaluating her D.C. life, her career, and maybe her relationship, in light of her dad's interference. Dear old Dad might have had a hand in choosing her D.C. plus-one. No way would she divulge her suspicions to Heidi. She'd never hear the end.

Still, Heidi's insight made her think. Not often, did she and Wes do fun, personal things together. Over the last few weeks, she recognized their relationship was basically a plus-one designed to boost their public profile in a city thriving on who's who. She and Wes *were* good together…as professionals.

In two years, neither had taken time to learn the other's interests. Could the lack of personal connection be the reason she had the urge to escape and think, and now to ignore Wes's communication?

"No *thing*." If she didn't repeat her conviction, Heidi would relentlessly work to push her two dear friends together. Natalie wouldn't have space to gain perspective on Wes.

"Message received." Heidi flashed her palms and escaped to the walk-in.

The rest of the morning blurred.

The promise of a slow day was anything but a sleeper, starting with three more reservations for Wednesday night. She informed Heidi, then scheduled on-call staff. She emailed regular and seasonal staff regarding an early breakfast meeting.

Next, she caught up on emails and was amazed when the senior event single enrollees were excited over bunking together. She called Walter. He had enough on the wait-list to refill the vacant rooms and exceed her goal of twenty attendees. She suggested he post an "event filled" tag. Round and round she circled, checking off tasks with methodical accuracy, then adding more.

In no time, Mary returned from Sunday brunch with friends, ready to staff the reservation desk.

With the weight lifted concerning how the next month would play out, Natalie deserved a break. *Alone*. She strode through the lobby, intent on heading to her room to work on her studies, then reversed direction. "Mary, mind if I leave you alone this afternoon? I want to contact Chelsey shop owners to solicit donations for welcome bags and gather permission to promote their stores in our literature."

"Of course, dear. Sounds like a win-win."

The excitement of exploring Chelsey, to check off her to-do list, get acquainted with shop owners, and bask in alone time infused her soul. She never imagined innkeeper and event planner were in the stars. She might even become accomplished in this profession.

For a moment, guilt crawled through her. Her studies were far from complete. Still, taking a break buoyed her spirit. She vowed to boot up prep class and study after dinner. So far, after eleven years on the job, she was surprised the material covered was review.

Fifteen minutes later, loaded with lists, her tablet, and winter gear to face the *balmy* twenty-three-degree day, she headed toward freedom. The front door blew open, stopping her in her tracks halfway to escape.

"Brad." Her aunt's cheerful voice rang through the lobby.

Like a deflated balloon, she wanted to sink in a heap on the floor.

The *prodigal son* constantly had bad timing.

Chapter Twelve

Brad stood silhouetted, the bright winter sun firing off the gold and auburn streaks in his chestnut hair. As longing lodged in the pit of her stomach—a longing she worked hard to deny—the thump of Natalie's heart skipped a beat. Gripping the corner of the registration desk, to avoid tripping over her feet, she retreated.

She never stopped loving Brad. With breath trapped in her lungs, she had to consider ramifications of such a revelation.

Wes.

She and Wes were working on things, and she couldn't overlook her mission—gunning for promotion. Despite questions concerning her future, she would head home, to Wes, to work, and to…

They're interchangeable.

From behind the desk, she stared at Brad and worked to stuff her longing. A desire she never experienced with Wes. But, after two years together, she did owe Wes a fair chance, didn't she? She'd worked beside Brad the last few weeks. The man she knew today was the one she loved years ago. More mature, but with the same attributes—his care for family, his and hers, work, friends, community, and concern for Mary's livelihood.

With desperation, she shook her head to dispel the gloomy notion of what she once believed was a full life.

With Brad invading her space, for the life of her she couldn't fathom her D.C. existence beyond day-to-day tedium. Wes and work. Work and Wes. The drumbeat of her dreary reality numbed her brain.

She wanted more.

"Nat, ah Natalie, meet Jeff."

Brad's voice catapulted her from her musings. "Jeff?" A tall, wiry man grinned wide from over Brad's shoulder. "Oh."

His friend stepped forward, dropped his duffel, and offered a hand. "Stellar. Heard a ton about you."

"W-welcome. We, um, weren't expecting you until *after* Thanksgiving."

Brad flashed his phone. "I texted last night."

She manufactured a smile. She'd ignored his communication. "We haven't cleared the room."

"Two strong bodies ready to work." Jeff bent to retrieve his large bag and slung the duffel over his shoulder. "Lead on."

Natalie froze.

"What's up?"

Brad's warm hand pressed the small of her back.

His touch surprised her. Sparks shot along her spine, further frying her brain cells. "I, ah… I need to grab the master keys. And…find Abby. The linens. Cleaning." Why couldn't she speak full sentences? She ducked behind the desk to stash not only her escape plans, but the butterflies winging through her stomach.

Mary emerged from the office and extended the keyring. "I'll organize Abby. You go ahead."

After introductions between Heidi and Jeff in the kitchen, she led the two to the carriage house.

Brad stopped short at the staircase and looked

toward the second floor.

Jeff slammed into him. "Whoa, an old carriage house. Big."

She turned. "Once the stables until Uncle Harry raised the roof. He added rooms for the family and built a small barn. I believe he yearned for a horse or two." Jeff, quick-footed like a mountain lion, climbed the steps.

He turned at the top. "What's below?"

"Storage." She huffed up the stairs after him.

Brad trailed.

"Snow blower, tractor lawnmower, snowmobile, the trail groomer…and a lot of junk."

"Sign me up for the trails."

On the landing, Natalie drew a deep breath and raised her gaze to Jeff. His shock of golden hair brushed one eyebrow and dusted his neck, as though he emerged recently from a wilderness trek. His warm, brown eyes flecked with sunshine signaled sincere excitement. "Really?"

"For real. I'll tackle the groomer. I'm in for exploring the grounds"

"And you want to groom trails?" As a teen, helping her uncle, grooming wasn't a *fun* chore.

"Gives me opportunity to understand the land."

Jeff beamed a wide-open grin.

Natalie understood why this affable guy was Brad's good friend.

"Brad has assigned me to lead the event outings in December. Any opinion on dry runs before your event?"

"Dry runs?" She was out of her element.

Jeff anchored a forearm against the doorjamb.

"Leading a few brave souls helps me practice the trails. We can push advertising for your facilities. Kids are school-free over Thanksgiving. Run a holiday special in the local paper—family cross-country skiing at the inn. Hot chocolate and Christmas cookies included. Holiday events get people pumped."

Brad stood on the top step. "I'm in."

He flung his arm over her shoulders. A quiver of excitement slipped to her belly.

"What do ya' say, Nat? I'll contact the Y regarding flyers. We'll add promo to our websites and run quick ads this week."

"Whoa." She shrugged off Brad's arm. Striding past Jeff, she flung open the large wooden door and was halfway down the hall, before the guys caught her.

Brad palmed her shoulder to stop her momentum. "Nat. Great idea. What's the prob?"

"We—*I* don't need more on my plate."

"Not your plate." Brad moved in front of her. "We'll run the program and handle advertising. Heidi can provide hot chocolate and cookies…"

His mouth turned up at the corners. Adding to the coziness of being inside, his grin sent a warm wave of comfort through her, despite the mad she had going.

"You already have them for guests."

She faced the men, arms crossed, ready to stand her ground against more tasks. "You add people and work increases."

Brad eased forward and cupped her chin.

Despite the scorch of his touch, a shiver slipped through her.

"I'll plan everything and absorb the costs."

"Not the problem—it's just… Never mind." She

stepped from his reach and inserted the key for Jeff's room.

"Special activities puts the inn on the map, Nat."

He moved alongside her.

"Thanksgiving weekend attracts people to town. You'd showcase the inn to residents and tourists. Ten dollars a person covers your snacks and our labor. They lug their own skis or rent from GMS. And they might stop for lunch or breakfast. Win-win."

She drew in a deep breath, ready to protest again.

"The moon will be at the three-quarter mark and moving toward full. Saturday, we could lead a late-night trek after the Christmas tree lighting. The townies will love the idea."

She released a soulful sigh. Why bother arguing? He was right. Not her stress, so why say no? "Do your thing." She flipped her wrist.

Abby bounded up the stairs with an armful of linens.

Tina followed and headed for the vacuum in the utility closet.

"This one needs a good cleaning." Natalie toed open Jeff's door and gasped. Without an audience, she'd have pounded her head against the doorjamb. The room was far from ready for a quick vacuum and linen change. She glanced over her shoulder. "Jeff, leave your things in my room while we ready yours. We'll be done by the time you finish work with Brad."

The tower of chairs and extra bedside tables stacked along one wall taunted her. Forget her afternoon escape plans. Today's new agenda, lug furniture.

"No way." Jeff dropped his duffel in the hallway.

"This'll take us no time."

Before she could protest, their jackets landed on top of the bag.

The two men started hefting furniture.

Brad filled the doorway. "Where do you want this stuff?"

"Give me a sec." She strode to the end of the hallway, praying the next room had space. Why hadn't she cleared the room earlier? An avalanche of goose bumps dove over her skin, as a palm wrapped the curve of her shoulder. Brad's scent and heat fogged her mind. How was she supposed to ignore his presence when he shadowed her?

She concentrated on twisting the old key. "This room has the most storage space." She shoved open the door. The room was jammed. "How will we ever—" She swallowed a frustrated growl.

"We'll rearrange." Brad seized the key ring. "Let's see the other room." He strode to the end of the hall and opened the door. "We can consolidate and fit everything."

The angry whirl of worries hit her gut, zapping her energy. Righting the troubles of running the inn would take more hours than she had left. She slumped against the wall. The crack of her elbow on wood sent a slice of pain radiating to her fingers. She suppressed a *youch*, before fumbling for the ever-present water bottle hanging from her belt.

"Look."

Brad's voice echoed through the cavernous hallway, pulling her from her pity-party. Straightening her shoulders, she sucked down a deep breath and stalked down the hall.

Brad looked up and grinned. "We found two twin bed frames and mattresses, plus a bureau. We'll set up one extra room like this for emergencies and put the rest in the last room."

"You think?"

"I know."

He tugged her close and lifted her chin, as his gaze met hers.

"We'll get to work. Later Jeff and I will check the grooming equipment and trails."

"What happened to running your store?"

"Will is staffing, and Gretchen is home for the holidays. Take advantage. By week's end, the store will be slammed. Today, I'm all yours." He winked.

A frisson of heat worked through her, and the fire of a blooming blush settled on her cheeks.

All yours.

For a mere moment, she allowed her mind to roam to what-ifs.

No.

She shifted. No contemplating the past—or the future—in Mistletoe Falls. Her future was a promised raise, new responsibilities, and a resurrected long-term relationship. Despite her hiatus, she'd return with a renewed sense of self and hope for creating a relationship that would be solid and equal, and more than an interlude—a shiny preoccupation of long-ago moments from her childhood in Vermont.

A pipe dream? Maybe?

On her return to D.C., she'd up the game and ensure Wes understood her—her work, her ambitions, and her passions. She'd instill the concept of an equal partnership. She doubted Wes appreciated her zeal for art, her wish to learn graphic design, or the simple pleasures from roaming antique stores, Georgetown boutiques, and the halls of the Smithsonian and smaller D.C. galleries. If he cared, he'd bend and enjoy her interests, too.

She realized she'd allowed Wes to dictate the boundaries of this relationship. Time to take charge of her own fate. She had to try.

Brad helped her realize what she missed. At his insistence, he'd *dragged* her from the office to clear her brain. He urged her to breathe deep the scents of winter air and watch the sun set majestically over the Vermont mountains. She owed him gratitude for opening her eyes to the value of discovering life beyond work. The sparks of passion she experienced with Brad would corrode easily, unless the two worked to build a solid foundation…together. Too little time and long-distance were factors they could not overcome.

She shook images of Brad from her mind. Vermont was a pit stop.

Numerous activities and interests about things she could do in D.C. buzzed through her head. How long since she ice-skated? Not since she was a child in Boston, and then during the one winter she spent in Mistletoe Falls. Perhaps she and Wes could experience the magic of skating together when the canal froze in Georgetown or the man-made ice rink was installed with twinkling lights and holiday music along the National Mall.

She and Brad skated arm in arm on the flooded and iced-over town square. Another magical memory, with the lighted gazebo and bench-surrounded bonfire, perfect for roasting marshmallows.

"Earth to Nat."

Brad gripped her elbow. She snapped from daydreams of what a perfect life would be—D.C. and a renewed relationship or Vermont and a revived relationship.

"I could hear your wheels grinding from the other end of the hall."

She obtained solid footing. "Ice skating." She breathed the two words.

His chin dipped, as his gaze swept over her face.

Traitorous color warmed her cheeks. She swore he could read meaning in every worry-line and the stiff set of her mouth.

"Ice skating, huh?"

She stepped back, hoping he wouldn't guess her thoughts pondering the past…and the two together. "I haven't been in years. By Christmas, the rink should be open. Do they still rent? We could take our guests."

"And you?"

"Me?" She stepped from his hold to escape the scent forever ingrained in her soul. For sixteen years she'd tried to forget the essence of Brad that continued to haunt her every time he moved close.

Like now.

"Not me. Our guests."

"The guests can wait. When was the last time *you* skated?"

"High school. With you." Not sure why she uttered the last part, she ducked her head and mumbled, "Long ago."

"I doubt a deep freeze happens before Christmas. However, if we get ice, I'm your man. Remember?"

She edged backwards. He sauntered toward her,

like a panther on the prowl. That lift of his right lip sent showers of sparks to her belly. She cradled her stomach to quell the riot of emotions. His weighty arm landed on her shoulders. The memory of skating, snuggled warmly in his arms, caused the last years to disappear in an instant.

He drew her closer.

She dug her elbow into his side.

He beamed a smile.

For a flash, in the semi-darkness of the hall, she shared a sacred space with him until otherworldly voices drifted from the far room, disbursing the momentary magic. She ducked from under his strong, warm arm and strode toward her room. At the door, she turned.

Brad stood, hands on his hips and his legs planted wide.

She couldn't allow herself to fall again for this guy. To diffuse the situation, she threw the only weapon she possessed—nixing any thought of a long-distance relationship. "I thought I might take my skates to D.C."

"Oh."

His pupils darkened and his lids shuttered, then he ducked into Jeff's room.

A momentary nudge of guilt hit her square in her heart. She had to protect herself. No way could she open herself to pain—not again.

"Let's haul everything to the hall so the staff can clean. Then we tackle the other rooms." The authoritative sound of Brad's voice boomed from the tiny room.

His message was loud and clear—time to work. She'd hurt him. Although, now her own preservation necessitated putting distance between them. Swiping her hands on her pant legs, sweaty on a chilled day, she strode toward the stairs. In the doorway, she turned and hollered. “Abby? Tina?”

Two heads poked from the room past Jeff’s.

“I’ve got a list of things to do. Can you help the guys? I’ll let Mary know.”

“Piece o’ cake,” Tina said. “We’ve got this.”

After blowing Abby and Tina a kiss, Natalie pushed open the heavy door, plunged into the cold Vermont air, and escaped to freedom. At the bottom of the staircase, she pulled in a blast of cold air.

Rule number one—stay far from Brad. Leaving ran contrary to her work ethic. Staying behind and working in close proximity to Brad and his scent and his heaving muscles, watching him haul furniture… She didn’t have the strength to endure that torture.

Escaping to Chelsey and giving herself much-needed breathing room from the lure of Brad ranked as self-preservation, pure and simple.

Now if she could ban him from the inn altogether, time spent in Vermont would go much smoother.

****

Four hours later, the sun disappeared behind the mountains, and dusk descended into the valley bordering Mistletoe Creek. Brad jogged the steps of the carriage house, heading straight to his truck, parked near the inn’s front door. He rounded the corner.

Nat jumped from the inn’s SUV. Carrying three shopping bags with another slung over her shoulder, she bounded up the steps.

He hauled open his truck door, then paused. Nat’s earlier annoyance over Thanksgiving week promo ideas was crystal clear. Then, she hadn't come clean about what wheeled through her mind. Not much had changed over the years. She tried to hide something, evident by the way she ducked her head and darted her gaze. Today, the only explanation she conjured up was some lame ice-skating fantasy. From the grimace plastered on her pretty face, she was upset. Skating in D.C.? He sure as hell could tick off a number of other things she might be upset about, including the fact he existed.

Period.

At times, he got in her face to elicit annoyance. At least she took notice. Not much changed since kindergarten. What was the saying? Everything you need to know about life you learn in kindergarten mirrored his plan. Keep putting himself smack dab in her path. Make a pest of himself, if necessary. Tug a pigtail, or that crazy point of hair. Like the child he was a *hundred* years ago—pulling ponytails, hiding pencils, taunting girls on the playground—he knew the method worked.

Sooner or later, she couldn't ignore him. His logic was lame, but he intended to be indispensable. Prove he wasn't a stupid, vulnerable eighteen-year-old *kid* who ran scared, rather than verify the truth of her father's words. Every small-town teen he knew wouldn't have the backbone to go head-to-head with a powerful and wealthy attorney from Boston.

With a ton to prove to Nat, showing he was serious from afar wouldn't work. In her face he'd be for the next six, short weeks.

The moment he first noticed her behind the inn's desk, the memories slammed him hard. He'd never stopped wondering why they broke up. These past weeks, he observed the same methodical attention to everything she did, had done, since she was little. Her unwavering concentration was one of the things he loved. Also, if he admitted the truth, one of the things that drove him insane.

Nat kept him grounded when all he wanted was to follow his heart, his emotions, and pursue what pleased him—trekking in the mountains, skiing along the banks of the roaring creek, or climbing a wall of rock. Because of her, he'd studied hard, elbow-to-elbow with her on the couch in the parlor.

Here he was elbow-to-elbow once more. Learning new ways to make his store profitable, recruiting new customers, and showcasing his merchandise to the best advantage. He'd ducked his head to concentrate on the day-to-day business, shoving away his desire to escape to the wilderness.

Okay, he hadn't quite mastered ignoring escape routes. Or quelling the fantasy of taking Nat with him.

Nat.

He refused to leave unsaid what needed to be addressed hours ago in the hallway of the carriage house. He slammed shut the truck door and jogged the steps two at a time. He burst through the door, stomped his snowy boots on the welcome runner, and strode toward the desk.

His noisy entrance had Nat peeking from the office, a smile on her face that turned immediately to a scowl.

"Reporting in." He saluted, then grinned. *Yup, kindergarten logic.*

She sighed.

She'd perfected that weighty exhale over the last

weeks. A few days prior, he believed he'd wiped sighs entirely from her repertoire.

They got along and made headway toward reconnecting. The past blurred, until he spilled the news her father, and his manipulative lies, broke up and kept them apart for years. He abhorred the avalanche of pain her father's behavior set off. He could relate. He understood *father* issues.

Brad intended to make up for her father's control and be ready to help—prove he was the good guy. Undaunted by her glare, he took the last steps toward the office where she'd ducked. He filled the doorway, blocking any idea of escape. "Jeff and I cleared two rooms."

She dipped her chin while staring upward.

He plastered on a grin to dispel the notion he was fazed by her doubt. "We set up twin beds, bureau, and bedside table in the room next to Jeff's. We discovered rolled carpets and a handful of lamps. After distributing to the two rooms, I set extra lamps outside the storage room. Bulbs are burned out. I'll replace them so you can divvy them between your rooms."

Her brow straightened. The corners of her mouth tweaked.

Was that a smile?

"Things fit?"

"Yup." He nixed *I told you so*. "Extra furniture is in the corner of the garage. We located and slid two long runners along the hallway. Tina vacuumed the rugs."

"I—ah, wow. You spent the day."

"Several hours. Jeff's moved in. I told Heidi one extra for dinner."

"I, ah, hadn't considered meals."

He ignored her comment. Jeff had done yeoman's work before he unpacked. Mary said room in exchange for work. In his mind, Jeff would be treated like Nat, Heidi, and her four-year-old son, Keegan—room and board.

"We started annual maintenance on the groomer and took a test run. Most of the trails are set. Jeff will finish tomorrow, first thing. And I'll advertise afternoon skiing. Heidi has plenty of cookies in the freezer."

Nat's eyes widened. "You've been busy."

She didn't know the half. Like the discovery of the small sleigh. Or his plan to refurbish the gem. "I'm off. Anything you need at the hardware—text me." He left her in the doorway, mouth agape. As he jogged the inn's steps, he hoped she'd reconsider their relationship.

Two hours later, he'd piled into the cart light bulbs, spotlights, and enough strings of outdoor lights to decorate the sleigh. He located red, green, black, and gold paint, primer, brushes, two grades of sandpaper, and various other supplies. He and Jeff would tackle sanding and painting tomorrow night. He added a giant, outdoor gold bow for the front of the sleigh from the selection by the register.

Loaded down, he headed to GMS to close shop. An hour later, he loped the front steps to the family home, dangling a carryout bag. His mom opened the door before he hit the porch. "Dinner."

"Oh, darling, I appreciate this. You know I can make dinner."

"Why?" He kissed her cheek. "I've got Ricky's

special—roast chicken, garlic mashed potatoes, sautéed seasoned Brussels sprouts, and a side of his famous red cabbage slaw.” He wouldn’t confess his need to constantly check on her.

“Smells wonderful.” A smile bloomed.

“And enough for leftovers.” He placed the bag on the dining room sideboard and removed aluminum containers. His mom followed him, the place settings already on the table for their usual Sunday meal.

“Ricky’s makes the best slaw, like my grandmother’s.”

“Ma, you make a heck of a slaw.”

“My mother taught me well. But these days…those darn cabbages are a beast to cut.”

He squeezed her hand. “Soon. Right? You can teach me the secret salad recipe. I’ll cut the cabbage.” He winked. “Deal?”

“Deal.” She smiled. “By summer I’ll be one hundred percent.”

“Atta girl. I love you, Ma.” He set containers on trivets already placed on the table. He drew his mom’s chair and sat cattycorner. “You’ve taught me to be strong. You know, right?”

Her gaze rose to meet his, her eyes shining with unshed tears.

He placed a hand over hers and squeezed. “Which means you’re the strongest woman I know.”

She sat straight, blinked, and removed her hand from under his, before she backhanded a wave in his direction. “I try to be strong. You’re lucky. You’re surrounded by strong women. Mary. Natalie.”

“You’re right. Both strong, as were the women I’ve worked with. Talk strong…” Before she could draw breath and steer conversation to Nat, he launched into adventure stories. Between chattering and filling her plate with food, he diverted her matchmaking. "Eat while food is hot."

Truth be told, he was already well into the mission of winning Nat.

Tomorrow, he'd ramp up by sanding the old sleigh.

Chapter Thirteen

"Mary? What's up?"

"I think plans are working." Mary wedged the receiver between her shoulder and chin, as she jotted notes in the registration book.

Sylvie giggled. "Do tell. Because Brad would not say a word regarding Natalie."

"You didn't quiz him?"

"No. He told me I was a strong woman—"

"Aww, he's a good son."

"Not the point. I told him he had many strong women in his life, like you and Natalie." He championed all the women he'd worked beside out west.

"Aha, don't you see, if he didn't care, he wouldn't have changed the subject." Mary planted a forearm against the counter. "You know the term they use in poker? A tell."

"Since when do you play poker?"

"Harry did. Want to hear the latest with the kids?"

"Spill, Mary."

"He and his friend Jeff spent most of the day working here and even offered to pick up decorations for the inn."

"Brad never mentioned the inn. His store—he can't neglect his business."

Mary laughed. "Natalie gave him the dickens, too.

He assured her his holiday help was onboard."

"What's next?"

"You and Brad come for Thanksgiving dinner." Mary sat back, pleased with the idea. "Jeff is living in the carriage house, so perfect excuse. You won't have to lift a finger."

"I'll check."

"Just tell Brad. You know he'll do anything for you. In fact, spend the night in my suite? Plus, we have an extra bed in the carriage house for Brad. Have him pack a duffle. We can keep the two together longer."

"Oh, Mary, sounds like fun. Remember our slumber parties? Seems forever since I left the house for more than a doctor's visit."

"I'll treat you like a princess."

"Any chance you invited Walter?"

Mary let the silence float. "I, ah, I hadn't considered—"

"Well, think, woman. A great excuse. Otherwise, he'll be alone."

"You're right. With you and Brad attending, I can say we're having a *friend-filled* Thanksgiving. Walter comes tomorrow to check on the event."

"Tomorrow might be too late. He's one of the eligible bachelors in town. I'd be surprised if Wanda hasn't called him. I'm hanging up. Call him."

"I, ah—"

"You want to miss the opportunity? Wanda could be dialing while we speak."

Mary pushed the disconnect button and dialed Walter's number.

****

Natalie crawled into bed at eleven.

Heidi sacked out on a rollaway cot nearby.

Evan, her ex, bunked with Keegan in Heidi's suite.

Every pore in her body oozed achiness. The next few days would be mind-numbing. The saving grace—all their guests were checked in, including a last-minute walk-in at nine p.m. With one single room left, Natalie sighed, sparking waves of relief to every muscle and brain cell. She sank into the pile of feather pillows. Already late, morning would skate in on a fast track.

Instead of counting sheep, she reviewed tomorrow's agenda. First thing, Heidi and Jeremy showcased the inn's famous continental breakfast, including a warming tray with breakfast croissant sandwiches and Heidi's inventive scones. Thanksgiving seatings were scheduled for one and three—serving the Vermont feast early, so staff could enjoy Thanksgiving with their own families. The remaining staff and family would later have their feast. Guests would graze into the evening on a buffet of soup, salad, and assorted breads.

Relieved the scrolling check-list had *done* checked off on each item, Natalie counted backwards as she visualized relaxing each part of her body. She snuggled under the goose feather comforter. Her worries eased. She rolled to her side to face Heidi. "Is Evan settled with Keegs?"

"Who knows." Heidi shrugged as she yanked the blankets, covering half her head like a cocoon. "He's complaining about not getting a bed in the inn."

"Ha…bet his cranky attitude went down like a deflating soufflé."

Heidi rolled over and hooked her hands behind her head, her nose peeking above the covers. "Ya' think? I gave him directions to the highway if he couldn't handle a few days bonding with his son…alone. Without me doing the heavy lifting, he'll have to deal."

"Yes, he will," Natalie dragged the covers to settle over her shoulder and cuddle her neck. "Keegs deserves to have Evan's attention one hundred percent."

"Uh-huh." Heidi's eyes closed the moment she removed her hands from behind her head.

In what seemed like seconds, a soft snore emanated from her exhausted friend. She, on the other hand, rolled to her back as her buried worries resurfaced. She envied the ease with which Heidi fell asleep.

She stared at the blank slate of ceiling. Just because today's list was checked off… A zillion details marched through her brain like the high-school drum corps. If she stared at the ceiling long enough, would her worries be allayed? In what seemed like a decade, she eased her eyes closed and drifted off.

A sharp buzz from her phone's security app had her catapulting off the bed. Plunging her bare feet into her boots and shoving her arms into her bathrobe sleeves, she snugged tight the belt.

"Wha-a-at?" Heidi sat up, her gaze at half-mast.

"Late check-in."

"Everyone's here."

"Walk-in. I'll handle registration." With her cell clenched in her fist, she raced through the hallway, thumbing on the security screen—the system she dug into her savings to install in time for Thanksgiving.

Wes?

She ran through the snow piled high along the pathway. Cold, wet flakes slipped into her boots. The chilled melt assaulted her bare toes. A shudder zipped along her spine. She keyed in the security code at the kitchen door, kicked off her boots, wiggled her toes to warm them up, and padded through to the lobby.

The continuous chirps off her app highlighted Wes's impatience. In between plastering his thumb on the doorbell, he'd texted her twice, the tinny gong clanging from her pocket. "I'm coming." She strode toward the door, tempted to ignore Wes and stomp to bed. The incessant bell-ringing and texting grated every nerve. Why did Wes think arriving with no warning was a good idea? She glanced at the grandfather clock in the corner. Eleven-thirty.

What was he thinking? Showing up in the middle of the night? In the snow? On the busiest weekend of the season?

Doing her best to beam a customer-service smile, she flung wide the door. She wasn't sure she'd ever seen a disheveled Wes, despite his usual, I'm-used-to-perfection scowl plastered across his face. His polished shoes were caked with an icy glaze. Water dripped off the divot in his chin, making a mockery of his need to be meticulous.

Wes's gaze skimmed her from head to toe.

"You expected me to be in formal wear? I was in bed."

He huffed a condescending sigh. "It's not even midnight. You've become a country mouse."

"Excuse me?" Her voice rose an octave. The urge to plan revenge overrode desire to roll her eyes. Wait until she woke him at the crack of dawn to refill the continental breakfast, wait on tables, and…kept him working until tomorrow night. He'd be ready for bed at seven. "What are you doing here?" Despite her forced smile, her greeting would not be construed as a gold star welcome.

He removed his fancy leather gloves and stuffed them in the pocket of his cashmere coat. His blond hair was sprinkled with snowflakes, and his dark eyes beamed his dissatisfaction with…everything. He stepped through the front door and brushed his ice-cold hand along her arm.

"I can't believe you're surviving in the boonies."

She shivered, not sure how to respond. Dragging forth her finesse, she shrugged off annoyance and pinned on her happy-to-see-you face. He'd taken the time to visit. His gesture had to have a meaning. "Come in. Let's get the door closed before the heat escapes."

Dragging his rolling suitcase, he stepped closer and fingered the tip of her blunt cut.

Natalie waited for the zing of excitement to spread. *Nothing.*

"You could use a trim." He dropped his hand.

Unbelievable.

How had she never noticed his self-centered side? No, hello kiss. No, "I missed you." No, "Wow, what a beautiful spot." In less than a minute, he'd insulted her twice and complained about his trip. "It's late, Wes. We'll discuss dress and hair styles tomorrow." *After I wake you up at five a.m.* Heidi will have a heyday with Wes and his attitude. "You're lucky I still have room at the inn. Otherwise, you'd have bunked in the stables with only the hay and a scratchy horse blanket to warm you." He didn't bat an eye at the Christmas reference or her dig.

"Stables? You muck stalls, too?"

The fact he understood about caring for horses

surprised her. She batted her lashes. "You can help tomorrow." No way would she confess the stable was now a carriage house. Only the two-stalled barn with no horses stood behind the inn.

She tamped retribution fantasies and the temptation to trot him through the snow to the half-finished, cold room in the carriage house. One room left in the inn. She hazarded a guess he wouldn't offer payment. She scooted behind the desk to retrieve the key. Then she opened the leather registration book. "Sign here."

He squinted and patted his breast pocket, then searched through his overcoat. "My glasses."

She drew a finger along the line. "All guests must sign in. Just scribble your name. Tomorrow, after you find your glasses, Aunt Mary can run your credit card."

A frown pressed his mouth shut.

She tried to contain her icy glare. She prayed for a better mood by morning, where she could appreciate Wes's gesture to spend Thanksgiving together. This minute, tired, wet, cold, and ornery as a cow without her bull, she wasn't in the kindest of moods.

The arduous climb to the third floor seemed as if she wore ten-pound hiking boots. She plodded to the last room.

"You aren't wearing shoes."

She stopped at his door. "My boots were covered in snow."

Flipping on the lamp and turning down Wes's bed was a gargantuan task. "Closet. Bathroom." She pointed at each corner.

He scanned the small room, his lips pursed.

Suddenly, she didn't care whether Wes was comfortable or approved of her family's rustic inn.

"Goodnight, Wes. I'll need your help in the kitchen tomorrow morning. I'll set the wakeup call." She eased the door closed behind her. If not for a full inn in the middle of the night, she would've relished a reverberating slam. Her feet were frozen, her sleep interrupted, and Wes had been as annoying as Wes could get.

Several hours later, the alarm yanked her from deep sleep and a dream—Wes showing up for Thanksgiving and hijacking her time with law work. Her dream was a desperate attempt to work magic with a law client who had a complicated cash transaction between the U.S. and Israel, while she juggled her phone and tablet, as she served breakfast to a full house. She swore she'd run a treadmill. She heaved a sigh.

"You all right?"

She jumped. "I forgot you were here."

"What's wrong?" Heidi tugged the covers to make her rollaway.

"Waking in the middle of a nightmare."

Heidi straightened. "Nightmare?"

"One of those keeping-up-with-work, gerbil-on-the-wheel dreams."

"You're juggling too much."

She frowned at Heidi's typical, hands-on-hips stance, not in the mood for motherly commentary, however well-meaning it was. She huffed as her climb from bed amounted to ascending Everest. "If we show profit this month, we'll add extra staff hours in December."

Heidi's exhale whistled. "Let's hit the road running. What do you need?"

"You have enough on your plate without—"

"Filling my hours with work means not dealing with Evan. Maybe he'll realize what transpires with fulltime childcare duties."

"And…leave you alone concerning custody—win-win. By the way, we have extra help today."

She raised a brow. "Who?"

"Wes."

"No shi—take." Heidi raised a brow.

Natalie laughed. "Is that what you say near Keegan?"

"Yup. So, Wes…?"

"The walk-in last night. Let's say he made enough condescending comments I figured payback was in order."

"Payback?"

She swatted her hand through the air. "As in washing dishes, shoveling, replenishing the breakfast buffet."

Heidi rubbed her hands together. "Oh boy. Can't wait."

"I knew you'd be up for the task."

Wes stood in the middle of the kitchen, by the time she and Heidi arrived at the main house. Natalie's eyes widened. "I can't believe you're on time—"

"Amazing thing—my room phone blasted auto wake-ups every five minutes."

"Whoops," Heidi muttered, before she pressed her mouth together in her signature evil grin. "Glad you can help. Grab the stack of trays in the corner and lay them on this counter. Wait! Wash your hands first."

"I just finished my shower," Wes said.

"Did you use the stair handrail on the way here?"

"Of course."

Heidi pointed toward the sink in the corner of the kitchen. “Then *wash* your hands.”

Wes narrowed his eyes and spun toward Heidi. “And *who* are you?”

Natalie wanted to throttle him. She tempered her own tone into sugary-sweet. “Wes, Heidi is our chef and one of my best friends.”

Heidi’s fists plastered against her hips.

Diffuse, diffuse. A stand-off between the two would not end well. Blatant animosity would rule the next four days unless she intervened.

If Wes lasted the weekend.

She swung her gaze between the two. The glares crisscrossing the kitchen didn’t give her hope civility would reign. Before she called in armed guards, Natalie opted for distraction. She set her features into a stellar fake, sweet smile. “Listen up. While I arrange the pastries, Wes, you fill coffee carafes.” She gestured toward the big electric pot. “Take them to the buffet. The cards show where to place decaf and regular. Do *not* mix them up.”

Wes blasted her with an I’m-not-a-moron look, then washed his hands. After two years of knowing Wes, today was the first time she directed him or called him on his behavior. Something she should have done last night…and long before this.

How had she never noticed the inequity?

With guests due for breakfast within twenty-minutes, she drew a breath, expelled the pent-up air in measured motion, and strolled into the dining room, carrying scone-filled baskets and sporting a wide smile. “Welcome to your first Vermont breakfast.”

The frenzied morning disappeared in a flash.

Heidi muckled on to her arm as she strode into the kitchen.

"You okay?"

She slid to stop. "Yeah. Why?"

"Making sure Wes isn't giving you trouble."

Her gut clenched. "None. You?"

"He's doing his job. Not exactly his bailiwick. Still, he's putting one foot in front of the other."

"Thank goodness. Neither of us has time to babysit. Dining room is cleared. Let's take ten and reassess needs." Thanksgiving weekend was such serious business, every brain cell and ounce of energy was focused on the end result—happy guests and a revived cash flow.

She and Heidi clutched mugs of coffee. The two scanned the work-flow chart, checking last-minute details. She scratched notes for a few changes to relay to staff. The front door groaned on heavy hinges, yanking her thoughts to earth.

Wes tromped in, the too-big LL Bean boots clomping against the wooden floors.

Earlier, Mary caught him before he fetched firewood in a pair of polished loafers. Her uncle's old boots came in handy.

"Uh, uh." Mary's voice echoed from her perch behind the desk. "Off with the boots. Then ask Heidi for the lubricant to oil the front door hinges."

Natalie peeked from the dining room. She couldn't help grinning at Wes's thin, black, executive socks.

"After you oil the door, Wesley dear…" Mary's voice rose in sing-song fashion. "Head to the parlor and prop your feet on the fireplace fender to thaw those toes."

With a sheepish grin, Wes glanced at Mary. “It’s obvious I’m not prepared for Vermont winters.”

He had the good grace to admit his embarrassment. Natalie wasn’t sure she’d ever seen him humbled.

“By the calendar, fall doesn’t end until December twenty-third.”

Without being condescending, her aunt pegged their visitors and got them to talk.

“Yeah, well…” Wes shrugged.

“This time of year, hot liquids are a must. Take ten and help yourself to the buffet.” Mary waved a hand toward the table stocked with afternoon pick-me-ups. “Go on. You’ve worked hard.”

Natalie ducked deeper into the dining room.

Abby, Tina, and a friend of theirs, recruited for the weekend, strode into the dining room. After tidying rooms and replenishing towels, they’d changed into server uniforms.

“Hello, ladies.” At the moniker, each displayed a varied hue of blush. “Heidi and I added to the list of items we need to be on top of this weekend. It’s attached to the office clipboard.

“We’ll check the instructions.” Tina turned.

The others followed.

“Hold up. You can check later. You three deserve a break. Once these tables are reset, head to the library and take a load off. The list can wait.”

“Sounds like a plan,” Abby said. “Okay if we grab hot chocolate and cookies.”

“Sure. You’ve more than earned a treat. Don’t forget to eat real food. Heidi has sandwiches and goodies.” Natalie breathed a sigh of relief. Except for Wes showing up, everything ran smoothly. This holiday weekend was the beginning of reclaiming the inn's old glory.

She gathered her phone and empty mug before striding into the kitchen with renewed vigor. Thanksgiving was off to a great start. For the first time in weeks, she had every confidence nothing could ruin the lovely plans.

Chapter Fourteen

Sylvie strode through the front door of the inn, like a queen on holiday. Brad followed, loaded with enough bags for a month's stay. His mom talked him into Thanksgiving dinner with her best friend. When her big, brown eyes signaled the importance, he'd succumbed to the harebrained, overnight plan, despite recognizing another *matchmaking* ploy. He hadn't yielded altogether.

First thing this morning, Jeff texted him regarding the late-night check-in. He indicated neither Nat nor Heidi was happy. The last thing Brad wanted was to share Nat, who was supposed to be taking a break from said boyfriend.

When he met Nat's guy at dinner, Brad would be expected to put on a happy face. Peanut butter and jelly on the couch at home in front of the football game was preferable.

"Where's your bag, darling?"

"Mom, I'm not staying. I'll pick you up tomorrow." He didn't let on he'd stowed his duffel in the trunk, just in case.

She sent him the over-the-glasses-rim, mom glare. "You *are* staying for dinner."

His mom turned and enveloped her best friend with a bear hug. He never had a chance to contradict the I-am-your-mother-and-you-will-do-as-I-say tone.

Mary leaned toward Sylvie's ear and whispered.

They both grinned.

Uh oh.

Mary turned to welcome him with a hug to rival a dancing black bear clutching a partner.

"So glad you're both here. Take your mom's bag to my room for our *slumber party*."

"You mean bags." Brad gestured to the luggage surrounding him. "Mom's planning to stay through Christmas."

"Oh, *pish*." Mary swatted his arm. "You know she's welcome to stay for days. I might put her to work so she can't escape."

Brad planted a kiss on Mary's cheek. "It would be good for her. Right, Ma?"

Mary blushed. "Brad, I've put you at the end of the hall in the room you and Jeff cleared."

Right now, he wouldn't argue or make excuses. Later, when the *happy-family* Thanksgiving dinner finished, he'd head home. He topped the stairs to the second floor of the carriage house, where, only a week ago, he rearranged rooms. Today, the small, antique washstands they'd stacked in the storage room zigzagged at intervals along both sides of the hall. Nineteenth-century, glazed washbasins, hand-painted in old-fashioned, soft pastel, garden flowers, sat on top of each stand. Electric chunky pillar candles in every bowl glowed, casting muted shadows, that gave the hallway a warm, sensual glow.

He fantasized kissing Nat goodnight in the subdued light by her door. Maybe he *should* stay the night. The thought skipped through his mind that he might owe the matchmakers a thank you. He bet Nat upgraded the decor. She'd always been a romantic.

Romantic? Jeez. Did she still embrace her romantic, artsy side? Nowadays, she was serious and by-the-book. The practical Nat added light to avoid lawsuits.

He strolled to Mary's room. The suite where she and Harry lived for as long as he could remember looked inviting. He deposited his mom's bag, then pulled shut the door, turned, and plowed into Nat. His arm wound around her waist to steady her.

"What are you doing here?"

Her accusation was a body blow. "I'm not breaking and entering." He pointed his thumb over his shoulder. "Mom's bags."

"What?" She pulled back from his hold and crossed her arms.

"For the overnight after dinner."

"Dinner?"

"What dinner do you think? Thanksgiving."

Her mouth dropped open.

"Mary *forgot* to tell you she invited us?"

"Are you *snickerdoodling* me?" Her fists settled against her hips, as she paced a tight circle before stopping toe to toe.

"Snickerdoodling?" He met her glare, then eyeballed the ceiling to contain his laughter. At age seven, she'd learned the term from Uncle Harry. "Do you use that expression in your big-shot, D.C. job?"

Her glare morphed to a frown.

His smile escaped, as he flashed palms, then yanked on her pointed lock of hair. "Lighten up. Teasing."

Her tight shoulders dropped an inch. "The term

fits. I'd wager my *immense fortune* Mary *and* Sylvie *snickerdoodled* you."

Using a forefinger, he tipped her chin, trying desperately not to react to her soft, vanilla-mint scented skin. Who did he kid? Being anywhere near Nat meant his body and mind leaped into high-alert. "I assumed, after years in law, you'd have learned to cuss like a linebacker, and—" he caressed her bottom lip with his thumb. "—anticipated any snickerdoodling."

She retreated.

He dropped his hand from the warmth of her mouth.

"You're here of your own free will?" She straightened with palms flattened on her hips. "No underhanded coercion by your mom *or* my aunt?"

"Does playing the cancer and get-out-of-home-bound-jail card count as coercion?"

Nodding, she withdrew a few steps, before she bit the tip of her already ragged nail.

She chewed her nails when they were kids. As a teen she begged him to help her stop. He circled her wrist and tugged on her hand, as he'd done years ago. The heat, from holding her, singed his fingertips. He released his grip. Regret slithered through him. "I—Mom and Mary, no doubt, have lined up tasks to keep me here."

"Tasks?"

"Mom convinced me you and Mary needed help."

"They're plotting for us to work together. Want to foil their plans?" Her brows lifted, and he swore she was about to flick a cigar in Groucho Marx style.

He didn't, but he nodded. "Count me in. Anything to thwart snickerdoodling."

"Good. You're in charge of directing tasks for our extra helpers, including Walter, Jeff, and Weston."

"Weston?"

"Wes. My, ah, sort of, ah, boyfriend showed up in the dead of night with no warning. And…" She heaved a sigh and dropped her gaze to her feet.

His heart plummeted straight to his stomach. *A sort of boyfriend?* "And?"

"Never mind."

Her features shuttered.

She headed toward the stairs, before looking over her shoulder. "Let's go. Work to do."

He caught her arm. "You want me to supervise your boyfriend, I deserve a head's up." No excuse for his frosty tone, except— Except…nothing. Nat stated her position multiple times. She showed no interest in exploring what they once had.

And now the boyfriend was in town.

Game on.

"He's a corporate attorney who showed up near midnight, unannounced and unprepared for a Vermont winter. Plus, an attitude involving my inn and what I do and wear."

"Oh-kay. Betting his middle-of-the-night arrogance didn't go over." Brad bit his lip to hide the grin that longed to escape. His Nat was not happy with the appearance of said, sort of boyfriend.

"I might have planned retribution."

"*Might* have? Or did?"

"Did."

"As in?" Again, she bit her lip. The gesture made him ache to sooth her mouth with the tip of his finger.

"Wake-up calls for five a.m. and every few

minutes after. He's been working since. I can't continue bossing him. So, you—" She took a step before turning fully to poke his chest with her ragged nail.

"Yeah?" He grinned. Wes had obviously won zero brownie points showing without notice or invitation. Score one for Brad's team, and the match had yet to begin. "I'm game."

"Fireplace logs delivered to every public space. Sidewalks and pathways cleared. The groomer needs a sweep through the ski course. Otherwise, guests won't be able to use the trails tomorrow."

"Anything else?" He ticked off the list in his head, assigning tasks.

"Keep the floors in the lobby dry. We don't need anyone falling on our watch."

"Aye, aye, captain." He saluted. "I'm on the job. My orders…keep Weston busy."

"Oh, and Walter is already assigned to keep the dining room and parlor stocked with drinks and snacks." Again with the raised eyebrows. He held tight his chuckle. "I want to leave him a bit of time to hang with Mary."

"Aha. Engaged in your own snickerdoodling?"

"Yup." She grinned.

His heart tumbled further into dangerous territory. Then she spun, to scamper into the cold and down the steps, leaving Brad wondering how the hell he ended up in the predicament of babysitting the *persona non grata* boyfriend.

He rubbed his palms together. Time to get started. Jogging the steps, he reached the path to the kitchen. The murky outline of Nat and the inn disappeared in a whiteout.

****

Natalie ran, slipping and sliding along the path. The snow descended thick and fast. As she closed in, the outline of the kitchen's door jumped like a ghostly apparition from the curtain of snow. She drew tight her coat. A prickle of fear zipped along her spine, an ominous harbinger their comfortable vacation weekend could soon become a nightmare.

Sheltered inside the doorway to the kitchen, she clicked through her phone to the weather app.

—BLIZZARD WARNING—

Brad barreled through the doorway and slammed into her back.

He gripped her shoulders, preventing her from toppling. A warm shiver, she didn't need or want when she was already rattled, slipped through her.

"Nat, what's wrong?"

Her phone trembled in her hand, as she turned and shoved the screen toward him. "Trajectory of storm shifted, due to Arctic winds plunging farther south than expected."

His gaze skimmed the message. "You check the local station?"

She shook her head.

"Come on." Grasping her hand, he hauled her into the welcome warmth of the kitchen.

"What in the world?" Heidi motioned between them. "You're covered."

"Blizzard." Again, Natalie showed her phone. "We're checking roads. We have enough meal supplies?"

"More than enough for the weekend. I've extras of freezer and dry goods."

Natalie slumped alongside the counter.

With Brad's hand still warm in hers, her tension eased, until she realized…their interlocked hands. She yanked—hard—and scooted to the middle of the kitchen, away from his heat and protection. "Brad will keep the staff on task. You and I need to talk."

Heidi's head tilted toward Natalie. Her gaze shifted to her hand, then locked on Brad's lone hand.

Caught with the hand-holding.

"I rescued the fair maiden from the blizzard."

Heidi rolled her eyes.

Brad shrugged one shoulder. "I'm off to ride roughshod on them menfolk."

His silly drawl crawled through her, warm and fuzzy. Still, she mimicked Heidi's eye-roll. Judging from Heidi's brow lift, his gallant attempt bombed at diffusing Heidi.

She sneaked a peek. Only a swinging kitchen door where Brad once stood. Her heartbeat steadied. She faced off with Heidi, hoping to capture the upper hand. "I slipped. Brad caught me. Don't even start. We've got an emergency." She shifted past Heidi's typical, in-your-face barrier of hands lodged on hips. "Wipe the grin off your face." She stomped into Heidi's small office and plopped in the swivel chair behind the desk. "Last-minute adjustments. With Wes, Walter, the waitresses, Jeremy, and the unexpected addition of Brad and Sylvie, we might have eight more people overnight and through tomorrow, depending on the storm track."

Heidi planted her palms against the desk. "We're set for the mid-afternoon seating. Jeremy is prepped for tonight's light buffet and breakfast. We always prep extra. We'll tweak tomorrow's dinner and supper menus, if needed. How long will the storm last?"

"At least twenty-four. Not good." She glanced toward the ceiling, counted to ten, and expelled a long, slow breath. "They're warning some roads are almost impassable, including Gooseneck Lane. The plows can't keep up."

"Stop worrying over stuff not in your control. We have food, firewood, gas for the generator, and many hands-on-deck. Consider the storm an adventure."

"Adventure?" She widened her eyes. "Not sure the word qualifies for one of the inn's most important weekends. Do we have enough wine?"

Heidi laughed. "You need me to crack open a bottle?" She held up a hand. "No worries. We've cases stacked in the carriage house. Enough to get us through any *adventure*."

"We better get hauling before the snow piles. Holler if you need me." Natalie held aloft the small walkie-talkies she pulled from the storage cupboard, in case their Wi-Fi connections stopped working. Once she found Brad and Jeff, she'd hand each a set and ask the two to lug wine cases. At this rate, the weekend would drag. Natalie slammed her palm against the swinging door.

"You holding hands with Brad put a smile on my face. Just sayin'."

Heidi's comment didn't warrant a reply. She allowed the door to slap shut. Two steps into the dining room, she came face-to-face with Wes.

"Who's Brad?"

"For goodness sakes. I slipped. He caught me before I fell. Heidi's just being…well, Heidi."

"And Brad?"

Wes's back stiffened, as it always did when he was homing in on a fact or grilling a witness. "He helps with our events. In fact, he's looking for you. A lot to do before the snow accumulates." Brad was her past. No explanation needed.

"Natalie?"

"Wes, I don't have time for chit-chat. Not with the storm—"

"One minute."

She retreated, not anxious to debate Wes.

He raised a finger. "One. Minute."

She tugged Wes deeper into the dining room, away from prying eyes and tuned-in ears. "What's so important you can't wait?"

"My apology. To you."

She straightened. Not what she expected. "A-apology?"

"Last night, I was rude and insensitive. No excuse. I was tired. Navigating dark Vermont roads is a bear compared to well-lit D.C. with street signs."

His mouth curved in the smile, which first attracted her, illuminating and softening his ice-blue eyes. "While we're apologizing, I'm sorry…the early wakeup call—er, calls. You woke me from a dead sleep. And then… Anyway, apologies all around, right? Look, I have a ton to do." She scooted past Wes, but he caught her wrist.

"We'll eat dinner tonight?"

"If nothing goes wrong." She flashed her fake smile, still not trusting his apology. "Otherwise, after dinner." She owed Wes a little together time. She wanted to hear his take on the inn, why he traveled to

Vermont, and give him a chance to redeem himself. Apologies spewed easy—all part of his charm with clients.

Until then, she'd reserve judgment. With an action plan in place, she strode toward the front desk. "Mary, where are Jeff and Brad? I need them A.S.A.P."

Chapter Fifteen

Natalie sucked in a deep breath, praying the family dinner would go without a hitch. With Mary and Sylvie's snickerdoodling alive and well, she had doubts.

Brad wheeled in the cart with the platters of thick carved, golden brown turkey slices, drumsticks, and crispy wings.

She and Heidi marched in behind. Heidi brandished the clove-studded sliced baked ham, while Natalie lugged an overflowing pile of stuffing in Aunt Mary's grandmother's, intricately patterned bowl.

Everyone sat shoulder-to-shoulder at the extended table.

Heidi reached over Jeff's shoulder to situate the ham platter, then rounded the table to sit beside him. She directed a quick wave toward her son. Heidi's gaze swept the table. Her eyes widened.

Why did Heidi seem surprised? Natalie surveyed the guests. A stranger sat wedged between Wes and Evan. She nudged Brad, as he positioned the cart at the opposite end of the table.

"Come on. I won't bite."

His whisper tickled her earlobe. "Not me. Who's next to Wes?"

Brad narrowed his gaze and growled. "What's Celia doing here?"

"You know her?"

"Yup."

"How?" Brad's face turned the same pasty white as the mashed potatoes.

"My ex."

"Your ex?" Her words emerged in a high-pitched squeak. "You didn't know she was here?"

"Nope."

She must have checked in with Mary. Natalie would have remembered a woman with bangles halfway up her arm, and bright red nails resembling curved talons of a hawk ready to scoop up an unsuspecting dove. "Why is she here?"

"Later."

Brad's grip on the platter turned his knuckles the same white as the tight lines surrounding his mouth.

"Sit. Everyone's staring."

Natalie scanned the table, before realizing the last empty seats were together across the end—she and Brad, the last two standing.

He scooted past to place the turkey platter on their end of the table.

Leaning closer, his shoulder brushed hers. His presence calmed her.

"Do *not* show your *fear*."

Natalie groaned, especially since fear was written on Brad's face in a ghostly pallor.

He laughed at his warped joke.

"Snickerdoodled again." She straightened her shoulders and held her breath in a desperate attempt to avoid inhaling Brad's woodsy scent.

"You okay?" He rescued the stuffing from her arms, before he drew back her chair.

She sat.

Brad seated himself and leaned close. “Breathe.”

“I could say the same.” She smiled through gritted teeth.

He speared a slice of dark turkey, then dropped the meat on her plate.

When his shoulder grazed hers, his heat radiated, warming her inside and out. Still, a shiver slipped through her, not from his touch, but because he remembered she liked thigh meat. She edged left, hoping to gain space.

Lifting her head, she caught Wes’s stare. His brow rose, reminding her of his ferocious attorney, grilling-the-plaintiff, defending-his-client stance.

She shrugged, hoping he got the message she was not responsible for seating assignments.

Mary stood, tapped her wine goblet, and set her fork on the placemat. She clasped Walter’s hand, then reached left for Jeremy’s.

Natalie held her breath.

“Everyone, hold hands for a moment of silence before we dig into the most wonderful feast.”

When Brad caught her hand, her heart rate tripled. After a bout of controlled breathing, she lifted her head to watch her aunt in her element.

“We have a family tradition of each person stating why they’re thankful.”

Please, please, please not today.

“But our food would be cold by the time we finished.”

Mary’s voice sang in delight. She did love a crowd.

“So, pass your plate to Jeff for ham and to Brad for turkey. Or both. Then we’ll pass the sides.”

The clatter of plates and silverware filled the room.

Both guys made quick work of fulfilling meat requests. Everyone else passed bowls of vegetables, potatoes, buttery rolls, and two types of cranberry sauce.

For the first time in forever, Natalie absorbed the sense of being with family during a holiday meal. She perused the table. Wes and Evan, with Celia sandwiched between them, caused Natalie to suppress a giggle at the picture of a family with wayward relatives who crashed last minute.

Celia leaned into Wes.

Not an ounce of jealousy oozed through her. The snickerdoodlers made their point by seating Brad's ex next to Natalie's current, maybe-we're-working-on-our-relationship boyfriend. She shrugged away their interference, refusing to let their meddling annoy her. She glanced at others and definitely spotted more snickerdoodling attempts.

The handsome new professor sat next to Sylvie. They couldn't take their eyes off each other. *Cute.* The close seating cemented her suspicion Sylvie also helped with the seating plan.

With Jeff at the head of the table, and Keegan and Heidi to either side, the seating setup was perfect. Jeff seemed enamored with both. The kitchen and wait staff, part of the inn family, were scattered around the table.

"Heidi and Jeremy, what a feast," Jeff raised his wine glass.

Everyone cheered. Voices dimmed when the group dug into offerings.

"Where's the salad?" Celia's high-pitched whine resounded.

Mary leaned past Jeremy. "With these offerings. we don't need salad, *dear*." Mary's syrupy sweet tone was anything but.

Brad's shoulder tensed against hers.

"But everything is covered in butter or sauce" Frowning, Celia gestured toward the laden table. "I can't eat any—"

Sylvie leaned forward. "It's Thanksgiving, *dear*. Calories are no concern." Her lips lifted at the corners as she mimicked Mary's *dear*, but her smile didn't touch her eyes.

"Or…if you just want salad—" Mary piped up. "You can excuse yourself and return later for the guests' salad buffet. Heidi and Jeremy do a wonderful job with quite a variety."

Natalie nudged Brad. "Uh oh, Mary and your mom are wearing their fake grins. I'm surprised your mom hasn't kicked Celia under the table."

Wes stood and headed toward the kitchen. Minutes later, he returned with a plate of vegetables left from the crudité platter from the earlier guest seating.

Again, Natalie elbowed Brad. "Seriously?"

"Rein in your suspicions." Brad leaned in. "Wes won't fall for Celia."

"The *last* thing I'm worried about." Natalie attacked her sweet potato casserole. The old family staple remained her favorite, seasoned with orange and cinnamon and at least a stick of butter. Let Celia eat those calories. She could stand to gain. She glanced at Celia, gazing at Wes, her shoulder wedged with his. She tried to conjure up a tad bit of jealousy.

Nothing. She glanced at Brad. "You're the one who should be worried."

"About what?"

"Your ex is almost in Wes's lap."

His reaction was to heap stuffing on his plate and ask Abby to pass the gravy.

Natalie worked to bury her grin, but the darn thing popped out, wide as a Cheshire cat's.

****

"Too many people in here." Natalie shooed four men toward the exiting kitchen door, while the wait staff carried dishes from the family dinner through the adjacent swinging door. The last thing she needed was Wes and Brad shoulder-to-shoulder and in her way. "You guys check walkways and firewood supply."

"On the job," Brad said. "And before you remind us one more time, yes, the generator is gassed. So are the snowmobiles. You need to relax."

Natalie wanted to slap the cocky expression off his face, until he leaned close, his warm breath skimming her collar bone.

"You're wound tighter than the vintage, wind-up Easter bunny on your bureau."

Shivers spiraled through her. Not the reaction she should have. Not when Wes made a special trip to make sure they were okay and still hovered in the kitchen. The problem remained that she couldn't be sure she and Wes *were* okay. They'd done the apology thing, so she owed him to see the weekend through. Time would tell if his apology was a simple overture because Wes perceived a rival.

A few weeks ago, she would've laughed at the idea of two men vying for her attention. Seeing Wes intimidated by an adversary amazed her. In the D.C. courts, his trademark was the tenacious bulldog, not afraid to bite or bully, and never one to withdraw.

Then Brad's whispered words hit her—*the bunny on her bureau.*

"What were you doing in my bedroom?" Her hissed whisper echoed through the kitchen, loud enough to be heard in the dining room.

Wes stopped dead in the doorway.

Brad flashed a grin and shrugged. "Hey, man. Jeff and I were lugging in an extra mattress."

Wes stared down Brad, then glared at Natalie.

Oh, boy. Brad baited Wes. Here we go. Defuse, defuse. "I-I forgot you helped Tina and Abby rearrange the carriage house."

"So, was the old toy your aunt's, or did you make a score at some antique shop? I know how much you love rummaging old yard sales and vintage shops. Remember—?"

She covered Brad's mouth with her hand. His *warm* mouth. As if scorched, she dropped her arm. At least she'd curtailed the monologue of shared memories—Brad's attempt to twist the knife in Wes's gut.

"The bunny?"

"*Mary's*." She gritted her teeth, hoping Brad would stop yammering. "I was seven when she gave me the toy."

"Stellar. Hang on to the gem. One day you can give the bunny to your kid."

If she hadn't been watching, she would have missed the lift of his brows. Yup, he taunted Wes on purpose.

She glanced at Wes. His pallor hinted at how the mention of kids freaked him out. In an instant, he schooled his features, leveled his shoulders, and straightened to his full height—a silent alpha-dog challenge. The bulldog prosecutor reared.

Realization hit her. Their D.C. lifestyle was so far removed from anything resembling family and everlasting, the subject of marriage and kids was never broached. None of their friends or colleagues had attained such a life-changing stage. Their relationship operated in a detached young professional's vacuum, where getting ahead was of the upmost importance. Working at an inhumane pace to build her career, she hadn't considered building a family, either. Her own upbringing by controlling and aloof parents played a part.

Now, in the soft, gentle folds of the inn and Mary's nurturing, she wondered why she'd forgotten how special family was. How special this inn, town, and Mary were, as well as Heidi, Brad, and Sylvie, her extended family since her childhood. Until…

Her phone bleated the formulaic weather alert tone, yanking her to the present.

The disembodied monotone computer voice beat a warning.

"Snow-covered roads. High winds. Low visibility. Granite Hill Road closed. Most Mistletoe Falls roads impassable. Gooseneck Lane Bridge washed out. Fallen tree, swift-moving water, ice, and rising creek causing damage. Do not traverse water-covered roads. *Turn Around. Don't Drown.* Governor instituted curfew for southern Vermont. Emergency personnel only on roads."

A high-pitched beeping tone ended the message, causing her stress to rise to equal heights. She was responsible for these people. Natalie listed.

"You're white as a blizzard." Brad gripped her waist.

Brad scooped her off her feet and carried her like a small child right past Wes, before Natalie could claim she'd be okay any minute.

Wes followed them through the lobby.

"Find Mary or Heidi, and get a cold, wet washcloth and blanket. Pronto." Brad's tone brooked no argument, as he strode toward the parlor.

Wes scurried off.

Natalie's head buzzed. She leaned her forehead against Brad's solid chest.

He cupped her neck with his large palm, while he cradled her tight to his body.

She closed her eyes, trusting he'd care for her.

He laid her on the plush sofa, seizing a throw pillow to shove under her head. "Glass of water. Stoke the fire." Brad barked orders.

Jeff plunked logs onto the glowing embers and prodded the fire to flame.

Natalie relaxed into the contours of the couch.

Minutes later, Heidi rushed in with a blanket and a chilled cloth. She handed them to Brad, squatting by the couch.

Between the coziness of the blanket settling the length of her body and the slap of cold on her forehead, Natalie blinked. "I'm okay. I've never fainted in my life." She tried to sit. "I need a minute."

"Stay put." Brad's deep voice settled her.

A strong, gentle, and familiar palm pressed on the center of her chest. Brad's scent swirled. She felt safe with him close.

"Give yourself a break, Nat. You've been burning the candle twenty-four seven."

Mary followed on Heidi's heels, carrying a tray with a pot of tea, a mug, a small pitcher of honey, and a large glass of water. "He's right. You got little sleep last night. Perhaps you're dehydrated. You must drink liquids, dear."

"Okay. I'm not moving." The fuss made her dizzy with too many bodies hovering. "I-I'll be fine. But…I need space."

Mary set the drinks on the coffee table.

Brad stayed crouched beside the couch, his palm stroking her hair away from the cold cloth. He lifted her head and brought close the glass of water. "Drink."

"Bossing me?" She gripped the glass in both hands.

"Yup. Someone has to."

"I do—"

He pressed his fingers to her lips. "No, you don't. Drink."

She did as ordered and had to admit she felt better.

He scooped the empty glass from her outstretched hand, then tugged the blanket to her neck.

Despite the warmth, she shivered from his gentle touch.

Jeff poked the fire once more, before grasping Heidi's hand and ambling to the lobby.

Natalie followed their path with half-closed eyes, thankful for the sudden quiet.

Wes stood stock still in the doorway, his hands jammed in his pockets, and his eyes wide. He might wow them in court but handling a personal crisis…not so much.

With reflections over Wes's incompetence zinging

through her mind, she expunged the scene. The things holding her and Wes together were doggedness, pride, and a common professional goal—not passion, not shared personal goals, and not love. As her head sank deep into the pillow, she knew what she had to do. She had to let Wes go. They had ended their run.

"You want me to take you to the carriage house?"

Brad's breath caressed her ear, his voice tender. "I need to close my eyes. I'll be fine soon."

"All right, folks, let's give Nat peace and quiet." He issued orders regarding shoveling, carting wood, and making a sign for the parlor door to read *Closed—Private Function*. Then he hustled everyone from the parlor.

The slow slide and click of the pocket doors resounded in the hushed room. For a split-second, worries whirled about the storm, before Natalie sank into the plush pillow and closed her eyes.

Chapter Sixteen

Two hours later, Natalie tossed aside the throw blanket. Standing, she raised her arms above her head, then lowered them to stretch, easing her stiffness. Hydrating and sleeping a few hours midday cured her lightheadedness. Lesson learned. Take care of yourself first, so you can care for others.

She folded the blanket and fluffed the pillows, then pulled open the pocket doors to slide silently into the wall recesses. Snatching the sign from the door, she dumped everything in the office. With renewed pep, she strode to the dining room. The kitchen doors swung behind Natalie.

Heidi strolled from her office and headed across the kitchen. Her apron hung askew, and wisps of hair straggled from beneath her bright, purple bandana. "You okay?" She pulled from the oven a sheet pan of cookies.

"Fine." Truthfully, she was embarrassed by the public display of her failings. She strolled toward the prep table.

Heidi placed the baking sheet on the counter and plated cookies.

"We've got the place covered so you can disappear." Heidi brushed crumbs into her palm and dumped them into the trash can. She laid the back of her hand against Natalie's forehead. "No fever."

"You're such a mother. Lack of sleep and storm stress. Nothing another tall glass of water won't cure. I'm ready to work."

"No need. With the roads closed, I have a full crew." Heidi filled a glass and handed the water to Natalie. "We're twiddling our thumbs."

"I'm taking over your kitchen. Take a break. Let the ladies know they can bunk in the spare room in the carriage house. I'll find Brad and Jeff. They can lug in folding cots to the spare room and to Jeff's."

"Jeff has two beds."

"Brad and Jeremy both need beds."

"Or…Brad could bunk with Wes."

Heidi flashed her evil grin. "Har, har. In his queen-sized bed? I can't believe you have enough energy to *try* warped humor."

Flipping her palms skyward, Heidi grinned. "I *was* funny." She waggled her brows. "Can you imagine the two sharing? If you could see tension, the hostility would be strung in red laser lights zigzagging the inn."

"Enough. You're imagining—"

Heidi propped her hands on her hips.

The intimidation stance didn't work. "I know. You're right. Not sure what to do regarding those two." Her little scheme with Brad to ride Wes hard had set this competition in motion. A twinge of guilt crept through her.

"Nothing. Their little rivalry is entertaining on a stormy night."

"For you. Not for me." Heidi picked up the plated cookies. She cupped Natalie's wrist and dragged her through the kitchen door to a table nestled in the dining room alcove.

"Sit. And before you open your mouth, the suggestion is an order." Heidi set the plate in the center of the table, then strode to the bar and grabbed a bottle and two shot glasses etched with the inn's pine-cone logo. She plunked them on the table and sat. "A little nip to celebrate a successful Thanksgiving dinner and full house." Heidi poured a thimble-full for each, then raised her glass. "Here's to The Inn on Gooseneck Lane's bright future."

"Here, here." Although Natalie questioned her wisdom, she followed Heidi's lead, swigging the tiny shot. The creamy, minty-chocolate whisky slid to her belly, leaving a path of relaxing warmth. "Dalby's?" She turned the heavy bottle to check the label. "Has a different flavor."

"The chocolate mint version."

"I haven't had Dalby's in ages. Perfect for a snowy night. Here's to getting through the rest of the evening with no complications."

"As long as you keep glugging water, you'll be fine."

"I'm not referring to me." She gestured toward the turret-shaped windows encasing the alcove.

The wind whistled. The snow swirled in a thick cloud. The lights dimmed, brightened, then dimmed. Natalie knocked her knuckles against the wooden table.

Heidi picked up the pillar candle ensconced in an old-fashioned glass and tin lantern. She struck a match. The light shined a flickering circle on the table. "Another bit of insurance to counteract your bad-Karma comment." Sporting a smug grin and arms crossed over her chest, she relaxed against the chair.

"No more jinxing. I promise I'll stifle any

negativity. So, how's everything going with Evan and Keegs?"

"You promised no negativity."

"Bad?"

Heidi leaned to fold her arms atop the table. "Keegan is having a blast. Evan is giving him much-needed attention. He has no choice, as he *sweetly* pointed out. He's stuck here in the boonies."

Natalie swatted the back of her hand in the direction of the carriage house. "He grew up here."

"Yup. Why do you think we're not married any longer? He wanted out of Mistletoe Falls and Vermont."

Natalie gripped the empty shot glass. "He and Wes should commiserate."

"Bad?" Heidi mimicked.

"No. Maybe. *Yes.*" Anger spiraled through her gut. Wes had ventured north, but he'd done nothing to prove he meant to save their relationship. "Face it, Wes doesn't want to be here. But because he's stuck, he decided to stake his claim—even though we're technically on a break. He and Brad act as though they're auditioning for who can be the best Natalie protector, like dueling superheroes."

"Kind'a cute."

"In what world is two men posturing deemed cute?"

"A world where I have no men who vie for my attention."

Natalie shook her head. "You are so blind."

"Me?" Heidi squinted. "No. What—"

"Jeff."

"No way."

"Yes way."

"You think?" A bright smile spread over Heidi's face.

"I watched you at dinner. He paid a lot of attention. And Evan kept peering around Keegan. Maybe they're not squaring off like Wes and Brad, but the dynamics are…interesting."

"I'll admit, I do kind of like the guy. He's got crazy energy and an adventurous spirit." Her grin slipped. "But he's not the kind to stick. He's already wrangled his next job in Wyoming in January."

"So, who says you can't do a bit of flirting while he's here. Once the roads open, drag him over to the Hazelton Peak Resort for music and a burger in their après ski lounge."

"I, ah—"

"Keegs can have an overnight in my room. You deserve fun."

The howling wind, like a slow, building roll of thunder, rattled the windows, curtailing conversation. The lights flickered and powered off. Within fifteen seconds, the generator roared to life, lighting the kitchen and common rooms on the first floor.

Heidi jumped up. "So much for a needed break." She strode to the bar, opened the storage cabinet on the far end, and withdrew a dozen-plus candle lanterns.

Within minutes, the two placed one with a matchbook on each table.

"We won't light candles until we need to conserve generator fuel." Natalie added two more logs to the dining room fireplace.

"I have a suspicion this room will soon fill. I'll replenish hot chocolate, coffee, and mulled cider.

Cookies are plated. Cheese and crackers?"

Natalie nodded. "You know this inn better than most. Can you grab the big flashlight and make sure the guests are okay? Flashlights are in their desk drawers. Help them activate the gas fireplaces. Once we grab the battery-powered lanterns from storage, we'll distribute them to each room." She glanced at the lobby's grandfather clock. "In the meantime, I'll gather staff to fix coffee and monitor guests."

Nine fifteen—a long night stretched ahead.

The back door banged, as Brad and Jeff strode in, followed by Evan carrying a blanket-wrapped Keegan.

Brad approached Natalie. "Put us to work."

"Lots to do." Natalie extracted from Evan's arms a sleepy boy rubbing his eyes. She shaded her hand over Keegan's face to block the bright lights. "You want to sit in my comfy office chair?"

He shook his head. "Where's my mommy?"

"Upstairs. She'll be right back. I bet we could find you a comfortable place on the parlor couch. The fire is going, and I have a flashlight so you can read your book." He nodded and snuggled deeper into Natalie's arms.

Jeff rubbed Keegan's head. "Hey, want me to carry you in? I can read to you."

Keegan jumped into Jeff's arms.

Evan flashed a glare, then shrugged.

Natalie turned to Brad. "Are Sylvie and Mary okay?"

Brad flashed a grin. "Mary fired up her wood stove and battery-powered lamps. Normal procedure for a Vermont country storm. I told them to stay put."

Natalie shook her head. "They won't."

"I alluded their job is to keep an eye on the carriage house." He winked.

"And they bought your line?"

"More like Mary poured each a snifter of brandy. They were settled in the two wingbacks by the wood stove."

Laughing, she shifted toward the others. "We need lanterns from the carriage house storage room. Attach the sled to the snowmobile for hauling supplies. Cart wood in from the porch and distribute to the common rooms. We have another wood pile under the eaves."

"Yo, guys," Brad said. "I'll start on wood. Jeremy, Evan, you're on lantern duty. Grab extra blankets from the storage rooms, will you? Jeremy, check the carriage house generator."

"Haul in some cases of wine, too," Heidi said.

Natalie scanned the group of wait staff standing by the walk-in. "Ladies, keep tabs on refilling hot drinks and snacks. Let's go, gang." She bustled toward the dining room.

Jeff shifted Keegan in his arms. "Wes and I—where the heck is Wes? Okay, I'll read Keegs a story, and when Heidi returns, I'll fetch wood. We need to find Wes. He can help."

Natalie bet Keegan would nod off long before the story ended.

"I'll stoke the first-floor fireplaces," Brad said. "Most folks will likely follow Heidi downstairs."

Walter and Frank, looking like abominable snowmen, stomped into the kitchen, shaking snow in their wake, as they swiped off their hoods.

"Need help?" Walter asked.

Brad wiggled his brows.

Walter grinned, then raised his palms. “We were checking on the ladies.”

“Sure.” Brad shook his head.

Natalie loved the sense of play between the two.

“Great. Reinforcements,” Jeff said. “Help Brad with firewood. I’ll be ready in ten minutes.”

“I almost forgot.” Natalie glanced between the two men. “We need a bed for Walter.”

“You have an extra cot? He can bunk with me,” Frank said.

Over the next hour, one by one, families and singles appeared. Natalie found old board games and puzzles in the parlor hutch to set at dining tables. They lit lanterns for ambiance. Heidi and the wait staff fixed popcorn on the gas stove top, filling bowls for each table. They set up a *buffet* of popcorn toppings, plated more cookies, and refilled the fruit bowl.

Soon the inn blazed in candle and firelight, saving generator juice. Chatter bounced off the walls.

“What fun.” Mrs. Edelston, one of their annual holiday guests, spoke up. “Reminds me of my childhood.”

Several other guests joined her to work on a puzzle. A few of the younger adults set up strategy board games. Several older kids lay a plastic mat on the lobby floor. They spun a dial, then each person on the mat entwined limbs from circle to circle, landing on like colors, and strained not to crash into another. Gales of laughter followed each tumbled body. Other kids chose the build-your-own skeleton game. The younger ones settled on the parlor rug in front of the fireplace and played a variety of age-appropriate board games. Keegan, wide awake, was in heaven.

Everyone seemed excited to ride out the storm with candlelight and roaring fireplaces. People, who had nodded in passing, carried on conversations, exploring commonalities, or making plans to meet here next Thanksgiving, Christmas, or summer.

Amidst the chaos of dealing with the lack of power, Natalie found time to make notes for promoting their family-friendly inn—a place to meet new people and experience life in the country, including a planned, *no-power*, old-fashioned evening.

Thank goodness, her laptop had juice. In the midst of recording ideas, a shadow crossed her desk.

Brad stood silhouetted by lamplight.

She closed her computer. “What’s up?”

“All rooms are set with battery-powered lanterns and extra blankets.”

“Wow, thanks for organizing the troops.”

He stepped closer. “Being prepared is the hallmark of my profession.”

His voice carried a deep, formal tone. His scent swirled. For a second, she held her breath to keep from leaping off the chair and flinging her arms around him. *Whoa, girl. Back off.* Just because Brad had been her mountain-man to the rescue, hours earlier—

Wes and Celia were both nearby.

She and Brad…they were no longer from the same worlds. High school memories starred as an exaggerated fantasy from years of inflating their significance. She shook her head. “I, ah, thanks. Your leadership is valued.”

“Hey.” He circled her desk, swiveled her chair, and knelt. “Don’t underestimate yourself. You’d have done the same.”

His finger brushed through her hair, caressing her ear on the journey. Shivers skittered. "I-I'm glad Sylvie talked you into coming today." She glanced around the tiny office…anything to avoid looking at Brad. "Wow, still today—not yet midnight. One long Thanksgiving."

"Should we begin to herd guests upstairs? Jeff stoked the fires downstairs and checked gas heaters in each guest room. We'll advise people of frugal use to get us through tomorrow."

She nodded. "Thanks. Did Jeff find Wes?"

"In his room working on a case before his computer gives out."

With Wes, work was always an excuse. "He didn't offer to help?"

Brad shook his head.

She wanted to ask after Celia, surprised the woman hadn't screamed bloody murder at the inconvenience. Unless she had a *rescuer*. Instead, she focused on running the inn. "We still have clean-up and breakfast prep."

Brad nodded. "I'm your man."

His words skittered warmly through her in a way they shouldn't.

Nearing midnight, the guests retreated, and family headed to the carriage house.

Natalie and Brad stood in the quiet and muted lights of a kitchen at rest. A knot formed in her chest as a flash of what-ifs reeled through her mind. What if she stayed in Mistletoe Falls? What if she and Brad ran this inn…together? In seconds, an image of Wes flitted though her head. Nope. By not helping, he proved he wasn't interested in being an equal or contributing partner.

"I'll lock up."

Brad's voice snapped her from her thoughts.

"Want to check the parlor to make sure the fire is contained and battery-powered lamps are switched off, while I check the lobby and dining room?"

Natalie nodded, too tired to utter another word. A few minutes later, Brad joined her as she warmed her hands by the parlor fireplace.

"You managing okay?"

She swept her gaze to meet his. "I hate to leave this fireplace, knowing we have to drag our way through snow to the carriage house. What if something happens at the inn while we're sleeping?"

Brad crossed to the far couch and removed the cushions. He threw them on the floor. Then he attacked the second couch and laid those cushions side by side with the first row.

"What in the world—?"

"Camping out. I'll grab the extra blankets."

Her heartbeat raced. "We can't—"

"Makes perfect sense. We keep the fires stoked on the first floor and start coffee early. I'll clear the path to the carriage house. Plus…we're here in case of emergency."

"Fine." Natalie bent to return the cushions to one couch. "We have two couches. One for you. One for me."

"Body heat."

Natalie stared at Brad. She recognized his expression—his teenaged, I'm-going-to-sneak-a-kiss-or-two grin.

He leaned toward her.

She flashed her palm. "No."

He raised a brow. “You’re not afraid of me, are you?”

“Fear is not how I would describe the potential outcome of this scenario.” She tamped her grin.

“Outcome? Ensuring we stay warm is my plan, darlin’.”

“We have fire and blankets. We’ll be fine, each on our own couch.”

Wrinkles creased his forehead. “You take the fun from camping.”

His drawl crawled through her, warm and enticing. “Where’d you learn to speak twang? Your days out west?”

“Twang?”

“You don’t fool me, Brad Matthews. If you think being cutesy will work to—” Heat crawled up her chest and into her cheeks. The color had to mimic the flickering flames in the fireplace. She closed her eyes, her weapon to battle the embarrassment.

“To what, Nat?”

His voice so close, his breath brushed her cheek. She popped open her eyes. Brad stood inches from her, hot, gorgeous, and smelling like memories of snuggling by a campfire next to Mistletoe Creek. She retreated a step.

He followed.

His chest touched her outstretched palm. “What are you doing?

“Something I’ve wanted to do since I walked through this door.”

He reached for her free hand, while her other palm tucked against his chest. His free arm half-circled her waist. He swayed, then danced them in a circle.

Memories assailed her. Homecoming, Christmas, and spring dances, then the prom—all in Brad's arms, all magical, and all sealing the deal. The one she hoped for when she spent senior year here, instead of at the snooty, Boston prep school her parents insisted she attend.

She leaned close, her forehead against his chest, and let the memories flow through her…soft, sweet, warm. He stopped dancing, let go of her hand, and lifted her chin. His lips touched hers—also, soft, sweet, warm, gentle, until reality slammed into her.

Wes.

Celia.

Sixteen years of nursing the heartache of betrayal.

She pushed her palm against his chest, but she couldn't make herself move. For those few magical moments, dancing in Brad's arms, kissing him, everything righted her world for the first time in…forever. The heat poured off Brad like a roaring fire, his touch firm yet gentle, and his earthy scent swirled as the muted classical music piped through the downstairs.

"Music?" Reality grounded her to the solid oak floors.

"What?"

"Is the power on?" She escaped Brad's loose hold. Then she rushed to the handiest lamp to flip the switch. Nothing.

"What are you doing?"

She stepped toward Brad. "Has the music been playing the entire time?" Brad scanned the ceiling as if he could see soft notes emanating from the hidden speakers.

"I hadn't noticed."

She shifted around him. "We need to switch off the piped-in music. We've been using up generator power."

"Stay put. I'll shut 'er down. Did you turn off your computer?"

He caught her wrist, morphing again into rescue mode. "N-no. I yanked the plug earlier to power off the battery."

"I'll shut off both and grab blankets. Then…" He stared.

His expression spoke of longing and heat and something else. Regret? Yes, regret. Matching her own. They never should have kissed. Neither of them had resolved entirely their most recent relationships.

He strode into the lobby, back in work mode.

What had she been thinking? She hadn't. Exhaustion, the exhilaration of a successful day, despite the havoc wreaked by the storm, and her proximity to Brad, who today had worked hard beside her, had addled her brain.

She'd kissed Brad and danced in his arms. And in those moments…she'd forgotten Wes. *Upstairs*.

Speaking of…he and Celia never showed. Neither pitched in to help. She hadn't seen them since dinner.

Had Wes worked the entire evening? Or…?

She shoved aside her imaginative musing over what-ifs and being in Brad's arms. She and Wes were supposed to be on break. They'd discussed the very subject before she flew to Vermont. Then why had he showed unannounced at the last minute?

And why did she feel guilty?

Tomorrow, she and Wes *would* talk. She'd put off this discussion long enough.

Chapter Seventeen

In the middle of the night, Brad woke from a fitful sleep. Tempted to throw the cushions on the floor and sleep as planned, he refused to spook Nat. Last night, his intention was a good night's sleep in front of the fireplace. Since he strode through the inn door weeks ago, he vowed to ignore the fire ignited every time he neared her. Until tonight, he'd stuffed his need to hold her.

He never stopped loving her.

She should be off limits. Reining in his protective side was no longer possible, after seeing her near-faint earlier. When he scooped Nat into his arms, danced with her, and kissed her, he'd blown his attempt at slowly rebuilding camaraderie and trust. Man, being so close had been like shooting straight to heaven or at least to the days they were tight and destined for a future…together.

Time to retreat.

As the wee, dark hours morphed to hazy, gray light, he stoked the fire, slid closed the parlor doors behind him, and removed himself from the temptation of a rosy-cheeked, sleeping Nat. Trying without success to put their kiss from his mind, with plenty to keep him busy, the easy solution was hard work.

He set the coffee to percolate, and once done, filled the warming urn in the dining room. He stoked the fireplace, then moved to the lobby. Glancing at the closed pocket doors, he stuffed his desires. The inn was quiet enough to hear a mouse skittering along the floorboards, if one dared set foot in Mary's immaculate home.

After throwing on his parka and stepping into boots, he flung open the door, and drew deep a breath of burning, frigid air. Tackling the mountain of snow drifting halfway to his thighs outside the kitchen door would clear the cobwebs from a restless sleep. He waded toward the snow blower, hauled off the tarp, yanked the cord to raise the ear-splitting roar, and attacked the piles between the inn and the carriage house.

In the middle of the path, blinded by snow flying from the blower, and the eardrum-breaking roar of his machine, he almost plowed over Jeff, wielding the other blower.

The pair of abominable snowmen, icy particles plastered to hair, lashes, cheeks, balaclavas, and waterproof snowsuits, switched off their machines.

"Crazy stuff." Jeff wiped caked snow from his googles.

"Bear of a job. I'll shovel the porch, steps, and hard-to-get areas. Hot coffee in the kitchen, if you want a mug first."

"If I go for coffee, I'll never leave. First, I'll tackle the front walkway, then plow the drive. Looks like sun soon."

Brad scanned the almost imperceptible shadows of huge pines dotting the pristine landscape. Early morning quiet after a storm held a special quality, appealing to his primal needs. The reason he loved trekking and living in the country. If only Nat could experience and appreciate the tranquility of the morning after a storm, maybe she'd consider staying. For a moment, he was tempted to wake her, help her strap on a pair of snowshoes, and pull her by the hand from her comfort zone to experience the icy wonderland.

Enough daydreaming.

"Sun is welcome."

Jeff scanned the horizon. "Yup. Get these folks outside."

"After breakfast, we'll groom trails. We'll soon have an inn full of antsy people."

"Heidi's on her way to serve breakfast." Jeff hauled on his gloves and flipped up his hood.

"And you know Heidi's schedule how?"

Jeff grinned, snapped his goggles in place, revved up the loud machine, and disappeared.

Brad smiled until his teeth froze. He bet his portion of his favorite, dark-chocolate chip, tart cherry scones that something brewed between those two. What were the chances he could convince Jeff to stick around through spring?

Making a last-ditch effort to purge hopes of keeping Jeff and Nat close, he threw his energy into shoveling. Half hour later, he found the parlor doors standing wide, the room pristine, like last night never happened. No sleepover, no close dancing, no kiss—only the hint of vanilla and mint hovering in the air.

He turned from musings of holding Nat and followed his nose to the dining room. Laughter and murmurs floated to fill the room with the easy camaraderie of guests who had weathered a blackout.

Baked goods, fruit, and hot entrees suspended in

steam trays covered the buffet. The salty, greasy aroma of fried bacon and melted butter hit him. Hunger pangs twisted through his gut. He reached for his favorite scone.

Nat swung through the door with a full tray, dwarfing her.

He took two strides, then stopped. She hated being rescued. Fact is, he'd wanted to rescue her forever.

Forever.

The notion wove through his mind that after a few weeks, he wouldn't have many chances to help. He tamped the rumble in his belly and bolted to the porch—the only way to maintain distance. The frigid air prickling his skin like icy needles, hung low on the now cloudless bright-blue, sun-filled day. Folks still needed wood-fire heat until they restored electricity. Time to haul more logs.

An hour later, Brad brushed clean firewood debris from his palms and strode through the lobby to the dining room.

Jeff wandered from the kitchen. The two claimed seats, filled their bellies, and planned activities. One hunger satisfied, Brad stood, another coffee refill in hand. "Listen up, folks. Our neighbors plowed the road to the bridge. The town is removing the fallen tree, repairing the wooden bridge over Mistletoe Creek, and restoring power. They anticipate we can use the bridge by tomorrow morning at the latest. Power—another story." He shrugged. Until the utility truck crews crossed the bridge, they were on their own.

A few groans mixed with a chorus of hurrahs heralded the skeptics versus optimists.

"In the meantime, we have snow." He grinned and

held up his palm, before the next set of groans exploded. “Snow means building snow barriers for an *epic* snowball battle. Right?”

The kids whooped.

“Then a snow-people-building contest between families.” He planned to upend the opinions of those playing-in-the-snow skeptics.

After more cheering, Jeff rose. “We’ll finish shoveling, then I’ll groom the trails. For those interested in skiing or snowshoeing, we’ll start after lunch. Heidi promises hot chocolate and cookies this afternoon. Those who want to relax, we’ll keep the fires burning. Books and games in the second-floor library.”

“Fun in the snow! Who’s ready to rally?” Brad grinned, ready for the challenge of keeping guests entertained. “Snowball battle at ten followed by building snow-people contest at eleven. Gather out front at the appointed times.”

As the dining room cleared, he drained his mug and refilled.

The wait staff cleaned and restocked the buffet with beverages, fruit, and breakfast bars.

He glanced at Jeff. “No one will go hungry on their watch.”

Heidi strolled toward them. “I hear we’ll have trail action. I’ve got cases of energy bars and bottled water. Any need for thermoses?”

“We can offer.” Jeff flashed his signature smile.

Brad was sure the smile was more than a frivolous flirt. He was happy for his friend but prayed he wouldn’t get hurt.

“People won’t be on the trails for more than a couple of hours. Sun dips behind the mountain early.”

Jeff stood with his empty coffee mug cradled in his palm.

"I'll set thermoses on the buffet, in case. Want me to take care of your mug?"

Jeff grinned. "I'm capable. First, I need one more cup."

Heidi grinned, then she turned and marched to the kitchen.

Yup, his pal was bitten by the lovebug. Brad related, totally. He cleared his throat. Jeff's expression changed from love-sick-puppy to don't-go-there.

"Back to work." Jeff charged toward the kitchen door, bypassing a refill.

Brad dogged his heels. "Uh-huh. Looks like sitting next to Heidi at Thanksgiving was a good thing."

"Stuff it."

"She know you're only here for six weeks?"

"Yup." Jeff tossed the word over his shoulder.

"Be careful."

"Yes, *Mom*. Time to groom the trails." The kitchen door swung in his wake.

Brad trekked to the front to snow-blow a pile of the white stuff, so the kids could build barriers. At nine-forty-five, he watched Nat herd the group to the front porch.

"They couldn't wait."

Jeff appeared, rubbing together his hands. "Ready for battle? My favorite sport—snowball skirmishes."

The kids jumped and hollered, then they raced down the steps.

"Whoa, careful, you guys," Nat called after them.

"Any chance you can help us build barriers?" asked Brad.

"I, ah…"

She glanced behind her, as if trying to find an escape route. "We'll finish faster and get to the snow balling. Fifteen minutes. Tops." He couldn't explain why he insisted Nat participate. Except, he hungered to see her let loose to have fun, like she used to. So much for distancing himself.

She hesitated.

Just as well.

"I'll get my coat and gloves."

Surprised, he grinned. Joining forces to battle snowballs with Nat…they could stand to do their own teambuilding.

With three adults and ten kids working hard, they constructed impressive snow barriers. Once Jeff co-opted Heidi into teaming with his group, and Nat agreed to even the playing field on Brad's side, the snow battle was epic. The adults packed a snowball arsenal, while the kids battled.

Afterwards, Jeff and Brad distributed prizes to the kids.

Nat picked up the yo-yo and executed *around the world.*

"How— Where'd you learn tricks?"

"From you."

He narrowed his gaze. "You sure?"

"You didn't *teach* me. I watched you and Evan, then puzzled the moves."

The last thing he expected was for Nat to throw like a pro.

Her hand shaded her eyes. "Where'd you get these?"

"In a box in the old barn. Mary suggested we hand

them out."

"The inn's name and phone number are printed on the wood." She dropped the toy into a *sleeper*.

"When the kids play with their friends, maybe a parent will notice and book a room."

She shuttered her eyes. "What are the chances a parent will notice?" Nat tried a *rock-the-baby* but tangled the string.

"Because these are the toys parents played with. They'll teach their kids. Maybe we should give them to the parents, too."

Her next throw was a colossal fumble. "Obviously, I'm rusty." She lifted her gaze to scan the snow-covered fields. "I hope our guests won't blame us for the weather and not return."

Brad slung an arm over her shoulders, as he pulled her tight to his side. Relieved she didn't stiffen, he held on. "Haven't heard complaints. Everyone's enjoying the old-fashioned ambiance without technology and other modern distractions. Tomorrow, we'll bus them into town for shopping and the tree lighting."

Nat sighed. "I haven't started decorating the inn."

"I'll grab decorations from the attic. Could be fun for guests not participating outside."

She widened her eyes. "You think so?"

"Why not? Walter and Frank want to help. We'll get Mary, Sylvie, and the guys to orchestrate the decorating."

"Your idea might work. You're good at this activity thing, ya' know." She jabbed playfully an elbow into his side.

"It's what I do." His fantasy was to take Nat on a trip, so she could observe him in action. An hour later,

Brad tromped into the lobby with the snow-people builders. He scanned the mantel and staircase, both embellished with greens, red bows, and various wooden, holiday-themed knick-knacks. "Decorations look great."

"My husband carved many of the ornaments." Mary blinked rapidly.

"I remember." Brad moved closer to run a finger over the smooth wood of a five-inch Santa. "Now you need trees."

"We used to cut them on the property," Mary said. "The last few years I've bought them at the Rotary Club booth."

Jeff ambled toward her. "Mary, we'll make tree hunting part of our afternoon cross-country skiing activity. How many trees?"

"Oh, Jeff, what a marvelous idea. What do you think, Natalie?"

Nat opened her mouth—

"You're brilliant." Mary patted Jeff's cheek. "Each year, we've had one for each downstairs room, so three. Then two on the porch, one on either side of the door. One upstairs in the library." Mary's forehead wrinkled. "Oh dear, quite a lot."

"I'll lead the skiers with the snowmobile and sled. We'll get what we can today, and the rest another day."

"The guests did love decorating." Mary perused the handiwork. "It's funny. Every year, Harry and I decorated the same. This year, I let people go without instruction. I like how the room looks."

She glanced at Brad. The sheen of tears, as Mary recounted a cherished memory, hit him right between the eyes.

Jeff circled Mary's shoulders. "Still, not having your husband by your side makes you sad."

"Change can be good, too, even when change isn't chosen."

He suspected Mary referred to their valiant attempt to preserve the inn. The good folks in town would work to ensure the inn remained open next Christmas. He planned to stay vigilant after Nat disappeared to the city.

Still, the thought of Nat leaving twisted his heart into a figure-eight knot.

****

"You coming?" Wes glanced over his shoulder.

Standing behind the registration desk, Natalie stared at Wes and shook her head. "Work." He was clueless concerning the time involved in running an inn.

He shrugged.

Celia glommed onto his arm.

His eyes widened. Then he smiled.

For a split-second, a boulder plummeted to the pit of her stomach. His grin was not like any smile he'd ever given Natalie. She suspected Wes was enamored with Celia, given their conspicuous absence during the storm.

In the next second, like a boulder flung, a weight lifted. Followed by guilt. *Stupid? Yes.*

Yes, Brad kissed her.

Yes, she'd kissed him. For those few magical minutes, she'd forgotten reconciliation with Wes.

And yes, during her restless night on the couch, guilt slid through her dreams. In the light of day, she admitted her relationship with Wes had run its course. The raw truth was, from the start, she'd never invested the energy or emotion.

Neither had Wes. Colleagues to friends, they shared a few kisses and hugs.

Not like the dance with Brad, the music drifting, enveloping them in a cocoon of unresolved what-ifs. Or the molten, far-from-simple kiss last night in front of the fireplace.

Right now, the present colliding with her past was more than she could handle. She wouldn't move toward a comfortable future until she summoned the energy to face frankly both past *and* present. She and Wes should talk.

But as Wes headed through the door with Celia wrapped around him in an inappropriate public display, Natalie sighed. To see the present placed in the immediate past, as the two disappeared down the inn's steps, seemed a neat and tidy wrap. She brushed off her hands. *One item checked off my list.* A little cavalier, for sure. But ending their relationship had been brewing. She felt liberated. Only one thing left…inform Wes. Although, she suspected he'd drawn the same conclusion.

"A quarter for your thoughts?"

She fixed her gaze on Brad's cocky grin. Had he witnessed the end of her relationship? He flipped the coin, prompting a shimmer of breeze to float by her ear, before he slapped the quarter against his other hand. "What's with the coin tosses—chocolate or otherwise?" A flash of memory slipped in to mess with her sanity. Brad flipping a coin, the first time she met him at age seven. *Heads, we play kickball. Tails, we play tag.*

Maybe having her own coin to flip was the solution. Wes or Brad? Washington or Vermont? Law or Innkeeper? Big city anonymous or fodder for the small-town gossip mill? Independent or dependent on her aunt and a building?

A few weeks ago, she would have checked option A straight down the list. Today, one item was placed in column B. *No!* Brad was *not* her future.

"Well? What's with the heavy sighs. Wiping hands to dislodge…what? Dirt? Problem? Maybe I can help."

She shook her head and stared at the ceiling. No way would she play games with him. Drawing another deep sigh, she shot a brook-no-argument stare. "Mentally checking off lists. Nothing concerning you."

No, not column B. She needed a column C. Undecided. She straightened, wanting desperately to glare at Brad, like she'd done as a kid when he bugged her. Unfortunately, acting like a recalcitrant child would play into his little game.

"Come on, Nat."

He fingered a lock of her hair. The little pointed strand that, according to Wes, was in urgent need of a haircut. At his gentle touch, an unwanted shiver slipped down her spine.

"Let me help. You have too many burdens to bear."

"Aren't you being a bit dramatic?"

"Am I?"

She stepped from reach. "Brad, you know how I work. I have to check off my to-do list." She tapped her forehead. "I've got this." She strode past him. A strong palm landed on her shoulder, comfortable and protective. She shrugged off his hold. *Remember*, he remained here because until they repaired the bridge, he couldn't leave. If any rescuing was to be done, she'd be the heroine of her story.

"Nat. Talk to me."

She spun to face him. He was persistent—one reason he was good at leading crazy outdoor adventures. He would've made a good lawyer.

Funny how their roles reversed. She'd been set on making her way in the world of art, and he in law. She settled her hands on her hips and bit her bottom lip. "Brad. I'm tired. I'm overwhelmed. I'm caring for an inn full of people. The priority list swimming through my brain is food, amenities, and keeping customers warm and entertained. Put away your quarter." She attempted to skirt him a second time.

He tapped her shoulder.

Not the rescue-hold of earlier, but a light touch, enough to cause her pause.

"Let me help."

His voice skittered across her neck in a wisp of warm breath. "You've done nothing but help since you arrived." She looked over her shoulder. "Not what you signed up for."

"Nat, I'd do anything for you and Mary. So would Mom. You think you'll help your aunt if you end up in bed for a week from exhaustion?"

With a hand on either shoulder, he spun her and drew her close for a hug. And dang if she didn't melt into the comfort he offered. Her sort-of boyfriend, who hadn't ended their relationship in any official way, skied off with another woman. Brad remained here, big and strong and concerned over the inn and her family.

Deep down, she realized accepting help was not a weakness, but a strength. Although she wanted to absorb his warmth and energy for another few minutes, she withdrew. "Thank you. I need to powwow with

Heidi, then I'll meet you in the office. We'll go over the to-do list." She ignored the drumbeat pounding through her head, repeating *what are you doing giving up control*? Instead, she escaped to the kitchen.

Chapter Eighteen

Jeff's snoring echoed through the cramped carriage house room. Brad rested on the extra bed, staring at the ceiling hovering somewhere above him in the pitch-black night. Still no power, but soon he'd head home.

Contemplations about Nat, Wes, and Celia scampered through his brain, like a mouse playing hide and seek in a wood pile. No way could he reconcile his concerns or solve the problems weighing him to the unfamiliar, lumpy mattress.

Not tonight.

Using every mental exercise he could conjure, he willed his body to calm. Instead, his muscles twitched from the mountain of shoveling and snow blowing. His heart tattooed an uneven beat, while worries piled up, and then let loose to tumble and roar through his mind like an avalanche.

He shifted to his side, facing the wall, and counted Belted Galloways. They moseyed through green pastures, just beneath his eyelids, in a vain attempt to lull him to sleep. Between the roaming cows and the whistle and moan emanating from Jeff, which should've been rhythmic white noise, the large mattress lump prevented relief.

After years of bunking with many different people on treks, and lying on every uncomfortable surface he could imagine, he shouldn't have trouble sleeping.

Instead, the last few days, his worries had mounted. At this inconvenient moment, his subconscious worked to find solutions for his problems and Nat's.

The roads will open. Soon, if the snow gods were appeased, he'd manage the first day of GMS's busy season and spend tomorrow night in his own bed. And he'd be free of proximity to Nat. After two more minutes of wide-eyed, brain-racing, tossing, he rolled over, climbed from bed, and prayed he wouldn't wake anyone. Brad laced up his boots and snatched his outdoor gear.

Jeff's bed creaked. "What're you doing?"

"Nothing. Go back to sleep."

"Can't. You need help, I'm there."

"No sense in two of us being exhausted tomorrow." Truth was he needed alone time.

"Problem at the inn?"

"Nope. Just me with too many thoughts scrambling my brain. Sleep."

"Un-huh." Jeff's mattress sighed and settled.

Brad tiptoed through the hall, avoiding the squeaky floorboard near Mary's room, and shoved the door wide. In the carriage-house workroom, he flipped on the ceiling heater fan, hoping to blast enough warmth to keep his fingers from numbing. The generator's gas would last through tomorrow. Within minutes, the blowers did their job.

He stripped off his coat, rolled up his thermal shirtsleeves, and began sanding the front end of the old, two-seater sleigh. He'd already scraped off old paint chips and sanded the rest. The job should take an hour or so, then the space would be heated enough to paint.

The repetitive work soothed his brain, dispelling

worries streaming through his head over the last few hours. He dispensed a figurative slap on the back. Smuggling in primer and Christmas-red paint had been brilliant. For sure, he'd surprise Nat.

In the zone, he finished the last square foot of sanding. The door at the far end of the garage squeaked. He jerked to attention.

"You planning on spending the night?"

Brad glared at Jeff. "Maybe."

"Where're the paint brushes?"

"I don't need help." Brad turned away.

"Maybe I *need* to help."

He swung back to face Jeff. "Why?"

"You don't have a corner on worries."

Brad tossed the used sandpaper, then found a cloth to brush off sawdust. He waited.

Jeff picked up another cloth and brushed the opposite side. "Heard from my next gig, Aaron's Outdoor Adventures."

"Montana?"

"Wyoming." Jeff's palm swept toward the wall.

"And?"

"Not enough sign-ups for the January and February outings. So, I'm stuck hustling for work."

Brad breathed a sigh of relief. Would his buddy stick around? "You like this gig?"

"Vermont?"

"The inn and Green Mountain Sports."

Jeff straightened. "You serious, man?"

Brad nodded. "I've been trying to figure how to convince you to stay."

"Yeah. Sure. I'm in." Jeff pried open the paint-can lid. "You sure you're not just throwing a bone?"

"No bone."

"Good."

"One worry eliminated. Then check off the next twenty-seven."

"Spill." Jeff stirred the paint. "Two tired brains are better than one."

Over the next hour, the two slapped on red paint and edged the sleigh's scrolled tops in black and gold. Little was said after they worried through a few of Brad's concerns. Knowing his friend would be here lifted a massive weight.

"Forgot to tell you…" Jeff finished the last black edge with a flourish of his brush. "After I finished yesterday's ski lessons, I trekked the trail. I dug up four small trees—one each for Mary, Nat, and Heidi's rooms. And…one for mine. I'll pot them to surprise the ladies."

"Keegan will be thrilled. You see him circling the lobby tree?"

"He's wondering if Santa will find him. I remember…" Jeff tapped the top on the paint can and wiped the extra paint off his brush on a stack of newspapers.

"Yeah?"

"We moved a ton." Jeff's shoulders moved toward his ears. "Wasn't long before I gave up believing in the big, red-suited guy."

"So, you want to make sure Keegan doesn't have the same anxiety?"

"Something like that."

Brad stepped from the sleigh, wiping his brush on the paint rag. "You over your head already?"

Jeff glanced at the ceiling. "Not over. Close." He

tapped the edge of his hand against the tip of his nose.

Brad laughed. "Darn close to being over your head."

"Yeah, well…glad I can stay longer."

Brad expelled the breath he'd been holding. He'd been close to offering a bribe he couldn't afford to keep his buddy working in Mistletoe Falls.

****

Natalie blinked, stretched, and glanced at Aunt Mary's wind-up clock. *Holy moly.* She threw off her covers and hit the floor running. She flipped the light switch, praying power was restored. *Nothing*.

With a filled inn and no juice left on her computer, worry wormed through her and lodged beneath her heart, like a tight fist to her solar plexus. They could manage the inn and guests for another day by occasionally hooking up to the generator. But no way would she waste fuel on law review work. Several times, she sucked in a lungful and expelled in slow motion, until she was afraid her lungs might collapse. A few shallow breaths, and relaxed control, settled her body and brain.

Inn first, then once power is on, deal with law. For a flash, she allowed the fantasy to take hold concerning what her life would be like if she didn't pursue her long-fought-for promotion.

Her father would be livid.

Wes would be on her case about priorities—as if he didn't already question her *blind* devotion to Mary and the inn.

She simply needed to stay true to herself. She waved off doubts, dressed, and dashed toward the inn. From the looks of the kitchen, Heidi and Jeremy had been working for several hours. “Why didn’t you wake me?”

“No need. Everything’s under control. You needed sleep.”

She stared at the ceiling and drew in a cleansing breath. Did no one remember she was an important cog in this rapidly turning wheel. “I needed to be here. I have to stay on top of things with no power. Any word on the bridge?”

“Nope.”

Natalie stifled a groan. She’d used up her entertainment ideas yesterday. Now what? “I’ll be in the office.” As she flew through the lobby, a list of to-dos raced through her mind.

First up, plan the day and evening.

Second, pray for power and open roads.

Third, while Walter and Brad were a captive audience, lock-in point people and confirm final tasks for the December event.

Then, forth, if time allowed, she’d pick their brains for future senior-college study weeks and events aimed at other generational cohorts, then mock up a template. If they wanted to keep momentum going into spring, they’d better jump on advertising before the holidays. Maybe offer a discounted price—perfect family Christmas present or fun Valentine gift for a singles’ outing. As she paged Heidi, she clutched the walkie-talkie. “Any sign of Brad or Jeff?”

“Coffee on the run over an hour ago.”

“If you see them, will you send one to the office? I have a few more to-dos. Also, if you see Walter…” With her head bent over her laptop, charging on generator-powered juice, she jotted meeting notes.

Without Wi-Fi, she couldn't check the Internet. She finished the notes and unplugged the computer. Pencil and paper would work until she knew the status of roads and power crew repairs.

"Morning, Natalie. You need me?" Walter's shoulder touched the doorjamb, his pepper-and-salt hair standing on end from the knit cap he'd dragged off.

His sky-blue eyes shone. No wonder Aunt Mary had a crush. He showed the heart of a kind gentleman, smart and handsome, with an adventurous spirit. "The ladies arrive yet?"

"They're in the dining room regaling guests with Mistletoe Falls stories of yesteryear."

"In other words, in their element." She clapped her palms together.

"You're so right."

"I want to nail last details for New Year's week."

"Since you have a captive audience." He rolled his eyes.

She laughed. "You caught me."

"Makes sense."

He flashed the sweetest smile. In an instant, Nat pledged she'd do whatever she could to encourage Mary to have fun.

"Name your time. Until the bridge opens…. Want me to recruit Frank?"

"He doesn't have a stake." She tapped the pencil on the desktop.

"Since he's new in town, and he'll be working at the college… He's expressed interest in helping the senior college." Walter grinned. "And…if Sylvie says she'll help, I'm sure Frank will volunteer. Do him good, and help him get to know folks."

"You're right. Great idea." She grinned and winked. "Sounds like a little matchmaking." The red rising on his cheeks met blue eyes sparkling with mischief. "Ask Frank, and let Mary and Sylvie know. Once I find Brad, we can meet."

"Last I noticed, he and Jeff were in front."

"I'll check. I'll double back to the dining room once I find them." Natalie scooted from the office. A guest tapped her arm.

"Any word on bridge repairs?"

She shook her head. "I'm at a loss what to tell you, until I get a Wi-Fi signal." She cursed her phone. Normally, she only picked up signals in a few random spots, but the storm wreaked havoc on what little access the inn did have. "I'll inform everyone, once I know. Then we'll load vans for town. The Mistletoe Falls tree lighting is at five." Ending with a note of optimism, she plastered on a smile, hoping the teaser for afternoon activities would placate the guests…and happen.

Strolling to the wide porch, she scanned the gardens buried in snow to take in the pristine white fields dipping toward Mistletoe Creek. The guys had worked hard from the looks of the plowed circular drive and cleared paths meandering around evergreens and bushes. Snow walls, from the snowball fights, and a variety of snow-people decorated the front lawn.

No sign of Brad or Jeff.

Laughter floated from the end of the drive. She tugged her heavy sweater tight. Aiming her face high, she absorbed the warm sun sparking off the sea of white snow. Deep male voices drifted toward her. She rounded the curve of the drive leading to the main road.

Jeff and Brad stood by a bright red sleigh.

What in the world?

The sleigh seat sported small, emerald green pines entwined in miniature white lights, each tree wrapped in a blanket of burlap. The effect resembled a monstrous bouquet of flowers—simple but elegant. Setting off the front of the sleigh with the glossy black runners, and a backdrop of snow, perched a huge gold bow. She stood rooted to the hard pack of snow-covered pavement.

Brad knelt in front of the display. He lifted his head to meet her gaze, his smile climbing to light his eyes. "You caught us. I hoped to have these spotlights set before we showed you."

"How did you create this incredible exhibit without me knowing?"

"Stealth." Jeff circled behind the sleigh to tuck from sight the cord on the lights.

Brad grinned. "Remember the old sleigh I found in the carriage house?"

"The same one? How beautiful." Like a warming breeze, a shiver of excitement slipped through her. The inn and its grounds resembled an old-fashioned Christmas card.

"One and the same."

"How did you find the time?"

Jeff's laughter rumbled from behind the sleigh. "Try the middle of the night."

"Y-you shouldn't have."

Brad jumped to his feet. His expression shuttered. "I should've asked."

"No, no." She shook her head. "I meant you've already done so much."

His cell beeped. He flashed a wait signal and

swiped in the call. "Yeah? Great news." He slipped his phone into his pocket and whooped. The sound reverberated from the fields. "Bridge opened. Power trucks will round the curve any minute." Brad closed in, to lift and spin her in a bear hug.

Her arms circled his neck as she held on for dear life. The old excitement from being in his arms years ago filled her. *No.* She didn't need complications.

"Sorry. Pumped." He set her on the ground.

She held tight to regain balance and…because, despite common sense, she wanted to stay put. Brad cupped her elbow. Her palm slipped to rest against his chest.

"Nat, you can bus the guests to town. The inn can return to normal operations."

A twinge of regret crept in. They'd no longer be *held captive*…together. She released his neck, gliding her other hand down his parka. She smiled. "I-ah, great news. Great, *great* news."

"I've looked everywhere for you."

Wes's familiar, calculated voice sounded behind her. She dropped her hands and swung to meet his scowl. His mouth set in controlled, slow-burn fume of an attorney whose underlings bungled a case. Her joyful smile, that moments earlier had matched Brad's wide grin, crushed. She'd known Wes long enough to sense his ire, so she chose an offensive maneuver. "*Where* have *you* been?"

He held up both palms. "You've been occupied, so I kept myself busy."

"Busy not pitching in." The words spewed before she could temper her anger. Had the roles been reversed, she'd have done anything to help Wes. In fact, she had numerous times.

Instead, he'd hidden throughout the storm, then taken off with Celia. Neither offered one ounce of help toward the cause—her cause—her family's cause.

"And you—" Wes shifted into her space and grasped both wrists, "—have spent way too much time dealing with this inn. And..."

Jealousy spiked his speech. His glance bounced off Brad and skidded to land his full attention on her. Message received.

"You've people for *that* sort of thing. You need to delegate." He glanced over her shoulder and tipped his head toward Brad and Jeff. "What you pay these people for."

She straightened her spine. "I don't pay either of them. I didn't pay Walter, Frank, or Evan either." Heat spiraled up her spine. She no longer downplayed the bite in her tone. She'd had enough of his condescending attitude. "They helped free of charge because they saw the need. The *common good*, Wes. Do you understand the concept?"

She chastised herself for not tempering her response in front of the guys. Still, how had she not ever recognized Wes's character? She'd been blind. Over and over, he showed his true colors. "You'll be happy to know the roads are open, and you can head to D.C."

"I'm leaving tomorrow."

Natalie looked behind her.

Jeff ducked his head.

Brad tweaked a row of tree lights.

She tugged on Wes's arm and marched him around the stand of firs and up the drive. "We need to talk."

She looked him in the eye. “I’m not sure you should stay.”

“What?” His mouth stretched into the fake smile he used on a jury. “I traveled a distance—”

“For what, Wes?”

Leaning in, he plastered his hands on his hips. “To spend time…with you.”

“And have you? Spent time with me?”

“You’ve been consumed with your aunt’s inn. You’ve had no time for me.”

She smothered her retort over the childish whine coloring his voice and drew in a deep, calming breath. “You could have spent time with me. Working beside me. Life isn’t fun and games. Two people who care for each other help the other through challenges.”

He narrowed his eyes. “I-I…”

Natalie raised her forefinger and tempered her voice. He wasn’t used to being chastised. The last thing she needed was to hear his entitled excuses. “For the last two years, I’ve gone to every work event where you needed a plus-one on your arm. I delayed my own work to read briefs or research a case.”

Inhaling deep, she prayed for calm. “I needed your help during the weekend. Not just me, *we* needed you. My family…and the employees and guests. Thanksgiving weekend is make-or-break for my aunt and the inn, which has been in my family for generations. We can’t lose our home. And y-you disappeared on a weekend supposed to be about giving.” She stepped aside. “I needed you. I think you should take the opportunity before the next storm blows through to return to Washington.”

The moment she mentioned *storm*, the fear

skittered over Wes's features. She held in a laugh.

He took a tentative step toward her. "Natalie."

"Wes. Don't. I won't be home for another five weeks. Not until after the holidays. Letting you go will be best for you. You won't have to spend the holidays alone." For an instant, a stab of pain gutted her at the notion of giving up her reliable companion and friend. A friend, who in the end, proved not to be much of a friend. A clean break would be best for both of them.

She withdrew from the guy who had been her security at work. Dissolving their relationship was right. She had no doubt he'd find her replacement soon. Once word spread, every single woman in the law firm would line up…and Celia. Natalie would bet the future of the inn they'd spent a lot of hours during the blackout getting better acquainted.

The realization both had vanished, together for the entire weekend, cemented her decision to let go. A decision she should have made prior to leaving D.C. She didn't need the distraction of Wes or a relationship which had been going nowhere for longer than she cared to admit.

Wes started to speak, then shut his mouth…tight. For a moment he stared, then straightened his shoulders. "Whatever you wish."

She shivered at the drip of sarcasm lacing his voice.

"But Natalie, we will talk once you return to work. In the meantime, you might want to adjust your priorities. Your future at the firm depends on you getting your work done." He pivoted and strode up the driveway.

Celia stood on the porch, waving. "Yoo-hoo."

Her high-pitched voice echoed over the fields. Natalie swore her screech scared the snowshoe hares and deer toward the safety of the woods. She envisioned a snowy owl swooping from the sky and plowing her down. She read how their strength flying full speed could topple a man. Her wildlife fantasy afforded her a nanosecond to smile, before she schooled her features.

"Nat?"

Brad's voice sounded steps behind her. His hot breath feathered her neck, spiraling shivers straight to the tips of her toes.

"You okay?"

She should withdraw. Instead, she turned and swayed into the comfort of his arms. He didn't say a word as he rubbed a large, warm palm against her back.

Brad was the man who stayed up half the night refurbishing the old sleigh to surprise her. He'd orchestrated games, snowball fights, and decorations to keep guests busy and happy. And, in case guests needed assistance in the middle of the night, he'd slept on a couch too small for his tall frame.

He never ignored the taunting of other kids or the veiled innuendoes they tossed her way the year she attended high school as the new kid. Instead, Brad stepped up and rescued her. This weekend, he rescued her once more. Brad proved himself every day to those he cared about, and had since the moment they met as kids. He did still, years after she first fell in love with him.

She settled her cheek on his chest. Even though his strong and gentle gesture might hurt her heart in the end, she accepted his offer of comfort. She'd pay the price later for leaning into him, depending on him, and accepting his comfort. Right now, she couldn't ignore the racing of his heart beneath her cheek, or the dream of what might happen if she opened her own to possibilities of the two of them…together once more.

Chapter Nineteen

Natalie sent the inn's visitors to town in vans, some before lunch, others after, so they could enjoy the day. Most planned to watch the tree lighting and later enjoy dinner. Mistletoe Falls went all out. After the ceremony, tradition dictated families stroll the holiday-lighted square and surrounding streets lined with open shops and sidewalk vendors hawking hot chocolate, roasted chestnuts, and candy-cane chocolate fudge or eggnog-frosted meringue cookies.

Catching the last van, she was as happy as the inn's guests to escape the confines of Gooseneck Lane. Who knew wandering downtown equated to a get-out-of-jail card after enforced captivity? The guests acknowledged the storm adventure was fun, but enough was enough.

Whiffing drifting scents, she strolled toward the first booth. *Ye-e-es.* The stuff of her fantasies. She hadn't tasted chocolate fudge, laced with bits of candy cane, since the Christmas she and Brad were in blissful, innocent, teenage love.

With joy in her heart, she proffered payment. Clutching the morsel of heaven cradled in bright green tissue paper, she'd savor the treat while sauntering and window-shopping. She nibbled a corner of fudge and sighed. The weight of her problems floated toward the stars. Tonight, she'd relish every bite and enjoy every moment of wandering this sweet town, displaying special holiday sentiments.

No inn business.

No law.

No Wes.

No Brad.

No worries.

She took another measured bite, treasuring the morsel, before she stopped. The jewelry store's lit window displayed a glittering, gold and royal-blue, enamel dragonfly pin. A perfect Christmas present for her aunt, she added the jewelry to her mental list. Next, she perused the toy-store window, showcasing a cute stuffed moose, perfect for Keegan. She imagined Keegan's excitement on Christmas morning. A shadow darkened the window. Wood smoke and pine scent wafted.

Brad.

A twist of excitement spiraled through her tummy.

"Chocolate and candy cane fudge. You couldn't get enough."

She circled to face him, pulling in an unhurried breath to ease her pounding heart. "You didn't help by buying me a two-pound box for Christmas. Until then, I could ration my bad habit to the few times I ended up downtown."

His lopsided grin reminded her of his teasing all through high school. "If you can't indulge over the holidays, what's the point of living?"

"You—" she poked her finger into his goose-down jacket, connecting with solid chest beneath "—have been a bad influence on me since we met."

"I would hope I still am."

"A bad influence?"

"Where's the fun in being good?"

His wide grin shot shivers straight to her toes. He clasped each end of her parka collar and tugged her toward him, straight into the circle of his scent.

"If my *wicked* influence helps you relax once in a while, I'll continue to be bad."

He brushed a kiss on her forehead, then grabbed her free hand. The sweet gesture shot warmth straight to her toes.

"Tree lighting? Will you be my date?"

She opened her mouth like a guppy craving oxygen from an algae-filled tank. She couldn't form a no but couldn't say yes. With Wes gone, could she relax a little and enjoy her last weeks in Vermont? Being Brad's date for one night did not a lifetime commitment make.

She nodded.

He squeezed her hand.

The two meandered hand-in-hand toward the pavilion. A light snow sifted over them like powdered sugar dusting her favorite almond snowball cookies. Once the two encountered the milling crowds assembled for the tree lighting, she inched closer to Brad.

He leaned in to hold her tight.

Once more his scent drifted.

"My favorite part of Thanksgiving weekend." He nudged with his elbow.

His warm breath skirted her ear, sending a thrilling skitter along her backbone.

"Besides the feast."

She laughed, remembering those exact words their senior year. "You do love a feast for *any* occasion."

"Have to keep up my strength."

"You're lucky you burn off calories with ease."

"What are you talking about? You haven't imbibed in enough calories to keep you going."

She nudged her elbow into his ribs. "You have to remember I'm used to a desk-job calorie intake." His hand rimmed her wrist until his thumb and forefinger touched.

"Brain power uses tons of calories. You've lost weight, Nat. Once those tree lights power on, we're going to Ben's Ale House to gorge on steak, twice-baked potato, and salad drenched in creamy, calorie-laden dressing."

"Used to be the day—"

"I remember. Dinner before the prom. I saved our entire spring semester to treat you like a queen."

He caught her other hand—now face-to-face. She sucked in a breath.

"Nothing's changed, Nat. I'd spend my last penny to make you happy."

Her fingers resting against his lips, she retreated. "Don't go there. Not tonight."

"I wanted you to know. I'm not trying to overstep—" His lids shuttered, before his chin dipped toward the ground. "You just sent Wes packing."

His head lifted, and his gaze caught hers.

"Come on. Let's venture closer."

End of discussion. Still, she couldn't tamp the direction of their conversation. Wes would have insisted they order baked fish—no butter—a dressing-free salad, hold the carbs. *"You have to keep your figure, Natalie."* If he'd discovered her stash of chocolate-covered caramels in her lower desk drawer—

her stress relief go-to—he'd have gone into cardiac arrest. With the all-consuming stress of running an inn, she hadn't had time to indulge in, much less shop for, her favorite candy. But peppermint-chocolate fudge? *Yes, sir-ree.* She nibbled another bite.

They stopped near the outer edge of the crowd. The gathering counted down. On zero, the tree lit section by section. Lights swirled and twinkled around and up, until the entire tree sparkled, to ignite the silver star in a blaze of colors.

Natalie exhaled. "Best tree ever. This ceremony steals my breath." Brad squeezed her hand, like a promise— a promise she wasn't free to accept. With only weeks before her return to D.C., she had to escape before her heart broke one more time.

Tonight, she would enjoy every minute, including the nostalgia of walking hand-in-hand with Brad. A magical comfort settled her shoulders to slip through her.

Tomorrow was soon enough to set limits with Brad.

****

Brad glanced at Nat. Her eyes were large with excitement and wonder. Transported to memories of long ago, when each believed in the wonder of Santa, he bet she still believed. "Come on." He grasped her bulky mitten and hiked through the mass of townies. "Dinner first. Then we'll check the tree after the crowd thins."

"Want to ease your stride?" She breathed hard. "No marathon workout needed. I've already built up an appetite."

"Sorry." He was anxious to get her alone. Ahead of

the hordes, he measured his stride to her stroll. "Better?"

"Thanks."

Her breathy answer squeezed his heart. He couldn't let her go. He needed her—wanted to be a part of her life. Reality hit him like a slam to his solar plexus. She ended her relationship with Wes, but she had no discernable plan to stick. She intended to leave. He'd *have* to put memories where they belonged—behind him.

Stuffing his defeatist attitude, he straightened his shoulders. Five weeks until New Year's Eve was his timeline to convince her to stay or at least try a long-distance relationship.

Tonight, dinner alone, the two of them, evolved to be the crucial first phase. Brad's stomach muscles tightened. Game on. Time to implement his strategy to win over Nat. The two neared Ben's and slowed. He glanced at Nat, as they approached the door. Without thinking, he pressed her against the wall bordering the entrance. Before she could react, he bent close. With his mouth touching hers, he grazed on warm lips, nipping the bottom one.

All he needed was one quick taste. When she shivered, he lingered. He longed for her to understand he was in one hundred percent. She couldn't leave until he showcased his dedication to rekindling their relationship. He lifted his mouth, despite hating the idea of leaving those warm lips. Crowding her did little good in proving his honorable intentions. Her sigh sailed through him, and he wanted to keep kissing.

Chatter and laughter swirled on the busiest Mistletoe Falls weekend.

Her lids fluttered, then her eyes widened.

He reached for her hand.

She escaped through the front door of Ben's Ale House.

Wanting to kick himself for ruining their tenuous relationship, Brad raced after her. He sure-as-hell prayed he could salvage what started as a beautiful evening together.

****

For the fifth time in an hour, Brad glanced at his office clock. Despite increased customer traffic with the beginning of the official holiday shopping season, time passed in an unbearable crawl.

His mind wandered from milling customers to Saturday dinner. The night he hoped to make inroads with Nat. She'd been congenial, but not open. Not the uninhibited girl who would tell him anything, show her raw emotions, and share her deepest secrets.

He pitched probing questions regarding life in D.C. and pushed for answers in the one-sided conversation. She replied in one-liners, sidestepping details. Was she tired or taken-aback by the public display of affection? Until then, she showed her delight with the lighted trees and fudge.

When he declared work a taboo topic, the evening morphed to a first-date-destined-to-doom scenario. Later, on the inn's front porch, he leaned for a goodnight kiss.

She moved past him and scurried inside.

Either he was rusty at this dating thing, or she wanted nothing to do with him—which didn't sit right after their nice evening and working closely during the storm. The last few weeks had been a ping-pong game, between burgeoning friendship and running for the hills.

Concentrate.

He strode to his desk, determined to dispel Nat fantasies, and eliminate thoughts about where the two were headed. Settling in, he tapped the computer to access his inventory spreadsheet. Income numbers saw a substantial rise compared to last year. His promotions for both GMS and the inn were working to bring in customers and convert their presence to sales. The train transported more visitors from Chelsey. The early Thanksgiving snowstorm elevated shopper's holiday spirit.

A light rap sounded at the threshold. He spun from spreadsheets and numbers, relieved at the interruption.

Jeff peered around the corner, his hands anchored on the door's head jamb.

"What's up?"

"Going to the inn."

"Already? Hey to Heidi."

Jeff rolled his eyes.

"Don't fool me, bro. You're hoping for a quick lunch in the kitchen."

"Beats the food here." Jeff gestured toward the half empty bag of stale popcorn by Brad's computer. "Man cannot live on snacks alone."

"What's happening on the floor?"

"Quiet. Will and Gretchen can handle the store. Want to hit the trails?"

"Hoping you'd ask." Brad closed his laptop and grabbed his coat off the hook as he strode toward the showroom.

"Hoping you'd get a decent lunch *and* catch a

glimpse of Nat."

"You know it, bro."

"Working your magic yet?"

"Slow but steady wins the race. Slow. And. Steady." He wouldn't get into the week of frustration at not seeing Nat, or the jumble of creek rocks crushing his chest.

" Getting nowhere fast, I suspect."

"I am nothing if not persistent." Brad shrugged on his coat and, holding his cell high, passed the cashier's station. "Call if you need me."

"We got the routine down, Boss." Will waved his get-outta-here gesture.

Brad grinned. Yup, he *was* the boss. A positive attitude, for the first time in weeks, coursed through him. Good employees. Good bottom line. Good prospects for an active spring with Jeff on board to lead trips. And a great partnership with the inn. And Nat—well…today, he planned to up his game. *Campaign Win Nat.*

Jeff parked by the carriage house.

He and Jeff strolled through the kitchen door.

"Hey, handsome."

Jeff chuckled and headed toward Heidi. "Best customer service in town." He pecked her cheek.

Brad raised a brow, as the two played googly-eyes.

"Because I feed your ego and your bottomless pit of a stomach." Heidi grinned and swatted Jeff on the arm.

"Life couldn't be better." Jeff winked.

Heidi swatted him again.

Jeff, never one to be intimidated by a swat-obsessed woman, flung his arm over Heidi's shoulder.

Certain things never changed. Heidi had been feisty since the day she and Brad bonded in kindergarten. A perfect match between his two friends. Brad hoped to hell no one got hurt.

"Any pre-registered customers for hitting the trails?" Jeff asked.

"We have seven book-club ladies from Chelsey. Natalie picked them up at the train station. They're eating lunch."

"Any indication on ski level or duration?"

Heidi wiggled from under Jeff's arm and checked the chart on the clipboard nailed near her workstation. "Three beginners and four intermediates signed up for two hours."

Jeff nudged Brad. "Want to take beginners? A quick lesson, then head along the short trail. I'll handle intermediates on the longer trail and return to meet you at the junction."

"Sounds like a plan."

Heidi shoved two bowls toward them. "Fuel up. I think this bunch might be a handful."

Jeff raised a brow. "A book group?"

Heidi swatted Jeff again. "Feisty people like to read. *Men.*"

"You gotta love 'em." Jeff scooped up his bowl and jumped out of range.

"A few. All? Not so much." This time, Heidi backed away.

Brad picked up the steaming bowl filled with herb- and garlic-scented chicken stew. "You've got his number already?"

"You bet." Heidi shrugged. "An open book. I'd say junior-high reading level."

" 'Bout right." Brad winked, threw a "thanks" over his shoulder, and followed Jeff from the kitchen. After lunch in the parlor, the two ambled into the dining room to greet the ski group.

Nat looked up and tilted her head.

Brad diverted his gaze to the ladies. Playing hard to get? You bet. As he greeted the group, he guessed their ages ranged from twenties to fifties. Judging from the earlier chatter and raucous laughter echoing from the dining room, they were full of energy and ready for adventure.

Jeff anchored his palms on Nat's chair. "What enticed you ladies to the inn?"

"We finished reading Peggy Shinn's book." Helen planted her palm on her heart.

"About the making of the women's cross-country skiing Olympic team," another woman added.

"And the history of women's cross-country skiing in general. Our Vermont women are pioneers in the sport." Helen flashed a smile.

"What's the title?" Jeff asked.

"*World Class, The Making of the US Women's Cross-Country Ski Team*," the entire table of women chorused in harmony.

Helen's gaze circled the table. "Our U.S. team made a significant splash. Quite a few are from Vermont."

"Sounds like this book jazzed you to journey here to trek our Vermont snow."

The group echoed a chorus of "yays."

"Stellar."

From the smiles, Jeff wowed the women with his dimple. "You ladies ready to hit the snow?" Jeff asked.

"Ten minutes? Out front."

"I, for one, need to work off the chef's fabulous dessert." Helen stood and clapped. "Three cheers for Heidi's dessert."

Brad opened the kitchen door and beckoned. "Come take a bow."

Heidi stepped from the kitchen and saluted the table. "Thanks, ladies." "Wish I had time to join you this afternoon."

"You share recipes?" asked one woman.

"I'll print you each the recipe for my mom's peppermint-chocolate-chiffon pie."

"Hey, we never got a piece," Jeff jammed his hands against his hips.

"You'll get your reward after you ski." As the kitchen door swung shut, Heidi lifted her brow.

After the ladies teased a red-cheeked Jeff, they headed to freshen up and retrieve their equipment.

Quiet settled over the dining room. "Successful lunch." Brad nudged Nat's shoulder.

"Amazing." She retreated a step. "Snap photos of the ladies on skis. I took a group picture of them holding up the book."

"Great idea. With permission, we'll add photos to our websites. We could write a publicity piece for the weekly paper and the information kiosk. You have information on the author?"

"Lives nearby."

Nat's eyes lit like the Christmas tree at last week's lighting.

"Maybe the author can have a book signing for our senior-college group. Or…maybe have the library host the general public that same day. Both our businesses could sponsor, along with the senior college."

Brad bit his lip. Nat, enthusiastic, acted as though the chill-out from last week never happened. *Stick to business, dude.* "We might need to pay a stipend or travel expenses."

"I'll check on registration for an open room." Nat waved toward the lobby. "We could comp the author room and meals."

"GMS can chip in for gas. You want me to ask Helen? She's in my beginner group today."

She leaned within touching distance. "You're helping Jeff lead?"

"An excuse to get outside on this gorgeous day."

"Like you need an excuse."

Her musical laughter rushed through him like a springtime roaring creek after a mountain thaw—a sweet challenge of *man* versus the elements. "Come with us. I haven't given you a lesson yet. I'm sure the ladies won't mind."

Nat scanned the lobby.

Did she hope an excuse would materialize? He stepped so close the whiff of vanilla and mint swirled around him. "What's wrong?"

"I haven't had time to work the treadmill or elliptical in weeks."

"You run all day. You think you can't keep up on skis?"

"Last time I skied was in high school, and then I bombed. Remember?"

"You weren't bad. You've always been athletic. I bet the women in my beginner group have never skied. Come." Brad tugged on her short hair, getting longer by the day. "You'll need a big-city haircut soon."

"What's your jab supposed to mean?" She retreated a step, her face a blank canvas.

Shoot. Nat always took things wrong. "Teasing. Your cut is okay." He flashed a grin. "Come on, Nat, you know I loved your hair long."

Her shoulders drooped. "Almost twenty years ago."

"It wasn't a critique. Your hair is beautiful, either way." He fingered the silky tress. "Go skiing with us."

"I don't remember how."

"Like I said—lesson first. You'll remember the glide and rhythm. We're skiing the short course." He lowered his lids and shot his best seductive glance. One he hadn't used in eons. His attempt at cajoling would either entice or send her running. "Come…on…"

"I need my boots and coat."

In his head, he pumped his fist. Tiny pebbles, lodged among the pile of rocks in the pit of his stomach, floated free.

Could his little jaunt with Nat be a breakthrough? He'd have to up his game over the next hour—convince Nat they belonged together. "You and I can double-team Helen over contacting the author. Don't forget your camera."

Chapter Twenty

Two hours later, Natalie skied into the carriage house field. Despite rubbery legs and flaming arm muscles, joy swept through every cell. She looked at Brad. "The trek was wild. Thanks."

Brad drew close to lift her chin.

The tips of her skis slid between his straddled legs. As he leaned, his eyes sparkled like the sun off the snow. Did he plan to kiss her? She bit her lip.

"As partners in the senior college, skiing together is mandatory." His deep voice dipped to soft.

She shoved her palms against his chest, then extended her elbows. "I had fun. What about other outdoor adventures?"

He wiggled his brows and smirked.

She wondered what wicked ideas he conjured.

"I thought the two of us… Winter camping?"

"For our guests. You haven't changed a bit, Brad Matthews. I refused to go years ago, and I refuse today." She slugged him on his biceps with her mittened hand.

He doubled over and moaned.

"Such a faker."

"Ice skating?" He straightened.

"Maybe."

"Downtown? Tomorrow night for family skate night? With cold weather, they set up the rink in the town square. Skating could work for the Outdoor Adventure Con."

She moved, causing her skis to tangle with his. He caught her arm before she tumbled.

"Nat?"

His breath feathered the wisps of hair escaping her knit cap.

"The local swing band plays in the gazebo. They'll keep us hopping."

"Swing Band. Local? Does Mistletoe Falls lack for anything?" She withdrew from the sphere of heat and his piney, fresh-air scent, reminding her of his kiss. The one that sent tingles shooting straight to her toes.

Nope. Banish thoughts of tingles and scents. With the pole tip, she released the rear bindings and stepped off her skis.

"A true wonder, our little town. Nat, we'll have fun." Brad pantomimed a silly face.

"Fine. You're on. Research for the event."

His eyes widened.

She couldn't fault his surprise with her quick acquiescence after the disastrous end to last weekend's non-date when she avoided another kiss by charging inside.

I'm leaving.

Soon.

"Any chance Heidi and Keegan can join us?"

His surprise question jolted her from daydreams of delicious kisses and skating dates. "I'm sure Jeremy can handle the few guests we have."

"I'll ask Jeff."

"Great."

"The five of us can hit the Burger Bar drive-through first. I haven't been since…"

Maybe she shouldn't have opened this particular basket of brook trout. She'd spent too much of her day ignoring her D.C. workload. And here they stood, reopening their past… "Fine. Yes." She turned, waved a hand over her head, and skedaddled before he could remind her of the last date at the Burger Bar.

****

For the third time, Natalie adjusted her parka, then willed herself to sit still in the front seat of Brad's cab.

During the ten-minute drive to the Burger Bar, Brad threw furtive looks. On the rear bench seat, Keegan, stuffed between Jeff and his mom, bounced with excitement. A needed distraction as Natalie ignored Brad's glances. He parked after what seemed like the longest drive ever.

Brad flashed the headlights for service and placed the order. He cranked up the radio.

They all sang, sometimes botching the lyrics and laughing.

"I am so-o-o hungry." Keegan was overexcited and in his whiny mood. "Is my hot dog ready yet?"

"Keegan. Patience." Heidi's stage whisper broke the tension.

"But, Mom, I'm so, so, *so* hungry."

Natalie reached behind to pat Keegan's boney little knee. At a gangly age, he was in constant motion. "Keegs, look."

Brad rolled down the window to accept the heaped tray from the server.

The blast of cold air sent shivers along Natalie's spine.

Brad tilted his head to throw a side glance and

adjusted the heat.

He knew her too well—constantly running cold. “I’ll hold the food. You close the window. Then you can dispense.” She clutched the tray.

The server wrapped her sweater close and scurried toward the warm building.

Brad distributed food. “I can’t believe they’re open in the winter.”

“Through the holidays, then they close for January and February.”

Brad glanced in the rear-view mirror. “How’s the dog, Keegan?”

“Um-moph.”

Heidi leaned toward her child. “Wait until you swallow before you answer Brad.”

“Yummy in my tummy. Wish I had two.”

“You have carrot sticks to eat. And I’ll give you a few fries,” Heidi added.

Keegan’s face transformed into a-kid-who-hates-veggies grimace. Natalie held tight to her grin. “Want to trade your carrots for my coleslaw?”

“Nah. I guess—” He glanced at his mom. “I’ll eat my carrots.”

“Sounds like a plan. I’ll eat my vegetables, too. We’ll have lots of energy for skating.” She took another bite of her burger and caught Brad staring. “Mustard?” She slipped a finger along the edge of her mouth.

Brad blinked. “What?”

“Mustard on my face?”

He leaned toward her seat. “No. Nothing.”

“Then why—” Remembering they had company, she met him halfway. “Why do you keep staring…at me?”

"Later." Brad shifted his glance toward the windshield and stuffed fries in his mouth.

Soon, Brad headed to the town green.

At the rink, Natalie strapped on skates and slid onto the ice. The chill engulfed her. Despite being surrounded by skaters, she was alone with Brad, her hand clutched in his. As the two executed their first loop, she worked to steady her long-neglected skating legs. The icy air slipped over her, and a shiver prickled her toes despite heavy socks.

"Cold?" Brad dropped her hand, weighted his arm over her shoulder, and stood hip to hip.

Another shudder, having nothing to do with the cold, skittered through her. She caught him staring. His gaze shifted to her mouth. She wondered if he noticed the zing or remembered their recent kiss.

This attraction— Were her reactions real? Or residual from recalling their teen years? Either way…she needed distance. Being close to Brad in the truck, her heart beat a steady, fast pace. Now, skating beside him, her heart ached to explode.

She steadied her legs and ducked from his embrace to glide ahead. Lengthening her stride, she hoped to burn off her reaction. She never should have mentioned interest in skating, nor should she have allowed her heart to overrule her head. Soon she'd be home and have to face Wes. She had *not* left Wes for Brad.

Her head spun faster than a triple axel, as she skated backward into the unknown. In her heart, she'd never forget Brad or the bond they'd developed these last weeks. Being here, reconnecting with Brad, watching him interact with her aunt, Keegan, and guests was an eye-opener. He exuded the same cocky confidence as Wes, but in a different way. Brad helped everyone, cared deeply for those he loved, and worked hard.

Wes worked hard, but he calculated every move to attain his long-term goals.

Brad acted from the heart.

She could get used to being with a man like Brad—both what he represented today and from their past. *Huge* difference between the two men.

After her sprint, Natalie slowed her pace. Her breath raced from her in short puffs as she skated toward the bench and skid to a stop. Bending, hands on her knees, she breathed in through her nose to slow her panting and dispel strong reactions from skating with Brad. She sucked in the stinging cold air and control, then stood and squared her shoulders. Removing her gloves, she tucked stray tendrils under her knit cap, then eyeballed the rink.

Heidi skated the perimeter on the far edge.

No sign of Brad.

A warm hand snagged hers from behind. Brad spun her. His gloves tucked under one arm and grasping her other hand, his skates zigzagged backwards in slow motion, as he pulled her along. All her work to expel Wes *and* Brad from her thoughts took a spill on the ice with the tug of Brad's warm hands.

"You were deep inside your head."

"Catching my breath."

"Un-huh. I know better, Nat. Tell me what's wrong?"

A churn moved through her belly. "Why does anything have to be wrong?"

Brad's eyebrows met in the middle.

She'd been hot and cold with him. No wonder his confusion. "It's a beautiful starry night, and we're skating under the festive lights of the Christmas tree. A night off. What could be wrong?" She blathered, until she realized she sent up red flags meant to be buried.

His stare drilled her.

"Fine. You want to know?" He'd always had the effortless ability to extract confessions, especially when he stayed stoically silent. "Why are we doing this—this thing? Here. Together."

He squinted, then with a slight bend to his knees he straight-on met her glare. "We're skating under the festive lights of the tree."

"Stop mimicking me." She yanked on his hands and dug her skates into the ice.

He stopped short.

They stood inches from each other…torso to torso. "You and me, Brad. We're not an *us*. Why are we on a pretend date night?" His features transformed into a caricature of a stone mask.

"Pretend? I recall you're the one who suggested ice skating."

"Not a date."

"A date?" He pressed his lips tight, then he huffed a breath. "You think I would drag Heidi, Jeff, and Keegan along on a date? Give me some credit for knowing what it takes to romance a woman. It's not *dragging* along friends and their kid."

"I, ah, I—" The heat streaked over her face. She was unable to form a coherent thought. Despite condensation clouding the air with each breath, heat spiraled through her. She ducked her head before Brad noticed the splotches sure to adorn her cheeks. She prayed Brad would mistake the flush as a byproduct of skating on a frigid night.

He traced a finger along her cheekbone and circled to caress her earlobe.

The rasp of the rough pad tingled.

"You're nice and warm." He winked.

Busted. Despite the years, he knew her too well.

"Come on."

He grasped her hand, towing her toward a kiosk. The scent of hot chocolate and fudge tickled her nose.

"We'll have two cups, plus two squares of pink peppermint fudge." He pointed at the tray drizzled with dark fudgy frosting. He handed her one of each, then skated toward a bench near the flickering and crackling bonfire.

She followed. He still scrambled her senses.

"Sit."

She settled on the bench. Brad sat close, his body heat keeping her toasty.

"Can we talk this out?" He wagged his finger between them. "This…whatever is going on between us."

Despite the warmth of the fire, goose bumps pebbled her arms. Brad's forearm weighed like an anchor against her back, a bit scary, but warm and protective as she succumbed to the comfort of the physical connection.

"Drink up before your cocoa cools."

Natalie sipped, relishing the warmth sliding deep. She could adapt to relaxing beside Brad. Searching the rink, she hoped Heidi would race to the rescue.

Holding hands and gazes on each other, she and Jeff skated by with Keegan perched on Jeff's shoulders.

Keegan waved. The adults remained lost in each other's company.

Brad nudged her shoulder with his. "Think we can get past *this*?"

"Past what?"

"*You* not acknowledging we care for each other…still."

She leaned away and sipped more chocolate before mustering courage to face him. "It doesn't matter. I'm leaving. You're staying. And…we hurt each other. I-I'm not allowing myself to fall for you." She stared over his shoulder, as if doing so could remove her from this difficult conversation.

"Who says I plan to hurt you? Look at me."

She took another sip before she met his gaze straight on. Anything to distract from his strength and warmth and tantalizing smoky-pine scent, or admitting she was past the point of not *allowing* herself to fall for him. The deed was done.

"The wedge your dad drove between us happened to two different people."

"Exactly." The ache bubbled and churned in her tummy. She loved fiercely at that young age. She rubbed her sternum to ease the present pain. "Even if we'd followed our plans, we would've ended up in opposite directions. We are too different."

With pressed lips, he glanced toward the ice, then twisted to stare. "We'll never know. Following your logic, who can't say we've crossed paths because our paths are meant to collide at this precise moment? We've both learned and grown. We're thrown together, Nat. For…a…reason."

"You know I don't believe in Karma baloney."

His arm gripped her waist as he hauled her close. "Ye of little faith."

"Hogwash. We're together because of human intervention. *Snickerdoodling* I believe in. Karma, not so much." Despite her protests, she couldn't deny the warm, safe sense of security of leaning into his side.

"I'll admit Karma had help from two interfering, well-meaning ladies."

"True. Now leave me alone and let me enjoy my favorite, *very pink* fudge in peace." She nibbled and sighed. How had she lived these past years without chocolate peppermint fudge?

Brad captured a speck off her lip. As he showed the tip of his finger, he grinned. "Very pink. The color looks good on you."

She nudged over, leaving space between them.

He scooted beside her. "I'll leave you in peace to indulge in fudge, *after* you agree to go on a real date. Keep an open mind. Let's see where this leads."

Despite the pounding of her heart, she shook her head. "Whatever is between us can't continue. I'm going home."

Brad bit his lip. "To Wes?"

"No. *No*." She pictured her solitary condo where she spent little time. The few friends she seldom hung with. The *dates* with Wes that weren't really dates. The mountain of work that grew higher. The endless hours in her sterile office, where everything revolved around numbers, law references, and smiling for an endless parade of entitled clients who wanted everything yesterday and paid a hefty fee for the service. Countless hours spent on the treadmill to counterbalance time sitting at her desk. The traffic and ambient light never allowing an unfettered glimpse of the stars.

The job she bet her father orchestrated, like he manipulated her life throughout her school years. What she experienced since college remained a far cry from her original plans. Today she pursued a promotion in law, rather than art.

Art. She hadn't picked up a paint brush, thrown a pot, weaved a wall tapestry, or wielded a camera, except her cellphone, in years. Designing the inn's website, planning promo, and painting guest room walls came the closest to practicing art. She glanced at Brad's chiseled features—his kind eyes and a mouth she'd dreamed of since high school.

His gaze homed in. The firelight danced and sparked in his eyes.

A sense of peace and anticipation settled over her. Brad didn't demand anything from her to benefit his standing in the community. Plain and simple, he wanted to spend time with her.

Equally, she wanted to spend time with him. They had five weeks. Why isolate and deny herself fun? Why not say yes and go with the flow?

If she had to be in Vermont, while enduring the stress of rebuilding a business and studying at the same time, she should enjoy a bit of playtime. She nudged Brad. "Come on. Heidi and Jeff can use alone time." Before he could bug her about a real date, she plodded through the snow to the ice and skated toward the happy family.

Happy family.

She worried. Jeff remained for a few more weeks, then he'd leave for new adventures. She hated to see Heidi or Keegan hurt. "Hey, Keegs. Let's skate together?"

Heidi tossed her a grateful grin, before gliding off with Jeff.

She caught both Keegan's hands to twirl. His laughter shot straight to her heart.

Heidi hadn't had the easiest of times with an ex who at rare times showed up on a whim. The fact he planned ahead for Thanksgiving had been huge for Keegan. Despite her troubles, Heidi found her calling in the inn's kitchen, including a perfect home above the carriage house. Keegan gained an extended family who helped with his care.

The two were *her* extended family, as dear as Mary. Musings of family spun fast, like Keegan and Natalie's twirling. Spending more time with them was an unexpected huge bonus to her hiatus from her superficial and stressful work life.

She studied Keegan's pudgy, rosy cheeks and his bright blue eyes, full of wonder. In a split-second, her heart performed an Olympic-worthy backflip. She wanted kids. Her biological clock ticked.

Resolving to take more time for herself, she vowed to enroll in art classes, spend time at Smithsonian lectures, take in the nation's capital culture, and find ways to meet people outside the rat-race world of corporate law. She and Keegan ended their twirling session and skated an unhurried lap. A light drag on their momentum had her glancing sideways.

Brad joined their chain, gripping Keegan's small hand in his large one. His grin widened.

She imagined he read her mind over her longing for kids, real friends, and a job that didn't consume every ounce of her soul.

The string of three, holding hands, took a few more spins before Keegan tugged on each of their hands.

"You getting tired?" Brad asked.

Keegan shook his head. He pointed at the train circling the tree. Lights blinked, the whistle rang out, and real smoke curled from the toy stack.

"Let's go." Brad winked.

The three reached the edge of the rink. She and Brad swung Keegan between them to land him on the crusted snow where the three changed from skates to boots. She signaled Heidi, pointing toward the tree.

Keegan raced ahead.

Brad, on his heels, scooped him up and tickled him.

Peals of childish squeals, and a masculine, throaty chuckle, hit Natalie square in her heart as she caught up.

Brad crouched beside Keegan, his arm circling the kid's waist as he explained the different cars on a train.

"I read *Thomas the Train* you know." Keegan, in his grown-up voice, let Brad know he already understood all sorts of *stuff* regarding trains.

Brad poked a finger in Keegan's parka-covered belly, leaving an indent like the dough-boy. "No wonder you're so smart."

Keegan flung his arms around Brad's neck. "Can we go…?" He pointed toward the fire pit where kids brandished long twigs loaded with big marshmallows.

Natalie stepped toward the two. "Just to watch."

Brad squinted and mouthed, *really?*

"Until I ask your mom's permission. Okay, sweetie?" She patted Keegan's head. His bottom lip could float a jumbo marshmallow. She tamped her own laughter.

"Come on, kid. Until Natalie finds your mom, we'll watch the others. Do you like marshmallows burned black or toasted brown?"

Keegan looked up, up, up at Brad. "Brown. I don't like to taste the black." He grinned, displaying a gap in his front teeth. "But I love to watch them burn up." He tugged on Brad's hand, and the two trotted over the packed snow toward the fire pit.

Brad grinned at Keegan.

The kid looked up with hero worship shining from his eyes. A squishy, aww-worthy sensation lodged in Natalie's chest. Brad would make a great father. She wondered why no one had captured his heart. Maybe after she and Jeff both left, Heidi and Brad would get together. The two had been best friends forever.

Contemplating the possibilities of living without Brad, or having him hook up with someone else, snuffed her euphoric mood of moments earlier. *Stop daydreaming.* She caught Heidi's attention regarding marshmallows.

Heidi flashed one finger, then the A-OK sign.

Natalie made the return trip to the big tree, her attention on Keegan. Before she could tell Brad about Heidi's verdict on marshmallow consumption, she saw Keegan gobble in quick succession the three giant marshmallows off the tip of Brad's stick. Heidi would kill her. And she'd have to *kill* Brad for allowing the kid to eat so many. Soon, she and the group headed to Brad's truck.

Despite the excitement and marshmallows, Keegan wilted once they tucked him into his car seat.

Carolers serenaded, as the group drove from

downtown.

Natalie slumped in the seat. The magical night ended. How far would she go to stay clear of Brad and his talk of real dates, so she wouldn't get her heart ripped from her one more time? Part of her wished to fling caution toward the twinkling stars. The rational part vowed to put on the brakes, despite her earlier assessment of what-the-heck on giving a shot to the next five weeks.

Chapter Twenty-One

As the crew cab truck drove through town, Natalie stared from the passenger window. The town's holiday lights disappeared, replaced by twinkling stars. The waning full moon cast light over snow-flossed evergreens and pristine white fields swept clean by the wind.

Like the first sip of hot chocolate on a frosty day, warmth spread through her when she was caught off guard by the reflection of Brad's smile. She ached to return his smile. Instead, she hugged her midriff to stem her emotions. She attributed her nostalgia and unrealistic future dreams to the enchanted Christmas season filling every hollow, curve, and street in Mistletoe Falls. The newly installed, nineteenth-century lamp posts and residents' decorations enhanced the ambiance of Thanksgiving weekend, the magical start to the holiday season. Reminiscing boosted her dip into dejection. In five weeks, the holidays and her sabbatical would be over.

Brad pulled up to the carriage house.

He opened the passenger door and offered his hand, before Natalie could jump from the truck. She'd hoped to shout a quick thanks and flee.

Jeff would carry Keegan.

The storm no longer stranding him in the room at the end of her corridor, Brad would head home.

Too late.

Jeff, Heidi, and Keegan ascended the steps.

The child was still overexcited—no doubt his spiked energy due to the marshmallow and hot chocolate sugar-high.

Keegan's chatter faded as the door shut.

She was left stranded face-to-face with Brad. She swore her heart performed a twisting dive from the high board.

"Come on."

He clasped her hand, helping her from the high seat.

"The night is still young."

Instead of retreating, she rambled beside him along the lighted path and into the soft glow of the kitchen safety lights. Brad led Natalie into the darkened dining room. A shadowy light from the lobby lit their way.

Detouring behind the bar, he hoisted a wine bottle. "Okay? Put this on my tab." He handed over the wine key, then cradled two stemless wine glasses in his big palm. "Parlor."

Why she followed, she couldn't say. The whole scenario skewed toward end-of-date material. And despite her earlier protest, she'd instigated this non-date.

He set the bottle and glasses on the coffee table in front of one couch, before he ambled to the fireplace and prodded the embers into flame. "Close the door to keep in the heat."

And give us privacy. Wine, a fire, and the quiet parlor on a moonlit night—not a good idea. She shivered. Common sense ruled. She pulled the pocket doors together with a *thunk.*

Brad poured each a half glass and handed her one.

She cradled hers in her palm and studied the slow swirl of deep red wine. The aroma, bold and spicy, held a hint of fruity plum, blackberries, and black pepper. She trapped the first sip in her mouth before she rolled the liquid and swallowed. “I haven’t tried this wine. A delightful, chocolate finish. You know how to pick them, Mr. Matthews.” Heat rose on her cheeks when she realized she meant to think her last remark.

“So formal.”

His smile telegraphed his notice of her flirt.

Catching her free hand, he strode to the couch. “Sit. We’ve been on our feet the entire night.”

She stared at the empty couch. Between the soothing hiss and spark of the flames and growing warmth from the revived fire, she could envision settling next to Brad to snuggle against his solid presence, gather his warmth, and maybe lean in for a kiss. She chose the adjacent wingback chair.

For a moment, she transported to the excitement of young love. Anxiety clutched her midsection and consumed her desperate need to explore a close relationship with the man, no boy, she once loved. Adolescent love had been hard. What happened today didn’t seem any different. Sparks ignited and pulsed through every vein.

Love.

Why did that notion crowd her thoughts? She *had* been in love with Brad—but not anymore. *No*. This vibe stretching between them was exhilaration from a night of skating.

Brad sat on the edge of the couch, his knees touching hers. He leaned to trace a warm path between her brows.

The tip of his index finger scalded a path, before parachuting off the tip of her nose.

"You're thinking. What?"

Glancing at the chair, next to the fireplace on the other side of the room—a seat she should have chosen—she worked to relax her features. "N-nothing."

"Not nothing."

Her gaze veered to meet his.

He cocked his head.

He waited her out, as he used to. "Enjoying the quiet and the fire." No way she'd admit to the argument bouncing through her head. To love or not to love Brad didn't seem the right question. The issue—she was falling in love with Brad in spite of her cautionary self-talk. "Nothing," she repeated, to convince him…and herself. "Tonight was nice—with friends and watching Keegs' eyes light up—a treat. I haven't skated in years." She shifted her gaze to the fireplace. The flames whirled together in a fiery dance of colors. "Kids see the world in such a different way." She sipped more wine, relishing the warmth slipping toward her belly. "Innocent."

Babbling.

Chatter helped shove the idea of loving Brad deep, where memories belonged.

"We once viewed the world as innocents." He leaned to set his glass on the table. "Do you wish we could return to those few moments before your dad ruined everything? To the day we held hands, marching into the gym. We had our whole lives in front of us."

Going backward meant obliterating the last sixteen years about everything she studied and the college friends she made. Eliminating memories of the few relationships she had over the years, or her work, which she did enjoy…most times. Plus, admittedly, she was proud of rising through the ranks. Every experience shaped her. She studied Brad, remembering the boy. His own experiences molded him.

As he stretched to set his glass on the table, his forehead creased.

"No."

He straightened and stared.

At his wounded expression, her nerves twisted. "I meant…" How could she rationalize not wishing to return to their past? She set her glass alongside Brad's, stood, and weaved past the coffee table to the other end of the couch. Although, she distanced herself, she longed to edge closer and take his hand in hers. Turning to face him, she leaned against the sofa arm. "We're two different people. We've both grown to become interesting and accomplished because of our experiences." She straightened, planting her palm on the sofa cushion. "I don't regret any part of my life. I *do* regret, abhor is a better word, what happened because of my father."

He leaned to rest his hand on top of hers.

She absorbed his warmth, comfort, and shared experience from long ago, remembering in vivid detail the love they once shared. The curl of yearning slipped through her in tiny shivers—desire she hadn't understood at age seventeen. A swipe of his finger down her cheek, the light trace of his lips over hers, the nudge of a shoulder when they joked with each other—simple touches. All those emotions crowded through her as they did years ago, together in this very spot. Her aunt Mary lingered in chaperone-mode at the reservation desk. "I like getting to know the man you are today. I'd like to know more."

"Even as kids, we never showed the other the full extent of what we'd been through. Can we speak freely—learn to trust? Give us—" His finger waved between them. "—another chance?"

"I'm leaving, Brad. *Soon.*" The *soon* slipped in a whisper so faint, even she had trouble hearing her words.

His gaze dropped to the floor, then he drew a breath and looked straight into her eyes. "Five weeks—let's make the most of our time. On January second, we revert to the way things were."

"An end-date."

"Still friends. Stay in touch."

Allow her heart to be broken. The idea of leaving caused the first fracture to slice through her heart. With each day closer to January, the miniscule crack would widen. Then where would she be? In D.C., yearning for Vermont, while working with Wes, as he pleaded his case from the vantage of pure, stubborn pride.

She dropped her gaze. Could she hang with Brad and still return to D.C. unaffected? Sitting so close and sipping wine by the fire…would her heart recover? "I, ah…I'm not sure keeping in touch is a good idea."

He locked his gaze with hers. "So, this"—his finger wagged—"is worth nothing?"

Placing his strong, warm hand atop hers, his fingers worked gently between hers, until they curled into her palm.

His thumb rubbed the inside of her wrist, causing shivers to shoot along her arm, a cool reminder this—

whatever they had—would end.

"Our—this—is worth nothing?" His eyes darkened.

"I can't." She ached over what would follow.

His chest rose, followed by a controlled exhale.

"Where's the smart, gutsy woman I've gotten to know over the last weeks…Na—at."

Her name slid in a sensuous, long endnote to grip her heart.

He stared for the same long moment, before he expelled his breath in another slow measured note. He squeezed her hand and shifted closer. "Take a chance."

His whisper skimmed her cheek. "And get my heart broken…again?" If she let him in, and the relationship ended, she'd never survive. The widening crevice in her heart would split wide open.

"What happened to the trust I believed we built the last few weeks, Nat?" His voice lowered an octave. "I don't plan on breaking your heart. If anything, mine will be broken once you leave."

She ached to take a chance. Every pore, every nerve ending, screamed to give this…this thing a chance. Leaving would be no less painful. No stopping the agony yet to come. "The truth…" She breathed deep Brad's swirling scent. A whoosh of hot air emanated from the crackling fire. Neither the whiff of his smoky-pine aroma nor the fire's warmth settled her. "We're already in too deep. And, yes, I do trust you."

"We can't retreat. We move forward. Agreed?" His hand dropped, leaving the top of hers cold. His arm slipped across her shoulders and tugged her into the curve of his body.

She nodded, with her shoulder wedged against the

solid wall of his chest, as her stomach clenched, and her heart beat wildly.

They sat in silence, staring at the fire and breathing in sync.

She desperately desired to make their relationship work. Instead, dread coursed through her. This truce between the two would not end well.

****

The week had flown by. At her desk, Natalie bent over her long list and realized how much she'd checked off, despite accumulating daily tasks.

The inn phone jingled an antiquated tune, forcing her attention to the present. "The Inn on Gooseneck Lane. Natalie speaking. How may I help you?" Trying to contain a wide smile, she jotted a new, Christmas week, two-room reservation for a family of four. The recommendation came from Thanksgiving guests. Five minutes later, she strode to the empty lobby and pumped a fist. "Ye-ah-ssss."

"What's happening?"

Brad's deep voice echoed from the doorway. He'd been MIA since skating night. Heat skittered across her face. Lost in the excitement, she'd missed the telltale squeak of the door. Given Brad's propensity for unannounced arrivals, she should install a warning bell. "We're almost full for Christmas week, including our event clients."

"Huge." His grin filled the lobby like sunshine on a wintry day. "We still have a single left?"

She nodded. "Since our author is unable to come until spring. Walter calls the second he receives a reservation."

He strode through the lobby.

He invaded her space. Before she could react to the heat rolling off him, heightening his heady scent of pine and wood smoke, he tunneled a hand beneath her hair to caress her nape. His palm scorched like a hot brick against her skin. His gaze darkened, his breath featuring her cheek. She feared he'd kiss her in the middle of the public space.

"Proud of you, Nat. You've accomplished a ton in short order."

"Not just me." Her breath hitched from the close proximity. "T-the entire team."

"You drove the process."

She laughed. "Kicking and screaming."

Brad's grin widened. He squeezed her neck in a gentle caress, then dropped his hand.

She mourned the lost kiss.

"I agree a certain amount of nagging was involved."

His backhanded compliment tugged on her heart. She stepped away, but no distance could remove her from the lure of his scent. She was doomed.

Could she live through another month working and socializing with Brad, knowing the clock ticked down, steady and resolute? Reluctantly, she agreed to enjoy the month with him—no regrets and no looking back. She could never stay friends long-distance. Already, the pain hit deep from the resolve to leave behind the past, once she departed.

This time, leaving would be on her own terms, not her father's. His only motivation was to *save* her from the son of a local mechanic and town clerk. The folly of thinking she could abandon Brad this time without remembering hit Natalie. She left once. Could she run again?

The heartache twisted through every nerve. She loved the man, more than the high-school boy, who dropped anything to help his family and friends. He had grown. She had grown. No way could she leave unaffected.

Retreating behind the safety of the desk, she plastered on a smile and ignored her heart, breaking in two. She was convinced she would fill the gap with a calculated pouring of resolve and, once home, heal the ache.

Home.

She no longer grasped the meaning. Lifting her chin, she smiled at Brad, a ploy perfected after years of dealing with influential, moody, and entitled clients. "Why are you here?"

"A surprise."

"Surprise?" She struggled to hold her smile in place. She didn't want a surprise or his kindness to deepen the wounds.

"Jeff and I figured you need more holiday cheer."

She laughed. In an exaggerated half-twirl, arms outstretched to reach for the twinkle-light stars, she glanced toward the parlor, then the dining room. "You've got to be joking? Look at this place." Every corner was trimmed to the rafters with Christmas cheer, thanks to their stranded Thanksgiving guests. The heady scent of pine permeated the inn.

He circled around the desk and clutched her hand. "Come on."

The drag on her palm propelled her toward the front door.

At the bottom of the porch steps, Jeff flanked a

potted miniature evergreen topping his waistline. On the snowmobile-hauled sled, behind him, several small, potted trees stood regal.

The morning sun, warming her shoulders, danced over the tiny trees in a Christmas-magic ballet.

"For your rooms." Jeff clutched a little tree. "What do you think? Keegan needs his own. Right?"

Brad squeezed her hand.

"We found trees for you and Mary." Jeff shrugged. "Yeah, I need one, too. Time to make my room a home."

Natalie hugged Brad.

Lines crinkled from the corners of his eyes, and a tiny dimple cratered at the edge of one lip.

She was a goner. She loved his open smile. He could never imagine the potted pine was her first Christmas tree since college. Her heart expanded, she imagined much like the Grinch. With his surprise and sweeping smile, she'd never recover from the gaping hole widening in her heart. She hugged her arms to her waist.

I have to trust.

Have to believe.

Have to take a chance.

****

Standing on tiptoe, Nat encircled Brad's neck with her arms.

The gesture tossed him a ray of hope and released the weight of a baby elephant pressing against his heart. The little tree made her smile. He hadn't expected a scowl, but he *had* expected a restrained "thank you, how considerate." Not a smothering, warm embrace.

Jeff rated a huge thanks.

He bracketed her waist with both palms and breathed in mint and vanilla. Her scent reminded him of butter-mints and made him hungry. If he hadn't been standing in front of Jeff, he'd nip at the very spot where her neck met the slope of her shoulder.

Instead, he loosened his grip and stepped away. Still, his gaze roamed over her cheek's rosy hue to settle on her lips. In an attempt to dispel memories of their youthful love, he cleared his throat. Theirs was an innocent, and probably, unsustainable love, but love, nevertheless. He couldn't shake the emotion, heating every cell in his body, and overtaking every ounce of sense.

Was this real, adult love?

He distanced himself from butter-mint scents and heat and what-ifs and channeled his focus on distributing the holiday symbols to each private, family room. "Do you have time?" He cleared the breathless rise in his voice with a cough. "Jeff and I can lug yours to your room and set up Keegan's and Mary's at the same time. Surprise them."

"I, ah, yes." Nat gazed over his shoulder toward the creek, then stared at the inn's huge wooden door. "Mary is in the office, and Keegan's at school."

Brad nodded. "Meet you by the carriage house."

Jeff's gloved forefinger crossed his lips. "And remember—surprise."

He and Jeff dragged the sled to the carriage house.

Nat stood wrapped in a sweater at the entrance. The sun brushed-strands of her hair added a golden hue to the mahogany.

He shoved aside his wayward reflections and glanced at Jeff. "You ready?"

The two lugged trees potted in big black buckets, while Nat held the door. Next spring, they'd replant the saplings.

Jeff deposited his tree in Heidi's suite.

Brad stepped inside Nat's room. "Where do you want the tree?"

She pointed in the direction of the double window overlooking the field.

He caught a glimpse of Mistletoe Creek winding behind the inn, the edges frozen and the rushing waters leaping over to circle boulders. Winter creeks had a special rhythm. For a split second, the urge to kayak the narrow lane of rapids and breathe the earthy scent of evergreens and mountain air overtook him. His need to escape the scent of butter mints, and simultaneously lift Nat off her feet to twirl her in this tiny space she'd made home, overwhelmed him. Instead, he positioned the potted tree to the right of the window. "Here? The tree blocks your view if I position the pot any closer to the window."

"M-much better." She twisted her hands. "We should return to the inn."

Was she nervous or super busy? "Nat, I—" He stepped toward her but deemed the situation best not to brush the stray strand of hair from the corner of her mouth. The very idea of touching her ignited sparks fueling the fire roaring through him. "I need to haul Mary's tree. Show me where to put her surprise. I'll take care of the rest." Her subdued demeanor nailed him in the chest. He sketched a soothing circle on his torso with his palm. "You don't like the tree?"

Her head lifted. "I love the tree." She rubbed her hands together. "I haven't had one in years."

"Why not?"

"No time." She glanced skyward. "No need with no one to share."

His heart ached for her and had since they were seven. "The real reason?"

Tilting her head, her glare bored into him. She sucked in a deep breath. "Fine. I-we never decorated. We traveled. Or…" She fiddled with the collar of her Christmas-red, bulky sweater. "I stayed with Mary." Nat laughed.

Her stilted and nervous chuckle clutched his heart.

"Mary had plenty of trees."

"Your parents—they didn't care to see their child enjoying Santa's visits?"

She waved away his question, as if the effect of their parenting was no big deal. "Not their thing."

He noticed the sting of neglect etch her features, before the shrugged veil of happened-long-ago-and-now-forgotten tightened her shoulders. He had no clue how to react to her icy comment, waving off her parent's thoughtless actions, except drag her into a hug. She wouldn't appreciate the gesture of sympathy. "I've a little time. Want to decorate?"

"I don't have ornaments."

"We can search the attic."

"Or maybe I'll craft some with Keegs. I can run to town later for supplies."

His shoulders rose, feigning disinterest. The truth—all he wanted was to be part of the fun. Make a memory. Build a tradition. Let her know family and friends celebrated together during the holidays, rather than neglect their children. "I'm happy to help."

"I'll…we'll be fine—me, Heidi, and Keegs."

"Sure. Right." His heart dipped to the pit of his stomach and wedged tight. He scrubbed a hand through his hair, almost dislodging his ski cap. "Got to go. Store to run." He strode the wide hall, pushed through the outer door, and trotted to the bottom of the stairs, hoping to outrun the descending bad mood. Would she ever allow him close?

Halfway to town, he realized he'd forgotten to deliver Mary's tree. Jeff could deliver the surprise. He floored the accelerator, intending to outrun the hurt squeezing his heart.

Building trust with Nat was a work in progress. Rather than sulk, he'd build a plan to win her back.

Chapter Twenty-Two

Natalie stood in the center of her room, the cold arcing through her and chilling every nerve. She hugged her sweater tight. To say she regretted excluding Brad from her ornament-making session would be an understatement. But letting him in for this special moment would make leaving harder. She swore her heart tumbled and twisted and then slammed shut.

The little tree made her happier than she'd been in years, reminding her of the few Christmases spent with her aunt and uncle, Brad, and his parents. The first warm and welcoming Christmas lived on in her memory. She, a lonely child left at the inn while her parents skied Switzerland, was the best holiday ever. Since then…avoiding holidays became her mission.

She stared at the tiny tree, envisioning white lights and colorful decorations. She was desperate to erase memories of Brad's sweet smile as he staged her tree. Add to the grin was his warmth and scent, and the perpetual sparkle in his eyes whenever he glanced her way. His expression telegraphed a longing for what might have been.

Then she rejected him, and the mask dropped over his face. Despite telling him she would give the two a chance, this gift made her realize she couldn't allow closeness. The pain would be excruciating. Still, his smile and sweet gesture dogged her. Did he remember their little tree from long ago?

They'd hiked the trail through six-inch fresh powder with the winter sun pounding their shoulders. His cheeks were bronzed, and his blue eyes shone, as he winked and detoured off trail to yank the tiny blue-green fir, the roots included. Once on the snowy path, he bent to kiss her, his lips warm against her ice-cold cheek. Then he presented her with the foot-tall, scraggly, cartoon-sad tree. That tree had been the best gift *ever*.

With her help, he potted the tree in a container. The little tree survived the winter in her room. Today, she could see *their* tree standing tall and proud where they'd replanted the sapling the following spring.

Natalie inhaled a deep breath, and she swore she sucked into her lungs the cold, crisp air of a long-ago day. She'd avoided studying their tree, preferring, until today, to view the entire forest. She should strap on snowshoes and…do what? Touch the bark? Circle the girth?

The journey to the past seemed a foolish exercise. Obsessing over memories made her sad for what might have been. She meant every word when she told Brad their break-up was meant to be, so they could grow into the people they were today. Even after her bluster, she hadn't taken her own words to heart.

Natalie stepped from the window and the view, only to stare at another reminder—the potted tree gracing her bedroom. Gathering her gumption like a protective cloak, she concentrated on the tasks that lay ahead. Her unending mental lists evaporated, despite efforts to dislodge and replace memories.

Running from reminiscences, she dashed down the

steep steps toward the distraction of work. Immersing herself in holiday reservations and activities, she rechecked her to-do list, then assisted the dining staff. She planned to escape to catchup on review, once Mary took over the front desk after lunch. Tonight, she'd tackle her first online exam.

The noon rush ended. She and Heidi reviewed the week's menus and lists of supplies needed through New Year's Eve. They tweaked the employee schedule, adding extra shifts to seasonal help. For a moment, Natalie's fantasy included having a full inn employing these people year-round.

An hour later, settled in the office, she ran numbers and adjusted the budgets for December and January. Her heart sped. The November reconciliation beat projections. The Thanksgiving week activities paid off. Now they could order items on Heidi's wish list without borrowing and have a cushion going into January—a *miraculous* accomplishment in the last month.

Exiting her spreadsheet, she logged remotely into her D.C. work computer. Her replacement listed notes and questions concerning three projects. She tweaked Gina's work and sighed with relief the woman finally understood. She keyed a quick response to questions and an encouraging message. Today, long-distance work took half an hour. A first after working two to four hours daily.

The veil of anxiety, once the weight of a law tome, lifted from her shoulders. She slid behind the registration desk to rest her cheek alongside Mary's. Her aunt's soft palm patted her other cheek, like she often did when Natalie was young. A warm slide of comfort eased through her.

"What's up, Munchkin?"

The childhood name matched Natalie's youthful urge to lean on her aunt for a few seconds. "The books. They're looking good." She straightened. "Work is caught up. What if we have Abby fill in? We'll hit Mistletoe Falls for shopping and a cup of tea at the bakery."

Where had the spontaneous invitation come from?

Her need to spend precious time with her aunt overrode unexpectedly the intense pressure to review. She craved an afternoon to ground herself in a sane lifestyle.

"Oh, sweetie. An outing sounds like fun. We've barely spent time together."

She expelled pent-up air from her lungs. For the first time in forever, she realized what she'd neglected. Living close to family and friends soothed her like a crackling parlor fire. No matter what, her peeps would catch her. Plus, she would happily do the same for everyone in this sweet little town. A half-hour later, she and Mary were tucked into the car. What a treat to talk one-on-one with her aunt. Since her arrival, each had run a neck-to-neck marathon in opposite lanes.

"I can't tell you how pleased I am you're here to help during our busy season." Mary cradled Natalie's hand resting on the three o'clock mark of the steering wheel. "Your time off was fortuitous."

With the event bombshell the morning after Natalie arrived, she refused to ruin Mary's euphoria by confessing she had course work.

"I'm sorry you've worked so hard. I hoped you'd spend more time with Brad."

When would her aunt realize they weren't meant for each other? "We've seen too much of each other."

"*Oh pish*, dear. You two belong together. Since I discovered my brother is to blame for the long-ago fiasco, I—"

She snapped her gaze toward the passenger seat. "You knew?"

"Sylvie told me. I had no idea. I could wring his neck. I hope to never, ever lay eyes on him."

"I-I, ah…" How should she respond? Saying she agreed seemed sacrilegious to say the same regarding her own father and her aunt's only other family member. "One day, maybe I can forgive him."

Mary swung her torso to face her. "Why?"

"He's your brother. You should—" She bit her tongue. She couldn't tell Mary what to do. "He's my father. I, ah…maybe after this many years, we'll have an adult conversation. I must try to understand his motives and tell him how his actions affected me." A pipe dream—in the rare times she spent with her parents, neither treated her like a grown-up—ever.

"Honey, I'm sorry I raised the subject. Let's not allow old memories to ruin our time. I'm so glad to see you happy."

Natalie didn't respond. She wouldn't encourage Mary to hope. She and Brad had an end-date. She spied prime parking and spent minutes maneuvering into the tight space in front of McCarthy's. The five and dime, in spite of a fresh coat of paint, still looked as she remembered. Inside, the long aisles carried everything from toys to cooking pots, and steel-toed boots to snowboards. Only a few things had changed. Snowboards weren't part of the winter culture in 1904, when the store opened. "I need ornaments."

Mary frowned. "There're plenty in the attic."

"A surprise for Keegs."

"Okay then. I'm in search of a hoodie sweater, fashionable, to keep the chill off my neck when our front door opens."

"Good idea. If you find nice ones, holler. Or a cowl-neck. I could use one, too. Meet you at the register." Soon she had enough miniature ornamental balls in her cart for four little trees. Maybe she'd ask Jeff to join them in making decorations. Keegs would be over-the-top excited.

She hit the arts and crafts aisle, finding a colorful pack of construction paper, a six-pack of sticky tape, several, on-sale rolls of thin ribbon in various colors, and eight packs of ornament hangers. Overkill? Yup. She couldn't help the indulgence. A thrill shot through her—decorating her own tree for the first time in years. She grabbed several boxes of twinkling, mini white lights and strands of colorful wood-beaded garlands.

List in hand, she located the toy aisle, and found Keegan a plush stuffed moose. She searched for Heidi's present. Later, she'd hit the jewelry store to get her aunt's dragonfly pin. Gift certificates were ordered for the employees. Maybe next year they could afford year-end bonuses.

Next year?

A twinge squeezed her heart. By summer, she hoped the inn would have a general manager. She could visit Vermont for quarterly meetings and Christmas. A shiver of sadness engulfed her. She shook off the sorrow. Head in the present, she found Mary waiting by the door with a bag tucked under her arm.

Mary grasped her forearm. “Anything else you need to do, dear?”

“I’d love to wander. I haven’t had a chance to shop since I arrived. Do you want tea?”

“Let’s put these in the car. You continue to shop, and I’ll go see how Sylvie is doing and have tea there. Call when you’re finished, and I’ll pick you up.”

Natalie stared at Mary. Was she tired already?

Mary’s animated eyes sparkled. “Come on. Time’s awastin’.” With a spring in her step, she picked up her bags.

“Okay then.” That evening, after Natalie hid presents, she knocked on Heidi’s door and strode into the suite carrying the bag of ornament-making supplies.

One look at the stash and Keegan bounced off the walls—his excitement contagious.

“Good thing today’s Friday.”

“Still, I have to wake him before I start breakfast. Annie can’t get here until nine.”

The teenager from the nearby farm had been a godsend, watching Keegan on weekends while Heidi worked. “Rap on my door. I’ll come over and settle on your couch.”

Heidi shook her head. “You get little sleep without an early wake-up call.”

“Keegs can bunk on my rollaway, and I’ll sleep until he wakes—an adventure.”

“You sure? Not rousing him early makes my life easier. The Chamber breakfast is first thing, so extra pastries and coffee.”

“Need help?”

“Jeremy arrives early. Breakfast is continental. We need to keep the coffee filled through the talk. Easy setup." Heidi turned toward her son. "Hey, Keegs, Auntie Natalie has a surprise."

"Want a sleepover in my room? Before bed, we'll put lights on my tree." She bent toward Heidi and stage-whispered, "We'll do your decorations tomorrow night. With Jeff? He has a tree, too."

Heidi blushed and flashed the okay sign.

"Yay!" Keegan turned to his mom and jumped. "Can I spend the night? Plea-a-a-ase?"

Nat helped Keegan pack his cartoon sleeping bag and matching pjs for a jaunt across the hall. The two strung lights on her tree. The twinkling glow made the perfect night-light. By the time she got him tucked in, her energy had dwindled to a trickle. The second she pulled her sheet to her chin, the soft snores of her little roommate soothed her.

The next morning, she and Keegan skipped to the kitchen. The kid had tons of energy first thing. Natalie suggested a little breakfast party in the office.

After they dumped dirty dishes in the kitchen, Keegs tugged on her arm. "Can we go outside, Aunt Natalie?"

"Sure." She and Keegs stepped into the bright day. The sun glimmered off the fresh snow. Her heart soared at the prospect of enjoying a beautiful, crisp New England morning.

Jeff drove by on the little tractor with the giant brush, sweeping away the dusting of fresh snow.

She waved.

Jeff waved back.

She couldn't imagine how they'd have managed without his help. For sure, the inn had the better deal. Jeff might believe otherwise, with Heidi living close, and getting to take advantage of her tasty cooking. He now planned to stay through the spring. Win-win. Natalie grinned, happy for her best friend.

"Can we go to the creek?" Keegan clasped her hand. "I want to see how much is frozen."

"Sure. With the warm sun, the ice might start to melt today."

"Then we have to hurry."

She and Keegs plodded through the deeper snow in the field. Natalie drew a deep breath. The closer they got, the more magnificent was the view of the gurgling, half-frozen creek, skirted by the panorama of snow-covered mountains. She grabbed her phone and snapped photos, picturing this breathtaking scene on promo materials. She caught a colorful photo of Keegan, plunging through the snow in his bright red parka.

Keegan tugged on her jacket. "Can I touch the water?"

"Honey, you'll freeze your fingers."

He peeled off one mitten and raised a forefinger. "Just once. With one finger?"

"Fine, but you have to hold my hand."

He nodded and skipped toward the water.

Her heart dropped to her stomach. "Wait. Keegs. Stop." Her screech rose, seeing him skirting the sloped edge. "Wait."

He stopped. A pale face stared up. "O-okay, Aunt Natalie. Are you mad?"

She caught his arm and hauled him in for a big bear-hug. "Oh, honey, no, I'm not mad. You scared me. Okay, grab my hand so I can hold you while you touch the water. Be careful. The bank is slippery, and the water is very cold."

The closer they got, the tighter his little fist wrapped her hand. They reached a safe spot on the bank, and he grazed his finger along the edge of the water. He yanked his hand, his eyes bigger than his cereal bowl.

"So-o-o cold. See?" He presented his finger.

She kissed the icy tip. "Brrrr…you're right. I hope your finger doesn't fall off."

His mouth opened.

She laughed. "I'm teasing." She clutched his hand. "Come on. Annie should be here soon." On the way, the soft purr of cars meandering up Gooseneck Lane signaled the arrival of Chamber members. She and Keegan strolled closer. The line of cars snaked up the drive, causing a warmth to settle over her. The inn attracted more locals. A good thing, indeed.

She catalogued a mental note to contact more groups for lunch and breakfast meetings. Maybe one day they could renovate the bottom of the carriage house into a small conference center, after remaking the old barn into additional storage. So many opportunities. So little money. She rounded the curve, so Keegan could watch the parade of cars.

"Look, Aunt Natalie. What's—?" Keegan pointed toward the bright red sleigh.

"It's the sleigh Jeff and Brad fixed up— What in the world?"

"What's beside the sleigh?"

"I, ah, I don't know. Looks like a—a cow?" Natalie ran to keep up with Keegan.

"A big cow. Bigger than the sleigh." He halted near the huge sculpted statue. "See? I wonder who painted on the belly and the legs."

Brad's truck roared toward them. When the vehicle skid to a stop near the sleigh, the tires kicked up gravel. He jumped from the cab and spread his arm wide, as if he presented them with the grand prize of the day. "What do you think?"

His grin lit up his face, like a kid on Christmas morning. "Truth?" She gaped at Brad, then pivoted her glare to the cow, whose height topped his six-foot-two frame. The cow, adorned in a painted landscape, resembled their snowy fields, dotted with evergreens covered in red Christmas balls and topped with gold stars. Mistletoe Creek ran a vertical line in the center of the cow's belly. A few deer grazed beside the creek while rabbits gathered under one tall evergreen. The cow's legs were painted in twining holly sprigs with red berries. "There *are* no words." She shook her head. She was no longer in the city.

Keegan tugged on her hand. "Come on, Aunt Natalie. Can I touch the cow?"

Not sure how to answer, she glanced at Brad. He sported his mischievous twinkle.

"You bet, buddy." He offered his hand, as enchanting as the Pied Piper.

Keegan ran to him, tugging along Natalie. He clutched Brad's hand, linking the three like a human chain. When they reached the bovine, he dropped Brad's hand and stroked the cow's foreleg. "Wow. He's so smooth. And cold. See our creek, Aunt Natalie." Keegan faced Brad. "I touched the water in the creek this morning."

"By yourself?"

Brad's voice emerged like the bark of an angry dog. Keegan's grip tightened around her fist. "With my permission and a death grip on him."

His shoulders fell a notch. Brad knelt in the snow in front of Keegan. "Hey, buddy, I'm not mad. Trying to keep you safe, just like Nat. Remember, walking by the creek by yourself any time of year is dangerous. Right, buddy?"

Keegan nodded. "Aunt Natalie told me I have to ask." He glanced up and smiled.

"She's a smart woman. In fact, you shouldn't even cross the driveway without one of us. Right?"

Keegan nodded, his dark eyes narrowing as his gaze fastened on Brad.

Standing, Brad ruffled Keegan's hair, which stood at messy attention, like rows of his haphazardly placed toy soldiers. "Good. I know you're a smart kid and will never go over there unless you ask and take your mom or Nat or Annie or… Right? Okay, let's check the mystery cow."

Jeff appeared from behind the hedge lining the drive.

Keegan ran full speed. "Did you see the cow?"

"Couldn't miss the big guy, pal."

With one hand in Jeff's, Keegan ran his hand over the cow. "Look at all the trees. And they have those colored balls like I'll have on my tree. Can I touch the top?"

Jeff hoisted Keegan on his shoulders so the kid could explore the fiberglass sculpture.

Natalie sidled up next to Brad and watched Keegan check every part. She couldn't decide whether she hated the idea or found the cow unique enough that the inn could capitalize on this promotion. "And we have a cow in our yard because—?"

"Mary didn't tell you?"

"I wouldn't be asking if…."

"An annual fundraiser, sponsored by the Chamber. Local artists vie for the honor of painting a cow. They're then distributed to area businesses."

"How long does the cow reside?"

"On New Year's Day, the votes are tallied."

"Votes?"

Brad waved a hand in the direction of town. "The welcome kiosk and area stores have a brochure with a location map to the sculptures. Tourists and locals alike are encouraged to visit all locations and vote on their favorite. Each participating business sells vote cards for a dollar."

"And where does the fee go?"

"The winning artist gets a monetary prize. The rest goes to the Chamber for area promotion."

"I can't imagine people will drive to see our cow." Natalie propped her fists on her hips. She wasn't sure why she was upset over not being notified regarding this monstrosity in the inn's front yard. Yes, the cow had a beautiful scene painted across the belly. *But a cow?*

"Relax, Nat."

His finger grazed her cheek, setting off the familiar series of shivers.

"You'd be surprised. Cruising the painted cow route is a family weekend tradition. They also come from neighboring towns. A twenty-plus year tradition. Most buy a ballot for every person in the family."

"Hmm. I had no clue about this event. Can we do our own promotion?"

"Sure."

She grabbed a notepad and lifted her gaze. “So maybe we offer discount coupons at the kiosk—ten percent off lunch through December twenty-third.” She jotted a reminder. “After that, with a full inn, extra meal guests won’t be practical.”

“Great idea—added incentive.” He winked.

“What?”

“I’m glad you see the value of the town’s cows. Anyone stays for lunch, the inn picks up the cost of one ballot per family. Can you handle the expense?”

“Can’t be more than ten dollars a week. Any chance we could get the artist on premise?”

Brad shook his head. “Afraid not. Participants are anonymous until the three winners are picked.”

“How can I get permission to start promotions?”

Brad checked his watch. He arched his brow. “Shoot. I’m due at the meeting in five minutes.” He gestured up the hill toward the inn. “Will you be in the office later?”

She nodded.

“I’ll bring the cow parade committee chair to your office. Donald Ackerman can explain everything.”

He started toward his truck, before he faced her. “Hop in. I’ll give you, Jeff, and Keegan a ride up the hill.”

Natalie dropped Keegan off in the kitchen to meet Annie, then beelined to the office to jot cow promotion plans. She downloaded photos taken earlier. Then she logged into her design account to craft templates. An hour later, she scooted into the kitchen. “Can Jeremy staff the meeting while you come to the office?” she asked Heidi.

Heidi turned from the pot she stirred and waved a

wooden spoon. "Sure. The meeting is winding down."

"I don't suppose you have a few extra scones lying about?" On cue, Natalie's tummy rumbled.

"I'll plate them, pour coffees, and be right in."

A few minutes later, Heidi and Mary hung over Natalie's shoulder, checking design mock-ups.

"Oh, honey, what a great idea." Aunt Mary rubbed her shoulder. "I think you've missed your calling over the years."

"I agree," Heidi said. "And capitalizing on the cow parade event is just the beginning. We need to keep pace with what's going on in town—find ways to get locals and tourists to the inn for a meal or outdoor activity."

"There are so many things we can do." Mary waved a hand in the air. "Artists' receptions and book signings. We could start a book group, and they could meet here every month. Maybe coordinate with the library and the college."

"We could kick off the group with the Vermont author and her Olympic, cross-country ski book." Natalie jotted the idea on her promotion list.

"I've been meaning to read the book," Mary said. "I bet Sylvie and I can round up enough to launch the group."

"Plus business breakfast meetings—like with the Chamber." Natalie added more notes. "We need to get together one afternoon and include Jeremy, Brad, and Jeff. They'll have ideas."

"And Walter." Mary didn't even attempt to hide her grin.

She scrolled through her calendar. "Next Wednesday?"

"Sylvie and I'll make calls." Mary added comments in her pocket notebook. "Nine a.m. or three-thirty? Food as incentive for attending?"

Natalie glanced at Heidi.

"Either work for me. I'll scrounge up a late breakfast or mid-afternoon snack."

Heidi greeted Brad, as she departed the office.

Brad poked in his head. "Don can meet in a few minutes. Parlor okay?"

"I'll be right in."

A half hour later, the Chamber committee chair explained the post-event auction of the cows and that the money went to town social service grants. He loved their promotional ideas—anything to help fill the fundraising coffers. After giving them the okay, Don departed.

Brad hovered.

They were alone with no buffer. Natalie's insides jiggled like a Christmas gelatin salad. "Don't you have to open the store?"

"Jeff's opening. I'm closing."

"Oh." Silence stretched between them. Natalie rose to poke the parlor fire and put space between them.

Brad strolled close to the hearth.

His pine-forest scent, mixed with the hint of smoke from the crackling fire, swirled. He was so close tingles slipped through her body.

"Dinner? Tomorrow night?"

"I, ah…not a good idea." One hand gripped the other.

"Why?"

Why indeed? Telling him they could hang until she left had been a mistake. How could she admit she should keep her distance—her only defense as time whittled down? Otherwise, she'd never survive the separation. "I'm so far behind on my law firm work."

"You have to eat."

She motioned toward the dining room.

"Fine." He stepped toward her. "I'll meet you here."

The uptick of his mouth indicated he guessed her stall tactics.

"We've pushed through the last few weeks, Nat. We have to give this"—he waved a hand between the two of them—"us. Give *us* a chance."

She nipped her bottom lip, hard enough to taste blood. Sucking her lip between her teeth, she tried to staunch the trickle. She was desperate to give them a chance. But contemplating the heartache to come had her questioning her sanity. At least, she would enter the relationship experiment with eyes open, knowing she wouldn't be blindsided by underhanded interference from her father.

"I know you leave in a few weeks." For a moment he dipped his chin to touch his chest, before he lifted his dark gaze. "We've found each other for a second time. I'm not willing to let you go."

"What do you mean?" *How could he say that?* "I can't stay here, and you can't leave. We both have obligations."

"I know." He displayed his palms. "But we owe our past and the hand we were dealt to see where our relationship goes. To right a wrong."

"And what if we weren't meant to be?" Her stomach seemed to ride the waves, dipping, cresting, and dipping again.

"I know your dad did a number on you."

Natalie swept her gaze to land at her feet. "He did."

"We've gotten to know each other this time—as adults. You've trusted me to help. And I've trusted you. Don't you think what we have today is different?"

"I-I, ah, I do." She looked at him as she stepped forward. "I've spent my entire life keeping people at a distance. I've let Mary and Heidi get close, a-and you. And see what happened. I had my heart stomped on." The ache throbbed through her chest, as if the pain of loss happened yesterday and not years ago.

The sparks of gold dimmed in his deep brown eyes. "You don't think I relate. Your father destroyed both of us."

She drew in a deep, cleansing breath and scanned the ceiling. "I know. But you ran. Without…without talking to me."

"I think you did the same, Nat."

He lifted her chin with the flat of his index finger, a gentle gesture. Not one meant to intimidate. "You never gave me a chance. And, heck, I was a scared eighteen-year-old. I didn't give you a chance, either."

He chuckled. The uncomfortable kind of laughter signaling he too wasn't sure of the next stage. Like he retreated to his teenage, terrified self. Natalie did the same on a continuous basis. "We both ran." Her whisper floated, cloaking them in an intimate fog.

"Yeah, we both ran" He stepped close.

Relief sighed through her.

"Now we stand here, two different people, better people, people who are falling in love…again. We have to give our relationship a chance."

"In love?" His features carried his vulnerability,

squeezing her heart.

He darted his gaze beyond her shoulder. “Tell me you don’t sense this—this thing between us.”

“I-I do, but the idea scares me.” She stepped back from his touch.

His hand dropped. “You don’t think I’m frightened straight to my hiking boots? Worn out, I might add.”

Despite the seriousness of the conversation, his grin tiptoed across his features.

“I put a lot of miles on these babies. My way of working you from my system.”

He rested his hands, protective over her shoulders, and looked her straight in the eye. Natalie stepped into the circle of his arms. She planted her palms on his waist and looked up. “Ditto. I retired five pairs of sensible black pumps.”

“So, we’re on?”

She studied her feet, her forehead hitting his chest. “We’ll explore a relationship and see where we go.”

Cupping her cheeks, his fingers grazed her neck, as he lifted her face. He nibbled her lips.

The kiss worked through her, straight to her toes, like sunshine on an icy day. *Please don’t hurt me this time.*

He pressed two fingers against her lips. “We can say we gave our all. We’ll know. I refuse to spend another sixteen years wondering.”

His gaze drilled her, lodging in her heart and in her gut and in her head. The head drummed the same beat of *this romance can’t work.* But the gut and heart begged her to give Brad a chance. Did her heart and stomach not understand the pain to follow? Did they not remember the pain from the past?

"Dinner then? Say yes, Nat."

The shouted *no* bounced through in her head. "Yes. Okay, yes." Her heart did a little tap dance and her stomach a backflip. At least two of three were happy with the word popping from her mouth. She scolded the head for not being stronger. *I believed you were the leader of this crew.*

"I'll pick you up for dinner at seven tomorrow. I'll make reservations at the Hawthorne."

"I'll meet you at seven-thirty."

At least the head prevailed by setting limits and having the last say. She strode from the parlor and beelined through the kitchen to her room. If she didn't keep the upper hand, she'd be hurt.

Chapter Twenty-Three

Brad tapped his fingers on the tabletop, set in a secluded corner of the Hawthorne. The minutes ticked past seven-thirty, as he stared at his phone. The tapping morphed into drumming. No way would she dare not show. He hated to admit, but he was less than confident she wouldn't blow off this date.

He swirled his Scotch neat. The silky *legs* crawled the inside of the glass to join the golden liquid—sipping and swirling, sipping and swirling—the rhythmic motion calming and mesmerizing.

The server hovered by the station piled high with cups, glasses, and other accoutrements to soon reset a table, despite being used for nothing more than a cocktail.

He tugged on his collar. The tag of the button-down, he wore rarely, scratched his neck.

The front door squeaked.

Brad glanced over, but he only noticed the backs of a retreating couple. One party of four in the corner drank coffee and waited for dessert. Three singles sat at the bar, yucking it up. Small town and the sidewalks rolled early. He glanced at his phone once more, before he drained the last bracing sip of Scotch, tempted to order a second.

The door creaked again.

Nat strode toward him, a frown marring her

beautiful face.

"Sorry. Did you get Mary's call?"

"What? No." He glanced at his phone and flashed the call alert. "I didn't realize I disabled vibrate."

She pulled back her chair and sat. "We had a plumbing issue in room twelve. Jeff triaged until the plumber arrived."

"Any damage?"

"No." She twisted her hands together. "Except another bill."

"We could have postponed."

She tilted her head. "I wasn't sure you'd believe me."

"Wow." Fact was, he might not have.

Her shoulders lifted almost to her ears. She rotated her head.

He longed to offer a massage. "You okay?"

Her eyes filled with tears. She blinked—several times.

He almost lost his self-control. His heart begged him to squeeze her hand. His head told him to stuff the impulse and let her work through her tension.

"I go home soon." She released the grip of one hand over the other and stretched her fingers. "Mary can't handle everything. And we have no money to hire a general manager."

A chill attacked his spine—she would leave in several weeks. "Can you afford an extra thousand a month?"

"That's not much. What're you thinking?"

"Jeff's staying through the spring. He has no overhead right now, so anything he makes is gravy. Not much for him to do at GMS but run trips and restock.

Can you pay him along with room and board? I bet he'd take over most of the day-to-day, back-end duties."

She tilted her head and pressed her lips tight. "I need a person who knows books and customer service and…can keep Mary in check."

"Glance at his resume. We know Mary digs on him."

She flashed a tentative grin. "*Digs on*? Seriously?"

He plastered on his best boyish grin, hoping to settle her anxiety. The worry lines circling her mouth eased into a full-bellied laugh. "My employee Will's influence. Seriously, Mary worships Jeff."

"Jealous?"

"Not a chance. She *loves* me."

Her gaze dropped. She ran a fingernail along the crease of her napkin, still folded on the woven placemat.

He couldn't take his gaze off the movement of her hand or her nails. "Red."

"What?"

"Your nails. Kind of…wow."

She grinned. "Jumpstarting my holiday mood."

"And…gearing up to go *home*?"

"Sort of."

Brad sat against the chair. Should he drop the explosive topic?

"Truth is, the color gives me courage and makes me smile."

He hadn't realized he held his breath, until he whooshed an exhale. He sucked down a breath. "I'll send you Jeff's resume. His management skills include running satellite shops for adventure outfits. Check his creds, then broach the idea."

She continued stroking the napkin, this time with her fingertips.

For a second time, he fought the urge to save her, aching to cover her hand with his to stop the nervous caress. He focused on work instead. "If Jeff works and he's off leading a trip, Mary can call me anytime." Giving up restraint, he caught her hand. "You know I'll drop everything, right?" He patted her hand like a big brother, when all he wanted was to absorb her warmth and softness and act like a boyfriend.

Her shoulders dropped. "Having help would be one load off my mind."

"One. What else?"

She shifted her fork. Fiddling again with the edge of the napkin, then lifting the folded cloth, her gaze followed the starched material as it floated to her lap. "The list goes on and on. Routine stuff."

"Nat, look at me."

She did.

Her chocolate eyes deepened to a moonless, midnight-black, dark and vacant, like she wanted to shut him or the idea of the two of them from her mind. "You know you can depend on me." Not sure whether his comment was a statement or a question, he held his breath.

She smiled, tight-lipped at first, then widening, until warmth sparked in her eyes.

Her grin had hit him straight on since they were seven. *Every. Time.* The smile he couldn't get enough of and would miss with a crushing blow. He vowed to do everything in his power to convince her going to D.C. wouldn't—shouldn't—be the end of them. He planned to win her over and visit. "How I can help."

"Feed me." She picked up the menu. "I'm not sure I ate lunch."

"Honey, you have to take care of yourself." The endearment shot from his mouth before he could recall his words.

After a slight lift of her lids, her gaze drifted to scan the menu.

"What're you thinking?"

"A salad." Her words escaped in a mumble.

"With protein. You need to eat more than salad."

Her mouth gaped.

He'd stepped in the pile, telling her what to do. "So, sue me. Want to split a salad and filet?"

Her jaw dropped, before she leaned toward him. "You'd eat an arugula, bleu cheese, and pear salad?"

"Yup."

"And just half a filet, which by the way is small to begin with."

"Yup. Or we each get our own."

"I can eat a whole one."

He grinned. He'd won a major battle. "Medium-rare?" Her smile spoke wonders. He remembered how she liked her meat. He remembered every minute they spent together.

Once they ordered, conversation turned to their days at the inn and GMS. Dinner arrived. They each devoured a few bites, settling into comfortable silence, like an old married couple.

Nat leaned against the seat, her palm against her stomach. "Tell me more about what you and Jeff do in the wilderness job?"

Savoring the buttery flavor of the filet, he set aside his fork. His mouth opened to remind her to eat. He firmly shut his trap. No need to start a spat. "Basic stuff. Organize every miniscule part of a trip, plan for contingencies, and babysit." Her throaty laugh attacked him, like she'd flung her arms around him and held tight.

"Babysit?"

"Beginner trips, or for those who have experience but need a refresher. So yeah, we keep close tabs, every step of the way. In a nutshell, keep them safe while teaching them skills and love of the outdoors."

"Besides your day-to-day, what's the prep work leading up to a trip that lasts a few days or weeks?"

"Months of planning. Even though we do the trips over and over, each one is a different mix of clients, changing weather patterns, various individual needs from expertise to food allergies, fear of mice and spiders and snakes—"

"Ewww."

Starting with the shake of her head and shoulders to her fists clutched tight, her shiver spiraled. On a good day, he would've teased her without mercy. Tonight, he held tight his grin. "We use a basic trip plan but have to account for variables with each outing. One reason Jeff would be a good choice to help at the inn. He's used to the customer service side and the think-on-your-feet reflexes needed to shift priorities at a moment's notice. Plus, he spends a ton of time, prior to trips, planning everything from budgets, staffing, day-by-day details, equipment maintenance, and inventory."

"What do you love most?"

"Easy." His forearms crossed against the tabletop. "The people."

She widened her eyes. "How come I never saw this

side of you? I knew you were a people-person. But the outdoor trekking part… Your decision to abandon our plans hit me broadside."

He held up an index finger. "Not my decision. I was forced to save face, Nat. I loved camping and fishing trips with my dad. Trekking the wilderness was the one thing I could do to escape Mistletoe Falls." *Escape the memory of you.* He sucked in his breath. "You dumped me. Why would I owe you an apology?"

"I-ah, I understand. We both made mistakes not talking to each other." She glanced toward her lap, then she fixed her gaze on Brad. "We were kids and both were hurt. Still, I have a hard time forgetting repercussions."

Time to change the subject. "Can we set aside our bad memories for tonight?"

"I want to hear more." She picked up her fork and stabbed a piece of beef. "Your work is something I know little about. Did your father ever join your trips? He must have been proud."

The pain landed in a direct hit. "My dad never forgave my decisions. He had high hopes for me going into a profession where I could make a difference."

With her palms plastered against the table edge, she leaned. "Brad, you make a difference in people's lives."

"How?"

"You told me yourself. Every time you take novices and teach them to let go and enjoy nature and challenge themselves—adventure therapy—you help people learn and grow."

"It's not like—"

"What, Brad? Making a ton of money by suing

others or…" She flipped her hand, as if that would explain what she left out. "Every parent wants their child to succeed. I'm sure he—"

"Nat. No. We never spoke again. He wrote me off, and I was too stubborn and hurt to make amends. He died before I ever…" His appetite disappeared. Nat hadn't touched another bite. He eyed the wait station and signaled their server. "Dessert? Coffee?"

"No. Thanks." She slipped her napkin to the tabletop and tucked the neatly folded cloth under the edge of her plate.

She remained so precise, assessing everything. Instead of homing in on her meticulous mannerisms, he studied her face and saw the fleeting flash of pity flit over her features. He raised a hand to signal the server. "Check, please. I'm glad we got to go ice-skating." By the time he finished the last sip of wine, the check and containers arrived.

The server scooted off to process his credit card.

Nat slouched against the seatback.

Her unguarded grin reappeared. His reward of her sweet smile circled through him and gave him hope maybe the two had crossed a threshold.

"Skating was nice."

"We'll do it again. You want to take a stroll before you head home?"

She shuttered her eyes in a long blink. "You'd have to carry me."

He tried, but he couldn't contain his brow lift at the idea of hoisting her lithe, warm body into his arms and carrying her from the restaurant.

"Don't even go there, Matthews. I'm not in the mood for a macho fireman's carry down Main Street."

He held up his hands and laughed. "Not what I had in mind. My thoughts wandered to a lift-the-bride-over-the-threshold carry."

She didn't crack the barest of a smile.

He swallowed a groan. Back to square one. Would he ever learn not to tease a tired Nat? "I know. Not in the mood." He stood, pocketed the credit card, grabbed the leftovers, and clutched her hand. "Let's go."

The cold air hit him with force once he stepped to the sidewalk. He sniffed. "Smells like snow." At his truck, he beeped open the lock and held the door. He made his second macho move of the night, before she could protest. "Get in. I'm not letting you drive."

"No."

"I'll drop off Mary's car first thing. Jeff will drive me to work. In. Or do I have to drag forth the fireman's carry?"

She sighed, heavy and explosive.

He longed to lift her into his arms, but she climbed in. He placed the to-go bag by her feet. Once he buckled up, he glanced sideways. "My intention wasn't to go caveman. But you're exhausted."

"I'm fine to drive a few miles."

He nodded. "Once in a while, let a friend help." His truck roared to life, before she could respond. He endured the short, silent drive to the inn. After parking near the steps, he rounded the vehicle and took her hand. "I'm walking you." He pressed his finger against her mouth. "I need to touch base with Jeff."

She hooded her lids with a suspicious glare.

"Your car, remember?"

When the hell would she ever learn to trust? Maybe best to give up on trying. She planned to leave. He bet she wouldn't look back—just like last time.

****

Inn business increased over the following days. Diners with promotional lunch coupons trickled in. The inn disbursed complimentary ballots for the cow-sculpture contest. Natalie had to admit she grew fond of their resident fiberglass bovine. She could picture the inn's cow standing in the field, like a grand dame surrounded by wildflowers. Would the artist be willing to sell?

She wrote cows on her to-do list. If they added one cow each year, soon the inn could use the unique sculptures like a promotional calling card to draw people—one more cow pasture added to the Vermont-style ambiance and the state's perceived reputation of most cows per capita.

Plus, Keegan would be over-the-moon excited. Problem…next he'd want real cows. She grinned at the idea of an older Keegan herding a handful of dairy cows, and maybe some goats, from their tiny barn. Heidi could make signature Gooseneck Inn cheese. She and Heidi could traipse to area wineries and organic farms to source the best Vermont had to offer.

She'd stuffed her longings years ago. Now she shook her head to disperse the pipe dream. A fun place to visit and escape city living craziness, but she'd never dreamed of moving home.

Until now.

Leaning against the solid oak office chair, she keyed in more notes. Her phone beeped, dragging her from her on-the-roll-with-ideas session.

Wes.

Clear on her feelings, she'd sent him packing. He

continued to text and call. Why? Wes had *not* enjoyed his Vermont trip, except for meeting Celia. She had to deal, but she refused to call him. Upon her return to D.C., being face to face was soon enough.

To hold him off, she shot him a text.

—We will talk in January—

She noticed more messages.

Darn it all, she'd forgotten to take her phone off silent until an hour ago and hadn't noticed the pileup from Gina. The D.C. workload escalated. *What else was new?* She scanned the texts. More questions and requests for help. She returned Gina's text to arrange a phone conference. What did taking a sabbatical accomplish, if she remained responsible for a good portion of the work? Her frustration level hit the high-water mark, diminishing the elation from the inn's good financial news.

Natalie logged into the Internet, a daily habit she tried to avoid until her plate cleared. Distracted by apartment rental ads, she searched for good deals. With a new rental, she could market her condo. The sale money would be a huge cushion in her savings account, in case the inn needed a bailout. She marked off a few housing possibilities. Grabbing her phone, she dialed her realtor.

Now or never.

"Stella, what are the chances of finding reasonable, small square-footage rentals in the Georgetown or MacArthur Boulevard area if I sell my place?" Within a half hour, she had listed the condo. Stella assured her rentals were opening at the end of the month for occupancy in the New Year.

For the next few hours, she turned her attention to

the dining room. With extra coupon-carrying customers, dinners were busier. Beyond exhaustion, she locked the inn, pocketed her cell, and plodded the carriage house stairs. The ramifications of listing her condo hit her between the shoulders.

Entering the hallway, she noticed immediately a light shining beneath Heidi's door. In her room, she hoisted a sample wine from the start-up Hazelton Peak Winery, strode across the hall, and knocked.

Heidi stepped back from the open door. "You look like death." Her smile did not erase the impact.

"That bad?"

"You've been burning the candle for almost six weeks."

"I took steps to put an end to the madness." Natalie reached for the wine key tucked in her pocket and opened the bottle, while Heidi located glasses. She poured a splash in each glass. "Port with berry overtones."

Heidi swirled the wine, checked the tear marks on the inside of the glass, and lifted the glass to her nose. "Nice. Subtle."

"Blueberry, raspberry, and blackberry with herbal undertones. I heard the winery is working on pear, apple, rhubarb, and cranberry blends. They use fruit from local farms and vineyards. Aunt Mary took pride in her huge rhubarb plants behind the inn. She told me both Gramma and Great-Gramma Packard used to make rhubarb wine."

"So, your family tree has bootleggers?" Heidi laughed at her own joke.

Natalie winked. "I think the term pertains to selling on the black market. Rumor is my ancestors claimed use for medicinal purposes *only*."

"Have you checked the basement?"

Natalie straightened. "What aren't you telling me?"

Heidi snorted wine. "Joking. Can't you see Mary and Sylvie funneling into dark green bottles the newest batch of *medicinal* wine?"

"Clear as day." She sipped. The bold undertones of berries were replaced with a hint of earthy, dark chocolate as she swallowed. "Delicious. I'm envisioning this port paired with our local chocolate, cheese, and nut plate, or poured over homemade ice cream?"

"Topped with fresh peaches. Or in a parfait with my double-fudge sauce and blueberries." Heidi stared over her head and nodded. "I've tons of ideas. Plus, it's a nice sipping wine. I can't wait to try more varieties."

"Close by is convenient. If the other wines are competitive, we could offer a winter promotion, inviting the winery to pair their offerings with a menu you create. Beginning each course, the vintner could describe the wines and explain their blending methods. You could speak on why you paired certain dishes and wines. What do you think?"

"Great idea. A great way to pair, pun intended, with local businesses and farms."

Natalie sipped and savored the not-too-sweet hints of fruit. "Should we have Mary and Sylvie start using the rhubarb for a private label, The Inn on Gooseneck Lane wine?"

"Don't even tease." Heidi shimmied. "You know they'd jump at the challenge. Soon, we'd have the sheriff on our doorstep."

The two clinked glasses and laughed.

Natalie stood and paced. “We have a cluster of wineries nearby. We could organize a series of dinners in January and February?”

“Or one a month through April. Different wineries. This wine would be great in a marinade—maybe a spiced pork tenderloin. Except you won’t be here.”

“I know.” The longer she stayed, the more she hated to leave. “In the meantime, I vote for research to find which wines work best with our winter and spring menus. Road trip?”

Heidi tapped her glass to Natalie’s. “I like the way you think. You sure you don’t want to stick? You have great ideas.”

“Comes from dining in D.C.” Natalie almost bit her tongue. “I, ah, need to tell you—”

Heidi straightened, set down her glass, and frowned. “What? You’re not leaving early?”

“No. Today, I listed my condo.”

Heidi squealed like the next-door farm’s piglets. She jumped and embraced Natalie, before she plopped on the couch. “You’re staying here. I’m so excited.”

“No. *No*.”

“Then why?”

“I might need to rescue the inn. I’ll find a smaller, less-expensive rental and put my condo money into a savings certificate.”

“Oh, Natalie.” Heidi’s smile faded, like the sun slipping behind a storm cloud. “You sure? A huge step and a *huger* sacrifice.”

“I could use another splash.” She extended her glass. “I’m never home to enjoy the view or amenities. I don’t even own a car, yet I pay for parking. I work long hours. Have to commute. No point in paying exorbitant monthly fees for nothing."

"Are you sad?"

Natalie hesitated. "You know, I don't think so."

"Would you ever consider living here?"

She shook her head, but deep in her heart screamed a question—*would staying here be so bad*? "Each job has stresses."

"Besides the job. Natalie, consider moving home. You and Wes have split. You're selling your condo. Your work is stressful. I know you're good at what you do, but do you love your job? At college, corporate law was nowhere on your radar."

She leaned against Heidi's kitchenette counter. "Lives take different paths."

"That's your rationale? I can't help but think… You've mastered the graphic design end. Promotions. Website. You're in your element. And the event planning—you have a knack. Ideas are flowing. You've made a huge difference. And…Mary… She seems happy and relieved, and she's taking a chance on love. Everything happened because you're here."

"Heidi, don't."

"Hear me out. I know rejuvenating the inn was never on your radar. You took time off to study. Is this new job what you want? If nothing drew you to D.C., would you say you were happy?"

"Of course, but—"

Heidi narrowed her gaze. "Think, Natalie. Think long and hard. Not what you're supposed to do, but what you want to do, even if running an inn in Vermont isn't your dream. You owe yourself."

"I-I'm more energized, despite the exhaustion and stress."

"And where does the stress stem from? Dawn to midnight hours working the inn *and* keeping pace with D.C. work?"

"Working at the law office takes a different kind of problem-solving—training, correcting other's mistakes, or solving situations with clients. The inn—"

"I know, daily challenges."

Natalie smiled. "Totally. Regardless, I use creative thinking to make the inn more successful. Running an inn is more than just dealing with everyday problems. And I'm in charge. Puzzling solutions with a team—you, Jeff, Brad, Mary, and Walter—we're invested together to make our businesses shine. We bounce ideas off one another. The work is hard but fun."

"And D.C.?"

"Having people looking over my shoulder or calling on me to tackle an emergency…at the firm…life continually seems beyond control."

Heidi's fingers rimmed Natalie's wrist. "I know moving here would be a huge change. Affect your bank account. Take you from the things now part of your city life. But contemplate making a change. Not how your decision will affect others, but consider what makes *you* happy. You do owe yourself to consider various other opportunities."

Natalie gulped her wine and stood. "I have to get to bed."

The door shut behind her. She hugged her middle. Could she consider moving? Leave behind everything she'd worked toward the last eleven years—and take a chance?

Chapter Twenty-Four

Awakened by high-pitched beeps, Natalie's heart beat like a drummed warning. No one texted this early. Her feet hit the floor.

The first text came from the senior partner, her immediate boss.

—Need you in D.C. NOW Emergency case CALL—

Her sigh rivaled the height and girth of neighboring New Hampshire's Mount Washington. Afraid to glance at the second text, she sucked in a deep breath before she scrolled—her realtor.

—Three more offers. Bidding war. Might need you in D.C. Call me—

Dragging her carry-on from the closet, she did not relish reentry to chaotic city life. She threw in toiletries and a few essentials. Her closet in D.C. housed her work clothes. Next, she removed from the closet the dark suit she brought from D.C., along with the blouse and pumps to match. She'd wear the outfit on the plane and taxi straight to work.

She slung her carry-on and purse over her shoulder. The bags slammed against her back. She caught the stair rail to keep from tumbling on the stairs. A minute later, she tore through the kitchen.

"Whoa," Heidi caught her sleeve. "What's wrong?"

"Nothing. Busy."

"Too busy for your favorite cheddar-bacon scone? And what's with the bag?"

To regulate her breathing, she imagined the mellow music from her yoga class. "D.C. I'll report back once I make calls."

Heidi set two scones on a plate, poured coffee, and handed both to Natalie. "Now go."

"Tell Jeff I need him, ASAP."

"Will do."

Moments later, she booted the computer and booked her flight.

Mary scurried in and sat close.

Jeff strolled in, oblivious to both her frazzled state and Mary's spacey-aunt persona.

She filled both in on her imminent departure and tasks for today. "I'm not sure how long I'm needed, but I'll be home for the winter trip event."

Mary emitted a tiny sob.

Natalie enfolded her in a hug. "I promise. In the meantime, you have Heidi and Jeff to lend a hand."

"What can I do?" Jeff laid a palm on Mary's forearm.

She could only describe Mary's expression as adoring, all smiley and soft eyes, the way she'd looked at Natalie since she was a kid. She collected *her children* like a child collected favorite stuffed animals. And she bestowed love on every one of them.

Running the inn equated to being surrounded by family. No matter what, she'd do everything in her power to save Mary's home. Both for Mary and for her *children* who depended on the inn—including herself.

This inn was home. How could she leave? She

shook off the melancholy and focused on the task on hand. "Can you drive me to Boston? I hate to disrupt your day, Jeff, but I'm desperate."

"Sure. I'm not due at GMS until tomorrow."

"Leave in fifteen? I'll explain on the way."

Jeff planted his palms on his thighs. "Absolutely. Any time you're ready."

"May we borrow your car, Aunt Mary?"

"Of course, dear."

Jeff stepped forward. "Need help with suitcases?"

"Just my carry-on." She pointed to her shoulder, carry-on bag lying at her feet.

Mary and Jeff exchanged glances. Her aunt beamed a full-fledged smile.

She handed Jeff her aunt's keys. "Have breakfast while I finish this email."

"Heidi already fed Keegan and me, before I ran him to school. See you in front."

Once Mary resumed her position at the front desk, Natalie slugged her coffee. She wrapped her scones in a napkin and stuffed them in her purse. She zipped up her laptop bag, set it beside the carry-on, then hurried to the kitchen.

"Whoa. What's going on." Heidi set aside her chef's knife from the pile of carrots she chopped.

"Too much." A warm tremor slipped through her at her best friend's concern. She and Heidi reconnected as if the two had never separated. She knew Mary would be surrounded by those who loved her after she left for D.C. "I have three minutes." She poured more coffee into her mug, her spine rigid and feet spread wide. "Bids on my condo."

"Already? Have you told Mary?"

Natalie shook her head.

"What else?"

"The law office has an emergency case. I have to fly to D.C."

"Your firm better be paying airfare." Heidi posed in her riled, hands-on-her-hips, don't-mess-with-my-friends intimidating tell. "How long?"

"Three, four, maybe five days. Jeff will drive me to Logan. Can you make us sandwiches? Please."

"Of course. But you have to promise to text or call tonight. Deal?"

Natalie hugged her. "Deal. *If* the hour isn't too late. I'll know more soon."

Ten minutes later, she snatched two bagged lunches from the kitchen, plucked her purse and laptop from the office, planted a kiss on Mary's cheek, and crossed the wide porch.

Jeff waved from the driver's side. "I'll chauffeur so you can relax before you have to deal with the big city."

"My carry-on?"

"Back seat."

"I guess I'm nervous." She climbed aboard, set the bagged lunches by her feet, and clutched her hands to quell jitters.

In no time, the tall pines and blue sky faded into crowded highways, urban sprawl, and hazy skies. She spotted the *Welcome to Massachusetts* sign. She wiggled in her seat to dispel nerves and breathed in to release the residual stress of running the inn. Instead, her back seized, spreading to tighten her shoulders and neck.

Compared to returning to D.C., she'd been relaxed in Vermont. Running the inn became second nature in a weird way. She enjoyed being surrounded by family and extended family, including her coworkers and old friends.

"You all right?"

Jeff stared, like her transformation from country girl to city corporate drudge happened while he gawked. "Truth? I'm not sure." She imagined herself as one of Keegan's transformer toys, which he maneuvered with nimbleness from machine into otherworldly superhero in seconds. Only this time, she wondered if she could easily convert to who she'd been weeks ago. "I was positive if I returned to my old life, the change would be easy."

"Ha. Change is never easy."

His throaty chuckle seeped into her soul. She'd known Jeff a few weeks, but he was a good friend to Brad. Her best friend had fallen for him, and Keegan's eyes shined with hero worship every time Jeff paid the kid genuine and caring attention.

He shot her a look. "Vermont, or maybe rural life in general, has a way of easing into your psyche. Makes you see the world in a different way."

"Is that the reason you and Brad seem so settled—you know—like life is good no matter what gets thrown at you?"

Jeff's smile disappeared. "Life's not always good or tranquil, but living this kind of life makes handling stresses easier."

She glanced through the window at wall-to-wall development. "I get your point. I do. I never considered environment would make such a difference. You replace one stress for another and slog through." She pointed toward the never-ending miles of buildings, pavement, and traffic, representing craziness compared to rural Mistletoe Falls. "I'm content at the inn." She waved her hand toward the passing concrete jungle. "The pressure is closing in on me, and I haven't even boarded a plane."

"There's hope for you."

She started to make a snappy retort. When she noticed his wide grin and teasing voice, she swallowed. Already, her hackles were up, bracing herself for backstabbing and infighting and winning at all costs which permeated her workplace. She prided herself on her ability to claw her way to the top. Now disgust lodged in her stomach like the aftereffects of gobbling an unripened pear.

She shifted. "I spoke to Brad regarding transitioning from the inn—how I can still help Mary. He recommended you." The snap of his head when he lifted a brow caught her off guard. "He didn't mention the idea to you?"

"No."

"I'm thinking a temporary position through spring."

Jeff's shoulders rose, and his grip tightened on the steering wheel.

According to Brad, he liked the variety and challenge of new jobs in different *ports*. "Until you leave for your next job." Jeff was the one viable solution. She had no choice but to ask, even for the short-term. Jeff's assistance would give her time to explore more permanent solutions.

"Job duties?"

"Bookkeeping, reservations, staff scheduling, and working with Heidi on supply ordering. We can't pay much, but we'll pay on top of room and board. And work around GMS and trip schedules." She tried to read his face. "You'd be like a liaison. Keep an eye on Aunt Mary. I'm concerned. Yearend, I return to D.C. fulltime. I can't maintain day-to-day management from afar."

A few months ago, she never dreamed she'd be staffing an inn and helping from afar. "You won't have desk or dining duty. And I'll be available by phone."

"I'll consider your offer." Jeff's gaze remained glued to the road. "Once you return, we'll discuss."

"Great." Her stomach churned at the possibility Jeff might not accept the offer. "I'm home in a few days." *I hope.*

The skyline of Boston unfolded. Despite the metropolitan sprawl whizzing by the window, she did love her hometown. The old and new juxtaposed like the two styles belonged together—the grandeur and ambiance of New England, the history combined with the new and modern facades fused into one.

She loved D.C for many of the same reasons. What she didn't love was the cutthroat politics and corporate life ruling the city. Natalie gripped the door handle.

"My driving making you nervous?"

Her body shifted. "No. I can't believe I'm edgy going home."

"Maybe you have decisions of your own to make." Jeff veered off the exit toward Logan Airport.

Was she ready to upend her life? She opened the window, hoping the wind would dispel her troubles, until she dealt with the crisis and returned to Vermont where she could think.

****

Natalie staggered through her condo's front door. Between the early morning summons, rocky flight, and getting thrown into the wolf's den the second she walked into the law firm, the day had been endless like no other. Now her uncle's mantle clock struck nine.

Even the inn gave her moments to catch her breath, with Mary's hugs tempering bad days. She shook her head and wondered how she endured eleven years of non-stop hustle.

Flipping on the hall lights, she left her suitcase by the door and shuffled into the spacious, modern living room. She'd forgotten the size, compared to her intimate space in the inn. Ambient light from Old Town, Virginia, across the Potomac, cast shadows on the floor. City life wore on a person. Urban life neglected to envelop one in a cozy, dark blanket, to give the soul a chance to unwind. Apartment buildings rarely slept. Traffic crawled by, and sirens shrilled. Observing the stars was a rarity because the location of her condo, lit with streetlamps, twenty-four-seven, also caught constant strafing lights of flights from the airport across the river.

She stepped to the windows, spread wall-to-wall, to close the curtains. The river view seen from the open-concept, through to the kitchen, was the reason she bought the place. Tonight, she chose to leave the curtains open and imagine the twinkling city lights were stars on a clear Vermont night.

Plodding back to the entryway, she hefted her carry-on with the last ounce of energy and carted the bag to the master bedroom. She left the lights off and the curtains open. Counting on the timed nightlight emanating from the bathroom to guide her, she stepped to her bedroom. The play of lights from a city still wide awake on her side of the Potomac allowed her to experience the city views she so often ignored.

She unpacked her laptop and a few toiletries. While she rummaged in her bureau for a nightgown, her phone beeped. Another text. She wanted to ignore the ding. Brad? Was the hour too late to call him and apologize for running off without a word? She checked her watch. Brad woke with the birds and worked hard throughout the day. She'd get in touch tomorrow and contact Heidi, too. Tonight, exhaustion crawled through her muscles and hijacked her brain.

After showering, she changed into nightwear. Flipping off the light in the bathroom, she checked her phone. *Wes*. She counted the day a miracle, since she managed to avoid him at work. Never mind she'd had no time to lift her head from the project or eat Heidi's sandwiches.

—Dinner? I'm headed to Georgetown Bistro on K Street—

She rolled her eyes. *He texts me at such a late hour and expects me to join him, after we broke up*. He'd watched how hard she worked in Vermont from early morning until late at night, and today, once she hopped off a plane and headed straight to the office. She climbed into bed and hauled the covers high.

Halfway through the next day, still hunched over her computer with case files scattered everywhere, she explained next steps to Gina. Already the morning, spreading into a late lunch hour, had been grueling. She stretched with her hands against her lower back.

Wes strode in. He planted his palms against the edge of the conference table. "I see you're still alive.

Lunch. We need to talk."

She refused to fall for his arrogant posturing, nor would she chase him when he demanded she *jump*. She stood, posture straight, and glared. "Lunch was delivered. I'm on deadline." She flashed a candy-sweet, press-lipped smile. No way would she debate their issues in front of Gina. "I'll be in touch once we finish the case prep. Tomorrow?"

He straightened. The scowl remained. "You never answered my text last night."

"I was asleep."

He lifted his gaze to the ceiling. "Still on Vermont time."

"I wish." She focused her attention on Gina. "Next, you need to…" Her back to Wes, she reached across the table for another file and flipped open the folder. She didn't look until she heard the door slam behind Wes.

"If you need to go… You know, talk, I can wait."

"We'll talk later. He'll forget his little snit."

Gina gasped.

Natalie ignored her.

At nine the next night, Natalie sat at the Trattoria Athena bar on the first floor of her condo building. She'd lived here for four years and never once entered the restaurant. Oh, she ordered delivered take-out a number of times, loving the combination of Italian and Greek offerings.

The ambiance, cozy with low lights, enhanced the scented air wafting hints of herbs and garlic and roasting meats, a hallmark of the restaurant's cuisine. Her decision to sell and live closer to work had her wondering. She loved the area.

Wes strode toward her like he owned the place.

Slipping from the bar stool, she lifted her wine glass and pointed to a booth in the corner. She refused to carry on a discussion in the adjacent, well-lit dining area or settled at the bar where others could eavesdrop. His expression spoke loudly—he was inconvenienced at having to come to her. Usually, she paid the hefty taxi fees to get home.

Wes hit the seat across from her. "What are you doing?"

She opened her mouth to respond.

"Your behavior is incongruous, Natalie. If you don't get your head on straight, you'll lose the job you worked so hard to get…and lose me."

What? She sucked in deep breaths to gain control. Her temper simmered below the surface, bubbling and ready to explode. "Lose you?" Her tone was deadly low, her voice husky. She tried to control her temper. "I think you have your facts wrong, counselor. *You've* already lost *me*. Or have you managed to forget Vermont and Celia?" With a few sips of wine left, she set the glass near the edge of the table.

The server appeared in an instant. "Another glass, ma'am?"

Wes slapped his hand to cover the top of her glass and shook his head.

Natalie gripped the tip of his forefinger and lifted off his hand. "Yes, please. I'd love another glass."

The server's head bobbed between them.

"And he'll have a seven and seven. Please add both to my tab." Case closed.

Wes's mouth dropped.

She didn't dare flash a smile, even though a smirk loitered deep in her belly, aching to escape. How many times had Wes ordered for her without asking? And how many times had she let him? "Now, you were saying? Oh, wait. I think I had the last word—you and Celia? Explain."

Darn. I would have made a great trial lawyer.

He clutched her hand, palm to palm, and smoothed his thumb over the back.

She shivered and not from excitement.

"Celia was at the inn to see Brad. We kept each other company because you two were so busy—"

She yanked her hand from his. Swallowing slowly several sips, she calmed her temper. "Keeping the snow shoveled, the rooms heated, and the guests fed. And amazingly, you two were invisible, despite everyone, *guests included,* pitching in." She took another sip and leaned. "I think we already discussed your *excuses* in Vermont. Is this the reason you insisted on a chat? A rehash? Or a new spin on the facts?"

"I shoveled and hauled wood and helped in the kitchen."

His lower lip jutted like Keegan's pout after being asked to clean his plate or his toy mess. Natalie laughed. She finished off the wine. Either she was too tired to continue the conversation, or she no longer cared to go round and round with Wes regarding nothing. Although from his expression, he wasn't finished denying and obfuscating her version of his Vermont stay.

The server delivered their drinks. "Would you care to see a menu?"

"Yes." Wes extended a hand.

"No," Natalie spoke over Wes. "I'd like to order take-out please. *Carciofini Fritti* and *Kolokithokeftede*s.

Thanks."

"And, you, sir?"

Wes waved a dismissive hand.

Natalie smiled at the server. "I guess we're set." Her voice chirped with exaggerated glee. *Not becoming of a lady*, her aunt would remind her, even if Mary agreed. Asserting herself translated into a confident, rosy sensation swirling through her. "Now, where were we?" She swirled her glass and sipped. "Oh yes, the help you gave us on Thanksgiving Day. Wes, I can't tell you how much I appreciated you chipping in to help the cause." Did she sound insincere? Perhaps. Because she didn't mean a word. She, along with Jeff and Brad, spent way too much time tracking him and keeping him on task.

A neighbor sauntered toward a bar stool, nodded, and sat. She raised her glass in greeting. For a moment, she lost her train of thought. Oh, yes—Wes and Celia and the vanishing act.

"Amazing to me, in an inn so small, you and Celia managed to disappear. Although—" she studied her steepled hands "—I never sent anyone to rap on your doors."

Wes swallowed half his drink. "Natalie."

His tone sharp, his brow rose in his usual don't-try-to-challenge-me glare he used on a witness. She plastered on a sickly-sweet smile to irritate him.

"You were working so much and had no time for me. Of course, I tried to stay away. You were busy."

For the first time since she met Wes, his tone didn't intimidate her. She removed her fake smile and countered. "It's apparent, you were also busy. You know, being a plus-one—" she motioned between them.

"—was nice for a while. But our arrangement isn't working anymore. We discussed the reasons prior to my leaving for Vermont. And, once more in Vermont. This discussion is finished. If you'll excuse me, I'll wait for my order at the bar." She lifted her glass in a silent cheer, finished the last gulp, and slid from the booth.

"Natalie, we are *not* finished."

"Wes." She stood. "We were finished long before you arrived in Vermont. Only this time, I understand why you've been distant the last six months. We've been nothing more than each other's plus one. We have no *spark*."

"Spark?" He narrowed his gaze. "There is more to a partnership than spark."

"No, Wes. You're mistaking partnership for relationship."

He shoved his chair. "Derek will not condone your attitude. And know, once you say no to me, no going back."

Natalie stifled her disgust. How had she not noticed his vanity and sense of entitlement? She didn't care whether or not Wes had her boss's ear. If the guy wanted to fire her because of a romantic tiff, so be it. "*No,* Wes. Clear enough?" Proud she finally had the backbone, relief flooded through her like a cool, refreshing breeze on a Vermont summer evening.

He slugged the rest of his drink, slammed the glass on the table, and stalked from the bar.

Natalie pressed a hand to her stomach and emitted a long, slow, cleansing breath. One more weight lifted from her tired shoulders. Wes no longer occupied space in her life.

Her one regret—she had to be nasty to make him understand.

She brushed her hands, trying to dislodge the niggle of guilt. Next, she must decide what to do regarding other burdens still weighing. At least her condo would soon be sold. Tomorrow she'd discover whether she had a job. And if so, did she still want the job. Contemplating possibilities for her future lifted another weight. No matter what happened in Washington, she had a job…and a home. She strode to the bar.

The bartender handed her the bill, swiped the credit card, and presented the take-out.

She clutched the bag, inhaling the wafting aroma. For the first time since she left Vermont, she was starved.

Tomorrow, she would climb from bed, relaxed for the first time in forever. Although the ramifications of her actions might scare her, tonight she was happier than she'd been in eons. Yes, tomorrow would be soon enough to sort through her life decisions, post-Wes.

Chapter Twenty-Five

Mary and Sylvie hunched over tea at Brenda's Bakery. "I heard my Natalie tell Heidi she's selling her D.C. condo."

Sylvie squeezed Mary's hand. "Do you think she'll stay in Vermont?"

Mary shook her head. "I'm not sure. I've heard nothing. Now she's in Washington, working on a case at the insistence of her boss. Oh, Sylvie, what if she doesn't return? I find managing the inn by myself to be hard."

"Jeff is helping, right?" Sylvie pressed both palms together. "Bradley claims he's a crackerjack project manager."

"Jeff is wonderful. But we must get Brad and Natalie together. We started the process, but the work we've done is not enough."

"I know. I can't even mention her name in front of Bradley. He hasn't stopped scowling since she left without a good-bye."

"We need another plan. The Thanksgiving power outage worked wonders, but..."

"Divine intervention is one thing. I know we're good, but..." Sylvie laughed, then sipped her chocolate chai.

"Can we convince Brad to go to D.C.?"

"Not with the busy holiday season at the store. You

have the event, and with no word from Natalie, Bradley is under pressure."

"I've no ideas." Mary propped her elbows on the table and leaned her forehead against her clasped palms.

"Mary, quick. Out the window."

She lifted her head.

Celia clutched Brad's biceps.

"What is *she* doing here?"

Sylvie shook her head. "I hoped we'd seen the last of her. Bradley was certain she left."

"Can't he just tell her to scram?"

"He did, but she continues to force herself on him."

Mary straightened. "Get your phone. Snap a photo. If Natalie sees them together, she might be mad enough to charge home."

"Or not." Sylvie aimed and snapped.

Seconds later, the front door opened, and Brad stalked in, shaking his arm.

She clung like he was her last meal ticket.

Sylvie changed angles and took another shot. "If Natalie is mad enough, she'll fight for Brad. They belong together."

"Yes, they do. I'll send photos. You and I can devise a plan." Time grew short. Natalie and Brad had to get together.

****

"What're you planning?" Jeff planted a fist on top of Brad's office desk. "The photo is everywhere on social media."

Brad shrugged. "Who cares? We both know Celia's playing her games."

"Natalie might see the photos?"

Brad stood, pressed his palms against his desk, and glared at Jeff. “Nat and I aren’t together. She’s patching things with Wes. And Celia is not my girlfriend. I repeat—what’s the problem?”

“First, your *facts* are false. Natalie is in D.C., working on a special case, which you well know. I’m the person who drove her to Boston. I listened to her fume. She was reluctant to leave Vermont.”

“Why didn’t she let me know? She’s had time.”

“She hasn’t gotten in touch with Mary or Heidi either. She said to tell everyone she’d be working long hours.”

Surely, she had two seconds to shoot him a text. Or had she slipped right back into her old life without a thought for Vermont…or him. “Right.”

“You idiot, she took only a small carry-on. Her work clothes are at her apartment. Everything from D.C. is still here, including her toothbrush.”

Sucking down a deep breath, he rubbed the back of his neck to relax his tight muscles. “How do you know?”

“Heidi. Who else?” Jeff grinned. “She’s not happy in D.C.”

“How—”

“Broken record.” Jeff shook his head. “You *are* dense. Heidi.”

“So, Nat’s been in touch with Heidi—”

“Stop. She talked to Heidi long before she flew to D.C. No one has talked to Natalie since. Satisfied?”

Brad slumped in his chair and scrubbed both hands over his face. He needed to act the bigger man.

“The problem is, you won’t admit you love her.”

Brad drew a deep breath, stared at the ceiling, and

studied an errant cobweb. He wheeled his chair from his desk and stood. “Yeah, I do.” Jeff didn’t say a word. “Okay, I’ve never stopped loving her. Having her in town and knowing we can never be together is killing me.” He wouldn’t admit to Nat he uttered the *love* word. *If* she returned to Vermont, the sentiment might send her running.

“Bro, I suggest you find a good way to show her. Convince her Mistletoe Falls is the right place—not corporate D.C.”

“I know. I *do* know. What if she runs like last time?”

Jeff pivoted and strode through the office door. He paused just outside and leaned in. “You sure you want to rewrite history?”

Before he could rebut, Jeff’s heavy bootsteps faded. Brad contemplated the last weeks, his mind spinning like an out-of-control Ferris wheel at the Vermont State Fair. Had he allowed his version of the past to cloud the rebuilding of their relationship? And more. If so, no doubt Nat had done the same. Time each of them let go the past and consider the future. *Together.* He seized his keys and charged from the office and past the register. “Will. Hold the fort.”

Jeff was spot on. First, he must scrub clean his immediate past. Time to set Celia straight once and for all. On a mission, he stalked through the front door.

****

Natalie enlarged the photo on her social media App. Her glare widened, and her pulse beat like a timpani drum roll at the National Symphony Orchestra.

Celia clutched Brad’s arm, her head tipped, and her smile wide, like he was the moon and the stars in her personal galaxy.

Was the photo for real? She recognized the background of the downtown coffee shop. The picture must be recent. Apparently, he connected with Celia, the second she left?

Her head spun and stomach churned. She braced against being dragged into her worst nightmare—being abandoned by Brad…again.

With one stupid social media photo, her joy experienced in the last month vanished. The urge to throw something sparked through her. Not a tchotchke in sight in her unadorned apartment. Reminders of childhood in Boston and senior year in Vermont sat boxed in her hall closet. The starkness in her D.C. abode contradicted her Vermont life surrounded by memories and family.

How had she not noticed?

She clutched her tummy and closed her eyes. *Think.* Concerning Celia, Brad had been forthright. Why would he allow her into his life? The scenario made no sense. She understood why Celia sported a starry-eyed expression. Still, she willed her heart not to split in half.

Brad had been Natalie's moon and stars long ago. And in the past few weeks, she began to view Brad in the same quixotic way. He jumped in and helped at the inn, acknowledged her accomplishments, and showed his sweet, caring side. He resembled the boy she'd fallen in love with so long ago, sweet and strong. She had no time to analyze a social media photo with a work-numbed brain from long, tedious hours at the law firm. She wanted to trust. She really did. Sometimes believing proved problematical.

She glanced at the boxes surrounding her. Yes, she craved a change in her life. She'd begun to dream the change included Vermont…and Brad. She longed for a rehash with Brad, to remind him of his disavowal of Celia. Instead, she focused on settling her heart rate and scanning the bank of windows and the view beyond. She had to trust.

Both Brad and Jeff described Celia's deception.

On the other hand, Wes became enamored, if only for the weekend. Somehow this woman ensnared men.

If nothing else, she had to believe she learned a lesson from years ago, when she thought the worst without communicating with Brad. She and Brad *would* talk.

Natalie loved Brad. *Still.* A once in a lifetime-love. She stared at the photo and swiped a hand across her cheeks. Despite her internal lecture, tears waterfalled.

Stop. Speak to Brad.

She sank onto the sleek, modern couch. The one costing her several paychecks and spread twice the length of a normal living room. She swept her watery gaze across the tall windows with the magnificent view. Brushing over each piece of furniture and accessory she'd saved for and added one piece at a time, she assumed the fancy furniture and lifestyle would make her happy. These days, the stark coldness of her chosen décor spiraled a chill straight through her.

She missed scrounging through antique and next-to-new shops or driving through town with Brad to scout yard sales. Trying to stop the trickle of tears, she grabbed one more paper hankie. She added the rumpled tissue to the pile, leaving a soggy streak on the sleek, metal side table. At least the waterfall receded into a slow-moving stream.

The reality of what lay ahead hit her.

She relinquished her condo. With her job in jeopardy, where could she go? Not to Vermont, if the photo of Celia and Brad showed the truth.

Selling her place still made sense. For the rest, she would wait and see.

Quitting her job and moving to Vermont? Off the plate.

The photo—if the old adage rang true—was worth a thousand words.

The special case would soon conclude. She'd return *home* and work through the event. With determination, she counted to ten, and then another ten, to keep her tears at bay. She had a course to finish, a certification exam to ace, and a promotion to obtain, if Wes didn't first destroy her career.

First, she'd speak to Brad.

Resolution made to do the right thing, she gazed through her mammoth windows to take in the sun slipping behind buildings and arrowing a golden path across the Potomac. With no one to talk to, she must find a way to ignore the sinking sensation in her stomach and the ache in her heart. She focused on the scene, memorizing her view. The city had been her residence for years. This was still home.

The one blessing from returning to Vermont was she'd learned what she didn't want—a sterile life.

One huge step forward.

Brad and Vermont helped her remember she could be successful and follow her heart.

Straightening her shoulders, she grabbed her phone and ordered take-out from the building's restaurant. She relocated to the guest room, started a list, and sorted her possessions to downsize. Tomorrow she'd call her realtor to check on new bids. She'd accept one and authorize a search for new housing.

In two days, she'd head to Vermont, face Brad, and resolve to soon enjoy life in D.C. by finding a job she truly loved.

Simple, right?

Chapter Twenty-Six

The last person Natalie expected to see by the Logan luggage carousel was Brad Matthews. "What are *you* doing here?" His signature grin didn't quite meet his eyes.

"Meeting your plane. Taxiing you to Vermont."

"Why are *you* here? Aunt Mary convince you to chauffeur?"

"Jeff was on pick up detail. Last-minute change."

He didn't deny Mary's role. She gave him the silent treatment, dragging her carry-on toward the exit.

"No suitcase?"

"Nope." She refused to look his way or engage in chatter.

"Why am I meeting you by luggage?"

"Convenience." With her head held high, she stalked through the revolving door. In seconds, he captured the side strap of her carry-on. She held on to the top. "You don't think I can handle one little bag?"

"Don't be stubborn. I'm carrying your bag."

"Why?"

"My job—*chauffeur*." He ground the word.

She tugged the handle.

"Surrender, Nat. If you could see yourself with circles under your eyes. How many hours did your firm make you work?"

"I'm fine." She gave one more tug.

"Not what your *army* claimed."

She released her grip. The carry-on slammed Brad's leg. He didn't flinch. She didn't apologize. Instead, she teared. Exhaustion crippled every muscle. She listed toward Brad.

He clutched her elbow and guided her to a nearby bench. "Sit. I'll get the car."

She sank against the seat and closed her eyes.

A light tap on her shoulder made her jump. She scanned buses, taxis, and people dragging suitcases—the airport.

"Nat. You fell asleep."

Brad cupped her elbow and helped her stand. He plopped her purse on the pickup cab floor and guided her into the front seat. "Where's my bag and my computer?"

"Back seat." He rolled his eyes.

Brad wended through neighborhoods and industrial areas bordering Logan. Twenty silent minutes later, he merged on to Route One.

"What did you mean by my army?"

"Mary, Heidi, and Jeff defended you. I was mad you left without a good-bye."

"My army. My protectors." She stared from the window, refusing to react to his *mad*. "Jeff took a different route."

"Collecting a customer special order. Plus, this route is more scenic. Passing through those concrete cities stresses me."

She stared at his reflection in the passenger window, then turned to face him. "Hems you in."

"Yeah."

"Maybe the reason you refused to accompany me

to Boston so long ago?"

"I would've followed you anywhere."

She turned in her seat. "Reality—you would have been miserable."

"No." Brad shrugged. "Maybe."

"You think my father did us a favor?"

His glare scorched her. "I loved you. I would've done anything for you."

She noticed his past tense. The spring of their senior year, the wedge had lodged already between them, despite her internal denial. Her father took advantage of the fissure and widened the gap. "Seems to me, we were never meant to be."

"How can you say we're not meant to be? The last few weeks…" His gaze met hers. "What happened in D.C.?"

She shook her head. "Simple. I'm a city girl. You're a country boy."

"You sure?"

"Brad, you were raised in rural Vermont. You've spent your career trekking the wilderness."

"Not me. You certain you're still a city girl?"

She'd asked herself the same question. *Yes. No. Yes.* She locked her fingers. Her shoulders tightened. She rolled her head against the seat and squeezed shut her eyes—not willing to share her doubts. Breathing in through her nose and expelling in a slow beat of ten through her mouth, she conjured yoga visualizations

Spring fields arrowed off in every direction from the inn. The sun warmed her shoulders, and the green grass, a soft mat under the soles of her feet, tickled. She dipped her toes in the creek and sighed.

Emerging from a foggy dream of Vermont

summers, she opened her eyes and shook herself. How long had she slept? Glancing through the window, she was greeted with a wall of green fir with nary a car in sight.

Brad steered his truck off I-89 and turned left at the Route 73 sign.

She concentrated on the half-frozen stream running through the narrow valley.

As the truck started the steep rise, Brad ground the gear shift to third.

The *Green Mountain State Forest* sign flashed by. "We're in Vermont already?"

"Welcome back, sleepyhead. We crossed into Vermont once we exited I-91. The scenic route takes us southeast, just north of Chelsey and Hazelton Peak."

"I forgot how beautiful the area is." For the merest of moments, she caught and held her breath as tears threatened. She loved Vermont. She loved living here. She loved her aunt and her best friend. And Brad.

She swallowed…hard. And worked to rein in her emotions.

Brad glanced at her. "Remember our hikes? We never worked our way to the eastern side of the state."

She nodded. Evidently, the cat caught her tongue. She never understood the saying and giggled at the image floating through her mind.

"What?"

"Nothing." As she watched the scenery whiz by, she rested her forehead against the cool glass. Once, she'd enjoyed being a country girl. She spent years living in the middle of the city, among historic buildings and near Boston Commons and the Charles River. She did love the serenity of wandering the city's green spaces. Upon relocating to Vermont for high school, she breathed easier and experienced freedom for the first time in forever.

Didn't she breathe easier once she arrived *home* in November, and today, heading into the mountains? The evergreens passed in a green blur, and the intense sun danced off the stream's water rushing around frozen rocks—frenzied and peaceful at the same time.

"Nat? You okay?"

"Why are you so drawn to Celia? I can't imagine she likes the country. Has she ever hiked in her life?" She hadn't meant to erupt with jealousy. "You and I, we ran our separate ways because I'm a city girl and you're a country boy."

"You referring to that ridiculous social media photo?"

"Of Celia hanging on you. And you enjoying every second. And yet, you were so put off because I didn't have time to let you know why I left."

"Appearances are deceiving."

"A picture is worth a thousand words."

"Cliché, Nat. You didn't see the whole picture." His hands fisted the steering wheel until his knuckles turned chalky.

"What are you getting at?"

"One photo is a snapshot in time. A photo of the prior thirty seconds or thirty seconds later…you'd know the truth." He inhaled deep breaths.

Brad always stuffed his anger. "Tell me about those thirty seconds."

He turned toward her. His dark gaze tunneled from squinted eyes. He pressed his lips tight.

Both actions, told her a ton. Brad thought she

questioned how much to trust him. She expected an explanation, but she also owed him an apology. "I'm sorry I didn't take time to text you. I worked sixteen-hour days and was beyond stressed. The last thing I needed was to return to work and face Wes."

"Did you?"

The crush of a river stone slammed into her gut. He didn't trust, either. "Yes. I told him in no uncertain terms we were finished. I told him the same before he left Vermont. Now he understands." She shifted to face him. She almost divulged packing her condo. "Then I arrive home to find—" She swatted at an imaginary fly named Celia. "Seems Celia circulates. You. Wes. You, *again*." She steered the conversation to the photo.

"*Never* again. Banishing Celia from my life has been a years-long struggle. Ask Jeff."

"Then explain those thirty seconds."

"You mean the fact she approached me from behind, hung on, and put on her possessive smile, even though I told her to get lost—repeatedly? Words spoken don't come across in a silly, out-of-context photo. Understand?"

Like an arrow, his anger shot through her. She deserved every hurled word.

Trust goes both ways.

"What's your history?" Her voice, low and soft, begged Brad to stuff his anger and speak without reservation. "Why does Celia think she can waltz into your life? Or stay, once you tell her no?"

His sucked-in breath echoed through the truck cab.

"In Jackson Hole, we dated off and on for a few months. Most of the time, I trekked. We saw each other occasionally, in between trips. She thought we were in a relationship. I later learned she tended to latch on to people and not let go until she squeezed them dry."

"What do you mean?"

"Money."

"She wants your money?"

"She heard I invested in GMS. She figured I had money I could spend on her. So here she is, trying once more." He flashed a squinty-eyed scowl. "Do you think I could fall for a woman like her?"

She glanced at Brad, his face a mask of fury. "Concerning Wes? I-I assumed he and Celia were—" She twisted her hands, to grip them so tight her skin paled.

"I told her I'd get a restraining order. Wes probably rebuffed Celia, or she wouldn't have come back."

"Oh, Brad." Her stomach turned. "A…restraining order?" Rasped words caught in her throat. She rolled open the window a few inches, sucking in cold air to stem her nausea. She caught Brad's glance in the reflection on the glass.

"You okay?"

For a moment, she couldn't answer. The thought of a restraining order conjured awful situations she'd helped clients with during her stint at legal aid. "Aren't your actions a bit harsh?"

"Harsh?"

The word dropped to the pit of her stomach in a thud. She jerked her gaze to meet his glare.

"She demolished my bank account, Nat. She used me and left me for another target. And now, she's stalking me again."

Natalie gasped. "She can't—"

"Are you condoning what she's done?"

"O-of course not." She laid a hand on his arm. "I believe you. I trust you, Brad. I meant…" She shook her head. "I'm sorry this happened. I-I…hearing you mention a restraining order shocked me. I didn't understand how badly she treated you."

Shadows painted a dark swath under Brad's eyes. She'd been too tired to notice at the airport. "Will she leave, and let you be?"

"I don't know, Nat. I really don't. I can guarantee, she's here because she has no money. Once she fills her bank account, she'll leave Mistletoe Falls. My bet—she'll head to D.C. to make Wes's life miserable."

"Should I warn him?"

With a back-handed wave, he glanced at her. "He meant something to you once. Yeah, you should warn him."

She nodded. "So how do *we* get rid of her?"

"A one-way ticket to Timbuktu?"

"Is Timbuktu a real place?"

"Yeah. Mali."

"I'll buy the ticket. I have savings. Whatever bars her from your life and Wes's."

"*No.*"

Natalie jumped at his anger.

"Don't give Celia anything."

"But—"

"She's a dog pursuing a meaty bone. You give her anything and she'll return for more."

"You planning on allowing her to get in your way forever? What will you do?" His glare hit her head on.

"I have a restraining order in Colorado. I'll get one here. She comes near me, she lands in jail."

Goose bumps prickled her skin.

Brad's glare arrowed. "She should be in jail. She's hurt a lot of people." His voice softened. "None of us deserved what she did. I hope I've seen the last of her."

Natalie wasn't so sure. Rather than voice negativity, or negate Brad's wishful thinking, she bit her tongue. She tunneled through her purse for her phone to text Wes a warning. He might not have been *the* one. And he might not have understood her love of Vermont. And he might've let Celia occupy his time while Natalie and Brad worked hard. However, the two had each other's back over the last few years. A text wouldn't be enough. Which meant making an uncomfortable phone call.

She plunked her phone into her bag. She'd wait to call once she arrived at the inn and had privacy. Maybe her gesture would smooth issues, so her return to the law firm wouldn't be awkward. She squeezed Brad's forearm and stared out the window.

Silence cloaked the cab's confined space.

Brad navigated the steep, windy roads.

Evergreens and birches and maples their only companions, except for an occasional sighting of a waterfall or a mountainside pond, the trees thinned. The truck crested the rise and started on the downward slope. A wall of azure sky opened ahead. She widened her eyes upon seeing the panorama.

"If you keep your gaze peeled, you'll glimpse Lake Champlain."

Natalie pressed a hand flat against her stomach. "Oh, my gosh, the view is unbelievable."

"See—past the lake? New York and the Adirondack Mountains."

Her breath caught. She couldn't stop staring at the

view almost a hundred miles beyond.

Fifteen minutes later, the truck exited the peace of the mountains and reentered rural Vermont civilization. A tall sign, *Welcome to Bradonville*, greeted the two.

At the bottom of the steep incline, Brad turned into town.

Victorian-style homes, several converted to bed and breakfasts and country inns, lined a wide, picturesque New England street. In a matter of minutes, the two wound through the quaint downtown, passing by restaurants and artsy boutiques until the truck dumped onto Route Seven, headed south. She said very little following *the Celia* conversation.

Brad remained silent. Several miles later, the route took them past the turnoffs for Chelsey and Hazelton Peak. Silence hovered in the vehicle as the miles passed. Brad hung a left to a narrow and bumpy rural road scattered with potholes and frost heaves.

The trip curled through the countryside, past dormant apple orchards, dairy farms, and evergreen forests, to end in the middle of Mistletoe Falls, where the creek ran off the mountains in a spectacular waterfall. The rough waters churned toward Gooseneck Lane, their creek, and the inn.

Home. She returned home. She lowered the window and breathed deep the bracing December air. The calm settled like a hug,

Yes, she *was* home. Now, what would she do concerning her future?

****

Brad lugged Nat's overnight case upstairs and deposited the light-as-a-feather piece by her door. He sucked in a breath to cool his churning gut. A sense of relief settled in his chest. The suitcase represented a symbol Nat hadn't planned on running to D.C. forever.

Not yet.

He'd been a boorish idiot the last few days, taking out his mood on friends. The solace that things between him and Nat would be okay didn't negate the boulder still crushing his chest as he strode toward Jeff's room. With a tight rap on the door, he twisted the knob so hard a blood vessel popped in his forefinger. The damn thing hurt like a bugger. He shook his hand, trying to dispel the sting. Brad barreled into his friend's room.

Jeff whirled in his desk chair, leaving his computer work behind. "Whoa, what the hell is wrong?"

"You should have been the one to fetch Nat."

"What went wrong?"

"Why do you assume—"

Jeff flashed both palms. "Don't start on me, buddy. I know you too well."

Brad plopped himself in the recliner, a new addition to the room, and slouched into the comfort of cool leather. "She's steamed."

"Celia? You set her straight."

Jeff's declaration wasn't a question. "We hashed out the entire episode from Colorado to Vermont."

"And?"

"She gets the picture…now."

"And…" Jeff huffed out the rest of his question as if Brad was thickheaded.

"You're repeating yourself." He anchored his fists against the chair arms, before he was able to reign in his frustration and relax. Truth was, he didn't want to discuss Celia or Nat.

"Dish. Natalie's okay?"

Brad scrubbed a hand through his hair and leaned forward to cradle his neck with his palm.

"Uh-oh. She didn't believe you?"

"She felt sorry for me."

"Why?" Jeff stood and paced the small room.

"More like sympathetic."

Jeff stopped in front of the recliner. "What're you goin' to do?"

Brad shook his head. "Spilling is emasculating."

"Aw come on, man. Women love to sympathize. Empathy is their way of caring."

Brad planted his elbows on his knees and rested his forehead against his palms. He stared at Jeff's feet, planted in front of him, and lifted his head.

Jeff grinned, like he was the wise sage of women and relationships.

"Really? Caring?"

"The ladies eat up this stuff. You're golden, man."

Brad stood. "I can't lose her. Not again. I have to make our relationship work. Even if I truck between here and D.C."

"She might come to her senses and decide Vermont is home."

He paced near Jeff to glance past the field to *their* tree. "She did seem to relax, the closer we got to home."

"If you'd seen her when we approached Boston, you'd know she longed to turn and hightail her pretty little self home to Vermont."

"No looking at my girl." Still, he grinned. "Ya' think she hated to leave?"

"I know."

Suddenly, his heart felt whole again. Brad strode

through the room and opened Jeff's door, then he glanced over his shoulder. "Yeah?"

"Yeah."

He marched toward his truck with renewed energy and determination to find a way to win Nat's heart.

Chapter Twenty-Seven

Natalie rolled and squinted into the darkening shadows. For the barest of seconds, confusion clouded her brain. The faint outline of the fading sun dipped below the cover of the mountain range. A glimmer of light arrowed through her window.

She blinked, rose, and stretched like a cat awakening from cozy slumber by the fire. Lowering her feet to dig her toes in the deep softness of the gray carpet, she rubbed sleep from her eyes. The dim outline of familiar furniture grounded her. Transported from the wide-open space of her D.C. condo, Natalie's familiar Vermont room *hugged* her in comfort. She was no longer in *Kansas*. Maybe coming *home* to Vermont wasn't such a crazy idea.

She scanned the room wall-to-wall. If she stayed, she needed more room. She considered removing the barrier separating hers from the next room to consolidate the two into a small suite, making space for a comfortable couch and a desk. What was she thinking? She couldn't stay. Could she?

Working away the twinges from cramped travel, she yawned. Her stomach rumbled. Red numbers flashed ten minutes past four from her bedside clock. Memories returned of her early morning flight from D.C. to Boston, and the tense ride with Brad. No wonder, she'd slept for hours.

She scrubbed her face and ran a brush through her hair. Time to wander toward the main building and reality.

Scanning her little space once more, she wished hibernation was in the stars. She hated the thought of facing work piled high from her absence. Stepping to the window, she strolled her gaze around the outline of the evergreen she and Brad planted. She traced repeatedly her fingers along the lines on the cold window, mesmerizing her—transporting her to her teen years.

Here in her sanctuary away from her parents' overbearing rule, she matured into the land of grown-ups with responsibilities. Even with Aunt Mary and Uncle Harry right next door, living in the inn's carriage house gave her the special sense of freedom and responsibility of an adult. The two expected her to be part of the inn's crew. Harry and Mary trusted her to get the job done. Despite expectations and mature responsibilities, the ultimate benefit came from unconditional and compassionate love her relatives bestowed on a confused teen.

She glanced at the door leading to the hall and plodded to the bed, not wanting to face the hustle and bustle at dinner hour. Scanning the ceiling, she mustered her energy to pour tired feet into clumpy footwear. Wiggling her toes, the comfort of roomy old boots made her sigh. A far cry from achy toes squeezed into her D.C. *uniform* of tall, tight heels. She donned her coat, hat, scarf, and mittens, overkill for a quick jog to the kitchen door, but she craved warmth.

At the bottom of the stairs, she stopped short. She glanced at the lights beaming from the kitchen, then hooked a right to plod through shin-high snow toward *their* evergreen. Unsure the reason for finally taking a close look, she hauled in a cleansing breath.

The tree's dense, green height rivaled the inn's roofline. In fewer than twenty years, the fast growth astonished her. She lingered under the branches and looked skyward. Removing her glove, she flattened her palm on the furrowed gray bark. Memories had swirled round and round since the day Brad and Jeff dug her Christmas tree. She scraped a palm across the coarse surface, then forced herself to step from memories of a long-ago spring day.

Circling under the outstretched arms of the beautiful, eastern white pine, she felt wrapped in protection from the elements. She scuffed her feet among scattered pinecones and needles atop the brown grass at the base of the trunk, untouched by the snow cover. With her head bent, she circled to the rear of the tree and spotted the perfect pinecone. She crouched to lift what would be a precious ornament fastened with a bright red ribbon to her tree. Twirling the cone, several inches long, she admired the symmetry, before tucking the treasure into her pocket.

As Natalie stood, she locked her gaze on a discolored patch in the bark. In the dusky, dim light, she squinted at the outline of a lopsided, carved heart. She traced a finger across the old scar and leaned to read the initials.

BM + NT

Moments later, reality hit her overloaded brain. An echo of her gasp boomeranged through the quiet of the surrounding forest. Had Brad carved the heart—and when? The two planted together their sapling the spring each graduated from high school. This heart had been carved in the mature tree. She calculated the timing of Brad's recent move to Mistletoe Falls.

For a second time, she lodged her hand against the rough bark. She traced the outline multiple times. A tremble slipped through her fingers. Pulling in the deep, breath-stealing lungful of frosty air, she held the gasp, then she expelled in slow motion, hoping to keep her heart from racing.

She wouldn't cry at what could've been. Too much time passed to undo the damage. Instead, she allowed possibilities for the future to circle through her head. "I love Brad." She backed from the tree and repeated the words. "I love Brad." The first step was to admit she loved this man with all her heart. The one who gave one hundred and ten percent to everything he did and for everyone he loved. The man who was kind and gentle and understanding had sacrificed the career he'd worked on for years to come home for his family and friends. The man who continued to drop everything to share her burdens.

The second step was to believe in her heart and gut that being with Brad was realistic. The carved heart was concrete evidence he'd carried his love for years. Despite the tawdry *proof* of the social media photo an idiot used to scare her off, he proved he cared. More than cared, if she read his silence and hurt when he asked why she hadn't informed him of her trip.

Were she and Brad meant to be, despite the many years apart—city girl—country boy?

How would the two make this relationship work? Staring at the carved heart, she had to try. Standing in the winter quiet, with the faint crackling from frozen tree branches swaying in the slight breeze, being a city girl was the farthest thing from her mind and heart.

She stared at the fields on the downward slope from the inn. Three deer stood in silhouette, their noses burrowed in the snow, as they searched for dinner. The awe of watching the silent, natural flow of winter life squeezed her heart.

Was her job so important she'd miss a chance with Brad to return to an unhappy life? Love, especially a lost love found, trumped aspirations for a career she never wanted. Following her previous footprints, she gazed skyward. The half-moon rose beyond the rooftop. Casting a light shadow, the moonlight battled with the last remnants of sunlight dipping to the west.

Speaking to Heidi to ensure a move to Vermont wasn't a lame-brained idea took on urgency. Natalie stormed through the kitchen door, intent on her mission. Instead, the commotion of activity accosted her.

Heidi shouted orders to her staff—the clamor of pots and pans the background percussion to the chaotic strains of the symphonic kitchen.

What in the world?

She hung her coat on a peg, ditched her boots, stuffed feet into her kitchen-duty sneakers, rolled her sleeves, and strode into the mayhem. Jeremy tossed an apron to land with precision on her shoulder. She washed her hands and waited for orders.

Heidi didn't blink while she plated three entrees and set them under the warming lights before she dinged the bell. "Three-top up." With the deftness of a practiced chef, she grouped five more plates. "Two-top first. Ready with the sirloin and veal special? Next, another three-top."

"Understood, Chef." Jeremy slanted a brow toward Nat. "Grab the container of radicchio slaw and the bowl of endive, already separated."

Natalie hustled from the walk-in with the requested items.

Jeremey shoved a small cookie sheet across the shiny, stainless-steel counter. "One endive leaf filled with two tablespoons of the slaw. Load the tray."

Natalie wouldn't ask questions until later. She worked her way into the flow of the kitchen, to fill two endive leaves.

Jeremy whisked the garnish off the cookie sheet and set one on each plate for the two-top. The next three landed on the waiting set of plates.

Soon she'd filled the cookie sheet with the last of the endive and slaw. "What next?"

"Prep more romaine. Heidi's special Caesar salad is tonight's hit."

"On the job." The din in the kitchen dipped to a dull hum with the two-top and three-top dinners delivered.

"Whoa. Intense rush." Heidi wiped her brow. "We still have a five-top and two deuces who just arrived. I think there are people waiting in the parlor. Dessert orders will roll in soon. We'll be fine now. Thanks for the help."

Natalie removed her apron. "What's going on? We're never busy on Wednesdays."

"Jeff placed an ad on the website and posted flyers at the information kiosk. Ski and eat, ten percent off both. Or enjoy cocktails in the parlor and eat." Heidi grinned.

"Cocktails in the parlor?" Natalie could picture ad

cost dollar signs swirling on the winter winds.

"Yup, he arranged the mini bar."

"Where?" She couldn't imagine where they found space for an impromptu bar.

"Jeff and I found a sweet butler's tea service cart in Burt's Antiques. Mary approved the roving bar expenditure."

Her gaze rocketed toward the kitchen door. "Jeff is serving drinks?"

"Ah, no. Jeff is leading the moonlit, cross-country ski trek."

She didn't ask how skiers could see with a half-moon skittering light through the tree cover.

"Tiki torches."

As usual, Heidi read Natalie's mind.

"Don't worry. Another tiny expenditure but well worth the few extra dollars. Don't you think?"

"Yes. Wait, who's tending bar? Not Mary." Natalie shoved her way through the swinging doors to the full-to-the-brim dining room. In the lobby next to the open pocket doors to the parlor stood Brad, smiling his addictive smile, pouring local wine, and handing goblets to a couple waiting for a table.

Other waiting diners settled on one of the parlor sofas.

She observed him schmoozing customers. He was good. But how in the world did he get roped into helping?

Brad glanced up. A smile crossed his face, then his expression masked. "You get any sleep?"

"Too much. I'll lie awake tonight."

"Once you hit the pillow… You were beat." He lifted the wine bottle. "Heidi's trying new wines from the Finger Lakes region. Want a glass?"

She nodded and pinched her fingers together. "A tad." Maybe wine would settle her nerves. Plus, having a taste would be a good excuse to stay on top of the research as the inn expanded the wine cellar offerings. The last two couples were escorted past her to the dining room.

Brad pressed a half-full glass into her hand.

She sipped. He placed his palm to the small of her back. The warmth of his touch heated her faster than the first sip of wine.

"Everyone's seated. Lobby bar's closed."

He guided her to two chairs obscured by the registration desk. The two sat in peace after the hurried pace of the last hour and sipped. Whispered voices from the office broke the silence. She laid a finger against her lips and beckoned to Brad.

Brad's head bent toward the opening between registration and the office, almost bumping hers.

"So, your plan worked."

Natalie mouthed *Mary*.

"*Our* plan."

Brad mouthed *Mom*.

She exchanged glances with Brad and leaned closer. Any time Mary and Sylvie had a plan, trouble followed. This plan had already happened. She raised an eyebrow.

Brad lifted his shoulders.

What were the two planning?

"You suggested I make sure Jeff was otherwise busy, so Brad would have to make the airport run," Mary said.

Natalie's heart plummeted to her tummy. She

locked her gaze with Brad's.

"And our plan worked." Mary's voice rose a note. "The two were in the same car for hours. I'm sure there was conversation."

Natalie bet the two each sported evil-villain grins.

"How do we know?" Sylvie asked. "I haven't seen Natalie since Brad dropped her off."

"She headed straight to bed. Why do you think I asked Brad to tend bar tonight? To keep him underfoot."

Natalie glanced at Brad.

Brad raised a brow, shook his head, and placed his warm finger against her lips. He leaned to mouth, *snickerdoodlers busted.*

Her gut hit bottom. Of course, the two orchestrated Brad's *chauffeur service*.

"Good thinking," Sylvie said. "We have to do everything in our power to throw them together."

Natalie stood and walked toward the office to confront the meddling *twins*.

Brad followed. In seconds, he clutched her arm and flashed a palm. "Wait. We haven't discovered the latest scheme."

The two hovered in the hallway.

"Well, at least I hope the photo lit a fire." Mary laughed in a high-pitched trill.

Natalie glared at Brad.

He shrugged.

"The two had time on the ride to resolve the Celia factor," Sylvie said. "She has made Brad miserable for years. Let's hope putting the photo on social media convinced Brad and Natalie to devise a plan against the ghastly woman."

Brad's scowl hit Natalie straight on. She opened her mouth. Brad's palm cupped her mouth.

In tandem, the two stepped closer to the office.

"And talk through their love for each other," Mary said. "They *are* in love, I'm sure."

"They are," Sylvie's voice mellowed.

"I've heard enough." Natalie straightened and raced toward the office.

Brad shadowed her.

The two wedged together in the doorway.

The guilty parties gawped like bulging-eyed fish skewered by a hook. Each slapped a hand against her own mouth like mischievous, and very guilty, twins.

She would have laughed at the cartoonish scene, if she wasn't furious. The two had gone too far. "How dare you. Frivolous matchmaking attempts are one thing, but plastering Brad's business on social media is unacceptable."

Brad elbowed past her to step into the office. "You don't need to defend me."

"Fine. Go for the gold." Natalie crossed her arms and glared at the two scoundrels. "But understand nothing has changed. Brad and I separated for a reason."

Brad spun on his heel, crowded next to her, and stared. "Really?"

Chapter Twenty-Eight

The pain from Nat's words speared his heart. Brad, his mouth close to her ear, repeated the word in a whisper. "Really?"

The two had been through a ton the last six weeks. Following the conversation in the car, he believed things were settled. His rant didn't help. Still, calling her out was necessary and, full disclosure, eased through his soul like a salve to his crushed heart. She'd been hot and cold since her arrival. He thought he and Nat had moved beyond the insecurity caused by the past.

Nat edged toward the door. She glanced at the co-conspirators, then she glared at him. "I can't stay here."

She curled her hand around the door frame in a tight fist, as if she could keep the wall and her world from crumbling. Her whisper, much softer than his, spoke of hurt and the return of mistrust plaguing the two over the last weeks.

She speared Mary and Sylvie with a glare.

When she hiccupped, the sound sent a wave of sadness and anger through him. His Nat didn't cry. She held her emotions close.

"I ignored…a-attempts at m-matchmaking. But this…this…scheme went too far."

Sobs sliced her voice. Brad wanted to pull her into his arms, despite her claim their long-ago breakup would never be resolved. He and Nat *had* moved past the pain. Who could blame Nat for not thinking clearly? Hearing her gasp for breath shredded his gut.

"You had no right to meddle. *Not* on—"

The catch in her voice sent a shot of hurt straight to his heart. He circled his arm around her waist.

She stepped away. "—Social media." Her voice hitched on the inhale. "The whole world knows our business. Consider what you've done. How can your public scheme be good for business—the inn or GMS?" She skirted past the door jamb. "Tomorrow morning, I'm going *home*."

Deathly low, her voice caught on her final word. *Home*. How could he convince Nat she *was* home? "This discussion isn't finished." Brad glared at the two *culprits*, before he followed her from the office to the lobby. "Nat. Wait." A cloying gardenia scent hit him head on.

"Yoo-hoo, Brad. Darling. There you are."

Can my day get any worse? "Celia. Out! Leave the premises. Now."

Nat disappeared through the dining room. The kitchen doors swung wildly in her wake.

Brad followed. Celia clutched his arm. He shook her off. "Unless you want me to call the sheriff, get off the property *and* leave this town."

"Oh, dear Brad, you wound me. I was so sure we had—"

"Nothing. Celia, go." He didn't wait. He had to catch Nat. On a mission of dire consequence, he shoved open the kitchen door.

Heidi's hand wound 'round his forearm, her protective-friend mode masking her face.

"Not yet. Give her time."

"We don't have time. She's leaving. Tomorrow."

"Brad. Stop. I'll talk to her tonight. Give her time. She's exhausted and stressed. But you better be here first thing in the morning with a good reason why she should stay." The corners of her mouth turned down, and she sighed. She threw a soft punch at his bicep. "You hear me?"

He scrubbed a hand through his hair. "I hear you. But what the hell should I do?"

Heidi's grip loosened, and she patted his arm. "You'll figure out everything. Whatever you do, you better go big. Grand."

Grand?

He had no clue what Nat would think was grand. He stalked through the door, on a mission to protect their love.

****

The pain of disappointing her niece constricted Mary's chest. Still, she held her head high and padded across the antiquated runner in her slippers. She'd allowed an hour to grind by. She leaned her ear to the door and heard sobs. Biting her lip, she tapped on Natalie's door.

This was her fault. If she and Sylvie hadn't interfered, both Natalie and Brad would be speaking. But the two thought the right thing was to bring these two kids together, Still, well-meaning didn't excuse embarrassing Brad. She straightened and put full force behind her knock. The sobbing turned to hiccups.

"G-go."

"Natalie, dear, please open."

"I can't t-talk."

Mary turned the knob and pushed open the door. She strode in, like the adult she was supposed to be, taking care of a niece in pain. "Well, I need to talk." One hand gripped the other.

Natalie sniffed, clutching a wad of tissues in her fist.

She leveled a look that reminded Mary of Natalie's teenage years, when she had been the only mother figure for her niece. She strode to the bed and settled beside her little girl—now a full-grown woman who deserved to be irate. She patted Natalie's knee. "I'm so sorry. We—Sylvie and I—didn't realize what harm this would do. We wanted so badly to see you and Brad resolve your differences and realize you loved and belonged with each other. Can you ever forgive me—us?"

Natalie glanced toward the window.

The darkness beyond, shrouding the forest, mirrored back the image of her darling niece's grief and anger. "Honey, you don't have to forgive me. Please, I need you to gather your courage and face the fact you and Brad love each other, need each other, and belong together. Don't let your anger obscure what really matters." She patted her niece's knee and kissed her cheek, then she stood to leave her niece to grieve.

Mary exhaled a long breath. She prayed Natalie would come to her senses concerning Brad, even if she never forgave Mary for causing her pain.

****

A sharp knock reverberated, sending another jolt of pain straight through Natalie. Now who invaded her privacy?

"Open up. Now."

Willing her friend to get lost never worked. When Heidi was on task, she didn't care if she woke the entire inn. She wanted nothing more than to shut out Heidi. She buried her head under her pillow.

Heidi continued to pound.

Swiping tear tracks from her cheeks, she padded to the door and released the lock. Heidi shoved open the door. Natalie jumped to the side.

"What's going on?"

Uh-oh, Heidi had her hands plastered to her hips. This could be a long night. "Nothing." Her voice hitched. No way could she hide her red-rimmed eyes or the hiccups.

"Brad said you're leaving. You call running nothing? Dish."

"I'm not *running*. I'm going home where I belong."

Heidi stood, legs planted wide and arms crossed.

Her stance mimicked the one she used following a Keegan ambush of the cookie jar. Natalie giggled. "Your poor kid." Soon her giggles mutated into hysteria. Sob after sob racked her body. Her chest throbbed. She fought to stifle her snivels.

Heidi's arm encircled her shoulder and guided her toward the bed. "What happened? We'll find a solution."

"There-there-there—is no solution." She held her breath to the count of ten. "I can't stay here. Celia has her clutches into Brad—"

"Don't even go there. Don't you dare blame Brad."

"I-I saw her."

"You didn't see Brad kick her to the curb and tell her never to return. He told me to call Sheriff Evans."

"H-he did?" She straightened. Her friend was a straight-shooter. A sparkle of hope bubbled.

"He did." Heidi held both her hands.

"Still, I can't stay.

"Really? You're blaming this on Celia?" Heidi narrowed her gaze, until her eyes were barely slits. She dropped Natalie's hands.

"No. No! I know what Celia did to Brad. This is about— Th-this isn't home." Her stomach knotted. She was so tired of feeling alone, even during her relationship with Wes. She'd finally reconnected with Brad, and…

"Aww, honey. Vermont and the inn will continue to be your home. This is where your heart has been since we first met at summer camp. Remember?"

She nodded and snatched a handful of tissues from the box Heidi held out.

"You were happiest here. You, me, and Brad—the three musketeers."

"I don't want to talk about Brad."

A puckered line formed between Heidi's brows. "Isn't Brad the reason for your meltdown?"

"No. Yes." She pressed her fingers to her eyes, hoping to stem the steady flow of tears. She hadn't stopped crying since she took the stairs two at a time.

"What is this really about?"

Heidi's voice was as gentle as a mother cajoling her child out of a tantrum. Not a normal Heidi tone. For a split-second, Natalie dropped her shoulders a fraction of an inch. "I've spent my entire life trying to please my dad. Doing what he wanted of me. Never what I wanted for myself. Now Mary—"

"Mary what? You can't compare a bit of

matchmaking to what your dad did."

"Don't you see? S-she—and Sylvie—are trying to manipulate the d-direction m-my life—and Brad's—should take." She sniffed and blew her nose.

Heidi winged a glance toward the ceiling. "Mary and Sylvie, in a convoluted way, are only getting you two to see what you had with each other—what, deep down, you know."

"What if Brad and I don't work?" Rather than see Heidi's you've-got-to-be-kidding-me expression, she dropped back to rest on the bed and stare at the chips of paint curling off the ceiling. She really should repaint this room. And Mary's, too.

"You love him. He loves you."

Natalie hoisted herself to half-sitting, resting on her elbows planted against the mattress. She swiped at her eyes with the wadded tissue. "I l-love him."

"A bad thing?"

She shook her head, then nodded. "It's the worst th-thing."

"Ah, o-o-kay?" Heidi crossed to the mini-fridge and snatched the half-empty wine bottle. She popped the cork and handed Natalie the bottle.

"I don't need wine." She sat, reached for the fisted pile of tissues crumpled on the quilt, and dabbed her eyes, before she sucked in a deep breath. *No more tears.*

"Yeah, you do."

Knowing better than arguing with Heidi, she gripped and tipped the bottle. The slug of wine slipped warm into her belly, cooling her temper and heartache. The strawberry, clove, and chocolate undertones gave her a cozy, loved feeling. She took another sip and sucked in a breath. "I'm so—so angry." Hoping to revive the snug sensation that disappeared when she voiced angry words, she slugged another swallow.

"Angry? At Brad?"

"No. Yes. No. Mary and Sylvie. I can't help feeling betrayed."

Heidi retrieved the bottle and poured each a juice glass full. "Then why are you venting your wrath on Brad?"

"I-I'm not. I can't do— I—we can't go back." The tears overflowed to slip over her cheeks and drip from her chin. She finally admitted she still loved Brad, and now the whole relationship was ruined. She plucked another tissue from the box, dabbed her cheeks, and swiped at her nose.

Heidi leaned against the wall. "What in the world did the Bobbsey twins do?"

"Social media."

"*Nah.*" Heidi's gaze widened. "Those two—*they* posted Brad and Celia?"

"Yup." She gulped half the glass of wine. "Brad explained. A-about Celia. And I *do* believe him. Did—Until she str-strode through the door."

"Did you not hear what I just said? She's gone. For-ev-ah."

"Beside the point—he and I are *not* compatible."

"How?" Heidi snorted the question, one hand anchored against her hip. "You seriously believe that? You're scared. Your parents have so engrained in you that to succeed you have to follow their direction—big city, law, prominent spouse—that you can't even recognize who you really are. That's not you—never has been."

"Oh, come on, Heidi. Brad lives—*lives*—for the outdoors and the country. I'm a city girl, born and raised."

"Uh-huh. Did you not listen to what I said? You having nothing in common with Brad is why you spent every summer in Vermont and refused to go home to Boston your senior year?"

"Nothing to do with the city. Everything to do with getting away from my parents." She waved a hand.

Heidi darted forward to grab Natalie's glass, before the last few drops of wine splattered on the carpet. "And Brad? You told me you love him. Tell me the reasons."

"Ah, reasons?" To stem more threatening tears, she sucked in a breath. "H-h-he'd do anything for anyone. He's smart and considerate and lo-loves his mom."

Heidi rocked on her heels and laughed.

"W-what's so funny" She swatted the air with a hand. "Any guy who loves his mom and t-takes care of her—a good thing. Right?"

"Right."

"A-all I'm saying—if he loves his mom, h-he'll be good to his wife and kids." She straightened and sucked in a deep breath. "And, he makes me laugh. He knows how to have fun." She couldn't stop her motor-mouth litany. "He understands if I'm stressed or have to work or… You know. The world doesn't revolve only in his orbit."

"Like Wes?"

"Yeah, like Wes." She extended an arm. "Give me my wine glass."

Heidi lifted the wine bottle and poured an inch. She proffered the glass.

"More."

"Honey, you might want to hit the brakes."

"More."

Heidi added another inch. "I'm shutting you off."

She breathed in the calming aroma, before she took a lady-like sip, leaned on one palm, and released a long sigh. "Brad is polar opposite in the best of ways. Even though he's driven by work, he's also motivated by play and helping others and seeing both sides o-of…everything."

Heidi crossed one arm and propped her chin on her other fist. "And those are the reasons you're not compatible?"

"I-ah."

"You see. Brad balances you out. You've had a chance to revisit your relationship. Sure, you've both changed, matured, experienced life…"

She sucked in a deep breath to steady her nerves and quiet her ramblings. Instead, her insecurities roared back. "W-what if my feelings for Brad are memories? Nostalgia? Wanting to return to simpler times when relationships and love were…well, simple. You told me. We've both changed. Cupid's arrow doesn't strike twice in the same place."

"Are you kidding me?" She landed her palms against her hips. "Cupid is your rationale? *Cupid*?"

"You're repeating yourself." Natalie stood and paced. "You know what I mean. How can you fall in love with the same guy…twice?"

"Try *still*? Admit you've never fallen from love."

"Y-yes, I have. Wes…and before—" She flipped a hand toward Heidi, like she could conjure numerous names of great loves.

"Wes?" Heidi shook her head, then flashed her I'm-on-to-you glare. "You two were never in love. You had things in common. You were friends. You *never* loved him."

"I-ah, true."

"You can't even name another, because you never loved any of those guys. From what you told me, I'm not sure you even liked most of them. And except Wes, you never dated any others for long."

"I liked them. I liked Wes, most of the time. His advice helped me advance my career—"

"Of which great loves are made."

Natalie stuck out her tongue. "Quiet. He introduced me to the right people. He considered us a power couple—me on my way to being the senior administrator for the senior partner, and Wes on his way to a partnership. I know I ended things in a snit—"

"He deserved that."

Natalie brushed off Heidi's critique of Wes. "He was good for me."

"Was! But you never loved him."

"My warning him regarding Celia means we can still work together without animosity—and maybe friends."

"Working together and loving someone are different. With Brad, you have both."

"But Brad—"

"No *but Brad*. No telling me you two are different. Consider what you've done—*together*—these last weeks. You organized an event, kept a full inn running despite nature's wrench, and created numerous business opportunities. Together you are an in-sync and powerful machine. Plus, in all you do, you help others, too."

"We did work well together, but being in sync on a project isn't a basis for love. We argue. Have different ideas—"

"You compromised and worked together to elevate two businesses. What do you think building a relationship means?" Heidi stepped forward. "Give and take. Brad loves you. He's proud of you. He's concerned and stands up for you. He's loved you forever. Believe me."

"I-I…" Natalie sank into the easy chair near the window. She hung her head and stared at her palms cradling the wine glass. "Even if he did love me once, I blew the whole thing."

Heidi heaved a huge sigh.

Natalie glared and prayed Heidi would leave her alone.

"Believe what you want, but be honest with yourself. Why do *you* love Brad?"

She held her breath. Another hiccup caught her off-guard. "I-I do love him."

"And…?"

"He's self-sacrificing. He's helped me and Mary with the inn every step of the way. He feeds me and brings me my favorite fudge a-and takes me skating. He holds my hand and dances and builds fires to keep me warm." She laughed, a bit high-pitched and edgy. The realization hit her smack-dab in the center of her thick skull. She did love him, but… The epiphany made their last encounter hurt more. She might love Brad, and he her, but a long-distance relationship had a snowball's chance of surviving beyond the spring thaw.

"Go on." Heidi patted her knee. "You can make a

relationship work, even long-distance."

Now she was a freakin' mind reader?

"Repeat the mantra, loudly. I love Brad, and I'll make our relationship work. Believe in what you two have. Then work to make everything right."

"I've made a mess of things, haven't I? He's never stopped loving me, Heidi. Have you seen the tree in the field? He could have severed the event partnership the second he set eyes on me—his unexpected partner. Instead, he's been kind and supportive. O-okay, the beginning was a bit rough. B-But since, he's shown his love in every way imaginable."

"And you've done the same for him—believed in his ability and ideas. You've supported him, helped him with social media, technology, and promo."

"B-But, is this enough to make *us* work—two people who had grown apart and now lead different lives?"

"Only you can answer. You've rebuilt a relationship. Isn't making an effort to explore all options worth any sacrifice?" Heidi looked down her nose and shook her head.

"I-I've taken everything that's happened out on Brad. Even Celia… And the matchmaking. Brad's as much a victim."

"Life threw you curveballs. But Brad's one of the *white-hat* kind of guys. Now you have a chance to make the right choice."

She nodded.

Heidi patted her knee. "I'm headed to bed. I *will* see you bright and early. Promise me you'll at least hang in here a few days. Escaping wouldn't be fair to Mary or the rest of us." Heidi slammed the door on her parting shot.

Natalie jumped. She stood, poured herself more wine, and set the glass on the side table. Too agitated to sleep, she set her suitcase on the bed and began to pack. Heidi's last words were her way of imparting tough love.

Yes, she loved Brad. Nonetheless, she couldn't convince herself blind love was enough to make a relationship work. Not when the two lived in different worlds, separated by hundreds of miles.

She pulled open her bureau drawer and gathered a handful of blouses. She placed them in the suitcase. For a change, Natalie would do what was best for her. Not what everyone expected.

Not anymore.

Chapter Twenty-Nine

Brad stopped in the kitchen on his way to the carriage house. He blinked at the bright fluorescents.

"You okay?" Heidi asked.

"Yeah. Armed and ready to take my best shot at winning the love of my life." He refused to mention his roiling stomach…or the fear squeezing his heart.

"It's six a.m. Natalie's light was still on at two. Armor yourself with coffee and a scone and chill. You wake her, your goose is cooked."

"What kind of scone?"

Heidi rounded behind the counter. "You being picky on me, Matthews?"

He linked his fingers together and stretched, palms out. "Want to know my options."

Heidi lifted a plate from under the prep counter. "One of each. Smoked Gouda and dill. Bacon and cheddar." She plucked each mini-scone with tongs. "Blackberry and thyme. Chocolate and dark cherry. Satisfied?"

He grabbed the plate. "Not until I snag a cup. Short night." At the espresso machine, he prepped a triple. He'd gift one to Nat in a while. Part of his winning-her-back strategy.

"What's the plan?"

"I'm not jinxing by telling you."

"Fair enough." Heidi grinned. "You got this."

Brad sipped coffee and peeled off chunks of scone. Anything to pass time. Finishing too fast, he stowed his dishes on the dishwasher rack and turned to Heidi. "I'll clear off last night's dusting."

"Give her another half hour." Heidi checked the wall clock. "Go get her. Half. An. Hour. Hear me?"

Brad flashed a thumbs-up. Once the doors swung shut behind him, he stooped and groaned. Wolfing four scones, while nervous as a man facing a mother black bear protecting her cubs, was suicide on his gut.

Sucking in deep breaths to quell his stomachache, he straightened and ambled through the lobby. At most, the chore to sweep the steps and front walk would take ten minutes. First, he'd set the fireplace logs. He stepped into the parlor. In less than two months, the sitting room held so many memories. The first night, he and Nat wanted to get on with business. Instead, the two ate a romantic, albeit tense, dinner, while Mary, the matchmaker, disappeared.

He stared at the fireplace. A shiver slipped the length of his spine, as if the ghost of Nat past haunted him—a warning he better nail this grand gesture.

Visions of the sweet, but tender dance in front of the fire played in living color. And last night as the two enjoyed a drink together, the intimacy returned, right before overhearing the plot-obsessed *twins*.

Now his mission was to hit the ball out of the park.

If he had to travel to D.C. every few weeks to spend time with Nat, he'd figure a way to make their relationship work. He finished removing the pile of ashes from each of three fireplaces and stacked logs. He could wait no longer. Once he swept away the snow, he stowed the push broom and jogged through the inn. He stopped to pour a large travel mug of coffee, slapped on the lid, and continued his jog through the kitchen.

"It's been twenty minutes, not thirty, Matthews." Heidi's holler echoed.

He allowed the back door to slam. Out of patience, he took the carriage house stairs two at a time. At the top, he drew in a deep gulp of air. Digging for calm, he strode the runner like he owned the place. At her door, he tapped twice, listened, and tapped again. The faint patter of footsteps neared the door. Slippers? Was she still in her pajamas?

The door swung open. Her eyes rounded and mouth formed a perfect *O*, before she yanked her robe tight. Her hair, much longer since her arrival, tumbled over her forehead, disheveled and beautiful. He ordered his hand glued to his side, rather than to brush the wisps stuck to her pinkened cheek. The other clutched his coffee offering.

"What are you doing here?" Her words were resigned and filled with defeat.

"We need to talk."

"I can't take any more." She stared at the floor and shook her head.

"I'll talk." His gesture had to work. He couldn't let her run. *Stick to the plan.* He shuffled his boot tip toward the edge of the runner. "Can I come in? I, ah, bear coffee."

She stepped aside.

Sliding through the doorway before she changed her mind, he stopped where she stood planted, so close her sweet vanilla-mint scent accosted him. He wanted more than anything to haul her into his arms and absorb her sleepy, just-out-of-bed warmth. Instead, he skirted past her. He caught sight of her bed where her filled suitcase lay open.

His heart rate tripled. She planned to leave. With a glued-on smile, he handed her the mug.

She sipped.

Her sigh slipped straight through him. He imagined her exhalation was over leaving him.

"Why don't we sit?" She beckoned him toward the recliner. She perched on the edge of her bed, her spine ramrod straight.

He ignored the chair, instead slipping a square gold box from his pocket. "This got a little beat up." Thrusting the tiny package, he prayed she would accept his gesture.

She widened her eyes and reached for the box, cradling the small offering to her chest.

"Open. Please. I'll explain."

Setting her coffee on the floor, she peeled the tape off one end of the tattered three-by-three-inch box in slow motion.

Excruciating. Brad held his breath.

She flipped the box and started to peel the tape on the other end, using the same tortoise-like pace.

Her methodical nature made him crazy.

After an eon, she removed the lid, lifted the tissue paper, and raised a silver charm bracelet. She smoothed a finger over the first charm sporting two numbers.

For a moment, Brad was jealous of jewelry.

"From the year we graduated." She glanced at him, then spun the bracelet. She touched the next charm. "An artist's palette?"

"I bought the bracelet and three charms for your graduation present. I never had a chance to give…" He swallowed the anger and hurt.

"When you didn't show at college sophomore year…" Her breath caught.

Pain sparked through every nerve. "When I didn't register for a year off between high school and college, I lost my scholarship."

"I abandoned my dream the same year." Tears pooled on her lower lid. "I did what my father wanted; my mother, too. Law—*carry on the family legacy*."

He sat beside her, the bed dipping under his weight. He planted a hand between them so he didn't crowd her, while all he wanted to do was draw her into his arms and hold her…forever. "You've proven how good your creativity is these last few weeks."

She huffed.

"Your promotional materials, for one. The decorative changes to the dining room. Your aunt still hangs your paintings and photos. One day, I hope you return to what you love. What we planned long ago."

"I wanted to call you. I wanted to know what happened."

"Why didn't you?" He'd ached to ask but never dared to rock the boat on their new-found closeness.

"My parents disconnected my cell and made sure there was no long-distance connection from hotel rooms."

Brad wanted to punch something—wanted to punch her father. He sucked in a retort and released the slow hiss of pent-up air. Violence never solved anything. One reason he escaped to the peace of the wilderness. A place he could commune with his reflections and not have to deal with many people…or his anger.

She balanced the third bauble on the tip of her finger, the anniversary charm depicting the inn in 1890. She stroked the fourth charm and laughed.

The musical sound of her open and throaty amusement danced through him. The last time he witnessed her full-out laugh had been in school. "I couldn't resist the newest one. The cow." He reached for the fifth charm, his fingers brushing hers. A spark tingled through his arm. He dropped his hand, leaving the long, slender pinecone resting on her fingertip. The crafted silver was an exact replica to the eastern white pine shape.

A glimmer of unshed tears shone in her eyes. She glanced toward the window.

Brad's gaze followed her sightline, landing on the pinecone hanging by a bright red ribbon from the potted tree, and just beyond, to the tall white pine silhouetted in the window. "Our tree."

"Our tree." She echoed, a slight shudder in each soft-spoken word. "You carved our initials. When?"

"You found them?" He snapped his gaze to meet hers.

"The other day. When?" She leaned and bumped his shoulder.

He couldn't ignore her question a third time. "The day we buried my father, three years ago."

"Why?"

"I hated myself for never speaking again to my father. I moved because of you. Once I came home, I realized I never stopped loving you—would always wonder why. For some strange reason, carving those initials gave me hope and strength to remember what we had." He touched the back of her hand, the one fingering the pinecone.

She leaned her head on his shoulder, holding the silver chain and watching the charms twirl.

"Those last two were to be your Christmas present. I couldn't chance you running before…." He pointed toward the cone, then dropped his hand to his lap before he swooped her into his arms and ruined the magical moment. "The bracelet was stashed in the attic among my football trophies and debate club certificates."

"I-It's beautiful. I can't believe you were so with-the-picture in high school."

"I loved you, Nat. I wanted to show you how much. I still love you."

A tear slipped over her cheek. A torrent followed.

She wrapped her arms around his neck in a hug rivaling a grizzly's. He held her tight, absorbing her scent and heat, and prayed she would want to work on a long-distance relationship. "I'll do anything, Nat. I'll come to D.C. often. Whatever makes you happy."

"I-I didn't mean to jump you." She stood and moved a few steps.

He followed, catching her hand.

"Brad, I need to think."

"First, may I ask a question?" He caught her other hand and drew her close. "Will you stay through New Year's Eve?"

She backed away.

His heart seemed to plummet toward his toes.

"I can't think while you're so close." A smile twitched at the corners of her mouth. "I'll stay if…"

"Anything." He straightened. The tap-dancing nerves morphed into a slow, sensual waltz.

"You convince Mary and Sylvie to nix the

matchmaking."

He scrubbed a palm across his chest. "I'll do my best. Neither is easy to corral."

"Your best is what I ask." She patted his chest.

The simple gesture slammed him. Her sweet grin was enough to make him believe in the fairytale.

"I have to unpack."

He hauled her in for a quick kiss. "Later." He strode to the door.

"Brad."

The hitch in her breath had him whirling 'round to face her.

"I love you, too. Never stopped."

He took three giant steps and pulled her to him. Her palms spread against his chest—a cushion between them. He lifted her chin. "Music to my ears." He leaned in and kissed her, long, slow, and full of the pent-up love he'd carried for years. She returned his kiss, at first gentle and sweet, then hot and all-consuming, He never wanted the kiss to end.

Her palm shoved against his chest. "Go." The smile eased from the slight lift of her lip to encompass her face.

His heart filled with hope. Now, to keep Mary and his mom in line.

****

Once the door closed, Natalie called her realtor, followed by a call to her boss. Her heartbeat boomed like a bass drum. She had more to do than unpack. She had a life to rearrange. *Hers.*

Chapter Thirty

The last guests descended on the inn the day before Christmas.

Today's the day!

Natalie chewed the tip of her pinkie nail. A muscular arm slung across her shoulder, keeping her grounded—sort of—if she ignored the kaleidoscope of butterflies flitting through her tummy.

"Hey, look at me."

Brad's soft growl signaled he was her partner. His presence evoked courage. She gazed into eyes she'd never stopped dreaming about.

"We've got the week covered. Every *I* dotted and every *T* crossed."

His company infused her with strength, as his presence had since the first day they met as kids. "I can't help the nerves. Cross your fingers the weather cooperates."

Brad's X'd fingers appeared. "Ten-day forecast promises weather will cooperate."

She twirled in his arms. "I'll have to trust you *and* the weatherman."

He squeezed her biceps, as the last guest stepped into the lobby. Warmth radiated from her heart to her belly to zip through shaky legs. Together—yes, all they'd planned would work.

Jeff followed, hauling the newest check-in's

suitcases.

"Good thing we hired a *bellhop*," she whispered in Brad's ear, before turning. "A pleasure to meet you, Mr. Gunderson." Once she registered the newest addition, she reminded him to attend the upcoming orientation in the parlor.

Brad hoisted suitcases and showed him to his room.

The morning ran like a finely tuned machine. The welcome and buffet lunch were followed by a van ride to Mistletoe Falls. In early evening, the group gathered downstairs for cocktails and a Christmas Eve, New England-style buffet. Luscious scents wafted through the inn. Thanks to the great kitchen staff, the guests were wowed by lobster stew, clam cakes, baked ham, individual Vermont Cheddar soufflés, a variety of local bakery breads, and farm-to-table vegetable dishes.

That night, Natalie snuggled in her bed. Tired to the bone in the best of ways, weight of worry dissipated after weeks of concentrated preparation. She slept soundly for the first time in months—no, years.

The next day, the inn's staff welcomed guests to a sumptuous Christmas morning brunch. In early November, Natalie would never have guessed this crazy idea would succeed. The teamwork and renewed spirit, a bonus, enveloped all who toiled tirelessly to ensure a bright future for the inn.

Leaning against the threshold, holding the gift-filled box, she watched the guests enjoy breakfast. The front door shut with a soft snick. She turned. "Brad," she whispered. "Come help."

Striding through the lobby, Brad reached her side, grinned, and took control of the box.

His scent and warmth swirled, disarming her. "T-thanks." In a flash, realization hit that in nine days, she headed to D.C. She clenched her jaw at the thought.

Brad nudged his shoulder against hers.

Her tension dissipated. She removed a mini-stocking filled with local vendor coupons and a small, flat box, a complimentary present for each guest. Natalie found the long-ago commissioned etching of the inn among boxes and had postcard-sized prints made and framed. Moving forward, she would print the drawing on note cards and sell both at the front desk. By next year, use of the etching for an inn calendar cover would include promo photos for each month. Full of ideas, the future possibilities excited her.

"Everything looks great," Brad whispered.

His breath tickled her ear. She shivered, then focused on distributing presents to smiling guests.

He trailed, handling the box and issuing hearty Merry Christmas's.

Following brunch, everyone gathered on the wide porch for their first ski lesson. The day was vivid blue, and the air crisp.

Brad and Jeff answered a myriad of questions and demonstrated techniques.

Natalie sat on the wooden swing, adorned with new holiday pillows. She gazed at the guests skiing the front fields. She was so proud. A slight pang burrowed into her stomach. Soon, she headed to D.C. She'd not yet told Brad her plans. Even so, she would miss him during the next month, until…

She shook off the twinge of sadness shrouding the idyllic day. Today was Christmas. Tonight, Heidi would present a Vermont-style, holiday meal fit for kings and queens and other royal guests. They'd dine on grass-fed rib roast, wild brook trout, and other local delicacies. Rather than obsess over impending life changes, she concentrated on the moment.

Natalie shaded her eyes against the glare of sun off the pristine snow. The scene of guests enjoying themselves was idyllic. With assurance all ran smoothly, she headed to her room for much-needed space. Stepping aside for an hour to take care of herself resembled riding a weightless balloon. She could get used to this new outlook on life.

The next days flew, with activities going smoothly. Fingers crossed, this was a good omen for moving forward. She left nothing to chance, ensuing the crazy Thanksgiving weekend.

Now, midweek, the group headed to the arena for the final hockey tournament match between Mistletoe Falls' and Chelsey's varsity teams. The game conjured memories of Brad as goalie. He'd been a star, of course.

The crew of guests whooped and hollered like they rooted for their own high schools. Players from both teams joined the party after the game. The silver foxes were enchanted with the young folks.

The next day, Jeff and Walter drove the van caravan to Chelsey.

"We need alone time." Brad held open his truck's passenger door.

She shivered, knowing being alone with Brad would cost her. Excitement slipped through her like the warm, tasty slide of a gulp of cinnamon- and cayenne-laced, hot chocolate. So much changed between the two, the time had come to discuss next steps. Could she keep her secret for a few more days?

"We have reservations at Gray's Tavern."

"Brad—" She swept her hand the length of her body. "I'm not dressed for a fancy restaurant."

He tossed a side glance. "Lunchtime in Vermont. Christmas week. Nothing is dressy. You're...*we're* fine."

She picked up on his wordplay. "It'll be nice—just the two of us."

Brad pulled into a parking spot, jogged to the front, and issued his hand to help her exit.

"These two months have been intense having to be *on* twenty-four seven."

Brad shrugged. "It's the name of the game. Soon, we can reset."

The two climbed the three steps to the front door.

"The event is going well?" A tiny niggle of insecurity perched on her shoulder.

"Like clockwork. You're built for event planning, Nat. I couldn't have done this without you."

"You constantly plan trips."

"Those are easy." He squeezed her hand, as the two followed a server to a table beside the windows.

After ordering local brews to toast the week, she saluted him with her glass. "Easy?"

"What?"

"You call planning treks easy?"

"Well, yeah. Departure point. Destination. Map and stopping points between the two, staffing, and a packing and menu list. Fill in the blanks under each category. Cut and dried. You've juggled spreadsheets with a dozen events in different locations." He grasped both her hands. "This event was a full-time job on top of the inn and your D.C. job."

She appreciated his awareness and worry—neither of which Wes displayed...*ever*. Genuine and altruistic consideration of others was why she knew Brad was her one and only. "These last two months have been crazy. I can't believe my time is almost up."

His grip on her hand tightened. "I hate to see you leave. I wish..." He let go.

The absence of his warmth arrowed an icy shiver through her. This meal could be their last alone-time including New Year's Eve.

****

At the early evening cocktail and heavy hors d'oeuvre gathering New Year's Eve with the inn packed with mingling guests, Brad stood in the threshold of the front door and scanned for Nat. The group's chatter attested to the week-long bonding. A few singles paired up—a development he'd never considered. *Awesome*.

If only he and Nat could be a permanent couple.

His heart pounded so hard he feared the organ would explode. His dream of settling in this town, fitting in, happy and prosperous enough to build a family, rocketed into reach. Could he convince Nat Vermont was her destiny? Or would he tackle living in a big city?

He heard her signature laughter, low and mellow, before he spotted Nat talking to Frank and Walter by the fireplace.

Ted Gunderson sauntered toward her and draped his arm over her shoulder. She smiled at their new friend.

Mary Beth, another one of the singles, strolled over and placed her hand in Ted's.

Brad suspected both guests were sure to make another visit to the inn. He'd bet the two would arrive together. Hopefully, the guests would inform friends of next year's holiday event, already in the planning stages. Finally in sync, after the first few weeks of tension, he and Nat planned what he once believed would be a colossal failure.

Walter gestured wide.

Nat laughed.

He loved seeing her big smile. Usually so reserved, she'd emerged from her shell.

Turning, she spotted him, grinned, and waved.

Afraid he'd ruin his surprise if he locked gazes with hers, he returned her wave. He twisted to speak to the two ladies who registered from the same town. The two had become fast friends.

Soon, dark descended. The guests headed toward the driveway. The hay wagon, led by four horses, was ready for the trail sleigh ride. The bells on the horses' leather harnesses jingled with each snort, head toss, and hoof pawing the frozen ground. The scene set a festive mood.

Mary rushed toward Brad. "We have to use our small sleigh. There's not enough room in the hay wagon, and Martha's little sleigh has a broken axle. You two are on duty."

Thanks to his plan, the refurbished sleigh was hauled earlier to the barn. He and Jeff readied the horses who would later drag the sleigh, once he unveiled his surprise. Now, he'd have to retrieve the sled early…and change his timing. He touched Mary's arm. "Can you have Nat meet me in the little barn, while I hitch the horses?"

"Sure." Mary raised to her toes and kissed his cheek. "Good luck."

"I've handled many horses."

Mary winked, before circling to mingle.

How did she know? Which meant his mom was involved, requiring him to revisit his timing to avoid snickerdoodling. Brad shook his head. Would he ever get used to their interference? Given his plans, he had no choice.

Maybe he should pack and head to D.C. He couldn't help but love them both. And, no way did he want to ever live in a city. But enough was enough.

Nat appeared in the doorway of the inn's little barn. "What's up?"

"Time to lead the group on the moonlight ride."

She crossed her arms over her chest. "In this little thing?"

"Yup. The other sleigh broke down."

She scanned the front of the barn.

The guests' voices carried from the group by the hay wagon. He tipped her chin. "I can see your wheels spinning."

"I can't believe the week is almost done."

"The event, yes. Us, no."

She shoved her hands in her pockets. "I, ah, I know."

Brad hauled her in for a hug. He'd give anything to stay within her circle of warmth all night and ignore the gathered crowd.

Her gaze caught his. "So, the plan—"

"We've checked the plan. Many times." He pulled her closer. "You just want an excuse to prolong our snuggling."

The tease sparkled from her eyes. “Tell me one more time, and keep me warm while you talk.” Her arms rounded his waist.

“We’ll circle through the trails and Ben’s property, before following Gooseneck Lane to the inn.” He pulled her closer. “Heidi, Jeremy, and the rest of the crew are outside, assembling hot chocolate and s’mores fixings. I’ll text Jeremy once we start home. He’s supervising the bonfire lighting in the field. I want the fire engulfed, so our guests experience the wow factor once the sleigh arrives at the inn.”

“I guess I’m nervous. I realize you know what you’re doing…most of the time.”

“Hey.” He chucked her under her chin. “And, yes, at midnight the pyrotechnics crew will set everything off by the creek so the fireworks will explode over the field. The display should be spectacular. I’m glad we opened the light show to the townspeople to watch from the farm next door. Good PR.” Brad dipped his head, kissed her cheek, dropped his hand, and stepped from the circle of comfort Nat brought.

She stepped away. “What? You’re not excited?”

“I’m pumped. But…I’m sad the week has ended.”

She glanced up, a line of worry sketching her brow. “I know time is growing short.”

No way did he want to get into a maudlin conversation regarding Nat’s impending exit to D.C. He strode toward the two stalls in the corner of the little barn. “I need to hitch up these guys.”

Fifteen minutes later, snuggled close to Nat, with heavy blankets pulled to share body heat on an icy-cold night, he guided the sleigh through the trails. The orange moon rose above the horizon. The orb’s dappled light served as a spotlight to guide them along the path of tall pines on a clear, crisp night.

Behind them, the revelers began to celebrate. A chorus of "Dashing through the Snow" broke out, followed by other renditions of sleigh-ride songs. The sled moved smoothly across the packed snow.

Time flew. Brad glanced at Nat, her cheeks rosy from the cold, her eyes wide with excitement. He wanted this night—this moment—to last forever.

An hour later, the sleigh glided to a stop by the barn. "I'll take care of the horses while you check the guests." He jumped from the sled, circled, and offered his hand. Once her feet hit the ground, he drew her in for a quick kiss. "See you in a few." Fifteen minutes later, he found her standing at the end of the dessert line.

Their guests proceeded through the pre-midnight buffet line in the dining room, after the group enjoyed s'mores and warm liquids on the lawn. Heidi's idea of a fun way to ring in the New Year included dessert first.

He circled his arm around Nat's waist. Her tremble traveled through him. He couldn't wait to get her alone. "Been quite a week. You executed a stellar event." Her head lifted, and her smile speared him. He had to believe the two of them together would work.

"I did have help." She snuggled under his arm.

He wished he was alone with Nat. Soon. "Remember our previous New Year's Eve?"

"The kick-off to our last semester together. Magical."

Brad kissed the top of her head. "We shouldn't have lost track of each other."

"Life took us in different directions."

"You think we can stay put?" He pulled on the wisp of hair in her angled cut.

"As we go between two locations?"

"I wish—"

"No." She touched her palm to his cheek. "We'll work out everything. You'll see. Let's enjoy our last night together with no what-ifs."

"Come on." He clutched her hand.

"Where?"

"A surprise. I want to show you—"

"Brad, we can't leave. The fireworks—"

"—will get set off by the experts. Without our coaching."

"But…"

"Mary and Walter have everything in hand. Jeff's working with the pyrotechnicians. We'll be at the inn in time to see the display. No one has dressed yet for outdoors. At this moment, I need *your* hand."

She lifted their linked hands. "You already have my hand."

He winked and tugged her outside to stride toward the barn.

His gut churned with worry. He knew he and Nat belonged together. He also knew Nat felt the same. But, was she ready to commit to a two-career, two-location relationship? More importantly, if she wasn't, could he give up his dream of owning Green Mountain Sports and living in Mistletoe Falls?

Chapter Thirty-One

A gust of wind sent shivers spiraling through Natalie. Despite the cold curling through her, she sensed something important would happen. That niggling *something* compelled her to charge into the winter wonderland without a coat, mindless of consequences. She yanked on Brad's hand to stop his momentum.

He traversed the frozen ground without breaking stride. Once he hauled open the rolling barn door, he released her hand.

"We'll stay only a few minutes. Promise. Then, the fireworks."

The horses snorted and huffed in their stalls.

All the comforting sounds warmed her. She wished Uncle Harry could see this.

Brad flicked on the light switch by the door. Tiny white lights sparkled throughout the building.

Her intake of breath shot through her in a full-body shiver. The sleigh sat in the middle, facing the door. The horses were rubbed and in their stalls with their favorite snacks. Their neighbor, Ben, would take the horses home later. The large animals added to the enchantment of the still barn on the cusp of a new year. She followed Brad to the sleigh.

Brad climbed the two steps and extended his hand.

She tilted her head.

"Come."

The sparkle in his eye gave her pause. *What was he up to?* She gripped his outstretched hand. The warmth licked her arm, as she ascended.

He tossed a red wool lap blanket around her shoulders. Holding the edges, he drew her close. His body remained toasty, despite the frigid air.

"Warm enough?"

"Almost." She pressed closer.

He added a prickly horse banket for another layer. "Now?"

"Toasty." She strolled her fingers across his broad chest, before her palm flattened. As she cuddled with the strong, caring, and thoughtful man who held her tight, love tapped a happy song in her heart. "Do you want to share the horse blanket?"

"In a minute." His forehead bent to hers.

The caress of warm lips sent sparks everywhere. She tiptoed her fingers to circle his neck and kissed him, long and deep. Pressed against his warm, radiating love was coming home. He straightened too soon. His breath brushed her mouth.

Then he stepped back.

"Brad." For a moment, she sensed she'd been locked from her safe space—her home base. The chill engulfed her. She touched her lips to his…again. Now she was home. She couldn't get enough.

"Not yet." He gripped her forearm to dislodge her hand massaging his nape.

"But you're keeping me warm."

"Oh, I intend to light your fire. First, sit."

Still holding tight to his hand, she settled on the hard, cold bench and shivered.

In the cramped space before the driver's bench, he dropped to his knee and tilted his chin to look into her eyes.

Natalie sucked in a breath.

"Sixteen years ago, you and I planned a life together. Maybe our relationship would have worked. Maybe not." He heaved a sigh. "We were young with much to learn. Nat, I believe we're each ready to take the next step. I love you more each day. I've loved you since we were seven years old."

"I-I love you, too, Brad." Her heart beat so fast, she swore she would burst open with the bottled love that ached to escape these last two months—for years. "I've loved you forever. But you already know." In the dim glow of bare bulbs lighting the way to the stalls and the twinkle lights above, his eyes sparkled with warmth and true affection. Those eyes she saw, these last sixteen years, in multiple dreams. She wanted to shout yes to the rooftops, but he'd yet to pop the question. No way, would she ruin their moment. Besides, she hoped he squirmed a tiny bit, after what the two had been through, together and alone throughout the years.

Rooting in his pants pocket, he dropped her hand. "Shoot."

A chill slipped through her.

He dug in the other pocket.

Biting her lip to keep from laughing, she tapped the shirt pocket with a square-shaped lump to save him from misery. His award-winning grin shot through her.

"So, I'm nervous. Who wouldn't be?"

"And I'm freezing." She tugged one end of the blanket closer, before she kissed his cheek. That tiny touch of warmth sustained her, until she could again fling her arms around his neck.

"Where was I?" Retrieving the box, he flipped the lid.

Her breath caught. The box held a white gold ring with a teal sapphire, the color of his eyes.

He plucked the ring from the red, velvet nest. "Will you marry me? I'll make our engagement work long-distance, until I can sell the store. I want to be with you, no matter what I have to do to have you in my life. Nat, will you be mine forever?"

Her heart pounded. He intended to sacrifice everything for her. She slipped the scratchy horse blanket off to land on the bench. Kneeling next to him in the tight space, she breathed his scent. "If you'll be mine forever."

"I will. Yes, I will—forever."

The word seemed to catch in his throat. For a moment, she swore her heart grew twice its size.

He slipped the ring on her finger. Holding tight to her hand, he kissed her.

Gentle. Sweet. Full of forever promises, she returned the kiss.

A roar of applause and shouts of congratulations rang out.

Each twisted toward the wide-open barn door. The entire inn must have emptied. The staff and guests assembled outside, others poured through the barn doors, led by Mary and Sylvie and their partners-in-crime, Walter and Harry.

Brad extended an arm to help Natalie stand, bowed, and shooed the crowd outside.

One last chorus of cheers erupted, before the shadows faded into the moonlit night.

"My aunt and your mom couldn't help one more snickerdoodle." He pulled her close.

"Let's get your coat, before you freeze."

"Wait." Natalie's heart beat so fast she wasn't sure she could speak. "I-I have a surprise for you too." She searched her pant pocket, before she presented the long, slim, shimmery-gold packet she had planned to gift at midnight.

His smile dimmed.

She laughed when he didn't proffer a hand. "Envelopes don't bite. I promise. Happy New Year, Brad."

He accepted the offering and slid his finger under the flap.

She'd seen him rip open bills and inventory boxes, but this particular envelope held her heart within and everything that came with her love.

Easing open the flap, he glanced above her shoulder.

Was he afraid whatever lay inside might wound him despite her assurances?

As he removed the sheet of paper, he looked into her eyes.

She tried to keep her features neutral. "I can't help smiling. I can't wait to see your face."

He unfolded the left corner of the folded sheet.

The splashes of color from the fireworks watermark peeked out when she peered over the top. She designed the present to mimic a gift certificate.

He drew open the bottom third and scanned the sheet.

His wide grin and tiny crinkles at the corners of his eyes caused butterflies to flit through her belly and sweep toward her heart.

"For real?" He waved the certificate. "This gift entitles me to having you in Vermont forever?"

With her heart exploding with love, she nodded. "We'll be together in Vermont forever, once I train my replacement and pack the condo. For which, by the way, I received far above asking price."

His palms anchored her waist, and he twirled her in the tiny space. "I'm the happiest man alive."

His mouth descended to hers as magical as a sleigh ride on a moon-lit night.

Setting her on her feet, he glanced at the paper one more time. "This-this promise is for real? I need to pinch myself."

She tweaked his cheek. "Does the promise seem real enough?"

"I have to process."

Her heart dipped.

"Nat, I'll leave Jeff in charge and help you pack."

"Oh, Brad." She flung her arms around his neck. "I can show you the city. And once you've seen enough, the time will arrive to haul my country boy home…to Vermont." His beautiful eyes sparked like the firework display.

"I knew my city girl loved the country."

His mouth found hers—the kiss warm and strong. As she ushered in the New Year with her love, fireworks erupted outside and in her heart.

Stepping aside, he flashed a big, sappy grin.

With her hands gripping his lapels, she dragged her country boy toward her for one more luscious kiss.

A word about the author…

~ cottages to cabins ~ keep the home fires burning ~

Delsora Lowe writes small town sweet romances and contemporary westerns from the mountains of Colorado to the shores of Maine.

Author of the Starlight Grille series, Serenity Harbor Maine novellas, and the Cowboys of Mineral Springs series, Lowe has also authored short romances for Woman's World magazine.

She is a Published Author Network (PAN) member of the Romance Writers of America (RWA), and an active member of several state chapters as well as on-line industry groups related to various topics including writing for Woman's World, seasoned romance, contemporary western romance, and New England Indie Writers.

http://www.delsoralowe.com

Thank you for purchasing
this publication of The Wild Rose Press, Inc.

For questions or more information
contact us at
info@thewildrosepress.com.

The Wild Rose Press, Inc.
www.thewildrosepress.com

CPSIA information can be obtained
at www.ICGtesting.com
Printed in the USA
LVHW012038111022
730464LV00001B/20